THE
GOOD
GUYS

THE GOD GUYS

BILL BONANNO
Former Head of the Bonanno Crime Family

JOE PISTONE
Former FBI Special Agent, a.k.a. "Donnie Brasco"

with DAVID FISHER

Ⓦ
WARNER BOOKS

NEW YORK   BOSTON

Warner Books

Time Warner Book Group
1271 Avenue of the Americas, New York, NY 10020
Visit our Web site at www.twbookmark.com.

Printed in the United States of America

First Printing: January 2005
10 9 8 7 6 5 4 3 2 1

Library of Congress Cataloging-in-Publication Data
Bonanno, Bill.
   The good guys / Bill Bonanno and Joe Pistone, with David Fisher.
      p. cm.
   ISBN 0-446-52965-6
   1. Russian teachers—Crimes against—Fiction. 2. Russian American criminals—Fiction. 3.
Government investigators—Fiction. 4. Missing persons—Fiction. 5. Organized crime—Fiction.
6. New York (N.Y.)—Fiction. 7. Mafia—Fiction. I. Pistone, Joe. II. Fisher, David, 1946- III. Title.
   PS3602.0656G66 2005
   813'.6—dc22   2004009525

I would like to dedicate my contribution to this story to all those men who have understood and tried to live by a natural law that supercedes all manmade laws: The promise to pledge their faith and trust in mutual confidence, to transcend all injustices and be possessed with the ability to speak with honesty, think with sincerity, and act with integrity. To all the people who lived by our Tradition.

Bill Bonanno

I would like to dedicate my contribution to this story to the men and women in law enforcement and the armed services, wherever they serve their country. Brave people who have given of themselves to bring justice to a chaotic world.

Joe Pistone

The Good Guys is a collaboration between Bill Bonanno and Joe Pistone. The story is told from both points of view. These two narrators tell their story, which includes some personal insights, in alternating chapters. The story begins from inside the Mafia. Chapter Two begins the story as seen from within the FBI.

ONE

"Fuck that no-good motherfucking fucker, Tony," Little Eddie said, his face turning almost the color of the cherry Danish on his plate. "I ain't kidding this time. I swear to God, I see that fucking guy come around here again, I'm gonna fucking rip out his heart and stuff it down his throat till he's shitting it out. I'm fucking pissed off."

"Listen to me, kid," Tony Cupcakes said calmly. "You can't hold back like that. You got something to say, you gotta say it right out loud. Holding your feelings inside like that, it ain't good for you."

Everybody laughed, even Little Eddie. This conversation was taking place on a crisp September afternoon in 1985, inside the Freemont Avenue Social Club, which naturally was on Elizabeth Street in New York's Little Italy. The truth is that I grew up in social clubs just like this one. For made members and associates of our organization, the social club is the center of the universe. Years ago the social clubs were very important places in the neighborhoods. Almost sacred. This was the place people would come for help. If they needed three dollars so their child could visit a doctor, they could get it at the social club. If they needed a job or were having problems with the landlord, they would go to the social club to ask for assistance. And they would be welcomed there.

But as the neighborhoods changed, so did the function of the social club. It became the place where people in my business would hang out while waiting for the next deal; it became the office, our home away from home, the place for real men to be together. Every-thing in life that mattered started there. If the great poet Robert Frost had known the people in my life, he might have written that the so-cial club is that place that when you go there, if you're a friend of ours, they have to take you in.

Then they would probably offer you some cannoli.

My father, Joe Bonanno, the man who served as the model for *The Godfather*, operated out of two clubs, the Rex Spinola Democratic Club in Brooklyn and the Shoreview Social Club in Manhattan. The Rex Spinola Club was for our neighborhood. It had a large meeting hall in the front and several private rooms in the back. One or two days every week the local people would line up to meet with my fa-ther in a back room. They believed that he was a great man who was concerned about their problems and had the power to help them. And mostly they were right.

The Shoreview Social Club was on East 12th Street between First Avenue and Avenue A. It was a long way from the nearest shore, and the only view through the front windows was of the tenements across the street. My father brought me there for the first time when I was six years old. But I remember it very well; I remember the feeling of being someplace very special. From the first day I was there every-thing about it felt comfortable. Being my father's son meant that people were always bringing me small gifts as a way of showing their respect for him. So for me the social club meant candy, ice cream, and small toys. It was heaven.

It was there that I began to understand the importance of rela-tionships among good people, that I began to realize how few things really matter in life.

I don't know how many hours I've spent inside social clubs since then, but that feeling never went away. And I've learned that after a while all social clubs seem to be pretty much the same. The same things matter. Wherever the club is located, whatever crew hangs out there, the cappuccino tastes the same, the shafts of cold sunlight slant through the windows in the late afternoon the same way, the same

Sinatra and Vic Damone music is playing on the radio, and the scent of loyalty, friendship, and money is always in the air.

As the function of the social club evolved, the most important requirement became that it not attract unwanted attention. Which meant just about any attention. In fact, after John Gotti went to prison, due at least in part to his insatiable love of publicity, the family closed down all its social clubs and operated mostly out of restaurants and back rooms. Not that it made any difference in terms of business. The Freemont Avenue Social Club, which was located in the former King Television and Radio repair shop, satisfied the primary requirement. From the outside it looked about as inviting as a federal prison. People who lived on the block and the people who had business there knew exactly what it was. Everybody else in the world didn't matter.

Directly in front of the Shoreview was a fire hydrant that didn't appear on any city maps and was not connected to any water supply. Like the plugs in front of several Park Avenue buildings, it just appeared magically in place one night. Its only actual function was to guarantee that there would always be a parking spot available for Henry Franzone, the captain, or capo, of the Freemont Avenue crew. Two large bay windows on either side of the recessed front door were covered from the inside with sheets of faded white plasterboard from the bottom to about three feet from the top. The brown steel door had a fan window near the top that had been cloaked with colored plastic that was supposed to look like stained glass but served to make it impossible to see inside. Directly above the steel door a wheezing air conditioner was framed by unpainted plywood. This air conditioner leaked, so on hot days people who belonged to the club knew to squeeze left when they came inside. Next to the door was a buzzer rather than a bell, and in the name slot above the black button someone with a sense of humor had slipped in a piece of paper on which was written, in faded black ink, "J. E. Hoover."

The Freemont Avenue Social Club was never closed. What was going on inside was the life. The good and the bad of it. It didn't matter what time it was, almost always you could find several men eating and talking and drinking cappuccino and playing cards or dominoes and laughing and complaining and planning. Always planning. The next job, the next scam, the next split. In the end, whatever was going on, it was always about money. Someone told me once that the quality of a social club could be measured by the availability of food and the quality of the complaints. By that standard the Shoreview was a good place to belong. Food first, though.

On this fall afternoon Little Eddie LaRocca was griping about a street hustler they knew as Benny Rags. This was a guy who was always coming around with something to sell. Stuff that fell off the back of a truck, from cheap watches to ladies' shoes. Little Eddie was little in nickname only. He was a big, fat, tough guy. He was Little Eddie only because he was Big Eddie's younger brother; physically he was much bigger than Big Eddie. But Big Eddie had started bringing him around when he was a kid and he made some friends and proved he could earn and eventually was invited to become an associate of Franzone's crew. Nobody ever knew Little Eddie's exact weight, but it had to be two seventy, two eighty, and the guy wasn't quite six feet tall. But even carrying all that weight he moved quick when he had to, even gracefully.

Little Eddie was a matter-of-fact guy. What is, is. What isn't, wasn't his business. Once there had been a lot of people like him around, people who believed without reservation in the family. Men who found great comfort in structure and predictability. Good soldiers. It used to be a joke that in some crews you were allowed to do anything you wanted to do. First the capo told you what you wanted to do, then you did it.

In fact, some clubs were run pretty tough; for example, you weren't allowed to change the station on the radio unless you had permission. But Freemont Avenue wasn't one of those places. The club belonged to Henry Franzone, who ran things pretty loose. As long as his people kept earning, and as long as he got his piece of every deal, his crew had a lot of independence. But when the bosses needed something done, it got done first. Everything else was tied for second.

The thing that was pissing off Little Eddie were the Banlon shirts he'd gotten from Benny Rags. "You wear the fucking things one time, the threads start coming out. Makes me look like shit."

From across the room Georgie One-Time asked, without looking up from the cards in his hand, "How much you pay him for those shirts?"

Everybody knew that Little Eddie never paid Benny Rags for anything. "That ain't the point," Little Eddie said. "You don't embarrass me by letting me wear this shit. What if somebody sees me?"

Fast Lenny said casually, "Hey, don't worry about it, Eddie. I see you. And you look okay to me. Honest. Well, except maybe for that thing what's hanging over your belt there, what do you call that?"

Tony Cupcakes answered, "Holy shit! You mean you got a name for that thing?" And again everybody laughed—except the Duke, who just went about his job, cleaning and serving. Duke was the aging deaf-mute who had done all the cleaning and most of the cooking in the club for the past quarter century. No one even knew if he had a last name. Or where he came from. Everybody just assumed he was Italian. He'd been "the Duke" for all that time, named in honor of Duke Wayne by the late Frankie "Fat Fingers" Ianiello after he'd seen Wayne playing *The Quiet Man* on TV. "Ain't nobody quieter than that guy," he'd supposedly said in bestowing the nickname.

Duke had been the perfect choice to take care of the club. He lived in the back, sleeping in a windowless converted storeroom, and left the place only to shop and occasionally visit a sister in Rego Park. Apparently his sister really was a Sister, Sister Mary Rose or something like that, which once caused Fast Lenny to wonder, "If the Duke could talk and his sister came around, would he introduce her as his sister Sister?" Because Duke lived in the club, nobody could come in without him knowing about it. No FBI, no cops, no DEA, no nobody. And because he was deaf and dumb, people could talk around him without worrying that something they said would be repeated. They used to tell a story about an old-timer named Danny Boo-Boo, who objected to the Duke being called deaf and dumb, pointing out that "Just because the guy can't say nothing don't mean he's dumb. Who the fuck knows how smart he is if he can't tell you?"

Following Little Eddie's Banlon shirt eruption, Duke was the topic of conversation. Fast Lenny wondered aloud if foreigners spoke some kind of foreign sign language. "Like, I mean, you know in English that a chair is called a chair, but in French it ain't a chair. It's a whatever the fuck it is. So if Duke were speaking to a French guy who couldn't speak too, how would he tell a French guy what was a chair if he needed to?"

"He could just point to it," Georgie One-Time suggested.

"No fucking shit," Fast Lenny snapped. "I know that. But all I'm saying is that if people from wherever the fuck they come from can't talk, do they all have the same signs? How hard a question is that to understand?"

Nobody knew the answer. Little Eddie started to suggest that they ask the Duke, then remembered why the conversation had started in the first place.

Right in the middle of this conversation Bobby San Filippo, or Bobby Blue Eyes, or Bobby Hats, as different people knew him, silently slipped in smooth as a Sinatra song. Even this early in the afternoon he was handsomely dressed in a tailored Kasper business-gray suit, a Burberry overcoat, and an Elite gray fedora with a black silk band, all from Brooks Brothers. This dressing expensive was a new thing in the organization. In the old days everybody dressed neatly, but nobody wore designer clothes. And while some people might have worn hats, that had gone out a long time ago. In those days people just didn't do anything that would attract attention. There was no future in it. But some of the up-and-comers, the John Gottis and Bobby Blue Eyes, had started dressing to kill. So to speak.

As Bobby walked toward the card table in the back of the club, he caught Duke's eye, squeezed his thumb and forefinger together, and tipped them to his lips. Duke nodded. Then Bobby turned up the volume on the radio sitting on top of the refrigerator and joined the group at the table. One of the many things people liked about Bobby was that he always acted like one of the guys, while everybody knew he was going to the top. There was no big shot inside Bobby Blue Eyes. The Duke placed a cup of cappuccino in front of him. "There's the man," Little Eddie said, then without even a slight pause changed the subject completely. "So, Bobby, who's this fucking guy we're supposed to find?"

Bobby shook his head slowly, as if wondering what he was going to do with this *cafone*. "What do I look like—Mr. Jeopardy? How the fuck do I know? He's the guy that Franzone told me to find. What else do we need to know?" Bobby San Filippo was clever in every area in which it was necessary to be clever. But even more important, he had an understanding of history. He was third-generation, and although he'd graduated from the University of Miami, at thirty-four years old he'd already risen higher in the ranks than either his father or his grandfather. Both of them had been reliable earners and stand-up guys, although neither of them had ever been made. His grandfather died of the Big C with a smile on his face after the Miracle Mets won the World Series in 1969. Five years later his father left his house in Rego Park one night and they're still waiting for him to come home.

"No disrespect, Bobby," Little Eddie continued, "but how we gonna find this guy if we don't know nothing about him? You can't find nobody if you don't know his right name, know what I mean? It don't make no sense. Like, if you don't know his name, how you gonna know when you found him? Maybe you find somebody else and think it's him. I mean, that's a pretty tough thing to ask a person, am I right or am I right?"

Bobby was always diplomatic. "Well, you know, Eddie, sometimes you just gotta do what you gotta do without asking too many smart questions. And we know he's a teacher and we know where he teaches and what he teaches. I mean, that's a pretty good start right there. We'll go talk to some people, that's all. We find him, we find him." Bobby would never admit it out loud, but he was a little puzzled by this one himself. Usually the job was explained pretty carefully: Meet with this guy and do this, go there and do that. Pick up a payment for a carload of cigarettes, find a buyer for thirty thousand rolls of Fuji film, see this dentist and remind him to pay his debts—the work of everyday life.

But this was different. All Franzone had told Bobby was that the boss of another crew, Tony Cosentino from over on Bath Street, needed to find a man real quick. And that the job took precedence over everything else. Actually it wasn't all that unusual. In the organization people did favors for people all the time. And often without knowing why it was being done. Once many years ago, when I was active, I was told to fly from New York to Florida, go to a certain restaurant and eat dinner. That was it, eat dinner at this restaurant. Then I could return to the city. I didn't ask, I ate. It was steak and potatoes and no questions.

Much later I found out that some people had been having problems with some other people, and they needed to show off their bona fides. They needed to prove that they had reach. Getting Joe Bonanno's son to show up for dinner was a demonstration of power. My presence alone solved their problem.

Back then life within organized crime was pretty simple. What mattered was loyalty first, and earning money tied for first. But you couldn't have one without the other; they were tied together. People did what they were told to do for the good of the family. It was like the Musketeers: one for all, all for one. That started changing when the people who had been in control for decades, people like my father, got old and had to step aside or were pushed. Then the lines got a little blurred, and the thing that mattered was loyalty to money. This search for a teacher with no name took place in New York right about the time things were beginning to change. On the surface, though, the waters still looked calm. So when a man like Bobby Blue

Eyes was told by his captain to do something, he did it without asking questions.

In this particular situation Tony Cosentino had asked Henry Franzone to help find a guy known around as the professor. Or Professor G. Somebody had to know his full name and who he was—otherwise he would never have been permitted to hang around—but the people who knew didn't tell it to anybody. In this world last names don't matter. People can know each other for years without knowing each other's last name. Unless, of course, your last name is something like, say, Bonanno. Or Genovese. Then people know it and respect it. But the professor was just "the professor." About all Bobby was told was that the professor really was a professor and that he taught Russian at Columbia University. A college professor. That was it, that was what they knew. If anybody knew where he lived or what he looked like or if he bet the horses or shot smack or anything at all, nobody was talking.

"The Professor" is a pretty common tag, although the one thing every "the Professor" had in common was that none of them were actually professors. It was a nickname usually given to people who thought they were smart guys. People who acted like they had all the answers, sometimes even when nobody asked the questions.

When all this took place, I was already retired from the family business, but I still had friends. So I know this story from the people who know the people. The people who were there.

I have to admit that when I first heard about this search, I got very curious. I wondered why it was so important to some connected people that this college professor get found. The professor wasn't a made man, he wasn't an associate, he wasn't even really connected. What was known was that he had gotten himself involved with Tony Cosentino and for whatever reasons he needed to be found. There wasn't necessarily anything ominous about it. He just needed to be talked to and apparently was making himself hard to find. One thing for absolute certain in this business: The less somebody wants to have a conversation, the more important that conversation usually is.

Little Eddie sighed. "This is bullshit. Who got time for this?" Without turning his head to get Duke's attention he said, "Duke, give me some more coffee, please."

Duke continued washing the dishes, oblivious to Little Eddie's request. Georgie laughed loud and deep. "It ain't ever gonna work, Eddie. The guy can't hear you."

Little Eddie had never trusted the Duke and was always laying traps for him. The day the Duke responded, proving he really could hear, would be his last day on earth. Eddie stamped his foot on the floor a couple of times; Duke picked up the vibration and turned around. Eddie practically yelled, "Gimme coffee, you fucking prick."

"Caw-fee," the Duke agreed.

"Yeah, yeah, yeah," Little Eddie replied, "cawfee. But the prick part, that he don't hear." He shook his head in disbelief, then turned to Bobby. "So where do we start with this thing?"

Bobby Blue Eyes and Little Eddie weren't exactly partners—the family didn't work that way—but they had done a lot of things together and had become close friends. Eddie knew Bobby was a mover and had decided a long time ago to swim along in his wake. So unless Bobby told him different, Eddie just assumed he'd be helping him out on this job. "I don't know. I guess we go up to Columbia and see what's going on."

Georgie laughed out loud. "Jesus H. Christ, that's all the world needs. Little Eddie goes to college. That's like me sending my wife to cooking school."

"Yeah," Little Eddie agreed enthusiastically. "If my mother heard I was going to college, she'd have a cow."

"Eddie," Bobby said matter-of-factly, indicating Eddie's huge frame, "I think she already did."

Everybody laughed again. That was the kind of insult that only someone like Bobby could get away with, because everybody knew he wasn't serious. "What are you talking?" Eddie responded. "You saying that diet book I'm following ain't working? Fuck you, I lost about two pounds yesterday."

Mickey Fists walked in just in time to hear Eddie make that claim. "Yeah, sure you did," he said.

"I did," Little Eddie insisted, "swear to fucking God." And added with perfect timing, "I threw away that fucking diet book."

Fast Lenny tossed down his cards in frustration. "Fuck this shit. You guys wanna play some cards or you wanna be fucking comedians? I'm dying here and it ain't that funny to me."

"Yeah, me too, I'm out," Tony Cupcakes said.

"Hey, Eddie," Bobby asked, "what do you say, you ready to go up to Columbia? Let's see what this thing is all about."

"Columbia?" Mickey Fists said. "I thought that was a fucking country."

Bobby explained, "Yeah, well, it is, but I'm talking about the college. Up in Harlem."

Mickey paused in front of the refrigerator and turned down the radio. "What's going on up there?" Mickey had been made more than two decades earlier. He was a man who commanded great respect, so when he asked a question, it got answered.

"The Hammer wants me to find some guy, a professor. He worked up there. We're just gonna go ask some questions."

Eddie stood up. "College broads, right? You kidding me? Boola fucking boola."

"Anybody else wanna take a ride?" Bobby was being polite. He knew that nobody was going to get involved in a job that didn't have the possibility of money at the end.

It definitely didn't occur to anybody that this might turn out to be something important. It wasn't that kind of job. It was just another favor being done in a business that functioned on favors being done. The way it worked was simple: You do this for me, then when you need something done, come and see me. It worked the same way whether it was an immigrant who needed three bucks to see a doctor or a boss who needed a missing college professor found.

What mattered was that it didn't interfere with the important business. And the important business was anything that earned a profit. The world of organized crime as portrayed in the books and the movies since *The Godfather* isn't entirely accurate. For most people working in this world, it isn't particularly glamorous, it isn't that exciting. It's a job. It's a hard job. There is a tremendous amount of pressure on every member of the organization to earn a living. Nobody gets paid a weekly salary. There's no health plan. You are what you earned last week.

The organization in organized crime is structured like a pyramid, meaning that a percentage of every penny earned by people at the bottom finds its way to people at the top. In essence that might be considered a franchise fee, because it is the existence of this vast support group that in many cases enables individuals to earn their living. People who otherwise probably wouldn't pay too much attention to a certain individual are careful to pay him the respect he has earned when they find out he's a member of this organization. It isn't about him, it's the people standing behind him.

Most soldiers in this world, people like Bobby Blue Eyes and Little Eddie, spend their days and nights looking for the next score, the big opportunity. At any time a soldier will have several deals in the works. Some of them he'll initiate himself, some will be brought to him by people needing the power and prestige he brings to a situation, and some will come from other members of the crew paying him a piece for doing some work. The range of opportunities is endless and indescribable. It's anything where there is the chance for money at the other end.

Bobby and Little Eddie took the West Side Highway uptown, although calling that particular traffic jam a highway was like calling John Gotti shy. At that time the road below 57th Street was a pothole-marred mess. The raised portion of the highway had been closed to traffic, but much of it hadn't been taken down yet, so big chunks of concrete still occasionally fell off onto the street. Personal-injury lawyers used to send people driving under it and then pray. But Bobby took the highway because he had a couple of stops he needed to make. When he got off the road on West Street, Little Eddie asked, "Where you going now?"

Bobby was one of those people who smile with their mouth closed. "Hell," he said.

"Right," Eddie said, "you're a regular fucking comedian."

"I'm not kidding you, Eddie," he said, "this is for real. I got a little piece of hell." About ten minutes later he parked in front of a seedy four-story building. Obviously to fit the property on which it had been built, rather than being rectangular, this building was constructed in the shape of a ship, with one square end and the other end of the building tapering to a point. The street floor was constructed of cement, which appropriately had been painted a battleship gray, while the upper stories were brick. A vertical neon sign affixed to one of the square corners identified the building as the *Terminal Hotel*. The *Terminal* was working its way down from fleabag. It was one of those short-stay places—two-hour minimum—a hot-sheet hotel, a place for street hookers to take their johns so they didn't have to work in cars or alleys. The only thing different about this place was that it was primarily for homosexuals.

There were two doors. A glass door with the hotel's name in an arc of gold lettering opened onto the lobby, but Bobby and Eddie went down a flight of steps and through the open second door, a windowless red steel door with no name or identification of any kind on it.

The door opened onto another world. The place was very dimly lit, the walls were painted either a deep red or black. As they walked in, Eddie said, "Gees, Bobby, this is a nice cheery place."

Sex has always been good business for organized crime. Nobody had any problems with it. There was a lot of money to be made in passion pits, and nobody was getting hurt, so what was wrong with it? Hurt? This was the business of providing pleasure. The mob, the Mafia, Cosa Nostra, call it whatever you want, has always been a service organization. We made available to people those things they desired but couldn't get legally, everything from playing a daily number to kinky sex. Little Eddie knew his way around this world. One of his first jobs—literally while he was still in high school—was working nights as a bouncer at Mello's on Seventh Avenue, an expensive strip club that catered to Garment District executives and their expense accounts. Through the years Little Eddie had seen a lot of interesting things in sex clubs and hooker havens—like he'd never forget the bachelor party in which the groom had been rushed to the hospital gasping for breath after being nearly smothered by a pair of 44 triple Ds—but almost all of it was the typical red-blooded American stuff. Tits and ass. But as he looked around Hell, he realized he was seeing things he had never seen before. "Jesus," he said disgustedly, "what kind of sick place is this?"

Even in the middle of the afternoon the place was busy. Many of the men in the club were dressed in black leather pants, and most of them had the crotch cut out. Eddie concentrated on keeping his eyes looking straight ahead at shoulder level and above. He wasn't embarrassed, exactly, but he knew there was something fundamentally wrong with men who wanted to be with men rather than women. When a man whose shaved head reflected the blue bulb hanging from the ceiling walked past, Eddie just couldn't help noticing that the guy wasn't wearing anything under his black leather chaps, his not-so-privates hanging right out there in public. As the man passed him, Eddie involuntarily reached up and tightened the knot on his tie. That was his way of reassuring himself that he was still completely dressed.

In one dark corner two men were having oral sex—they were actually doing it in public—and worse, one of them was dressed as a nun. "Ah, Bobby, this ain't right," Eddie said, following San Filippo through the quiet kitchen to a room way in the back. And as he did, he thought to himself, I don't care if I'm gonna bust a motherfucking gut, no fucking way am I going into the men's room.

Bobby knocked on a door marked "Private," and after being identified, he and Eddie were buzzed inside. A squat man with perfectly combed white hair was sitting behind a small wooden desk. Eddie took his post at the door and folded his arms on his chest, the traditional "don't fuck with me" pose. Bobby shook hands with the white-haired man but did not introduce Eddie. That was one way of making his point that this was not a social visit. "Hey, Bobby," the man said with obviously false enthusiasm, "I got it ready for you right here." He reached into the top drawer of the file cabinet supporting the desk and pulled out an envelope.

"What do you got for me?" Bobby asked, taking the envelope.

"Twenty-two," he said softly.

Bobby smiled that closed-mouth smile again. But this time there was no warmth behind it. "Gees, Mikey, that's not so good. I was looking for more than that."

The white-haired man frowned. "I know, but I couldn't help it. There was this big thing going on in town this week."

"What?"

"The fucking Village People were at the Garden. You'd think it was some kind of fucking holiday."

Bobby shook his head. "Look, Mikey, you gotta do a little better than this. I got bills, you know."

Mikey knew. "Look, I can throw another four hundred in there, Bobby, but you know I gotta pay for things here too. I mean, c'mon, I got expenses."

"Listen to me, you got a good thing going here. I'm telling you, as a friend, don't fuck it up."

Mikey understood the warning. "Bobby, Bobby, whattya talking? You think I'm fucking nuts? You think I'm gonna hold back on you? I'm telling you, the Village fucking People come to town, it's like the circus. It'll be better next week, watch."

"Yeah, we'll see. And I don't want to hear no 'Liberace's in town' shit either. *Capisce?*"

"Yeah, Bobby, I got it." Taking his wallet out of his back pocket, he removed four hundred-dollar bills and handed them to San Filippo.

This time Bobby didn't have to force his smile. "Pleasure doing business with you," he said, and turned to leave.

"Hey, hey, wait one second," Mikey said, as if he suddenly remembered something important. "You ever see one of these?" He held up a plump kid's doll made of fabric.

Bobby shrugged. "Yeah, sure. It's a doll. Big fucking deal."

Mikey waved off that answer. "Oh no, no way, José. This isn't a doll, this is a Cabbage Patch Kid. Every one of them comes with like its own name and birth certificate. The kids are going nuts for 'em." He checked the doll's name tag. "Meet . . . Penny Nichols."

Little Eddie finally spoke. "He's right, Bobby. My little nieces, they got 'em last year and they won't put them down. They treat 'em like little babies."

"They're going for more than the prices in the stores," Mikey added, handing the doll across his desk to Bobby. "They can't make them fast enough."

Bobby hefted it, bouncing it in his hand a few times. "And? So?"

"And so I got about sixty of them. Cost me six hundred bucks. I need a grand for 'em. You interested?"

"What the fuck am I gonna do with dolls?" Bobby asked, turning to Little Eddie. Eddie kept his mouth shut, which was the correct thing to do, but inside he was about to burst a vessel.

Mikey said, "You don't want 'em, you don't want 'em. I'll get rid of them."

Little Eddie nodded firmly.

"All right," Bobby said, turning back to Mikey, "I can go nine hundred."

"Oh, c'mon, Bobby, I need the grand. Do it for me this one time."

"Nine hundred," Bobby said, shrugging, "that's it." The deal was made. Everybody went home happy. Mikey was getting rid of the counterfeits from Taiwan that he'd bought for $350, and Bobby guessed he could get $1,500 from a guy he knew who sold whatever he could get his hands on out of the storefronts on Canal Street.

Go in to pick up some cash from a rough-trade gay bar and come out with five dozen kid's dolls. Actually it wasn't that unusual. This was a business with very little predictability. It was impossible to figure out what was going to happen next. It was a world where a big surprise wasn't so surprising.

When they got back to the car, Bobby tossed Penny Nichols into the trunk. Then he took the cash out of the envelope, handed two hundred-dollar bills to Eddie for the pleasure of his company, and put the rest in his pocket. The $2,600 was his cut of the previous week's business. In relationships like this the size of the cut depended on the extent of the individual's involvement in the business. Payment was always in cash—organized crime doesn't take credit cards. And Bobby would have to deliver a substantial piece of his end to Franzone, who would keep some of it and pass the rest of it along up the ladder.

Bobby had a nice piece of Hell. He hadn't had to put up any of the start-up money. But what he had done, which was even more valuable, was introduce Mikey to the banker who approved the loan needed to open the doors on slightly less than sufficient collateral. The banker was so cooperative because Bobby held his note for $23,000, which he'd borrowed to pay off some overdue gambling losses when he found himself on the edge of a broken arm. Bobby's association gave Hell a license to operate safely. Anybody came around learned quickly that Bobby Blue Eyes was in this place, and then they would walk away.

Bobby wasn't greedy; he wasn't one of those guys who squeezed every nickel from their joints. Bobby took the long-range view, as he did in the other aspects of his life. It was better that his places be successful, that the owners had a few dollars extra to keep growing, than for him to milk them dry. If he was short one month, he was known to declare a special dividend, but most of the time he got along just fine. Eddie hadn't noticed anybody looking real unhappy when Bobby walked through the place.

By the time they got out of Hell, it was getting late and the traffic to the George Washington Bridge was already starting to back up.

Bobby took a shot anyway, but he wasn't a guy gifted with patience. After inching along for a few minutes he decided, "Fuck this shit, we'll go up there tomorrow," and hung a U-turn.

Eddie agreed. "Fugetaboutit," he said, "there's too many fucking cars in this city. They ought to get rid of the traffic so people can get somewhere."

One of the few things in New York over which the Mafia had no control was the traffic.

TWO

Fuck that no-good motherfucking fucker, Tony. I ain't kidding this time. I swear to God, I see that fucking guy come around here again, I'm gonna fucking rip out his heart and stuff it down his throat till he's shitting it out. I'm fucking pissed off."

"Listen to me, kid. You can't hold back like that. You got something to say, you gotta say it right out loud. Holding your feelings inside like that, it ain't good for you."

"Who the hell is that?" asked FBI Special Agent Connor O'Brien, nodding toward the state-of-the-art TEK speakers. Every word spoken in the club was being recorded.

"Which one," wondered his new partner, Laura Russo, "Abbott or Costello?"

"The first one, the linguistics genius."

She checked her notes. "That is one Mr. Edward Peter LaRocca, a.k.a. Little Eddie, Eddie Black, Crazy Eddie." She looked up at O'Brien. "The original Crazy Eddie."

"What's he got, a cold?" O'Brien asked as he walked into the tiny kitchen. "That doesn't sound like him. Hey, you want something to drink?"

Russo stood up and stretched. From habit more than necessity her eyes stayed riveted on the front of the social club. "They leave any of my mineral water in there?"

"They" being Team II of the agents working the stakeout of the Freemont Avenue Social Club. Twenty-four-hour surveillance operations like this one required two or sometimes three teams rotating around the clock. As many as six people shared the one-bedroom apartment, which made it hard for anyone to keep their own food or drinks in the refrigerator. Maybe the question asked most often in the apartment was, "Who left the butter out?"

Believe me, there are very few assignments you can get in the FBI as boring as sitting on a wire. In this particular case, using information provided by an undercover agent who had successfully infiltrated the crew run by Henry Franzone—apparently stolen goods were being sold inside the social club—the bureau had obtained a warrant to bug the place. Among the stolen items the undercover agent had "personally witnessed being sold" were Banlon shirts. As much as anything else, though, this was an intelligence-gathering operation—although a lot of agents who have worked organized crime would tell you that what they heard could not properly be called intelligence.

Usually these assignments consisted of long hours spent listening to bullshit conversations, hoping to find a single nugget of useful information buried in a mine of boredom. Early in my career as an FBI agent, long before I went undercover inside the Mafia as a small-time jewel thief named Donnie Brasco, I spent what seemed like an eternity listening to old wiretaps, reading reports, and watching surveillance tapes to try to get to know how these people thought and spoke and moved. Combined with the education I received growing up on the streets of Paterson, New Jersey, this was the beginning of my education into the world of organized crime. I understand that some people might think it's exciting to be eavesdropping on real live gangsters who don't know they're being tapped or taped. It isn't. It wears real thin real quick.

Being an FBI agent is not the thrill-a-minute job portrayed by TV and movie producers. It's an always interesting, occasionally exciting job in a mammoth bureaucracy. The fact is that most agents spend most of their time collecting information. Everything from conducting interviews for government security clearances to picking up and analyzing bomb fragments in Africa. It's a career of watching and listening and tailing and interviewing, endlessly interviewing, gathering a mountain of information and trying to transform it into a molehill of evidence.

Being on-site in an observation or listening post is among the most tedious of all assignments. It consists of little more than endless hours spent watching and waiting for something to happen. Sometimes the most exciting thing that happens during an eight-hour shift is a pizza delivery. In organized crime investigations much of the time the people you're watching know they're being watched. They may not know exactly where you are, but they know they're being watched. And we know they know we're watching. In the old days agents used to be assigned to specific individuals for years at a time and the agent and the subject would actually get to know each other. On occasion they would even speak to each other. Everybody knew the rules and respected them.

The listening posts, observation posts, whatever you want to call them, are not what you would describe as immaculate. Probably "unbelievably filthy" would be more accurate. The way it used to be was that you had a small area with four to six men living there around the clock. Nobody was responsible for keeping it clean, so that's who took care of it. Early in my career I was working the Hijack Truck Squad and we were watching warehouses in New Jersey and Brooklyn. I guess I was a little more concerned about cleanliness than the other agents: I would take the garbage out once a month whether it needed to be taken out or not. One time, I remember, my partner pointed at a plate of melted butter on the table and said with disgust, "That butter's been sitting out since April."

"Oh yeah?" I asked. "What year?" That's how bad it used to get sometimes.

Things did get a little better when they started adding female agents to the teams. Some of these women were tough—they insisted that their partners pick up after themselves. This particular apartment was known as the Country Club. That was a joke. This apartment was as much like a country club as Sinatra was a heavy-metal singer.

It was on the top floor of a four-story walk-up. The building had to be at least eighty years old. New wiring had been installed to support the high-tech equipment the agents needed, but there had been no reason to upgrade the plumbing or the heating. The good news was that the plumbing and the heating banged and rattled and hissed only when they worked, which at best was erratically.

The Country Club exuded all the charm and style that the General Accounting Office could provide. It had one couch, an uneasy chair, and a kitchen set—a table with four wooden chairs that had been confiscated in a drug raid. A television and a transistor radio that had been provided by an agent assigned there for more than a year were known as the entertainment center. The tiny kitchen contained a refrigerator that dated from Eisenhower and a well-used microwave. Even the bravest of the agents wouldn't dare look at whatever life was going on behind the refrigerator.

But for Agents O'Brien and Russo this was home and office, eight to twelve hours a day, five and on occasion six days a week. On this particular afternoon they were a little more attentive than usual because two days earlier the body of a made member of the Genovese crime family had been found in the trunk of a stolen Ford coupe under the Williamsburg Bridge. What was unusual was that before he was killed, he'd been burned with cigarettes on his face, inside both ears, and on his prick and balls. Additionally both arms and one leg had been crushed almost flat by some extremely heavy object. This guy had been tortured, which was not the way the mob usually conducted business. The best guess was that the somebody who did him wanted to get some information from him pretty badly. The questions of the day were, who was that somebody and what type of information were they looking for? Was it family business? This seemed more like the way the ethnic groups, people like the Westies, a group of Irish crazies who controlled Hell's Kitchen, or the Colombians or even the newcomers, the Russians, who were trying to build a nasty reputation, did things.

There was a pretty good chance that this killing would be the primary topic of conversation in every social club in New York. Just like when there's a big fire, that's all firemen talk about in the firehouses; when there's a mob killing, that's what they talk about in the social clubs. So Little Eddie got Russo's attention when he started whining about the latest job—finding an unknown individual without being provided sufficient background information. "Just listen to him," she said, shaking her head with wonder. "I never heard anybody complain so much."

"Oh, you'll get used to it," O'Brien said loudly from the kitchen. "That's what they're experts at, complaining. When they don't have anything to complain about, they complain about not having anything to complain about." He popped open a bottle of mineral water and asked, "You want some ice with your water?"

"No thanks."

O'Brien noticed that when Russo shook her head, her tied-back light brown ponytail rolled sensually from side to side. They'd been working together in the Country Club for almost five weeks. The first few weeks were strictly professional, but the last couple of weeks he'd found himself stealing the occasional glance at her. He wasn't afraid to admit to himself that he found her attractive, sort of Lesley Ann Warren with the confidence of Katharine Hepburn, but he would never admit this to anyone else, and there was exactly no chance that he would ever act on that attraction. He'd heard too many stories about careers going down the chute for getting sexually involved with a female agent. This was right about the time that sexual harassment was becoming a serious occupational hazard. They had even started giving a warning lecture about it at the academy. He didn't need the reminder. Connor O'Brien prided himself on being much too smart to fall into that particular trap. Returning to the window with Russo's mineral water, he asked, "Who's he talking about?"

"Some Russian. A Professor G. You got anything about him?"

"A Russian, huh? That's pretty interesting." He began leafing through his notebook. Success or failure in just about any endeavor, he'd learned from his father, a very successful investment banker, was a matter of hard work and organization. It wasn't enough just gathering information, you had to be able to access it. You had to be able to find it when you needed it. So in addition to all the official forms he filled out for the bureau, he carried a small notebook and kept his own loose-leaf binder, cross-indexed by given name and nickname, by dates, by known or suspected involvement with groups of specific crimes. If he had previously come across any Professor G, he would be able to find out when, how, and who. He scrolled rapidly through the Gs with his index finger. While he found a "Doctor G," there was no "Professor G." "No. Nothing."

"How about anything in that book about the Russian mob guys?"

He glanced through the Rs, then shook his head. "You want to call it in?" When agents working a stakeout overheard anything timely, particularly interesting, or very unusual on a wire, standard procedure required them to immediately notify a supervisor. That way, for example, if someone was about to get whacked, they could do something to stop it. But nobody liked to report anything short of that because the inevitable result was that a whole lot of reports would have to be written. CYA, cover your ass, was the foundation of just about every successful bureau career. This was one of those close calls. A man was missing and a body got found. Maybe pieces of the same puzzle. It was probably nothing, but there existed that slight, tantalizing possibility that it was something.

The bureau had been struggling for more than three years to find a link between the five New York families and the growing Russian mob. It was well known that they'd had an occasional date, but no one had been able to prove that they had gotten married. So the combination of a missing Russian and an Italian body was at least interesting. "Let's just see where it goes," O'Brien decided.

Russo got up and stretched, clasping her hands behind her neck and thrusting out her elbows. Russo wasn't naïve: She knew she was an attractive woman and, more important, she knew how to use it for her own benefit. Within the regulations, of course, always within the regs. This was the first time Russo had worked with O'Brien, but the two of them had slid easily into a comfortable team. Both of them knew the rules and had learned how to get the job done without actually breaking them.

Organized crime was a new assignment for Russo, who had spent most of her seven-year career working undercover, first in HMO fraud investigations, then in counterintelligence. She'd requested an organized crime assignment primarily because it was an area in which few female agents had ever worked. It wasn't so much bureau policy as logic. The mob was so strictly a man's world that there wasn't much room in it for women. Russo was smart, though, and ambitious, so she figured out that punching the organized crime ticket would set her apart from most other female agents. As an additional bonus organized crime assignments generally meant staying put in the same city for a substantial period of time. So eight weeks earlier she'd arrived in New York City for the first time since her St. Louis high school senior class trip. This time she intended to stay for more than five days.

O'Brien and Russo made a good team. Just as in every other business, there were two types of agents in the FBI: those people who did the grunt work and made cases and those people who went along to get along. The workers tended to get the glory, but they also got the blame when things got screwed up. The bureau was not known to stick out its reputation to protect agents. The agents who put in their time, stayed out of trouble, and did their paperwork got their scheduled promotions. Both O'Brien and Russo were workers.

As O'Brien settled into the uneasy chair, a ripped leather recliner some previous resident of the Country Club had rescued from the sidewalk, he heard people inside the Freemont greeting Bobby San Filippo. "Hey, Russo," he shouted to Laura, who had gone into the kitchen, "your boyfriend's back."

Bobby Blue Eyes had become a continuing joke between them. The first time Russo had looked at surveillance photographs of San Filippo, with his perfectly styled hair, tailored clothes, Calvin Klein sunglasses, and large diamond pinkie ring, she'd said facetiously, "Hold me back, boys, my Prince Charming has just arrived."

In the background they heard the radio suddenly get louder, and a voice they could barely hear and was therefore impossible to identify asked, ". . . obby, who's this . . . ed to find?"

O'Brien sighed. "That bastard. He turned the radio up again. I hate that sappy music. Couldn't they at least play some rock music once in a while? If I hear that fucking Sinatra one more—"

"Hey!" Russo snapped. "Watch it there, buddy. I'm warning you right now, don't screw with Frank. I wouldn't want to have to take you down." Like every Italian off the Hill in St. Louis, she'd grown up listening to Sinatra coming out of every open window on the block. Except in her own room late at night, when she'd put her ear against the radio and listen to the Beatles. In fact, although she would never dare admit it to a living Italian soul, if she personally never had to listen to him singing "It Was a Very Good Year" ever again, she would light a candle to the Madonna. Maybe she'd even pop into a church one Sunday morning. But none of that mattered when O'Brien attacked the Chairman. It was her responsibility to her entire family, to all the Italians in the world, to defend Frank from the Irish O'Brien's heathen remarks.

There was almost always a radio or television playing loudly inside the social clubs, more to prevent conversations being overheard than for entertainment. Years earlier it had been very difficult to plant a bug inside a social club, but as the bureau's ELSUR—electronic surveillance—capabilities improved with the development of smaller and more sophisticated listening devices, and the engineers in the Technical Section of the crime lab got more creative, bugs had become as plentiful as . . . as bugs. Most mobsters just assumed that the clubs and their cars were bugged, and when they needed to have a serious conversation, they either took a walk outside or turned up the volume on the TV or radio to cover their voices.

When I was working undercover as Donnie Brasco, I never liked wearing a wire. Most of the time I just wouldn't do it. I hated the fucking things. One time another undercover I know, who was wearing a wire, was hanging out in an apartment with several members of his crew. These guys were stone-cold killers. Somehow there was a bug in the agent's bug, and suddenly every word spoken in the apartment was being broadcast through the television set. These guys went crazy trying to figure out what was going on. And not one of them ever suspected the most obvious reason—there was a microphone in the room!

I've seen mikes and even cameras planted in an incredible variety of places. The bureau has put them inside car dashboards, inside lightbulbs, in a sprinkler system. One time for a sting operation they hung a painting of a gorgeous nude woman on the wall—and installed the camera in the center of one of her nipples. There wasn't ever a guy who walked into that room and didn't look directly at her breasts, allowing the FBI surveillance team to get a clear picture of every single person.

The bug inside the Freemont Avenue Social Club had been installed in the very last place anybody would suspect: inside the radio. It had required the work of an engineering genius to figure out how to blunt the sound from the radio speaker. The actual scientific principle was explained to me once, but I didn't completely understand it. It had something to do with mirroring sounds, causing the sound waves to be canceled, supposedly allowing quality audiotapes to be made.

Russo leaned against the wall, sipping her mineral water. "So? What do you think about this Russian? Want to make a guess why they're looking for him?"

He shook his head. "You got me. I mean, c'mon, who knows why these guys do anything? The only thing you can know for sure is that whatever it's about, it's got something to do with money. Guaranteed. Chances are this guy owes somebody and doesn't want to pay it back or doesn't have it. Maybe he's a gambler, maybe he borrowed. But if the mob is looking for him, it's about money."

One of the first lessons young agents learn is to never suppose. In this kind of work people often surprise you. Profession isn't personality. I've seen kindergarten teachers who were degenerate gamblers, cancer researchers addicted to hard drugs, cops who sold intelligence to organized crime. O'Brien was smart enough to temper curiosity with caution. At least most of the time.

Russo smiled shyly. "Wanna find out?"

Connor O'Brien chuckled. The only time she let herself be a woman, he thought, was when she wanted help from a man. And he appreciated that. "You're some piece of work," he said.

"C'mon, O'Brien, it's right there in front of us. What can happen? Then at least we'd have some idea of exactly what's going down."

He hesitated, then said, "You know what the three worst words in the English language are?"

"Absolutely," she said firmly, and then guessed, "Are you awake?"

"Nice try, but no. The three worst words in the English language are 'What could happen?' Because if it can happen, sometimes it does."

"Oh, please. That's just ridiculous. We're not doing anything . . ."

Connor listened, but he was pretty certain he would go along with her plan. Whatever it was. In the few weeks they'd worked together he'd been impressed by her abilities. Laura Russo was an aggressive, shoot-from-her-very-attractive-hips agent. She knew her stuff.

I knew the argument because I knew the temptation. This was the other side of going along to get along—go ahead to get ahead. Good young agents were rarely satisfied with passive assignments. They wanted to get into the action. Early in my career I'd felt the same pull. Take a chance and if you're right, they know your name in Washington. You're on your way. There were real benefits available to aggressive agents who got the job done. Stars shined. But there were also penalties for failure, penalties that involved transfers to small offices in cold places.

"Tell you what," O'Brien decided, "you really want to do this, I'll call Slattery. As long as we're just doing a simple background check, I don't think he'll have a problem with it. But that way, whatever happens we're covered."

Russo straightened up, once again the asexual FBI agent. In that instant it actually looked to O'Brien that her hair had gotten shorter. "Good," she said, "real good."

In the background every word spoken in the social club was being recorded. ". . . heard I was going to college, she'd have a cow."

"Eddie, I think she already did."

The official transcription of that dialogue would be followed by the description: (Laughter). But Russo didn't think it was the slightest bit funny. She didn't think any of them were particularly clever or even slightly amusing. Unlike some agents who became fascinated by mob culture and read all the books and saw all the movies, she knew exactly who they were. She wasn't fooled by the image created by the media; Laura Russo had known them just about her entire life. She could remember them sitting at the big round table for ten in the rear of her Uncle Joe's restaurant, night after night, boorishly taking over the place. She remembered them making a big fuss over her when she waited on them, making jokes she didn't quite understand. In fact, when she really thought about it, she could almost taste the foul smell of their cigars that filled the place. As far as she knew, her Uncle Joe never had any problems with them. They had paid in cash and were reasonably friendly with the other customers. But from the moment they walked in until they left late at night, the restaurant had an unpleasant feel to it. They sucked in all the warmth.

O'Brien and Russo went to see James Slattery the following morning. Jim Slattery was running the surveillance operation. Slattery was the best type of supervisor, an agent nearing the end of a solid if not spectacular career. After twenty-six years in the bureau he'd made enough friends and lost enough ambition to not be overly concerned about every decision he made. He had a reputation for giving his people a lot of rope, but holding tightly to the other end in case they slipped.

I knew Slattery. I'd met him about ten years earlier, when I first started working organized crime in New York. He was a big guy even then, six-four, six-five, maybe two sixty, toward the limits of the regulations. He was still big—he had to be touching two eighty—but what once was muscle had settled into a potbelly. Slattery was a son of the auld sod, the man had the Irish about him. He could tell a fine joke, finish a serious bottle, and charm the ladies. But the one thing he didn't have that mattered in the bureau was the luck. All his Irish luck must have come from Northern Ireland. He just never lucked into the assignment that could have made the difference in his career. I had never even considered working undercover, for example, but one little thing led to the next and the next and there I was inside the Mafia. Obviously that assignment made my career. But Slattery had realized, maybe ten years in, that he wasn't going to be so fortunate. He accepted it and allowed his passion for the bureau to drain slowly away. The good news was that he no longer regretted going home at five o'clock on Friday without a briefcase stuffed with paperwork.

His office was in the Federal Building on lower Broadway. It was small and neat, with a view of the office building directly across the street. But if you stood to the very side of Slattery's window and looked uptown, you could see a slice of the upper stories of the Empire State Building. His office was actually quite symbolic. It was right next to the larger corner office that commanded sweeping views uptown. Which was pretty much as close as Slattery ever got to real power in the bureau.

O'Brien and Russo sat across Slattery's government-issued wooden desk. O'Brien noted that he had placed photographs of his attractive wife and two teenage sons on a glass-topped table behind his desk so they would face anyone sitting opposite him. He also noted, from Slattery's appearance in those photographs, that they had been taken years earlier, when he had a full head of dark hair.

Russo earnestly laid out the situation for him: Information developed through a legally placed bug had revealed that the Mafia wanted to find a Columbia University Russian professor for reasons unknown. The teacher's full name was also unknown.

"Yeah? And?" Slattery wondered.

"Well, sir," O'Brien began carefully, "it's our feeling that if we—"

"We want to find this guy first," Russo interrupted. "Obviously he has some connection to the family and they can't find him. If he's running from them, he might just be willing . . ."

Slattery covered his mouth with his cupped palm. While that made it appear as if he were contemplating a decision, in fact he was trying to stifle a smile. He had been a vocal supporter of the bureau's begrudging efforts to eliminate gender-based policies, although he also knew that actually accomplishing that was pretty much impossible. Hoover's bureau had institutionalized machismo—the vending machines practically dispensed testosterone—and changing that climate was about as simple as melting glaciers with a hair dryer. It would take a long, long time.

But because Slattery still loved the bureau, even after all these years, he knew that doing so was not only fair, it was good business. He'd worked with several female agents during his career and almost unfailingly had found them to be as competent as men—and usually a lot more aggressive. Sitting there looking at O'Brien and Russo, he couldn't help thinking that years ago this would have been the basis of a great Tracy-Hepburn movie, the perky female agent pushing the somewhat reluctant male agent into the middle of an international mess.

Russo had finished talking and was looking at him expectantly. He took a deep breath and grimaced, then spun halfway around in his chair, actions that demonstrated clearly how seriously he was considering this request, although truthfully he hadn't really been paying attention and didn't know precisely what it was she wanted him to do. "All right," he said finally, covering himself, "suppose I let you go ahead. What exactly do you have in mind?"

Russo started to respond, but this time O'Brien interrupted, placing a cautionary hand on top of hers. "Nothing much. We just want to go up to Columbia and ID this professor. Then we'll run a background check on him. Maybe that'll give us some idea why the mob is looking for him."

"That's it?" Slattery asked.

"That's it," O'Brien replied.

Like everybody else working organized crime, Slattery had a body on his mind. "You think it might have something to do with what they found under the bridge?"

O'Brien grabbed his hook. "There's one way of finding out."

Russo added, pretty much unnecessarily, "You got to admit it's pretty strange that these people would be so interested in a Russian professor. I'm . . . we're curious, that's all."

Slattery asked what is arguably the bureau's most important question: "How long's it going to take you?" In the end, whatever the result of an investigation, time spent had to be accounted for and all the proper paperwork had to be filled out. The bureau lived on an annual budget voted by Congress, and that money bought time.

"Not more than a day," O'Brien said definitively, and then added with perfect timing, "Two at the most."

"Okay, tell you what," Slattery decided, "just make sure I get some kind of reasonable memo. But one day, that's it. One. You guys need another team to cover for you?"

Russo told him they had already made arrangements with the night team to switch schedules. That would give them most of the day.

"Just let me know what's going on," Slattery reminded them as he walked them to the door. "I'm too old for surprises."

Many of the bureau's most productive investigations have started with just such minor meetings.

When O'Brien came out of his brownstone on West 87th Street at eight-thirty the following morning, Russo was sitting on cement steps waiting for him. "Here," she said, handing him a cup of food cart coffee, "milk, no sugar."

"Why didn't you ring the buzzer?" he asked as they walked toward his parking garage. Sometimes he just couldn't understand what was going on in her mind. Waiting for someone in front of their building for who knows how long—without letting them know you're there? That made no sense to him.

"No big thing," she said. She'd never admit it to him, but she hadn't hit his buzzer because she didn't know who might be up there with him. And really did not want to know. Laura Russo had done an excellent job maintaining a strictly professional relationship with Connor O'Brien. She knew very little about his personal life: She knew he was single, that he had never been married, and from his often funny complaints about his social life it was pretty obvious he wasn't involved with anyone. And that he had a loving but somewhat combative relationship with an overbearing mother he referred to mostly as "the lion in Gucci." Conversely Russo made certain he knew only the bare facts about *her* life: that she was divorced from an FBI agent currently assigned to the Los Angeles office and that she lived by herself in a comfortable one-bedroom apartment in a renovated building on Spring Street in suddenly fashionable SoHo.

That was the ANK, as she would describe it: all necessary knowledge. And as far as she was concerned, that was exactly the way she wanted to keep it. Laura Russo took great pride in never making the same mistake twice.

Every FBI team is assigned a vehicle, usually a Ford or a Chevy, but O'Brien preferred to use his own car, a scratched and banged-up five-year-old Mercury Cougar XR-7 that he'd named Xavier, in which he had installed both bureau and NYPD radios, a siren and dashboard beacon. "I've put every single dent in this car myself," he told Russo with a New Yorker's obvious pride.

Looking at the car, she offered him congratulations on a job well done.

O'Brien drove Xavier Cougar up to the Columbia University

campus on Morningside Heights and parked at a meter on 114th Street. He put four quarters in the meter for the hour, then added one more but did not turn the handle. By city statute, before writing a parking ticket meter maids were required to confirm that the meter was operative. So if there was a quarter sitting in the slot, turning the handle activated the meter, buying a ticket-saving fifteen minutes. In most other areas of the city O'Brien probably wouldn't have bothered with the meter; he just would have left his NYPD-issued parking permit on the dashboard. But this was Columbia University. It wasn't that many years ago that anti–Vietnam War students had taken control of the campus, and Columbia's students still didn't exhibit a lot of peace and love for law enforcement of any kind. Several months earlier it had cost O'Brien forty-five dollars, the price of a new tire, to learn that lesson when he had to interview an NYU administrator about some security clearance problem.

The Slavic Studies Department was located in Hamilton Hall, off Amsterdam Avenue. Hamilton Hall was one of the university's original buildings and had been designed by Stanford White's firm. As O'Brien and Russo briskly walked up the stone steps on the way to another interview, past the statue of Alexander Hamilton, Connor wondered exactly how many interviews he'd conducted in his eleven years as an agent. He couldn't settle on a figure. Hundreds, he decided, maybe close to a thousand.

Information was the name of the game and he was good at getting it. Through the years he'd learned how to squeeze out as much of the important stuff as was possible. Being a good interviewer meant being a good actor, becoming the person the individual you're questioning is comfortable talking to. For example, if the subject was respectful of the bureau—and Connor could pretty much determine this by the expression on their face when he flashed his credentials—he played up his professionalism, intentionally throwing in a lot of the silly terms used by television cops. Like "perp." When it was beneficial, he perped away. One time, for example, a cop he knew had arrested a Peeping Tom who liked to defecate while watching through windows; O'Brien always referred to that as "the case of the peeping pooper perp."

When Connor had to question people who didn't like the bureau, he played up his regular-guy-just-doing-his-job. At other times he became a New York City street guy. And, when necessary he became the Ivy League college graduate. Whatever he had to be, he became. Truthfully he wasn't even above a pinch of flirtation when questioning a single woman. Interviewing was an art in which he fancied himself an artist.

The Slavic Studies Department was on the seventh floor. O'Brien and Russo shared the elevator with several coeds. As they rode up, Connor fixed his eyes on the lighted floor directory above the doors and never glanced away, so he didn't catch Russo stealing occasional glances to see if he was checking out the college girls.

As they approached the Slavic administration office, they heard a booming voice warning, "Get your higgin' frands off my potato chips." That voice, they discovered seconds later, belonged to Geraldine Simon, Executive Administrative Assistant, Department of Slavic Studies, who apparently had caught a student reaching into her bag of potato chips. "What do you think you're doing?" she complained to the student. "That's my breakfast." O'Brien guessed that she was sixty-three but probably admitted to fifty-four. She had a stack of bright red hair piled high on her head, an unusual color for a woman of that age, and matching lipstick. Her perfectly polished nails were a couple of shades darker. She turned to the agents and extinguished her cigarette in a ceramic sombrero ashtray. "Hi," she said, coughing once to clear her throat. "What can I do you for?"

O'Brien smiled casually. He was real good with older women, having had considerable practice with his mother and her friends. He smoothly took his notebook out of his back pocket and said, "I was just—"

"I'm Special Agent Russo," Laura said crisply. "This is Special Agent O'Brien. We're FBI and we need to ask you a couple of questions."

O'Brien's smile disappeared. So much for his roguish-young-man strategy.

"Can I see your badges?" Geri Simon responded.

Almost simultaneously O'Brien and Russo opened their wallets and showed her their bureau identification.

Simon shook her head. "No, not the cards." She laughed easily. "I mean, I know you gotta be what you say you are, because around here there's no advantage pretending to be an FBI agent. But I've never seen real FBI badges, except the one they show at the opening of that TV show."

Russo showed Simon her badge.

"My former brother-in-law once had a friend in the FBI," Simon said agreeably, "but that was a long time ago." She snapped the bottom of her cigarette pack with her forefinger and a single cigarette popped up. She offered it to both O'Brien and Russo, and after they'd refused she put the filter in her mouth and slipped the cigarette out of the pack. O'Brien picked up the red plastic lighter from her desk and lit it. "Thanks," she said, taking a deep breath, then coughing her throat clear once again. "You can call me Geri. So? What are you doing here?"

This was taking place in the midst of the cold war, when the Russians were still considered our enemy. O'Brien had expected to meet some sort of resistance, some claim to privacy, some attempt to maintain secrecy. Some form of protest. About the only thing he hadn't anticipated was complete cooperation. It had been his experience that people who had the least to hide often made the greatest effort to hide it.

Russo explained to Geri Simon that they were trying to locate a Russian professor known only as Professor G. "That's the only name we know, Professor G."

"That's Goodenov," she said.

O'Brien was a little confused. "What is?"

"It's Goodenov," she repeated.

"I know, I heard you," he said. "What's good enough?"

Simon looked at him with disgust. This was the best the FBI could do? Pronouncing each word distinctly, she said, "The professor that you want to know about. That's probably Goodenov, Mikhail Goodenov. That's what some of the students call him, Professor G. Or even Professor Gee-Whiz."

Russo bit down hard on the inside of her cheek to keep from laughing out loud. Generally it's considered poor form for an agent to laugh at her partner. O'Brien got the joke but was too embarrassed to laugh. That was the kind of ridiculous mistake other people made, not him. "I'm really sorry," he said, shaking his head. "You know, you said—"

"I get it," Simon said somewhat testily. "You know, you're not the first person to make that mistake."

O'Brien ignored her. "Let me ask you this, then: Is he the only one? Are there any other professors whose first or last name begins with a G?"

"O'Brien," she said, leaning forward on her desk and lowering her voice as if she were confiding in him, "this is the Slavic Studies Department. Half the professors in here have names beginning with a G."

Russo picked that moment to intercede. "Listen, Geri," she said, "here's what's going on. The man we're looking for probably hasn't been around in a few days. That's why we're here. A man we only know as Professor G is missing and we need to find out who he is. Then maybe we can find out where he is."

Simon let that sink in. "So then if he's here, he's not missing. That's what you're telling me, right?"

O'Brien agreed. "Right." Then he looked at Russo. "Right?"

Russo agreed.

"Then it's not Goodenov," Geri said. "I saw him leaving maybe an hour ago." She picked up a clipboard and began examining the sign-in sheet. "Oak-kay," she said, drawing in the word and then exhaling it in a great puff of cigarette smoke. "Let's see who we don't have here." She started humming a Russian dance tune as she skimmed down the roster. "No. No. Saw him. No. No. He's dead. No. No . . ."

"Who's dead?" Russo wondered.

"Professor Golotin. Harry Golotin, Russian lit. It can't be him, he died more than a year ago. He had a sudden heart attack"—once again she lowered her voice to a near whisper—"while . . . you know, doing it with one of his students. So that's the reason we haven't seen *him* lately." Then, once again at full blast, she continued, "They're just using up the old forms." She continued scrolling down the list, shaking her head as she passed each name. "I don't know, they all seem so . . ." And suddenly she stopped. "Oh, wait. Here." She hacked her throat clear one more time. "This could be your man."

"What do you got?" Russo asked, leaning over the desk.

"Professor Gradinsky. Peter. He teaches Slavic Linguistics and Contrastive Phonics."

"Oh," O'Brien said.

"But I just can't imagine Mr. Gradinsky . . . I mean . . . he's always so . . ." She searched the air for the right word and found it. ". . . Dependable."

"What's up with him?" O'Brien asked.

Geri Simon expertly knocked a long ash from the end of her cigarette right into the sombrero's brim, and still without looking at either agent exhaled a long thin line of smoke that would have made Bacall proud. Russo realized immediately that Simon had feelings for this Gradinsky a lot deeper than she would ever admit. "I know he missed a very important appointment two days ago and then, I mean, he hasn't shown up for his classes. That's just not like him. He's very . . ." She hesitated.

O'Brien finished the sentence for her: "Dependable."

"Exactly. Thank you." Clearly Gradinsky was very dependable. Completely ignoring O'Brien, Simon looked directly to Russo and asked with obvious concern, "Do you think something's happened to him?"

O'Brien also noticed more than an administrative assistant's apprehension in that question, and he responded with the correct answer. "I doubt it very much. Sometimes the strangest things have the simplest answers. We just need to check it out. You have his home address?"

He handed her his pocket notebook opened to a blank page, and Simon wrote down the professor's address and telephone number on it. "I won't really worry about him too much. I mean, if he really was missing, Grace—his wife—she would have called here."

"Maybe we could take a quick look at his office?" O'Brien suggested. "You know, that might tell us something. Maybe he's got a calendar in there or something."

Simon shook her head. "I can't let you do that without his permission. Besides, he always locks up and I don't have the key."

Russo asked, "Is there a picture of him around anywhere? Maybe a yearbook or something?"

Geri Simon stood up and walked four steps across the room to a steel bookcase and pulled out a thick volume. "He's in here somewhere." She leafed rapidly through the pages until she found the annual photograph of the Slavic Studies Department. "This is him," she said, pointing to a small, somewhat burly man with a stern look on his round, puffy face. His hair was thinning and he had a trim mustache.

One other thing O'Brien noticed about this photograph. In it Peter Gradinsky was standing right next to Geri Simon. His left hand was hidden behind her back—and she was smiling innocently.

THREE

The late great Frank Costello often said that nobody was ever late for their own funeral. Maybe that's true, but other than their own funeral, nobody within organized crime regularly follows any type of schedule. It just isn't that kind of business. Things get done when they need to get done. People show up when they need to be there. The days and nights are pretty fluid. And so finding this Professor G was not exactly a priority for Bobby Blue Eyes or the Freemont Avenue crew.

Bobby had a lot of running around to do the following morning. There was a typical breakfast meeting: A guy Bobby knew from around had asked him to meet a guy who wanted to open a vending machine business in Queens and needed permission to operate. They met at the West Side Diner on 51st Street and the highway. The person Bobby knew spoke for the other guy. That meant he was accepting responsibility for him, so if anything went wrong, it would bounce right back on him. For a small slice of the proceeds, Bobby explained, he would introduce him to the proper people from Queens. He couldn't guarantee that anything would happen; he didn't have the right to speak for the people who controlled that territory. The price of setting up that meeting was a thousand dollars. "That's earnest money," Bobby explained. "It shows you're serious about this."

From the diner Bobby drove down to Canal Street. On weekends Canal Street from Sixth Avenue to the Bowery became one long flea market. Most of the normal stores that had been there for decades had been replaced by discount shops. You could buy just about anything you needed there at a good price. Bobby knew one of the people who owned several of these shops, Solomon Thomas, known to friends and associates as So Solly Tommy, because he had mostly Chinese immigrants fronting for him in these stalls. Due to Solly Thomas's impressive rap sheet, none of the city licenses were in his name. Bobby figured that with Christmas coming he could dump the whole load of Cabbage Patch Kids on Canal Street and they'd be sold by Saturday night.

Solly bought mostly low-end merchandise. Stuff that fell off cheap trucks. He didn't buy expensive jewelry, and the only drugs he handled were pills and pot. Nothing hard, ever. Ever. But otherwise he handled whatever it was people needed to get rid of. It didn't matter to him; he had the outlets and he needed the goods. Particularly just before Christmas.

Solly's office was in the back of a plumbing supply store, but he wasn't there, nobody knew where he was, nobody knew how to get hold of him, and nobody knew when he might get back. Bobby shook his head. "Jesus, how the fuck you guys run a business like that?" But when Solly's secretary asked him how her boss could contact him, Bobby admitted, "He can't. I'll call him."

It was almost noon when he finally got to Pamela Fox's apartment on Sullivan Street. "What time did ya get in?" he asked. Pam flew international for Pan Am. She had only eight years' seniority, but this month she'd been able to hold the very desirable twice-weekly New York–Paris line.

"Not too bad," she said, kissing him easily. "We landed about eight o'clock." She was wearing the white flannel robe she'd taken from Caesar's when they were in Vegas the previous July, loosely belted. She went into the kitchen. "Want some coffee?"

"No," he said, following her. He stood behind her, grasped her shoulders, and gently squeezed. In response she leaned back against him, resting her long black hair against his shoulder. His hands slid down beneath her robe until they cupped her breasts, and he began massaging her nipples with his forefingers. When they hardened, he began pinching them, until she moaned. "Welcome home, baby," he said.

As far as Bobby was concerned, Pamela's relationship with him was not exclusive. They'd never discussed it, but as long as she was available whenever he wanted to see her and he knew nothing about anything else she did, she could do whatever she wanted to do. That was pretty much his philosophy: As long as he didn't know what she was doing, there was no problem. He really believed that was true. But if he had been confronted with the reality of another man, pride and tradition would have forced him to respond.

That was the price he paid for being married and having a child. And he paid it willingly. Pamela was special. After Ronnie and Angela she was the most important woman in his life, but he didn't waste anybody's time trying to define their relationship. They'd met when he'd flown down to Miami to check out a club someone wanted to operate. They were in bed an hour off the plane. A week later he found the apartment in the Village for her. He paid enough of the rent so that she didn't have to share a place with other girls. He wanted to be with her when he wanted to be with her. It would last as long as it lasted. For him relationships worked best that way.

He definitely tried it the other way. He'd been married to Veronica Buonaconte San Filippo for almost twelve years. He was twenty-two years old when they married and was as determined as every twenty-two-year-old to be faithful to her. But one morning about two months in he woke up and realized she was still lying there right next to him and would be right there every morning for at least the next forty years. He went out on her for the first time three nights later, when he met an actress-model-hooker and accepted the fact that he was not a man comfortable with commitment. It wasn't his nature, he'd told Ronnie the first time she'd caught him, so there wasn't anything he could do to stop it. It wasn't his fault. He was who he was. From that point on he wouldn't even buy multiyear magazine subscriptions.

He had no intention of getting divorced. He treated Ronnie with respect, meaning he tried very hard to keep his other relationships secret; he spent all the holidays with her, bought her appropriate gifts on the proper occasions, and always made sure that she had enough money to keep the house nice and buy a few things for herself. After their first couple of years together he accepted the fact that she wasn't going to have a child, so he was real pleased when she announced she was pregnant and absolutely thrilled when his daughter was born. For a time after Angela was born he'd spent more time at home. Which lasted until changing diapers lost its appeal. Ronnie turned out to be a good wife and a wonderful mother. He probably loved her in that special way men love their wives; what he didn't like was sex with the same woman night after night. He was an excitement junkie. He loved that feeling of conquest each time he slept with a new woman. Maybe later, when he had some long-term things going, when he had enough money put away, when Angela was a little older, then he'd think about spending more time at home. Truthfully he probably wouldn't mind having another kid. The first one was working out pretty good. And it did give him a little boost at the club.

Pam never pressed him about his wife. She didn't ask him a lot of questions; in fact, he wasn't even completely positive that she knew what he did for a living. But just as important, she didn't volunteer a lot of information about her own life either.

Having a strong marriage when you're already married to your family is a very difficult thing to do. The mob is the toughest extended family in existence, and some wives just never accept it.

One thing Bobby knew for certain was that at that moment in his life Pam Fox was the perfect woman for him. She never criticized him, she never asked for too much, she was beautiful and nice and appreciative of everything he did for her, and she liked the sex as much as he did.

Just as important, she never made him listen to that relentless relative bullshit. Bobby had serious problems that he had to deal with every single day; he didn't want to be rude to anybody, but he couldn't care less about some Aunt Blossom from Hicktown. Relatives weren't his thing. He had enough to do just dealing with Ronnie's family. After they found out he was connected, they constantly hounded him: Can you get me cartons of cigarettes, get me a good price on this watch, get me tickets to the World Series? Get me, get me, get me. The fact was that some of those things he easily could have taken care of, but he didn't want to encourage them. Get them a VCR and next thing they wanted a cheap two-bedroom apartment on the Upper East Side to put it in. So he told them they'd been watching too many movies, life wasn't like that in real life.

Even if a lot of the time it was.

He knew exactly as much as he wanted to know about Pam's family. Nothing. There was no reason for him to know any more than that. This was only a temporary relationship. Besides everything else, she was too young for him anyway. How old could she be? Twenty-six? Maybe twenty-seven? Whatever, he figured she was easily eight or nine years younger than him. And he was already married. But when they got into the bed? Fugetaboutit. That's how good she made him feel.

He knew he wasn't in love with her. At least he didn't think so. What he felt for her was different than the love he felt for his daughter and Ronnie, the family kind of love. He'd kill anybody who hurt them without even thinking about it. But Pam? That was another kind of feeling. He wasn't so sure how far he would go for Pam, unless respect was involved, then he would have no choice. He'd go all the way, no question. But he really missed her when she was gone. When she was away for more than a day, the thought of being with her got him all excited. And when he thought about the way she talked and laughed, the scent of her, it all made him feel really good. That had happened to him very rarely. He couldn't remember the last time just thinking about a girl made him feel so good. Usually he tired of a woman within a few weeks and then it was *"adiós, amiga,"* but the truth he couldn't get beyond was that after almost six months together her perfect body thrilled him as much as it had the day they'd met.

And so it was almost four o'clock by the time he picked up Little Eddie and got up to Columbia. He parked at a meter, put in four quarters, and left his PBA card on the dashboard for the brownies to see. With that police union card he didn't really need to bother with the quarters, since when they spotted it, they'd extend him the necessary professional courtesy, but he liked to do things the easy way. Besides, the city needed the money and he was a loyal New Yorker.

As they walked across the busy campus, Little Eddie's head could have been on a swivel. "Fuck, look at that broad." Or "Holy shit, check out the knockers on that one." Or "Jesus fucking Christ, I shoulda gone to college."

Bobby reminded him that he'd dropped out of high school in tenth grade.

"So? What does that have to do with the price of tomatoes?"

Bobby stopped a heavyset coed and asked her where the Russian school was located. She didn't know exactly but suggested he ask in the administration office, in Hamilton Hall. Eddie watched with pure joy as she walked away. That was his type of woman. "Man," he sighed, "they even come in my size."

Eventually they found their way to the Slavic Studies office on the seventh floor. Sitting sternly behind the desk was an older woman with what looked a bit like a haystack of bright red hair sitting on top of her head. Bobby decided that if something died in there, it wouldn't be found for weeks. "Excuse me, darling," he said, politely taking off his hat, "I was wondering if you could help me out here."

The woman put down her cigarette. "What can I do you for?"

"Call me Bobby. This is my friend Eddie. And your name is . . ."

"Ms. Simon."

"Well, Ms. Simon, we're looking for a guy, Professor . . ."

She said it with them. "G."

"Gees," Bobby said, surprised, "how'd you know that?"

She snapped a phony smile at him. "Maybe I can read minds," she said. "Or maybe the fact that two of your people were here yesterday asking exactly the same question gave it away."

Eddie took a step forward. "Who was here?"

"A couple of other agents." She paused. "You guys are FBI, right?"

Bobby glanced at Eddie. The FBI was also looking for this Professor G? That definitely was bad news. Whatever it was that this guy had done, obviously it was important enough for the feds to be looking for him too. No wonder the bosses wanted him found so quickly. "Yeah, sure," Bobby responded, forcing a little laugh. "That's us, G-men. I mean, what do we look like?"

Using his most official FBI voice, Eddie asked Ms. Simon as casually as possible, "So, um, like what did these guys look like? I mean, you know, maybe they're friends of ours."

Simon tapped her cigarette on the brim of her cheap ceramic sombrero ashtray. "It was a man and a woman. The girl was nice-looking. He looked grumpy, like Walter Matthau when he was a lot younger. Like in *The Odd Couple*. Did you see that one?"

"You kidding," Eddie said enthusiastically. "I loved that pitcher. Like when he threw that spaghetti against the wall . . ."

Bobby shut him up with one look, then turned back to Simon. "Did you get their names?"

"Sure." She searched through the tray on her desk until she found the card. "Here it is. Her name was Russo. Special Agent L. Russo." She shook her head and sniffled. "The other one's name I can't remember. How about you guys, you got your cards?"

"Sounds like you got a little cold going there," Bobby said, making an elaborate display of searching his jacket pockets for his card.

"Sinuses," she explained.

"Ah, sh . . . shoot," Bobby said, snapping his fingers. "I left them in my other jacket. But lemme ask you this, Ms. Simon. What'd you tell 'em?"

When she hesitated, Eddie said, "We'd hate for them to find him first. That'd be bad for us."

"Inside the bureau, he means," Bobby picked up quickly. "There's a lot of competition goes on between agents."

"They give us big bonuses," Eddie lied, enjoying it.

Simon nodded, although not one hair moved. "I'm sure." She hesitated for just a few seconds, as if trying to figure out a complex problem. Finally she looked directly at Bobby in a no-nonsense way and asked with a plea in her voice, "I want you to tell me the truth, please. Those other two, they wouldn't tell me anything. Has he done something wrong?"

Bobby got the message. Whoever this professor was, he meant something special to this woman. The last thing she wanted to do was get him hurt. So he shook his head firmly. "Absolutely not." For emphasis he waved his hands palm-down away from his body, sort of like a football official indicating no catch. "This doesn't really even have anything to do with him. We just want to find him to ask him a few questions, that's all it is."

She took a long, contemplative drag on her cigarette and exhaled deliberately, watching the swirling smoke trail slowly dissolve. "They don't like me smoking in here, you know. But I've been here longer than the paint, so there isn't much they can do about it." She made her decision. "His name is Peter Gradinsky," she said as she reached for the yearbook, which was still on her desk, "and he's been missing for almost a week. Here, this is him . . ."

As they got ready to leave several minutes later, Geri Simon asked Bobby, "When you find him would you tell him to call me, okay? I just want to know he's okay."

"Oh, he's fine," Bobby said, dismissing her fears, "don't worry about it. We do this kind of thing every day. It always turns out good. But I'll remember to tell him. Thanks."

And just before they walked out, Little Eddie took an unopened pack of Salem out of his pocket, literally straight off the truck, and put it down on her desk. "Compliments of the FBI," he said.

Bobby had known Eddie since the day he'd walked into the club laughing about being soaked by the dripping air conditioner. And that was pretty much the nicest thing he had ever seen him do.

But in the car heading back to the social club Little Eddie was furious. "Fuck those no-good fucking bastards," he screamed, slamming his palm against the leather dashboard. "Who the fuck do they think they are, fucking with us like that? Jesus fucking Christ, that pisses me off." He leaned back and glanced at Bobby, who was calmly driving. "That ain't right, Bobby, and you know it."

"You're right, Eddie," he agreed. "It's not right." Bobby liked to keep his anger contained. When it got loose, he knew from experience, real bad things happened. When he lost control, he did stupid things, he didn't think things through. The last time he'd really lost it, when some motherfucking rope jockey at Xenon tried to make him and Pam wait outside, it had cost him almost $5,000 to square it. Losing his temper was a luxury he couldn't afford at the current prices.

But he definitely was angry. Here he was being a nice guy, doing a small favor for people he didn't know, and all of a sudden he was butting heads with the Federal Bureau of Investigation? The FBI? Where the fuck did that nuclear bomb come from? That was a problem he had not earned on his own. Franzone should have warned him that there was more to this than finding a name. That wasn't right, what they did. They should have told him the truth, given him all the information. Then let him make his own decision about whether to get involved or take a hike.

Now whatever it was that was going down, he was connected to it. For example, if this professor's body floated up onto the shore one day without a head, or if he turned up missing for good, both of which were reasonable possibilities, those agents might decide to have another conversation with the redhead. And where was that going to end up? Bobby licked his lips and told Eddie, "Anyway, there's nothing we can do about it now. They wanted a name, we got the name for them. Now we're out of it." He said it again, this time with finality. "We're out of it."

They drove in angry silence for a few more minutes, until Little Eddie asked, "What do you think this is all about?"

"Who gives a flying fuck?" Bobby snapped. "Let's just drop it, that all right with you? They want us to know, they would've told us."

In the world of organized crime curiosity can end up costing a lot more than a lost temper. In that sense it's like a military organization. Sometimes you do what you're told to do without asking questions. You be the good soldier. You do what you're told based on your strong belief that the larger organization exists for the common welfare, and you as an individual are not considered an expendable part. That the people who ask you to do certain things are going to protect you, whatever that takes. Things can get a little nasty . . . actually a lot nasty when somebody tries to stick out your neck for their business. So Bobby decided to pass along the information he'd learned, keep his mouth shut, pay attention, and see what developed.

That didn't mean he wasn't curious. He was. Surprisingly, in a world in which actions were based entirely on the reality of money—the bottom line is always the bottom line—there were a lot of people who still relied on faith, superstition, and gut feelings. Gangster intuition. Members of organized crime might not go to Mass every Sunday, for example, but religion plays an important role in their lives. They pray, they give the sign of the cross at appropriate times, a lot of people wear the crosses they've carried most of their lives—and will even kiss them for luck. They contribute regularly to their parish and invoke the help of the Blessed Virgin. Also, some of these people are superstitious. Maybe their things need to be put in exactly the same place every day or they knock three times on wood before leaving for a meeting or maybe they don't gamble on Friday the 13th. One guy, for example, was so superstitious that for luck every morning before he started his car he'd get down on his hands and knees and look underneath it.

But almost everybody pays attention to their intuition. If something doesn't feel right, there probably is a good reason it doesn't. The people in this business are all professionals. Experienced. Organized crime is one industry in which you don't survive and move up without being knowledgeable. This is a world replete with danger, so you have to pay close attention to what's going on around you all the time. You get to notice every ripple in the breeze. Or maybe you detect a slightly different tone in a familiar voice. Or somebody does something just a little bit out of their ordinary behavior. Noticing the little things, and responding to the slightest change, can be a matter of life and ending up in a trunk under the Williamsburg Bridge.

So Bobby paid attention to the uneasiness he was feeling. It was pretty much impossible to pinpoint the exact cause. It might have been the unexpected presence of the FBI, but it also might have been the body they found. He asked Eddie the question being asked in every club in the city: "What do you make of this thing they did to that crazy fucker, that what's-his-name, Skinny D'Angelo?"

At that moment in the office of the New York City coroner an assistant medical examiner was working up a sweat trying to saw through the breastplate of 320-pound Alphonse "Skinny Al" D'Angelo. A day earlier an anonymous telephone caller had informed the NYPD that they would find a "big surprise" in the trunk of a 1982 Ford Granada parked beneath the Williamsburg Bridge. After receiving that call, finding the body really wasn't much of a surprise.

D'Angelo had been shot several times at close range with a small-caliber weapon, although none of the wounds were of themselves fatal. But no effort had been made to stem the flow of blood, so D'Angelo died slowly, possibly conscious as his life drained out of him. But before he died, presumably he had been tortured. The killers, again presumably more than one, had stuck lit cigarettes in his ears, which burned through his eardrums, on his testicles and penis. Also, both his arms and one leg and foot had been crushed practically flat by some unknown method. The assistant medical examiner had never seen anything quite like this and could not even begin to speculate on the way this was done. The bones in the victim's arms and leg had splintered into flat fragments. The only detail released to the news media was that Alphonse D'Angelo, a reputed member of the Genovese crime family, had died of four gunshot wounds to his body.

What the coroner's office released to the media or tried to keep private didn't matter. As it turned out, the assistant medical examiner had a sister-in-law who sold inside information to certain city journalists. Everybody denied this kind of thing happened, but they also knew it was absolutely true. Reporters paid people for information. And it wasn't just those crazy weekly scandal sheets, but reporters for the mainstream city tabloids. The reporters, in turn, shared the purchased information with other sources, looking for a headline. So within hours every connected person in New York knew the details of the murder. It was obvious that this wasn't a sanctioned mob hit, this was somebody else sending a message. But only those few people for whom that message was intended knew what it meant. Or could guess who sent it.

"D'you know him?" Little Eddie wondered.

Bobby shook his head. "Heard of him. He was with Two-Gun Tony, over on Bath Street. You know him?"

"A little. He was around. I used to see him at the Oasis. Big fucking guy, I remember that. I swear to God, Bobby, this guy was so fucking fat that after he took a shower he'd work up a sweat drying off. Shit, a guy like that I woulda bet on him popping his ticker. See, the thing I can't figure out is how they fit him into that trunk. Even with the little guys that's tough sometimes, but with a guy that big . . ." Eddie was obviously impressed by the killer's persistence. "I'll tell you what, though," he added, "he must've pissed somebody off pretty good. They burned holes in his eardrums and pecker. That's a tough way to go."

Although the possibility of a sudden and violent death was a fact of life for everyone in the business, I never knew anyone who wasted time worrying about it. What could be prevented was prevented. But what is, is. People rarely talked about others being the victim of a hit, except as a matter of professional curiosity. Like the way stockbrokers might talk about ripping off investors. But this hit got their attention because it was so unusual. It wasn't a mob hit; the families didn't conduct business this way. They could be brutal when it was necessary, but this was a special kind of torture. It had to come from the outside. So the question became, who on the outside had balls big enough to take on the New York families?

"Colombians, you think?" Bobby asked.

"Who knows? They definitely got the *cojones*. You get in their business, they let you know." Little Eddie shook his head in wonder and laughed out loud at something only he found amusing. "There's a lot of crazy motherfucking people walking around out there."

As soon as Duke saw them walk through the door, he began steaming milk for the cappuccino. Bobby and the Duke had always had a pretty good relationship. For whatever reasons, Bobby had always watched out for him. Unlike a lot of the other guys, he never made fun of him, and he tipped him a few bucks extra on all the holidays. In the summer he made sure the Duke had a good fan for his closet, and in the winter he got him one of those compact space heaters. In return the Duke tried to do little extra things for Bobby.

"So, *bubelehs,*" Tony Cupcakes asked when they sat down at the card table, "you find that professor guy?"

Eddie answered, "What are you all of a sudden, Charlie fucking Chan?" His eyes settled on the full box of Hostess chocolate cupcakes directly in front of Cupcakes. "Gimme one of those," he said, reaching long across the table and grabbing at one of them.

Cupcakes pulled the box out of Little Eddie's range. "What is it, a big fucking secret? You either did or you didn't."

Eddie answered with his mouth full. "It's complicated is all. Trust me, you don't want to know."

Bobby agreed. "Hey, Cakes, trust me, the man's doing you a favor. If he told you, he'd have to whack you. Then where would you be?" Knowing that the FBI was involved, Bobby and Little Eddie had no intention of sharing their information with anyone except a boss. It probably was a wiseguy who once said you could know somebody forever, but you never really know them.

Bobby and Little Eddie were both connected guys, meaning they were involved in the family business but had not yet been made, or literally inducted into the Mafia. There is a formal ceremony, a very secret ceremony, in which the chosen man is made. The day I was made was one of the most fulfilling days of my life. For me, in addition to the responsibilities it carried with it, being made meant that I had earned the respect of my father. It wouldn't have happened without his approval. He believed I was capable of carrying on the family name. Personally and professionally.

It was pretty well accepted that Bobby was going to get his badge the next time the books opened up, which is what it's called when the heads of the families agree to induct new members. It's also known as being made or "straightened out." Maybe Eddie too. But as connected guys they were still subject to all the rules and had to pay a percentage of every dollar they earned to their family—although they were not entitled to share in the family profits and didn't receive the full respect or protection guaranteed to made guys.

Bobby had decided that the only person he would talk to was Henry the Hammer, Henry Franzone. Franzone generally came into the club to take care of business early in the afternoon and stayed as long as necessary. It wasn't like the old days, when the boss would sit at a smaller table in a corner of the room and one by one each member of his crew who had business with him would join him. They would share pleasantries, then discuss whatever they had to talk about. Anybody who was planning a job had to go through the details with Franzone, who would then—almost always—grant permission. There was no work done by a member of his crew that Franzone had not personally approved. And when the job was done, Franzone was paid his piece of it.

In a world where respect has to be earned, Henry Franzone was one of the most respected individuals. He had been around for a long time, ever since coming out of the army after World War II. He had volunteered in 1940 after emigrating to New York from Sicily and fought his way through the entire Italian campaign. He'd won a Silver Star on Monte Cassino but never talked about the details.

He was easily one of the oldest *capos* still working actively. As he liked to say in his Italian accent, most people his age were already dead, or at least permanently retired. Henry had survived all those years by keeping his mouth closed, treating people decently, staying clear of family politics, and being just a little tougher than his enemies. Some people said he was the living proof that the good die young.

Henry was a small man, almost frail-looking, but no one who knew his reputation was fooled by his appearance. Franzone was a stone-cold killer. It was said about him that he could open up a skull with one solid smack. No one really knew how much heavyweight work he had done in his career, but for a time in the 1950s he was considered one of the most ruthless killers in the city. There was nothing that bothered him; he was just as cool walking into a crowded restaurant and putting three slugs into a guy's head as he was standing out in the middle of a field looking a guy right in the eyes as he smashed his skull with one blow, then pulling out his brains with the claw end of a good Stanley. Around 1968 he pleaded to a trumped-up attempted-murder charge, mostly to avoid a trial that might have implicated an NYPD lieutenant, and did a quiet twelve years. When he came out, he was given control of the Freemont Avenue crew as his reward.

Most people in the crew respected Henry because he usually found a way to say yes to whatever jobs they were planning. And he had enough experience in the business to be able to offer sensible advice. In a world that was changing rapidly, Henry was a living reminder of the tradition that had brought them all together.

"I got the name of that professor and where he lives," Bobby explained when he sat down with Franzone.

"Dat's good," Franzone mumbled in a raspy voice vaguely reminiscent of Brando playing Don Corleone, but actually the result of a lifetime of smoking. "Here. You want some of this calzone? 'T's good for yas."

"No, that's all right. The guy's name is Peter Gradinsky. He lives with his wife on West End between 73rd and 74th. He teaches Russian grammar." He waited for Franzone to respond, but the old man didn't say a word. "There's one more thing," Bobby said finally. "Turns out the FBI's also looking for this guy. They were all over the place yesterday asking questions."

Franzone rested his elbows on the table, entwined his fingers, and took one very long breath. "Pay attention 'cause I'm gonna tell you something here," he said. "But this don't go no further. Right?"

Bobby nodded his agreement.

"See, Bobby, there's some things going down that nobody needs to know about the details right now, you unnerstan' what I mean? Big things."

Trust me is what he meant. Again Bobby nodded.

"Sos when I ask you do me something, you do it no questions. Now, I want you should do this for me. I want you to go to this guy's place and talk to his people. If he got a wife, you talk to his wife. Talk to the neighbors. See what you see. But you be nice now, you be good, because we don't need nobody making no problems for us. Maybe you find out what happened to him. You need to spend on this, that's all right, we got it covered. Just you be careful what you do. Bobby, listen to me now, this is an important thing I'm asking you. I'm asking you because I trust you. Don't go fucking up. *Capisce?*"

"It's done."

Franzone would never admit it, but the presence of FBI agents, while troubling, did not surprise him. When he first started working in the 1940s, it had been possible to keep the matters of the families private. *Omerta*. This code of silence was honored by everyone. Absolutely everyone. Betraying the family was the worst sin that could be committed, and for that there was no forgiveness. There weren't enough Hail Marys in the universe to make it right. You talked, you died. That simple. No appeals. Those were stand-up men, men who accepted responsibility for their actions, who did their time honorably. Now? Fugetaboutit. People get a hangnail they talk. You can't

turn around without bumping into some ambitious prosecutor looking to make his name licking the bones of the families.

For Franzone the questions to be answered were, how did the FBI
find out that this professor was missing and how deep was their interest in him? Admittedly there were several people looking for him, so
the information was around. It could have come from anywhere. But
for his own safety he would have to assume that it had come out of his
club. Either somebody had a big mouth or the government picked up
something on a bug. Maybe, he decided, this was a good time to talk
to some old friends of the friends who worked downtown.

But most troubling was the fact that the bureau was interested in
this guy. Tony Cosentino, the boss who had asked this favor of him,
had offered few details. A favor, that's all. A business deal that wasn't
going too good, that was what he'd said. The implication was that the
guy owed and skipped. That kind of thing happens all the time. But
ordinarily the FBI didn't get involved in those situations. Maybe they
would bust a hijacking once in a while for the public relations value,
but they really didn't waste time chasing bullshit. So the presence of
the bureau got Franzone real interested in learning a lot more about
what was going on. Henry the Hammer was a careful man. In his career he had put away a few dollars, but those years in prison had cost
him a lot of money that could never be recovered. He wasn't that
young anymore, and as you get older, you never know how much
you're going to need. You just never know.

Bobby wasn't particularly unhappy that he was still involved. Now
that he knew that the feds were on the trail, he'd have to be a lot
more careful, but if his feelings were right, if this was a serious opportunity, it could turn out to be a very good thing for him.

When once again he took his place at the card table, the Duke put
down a hot cup and smiled at him. But before he could take a sip,
Fast Lenny said to him, "Take a walk with me."

Few people dared talk about their plans inside a social club. Those
days were done. When the cops started planting electronic listening
devices in social clubs, a lot of people treated it as a joke. Those were

the talk-into-the-sugar-bowl years. Nobody took it very seriously until gleeful prosecutors at trial began playing the "best of" tapes of private conversations held inside the social clubs. That was the end of the joke, and a lot of time and money was spent protecting clubs against surveillance. But due to the extremely sensitive nature of their plans, a lot of people absolutely refused to talk business indoors. Fast Lenny, for example, was convinced that the walls really did have ears. On occasion he could still get a laugh by shouting at the wall, "You hear that? You no-good fuck."

So when Lenny had a proposition to make, he insisted on walking with it. "That's the way the Romans used to do it," he'd explained. "They were always walking around making plans."

To that, Mickey Fists had sighed and pointed out, "Of course they were—they didn't have no cars."

Lenny would walk up and down the block with the person he wanted to speak to, always walking on the outside and talking toward the buildings, so if the parking meters, pay telephones, fire hydrants, or lampposts by the curb were bugged, they wouldn't be able to pick up his voice. There weren't going to be any Best of Fast Lenny tapes played at some trial. "Listen up, Bobby, I got this guy, see, who's got this electronics store in the Garment District and he ain't doing so good. He's got a whole fucking truckload of TVs and VCRs being delivered tonight and he don't want 'em. You know what I'm talking, right?"

"Yeah, sure." Bobby seemed to be looking at something in the distance. He pointed to a building way down the block. "Hey, smile, Lenny, you're on *FBI Camera.*"

Lenny tried to spot whatever it was that Bobby had seen. "Where? Where?" All he saw was a large building with hundreds of windows. "What the fuck are you looking at?"

Bobby checked him with his elbow and laughed. "Come on, I'm just shitting you."

While both Bobby and Lenny believed—correctly—that they were being watched, which was an occupational hazard, the truth was that Bobby had absolutely no idea where the camera was situated. "Don't fuck with me like that, Bobby," Lenny warned, "it ain't funny." In disgust Lenny shook his head and muttered, "I swear to God, Bobby, sometimes I wonder where your fucking head is."

"It's a joke, Lenny, that's all."

"No, no, it ain't. A joke is something that's funny, and there's nothing funny about that, so it can't be a joke. So from now on, when you tell a joke, make it a funny one, okay?"

"Yeah, yeah, yeah," Bobby agreed dismissively, coming close enough to an apology to satisfy Lenny.

"Now, where the fuck was I?" Lenny took a few seconds to find his place. "Oh yeah. So this mook wants us to take the truck. We get the swag and he gets the insurance and everybody's happy. You want a piece?"

"You telling me the guy's got the thing set up?"

"Pretty much. Only the driver don't know shit. All he knows he's gotta be at the store at like nine o'clock. By then it's pretty quiet around there, 'specially if there's nothing going on at the Garden. When the driver gets to the store, he's gotta go inside and get all the forms and crap. We're gonna be waiting right there. That shit has gotta be worth fifty, sixty grand easy. So? You in?"

"Fuck yes, I'm in."

Franzone was gone by the time Bobby and Fast Lenny returned to the social club. He had gotten into his car and driven to a bank of pay phones by the basketball courts on Sixth Avenue and West 4th Street. The rumor was that every public phone in Little Italy was tapped. That was probably an exaggeration, but it was based on reality. The federal government does tap pay phones near government buildings and outside known mob hangouts. So Franzone wasn't about to play pay phone bingo. Instead, he used one of the phones in the Village to call his old friend.

FOUR

I'm sorry, I love you, sweetheart, but the indisputable fact is that being an FBI agent is simply not a suitable job for a Yale graduate. There are so many other schools you could have gone to for that."

Jamming the phone between his shoulder and his right ear, he worked at knotting his tie. "Hello, Mrs. Vader, is little Darth home?"

"Please, Connor, don't make me laugh. I've got all my makeup on and I'll break my face. I just want you to listen to me for one moment." She paused, and accepted the silence as evidence he was listening to her. "You know you have responsibilities. I'm the only mother you have and you're not treating me very nicely."

Someday, he swore to himself, someday when she got on this guilt roll, he was going to summon up the courage to tell her that he was a fully grown adult and she could no longer treat him like a little boy, and then slam down the phone in her ear. Someday, but not today. "Now it's your turn to listen to me, okay? I got the official word from Dear Abby. Here, I got it right here, let me read it to you. Dear Wonderful Son Who Loves His Sainted Mother, playing golf with your mother is not considered a family responsibility. There you have it. And Dear Abby doesn't lie."

LeeBeth O'Brien was not a woman who surrendered easily. "Even when that aging mother begs her only son to spend just a few small hours with her?"

"Nice try, Mops. I like that reading." She had become "Mops" about a year after Connor O'Brien Sr. had died at his desk at Chase

Manhattan. Adding her late husband's role to her own, she began coaching Connor's Little League team, taking him and his friends on camping trips, and even learned how to drive a manual transmission so she could teach him. And in exchange, all she asked from him was that she be foremost in his thoughts every single minute of his life.

Because LeeBeth was fulfilling both parental roles, mom and pop, her precocious son had created the appropriate title for her. Initially he had tried "Pom," but they both agreed that conjured up the image of a sad cheerleader, so "Mops" she became. This particular morning she was trying to convince him to come up to Chappaqua for the weekend to play with her in the club's annual parent and son tournament, which for years had been the father and son tournament—until she threatened a lawsuit, at which time single mothers and their sons were admitted. Thus far she remained the only woman to actually participate.

Very few people in the bureau knew that Connor O'Brien was the son of a successful investment banker and had his own trust fund. Or that he was a Yale graduate. While once all applicants to the bureau were required to have a college degree—and preferably an advanced degree—as well as three years of law enforcement experience, that had been slightly relaxed over the previous decade. The bureau now commonly made exceptions for individuals with desirable skills, from computer programming to the ability to translate Slavic languages. But while all agents were still required to have at least an undergraduate degree, very few of them had graduated from an Ivy League school with a major in philosophy, and even fewer of them had a trust fund fat enough to support them comfortably for the remainder of their lives.

If O'Brien's family and friends wondered at his choice of a career, he certainly never did. When asked by people who knew his background why he'd joined the bureau, he told them seriously, "Because I couldn't hit a good curveball." Connor really couldn't pinpoint the exact moment he decided to apply to the FBI. He realized it was an odd choice to make for a politically liberal Yale graduate at the height of the Vietnam War, but somehow it made perfect sense to him. "Bridging the gap," he'd explained to his mother. Bringing America together. Healing the societal wounds. He had used every cliché to explain it, but the bottom-line truth was that it seemed like it might be important—as well as interesting and fun. His father had provided him with financial security, which he interpreted to mean that his father had not wanted him tied to a desk doing a job he hated, the position in which he had found himself. Maybe more important than anything else, each day would be different.

So when he ended up with a high number in the draft lottery, he applied to the bureau and was accepted. LeeBeth thought it was an immature decision as well as a ridiculous thing to do. She brought in her heaviest emotional weapons to try to talk him out of it. Enlisting her late husband's friends, she managed to get him offers to join the management training program at Chase, Xerox, and the State Department—each of which he instantly rejected.

The night before he left for the training school at Quantico she told him honestly, "I tried very hard to raise you to be able to make your own decisions. And today I have to admit that I very much regret that." But she was sitting in the bleachers at Quantico the day he graduated from the academy. And completely true to her nature, she'd brought with her to Virginia an attractive young woman she'd met at a Bucky Fuller lecture at the 92nd Street Y. But even a decade later she still held tight to the hope that the FBI might just be a phase he was going through. A very long phase.

"One round of golf," she pleaded. "Is that too much for a son to do for his widowed mother? Just play on Saturday."

"I love you, Mops," he said, gently hanging up the phone. "I'll call you later."

Once again Russo was waiting for him outside the building with coffee from the cart on Broadway. "You know, you could come inside," he told her. "I had the apartment cleaned just last year. Most likely you won't get those diseases anymore." Then he added thoughtfully, "Just to be safe, though, you probably want to stay out of the kitchen."

Initially Slattery had turned down their request to spend a second day investigating the link between the missing professor and the mob. But when Russo started dropping phrases like "national security" and "communist involvement," he got the hint. Slattery put a relief team in the overnight slot. Team II was thrilled to work days. Watching a locked door at 3 a.m. can get pretty boring.

Conveniently O'Brien lived only a few blocks from the professor, so they took the shoe leather express. It was one of those good-to-be-alive-and-in-the-city mornings, with just enough chill in the air to snap you awake. Connor had proved to himself years earlier that he was not one of those lucky people gifted with the ability to sip coffee and move at the same time without spilling it on their shirt, no matter how small the edge they tore off the plastic lid. But he watched with admiration as Russo did exactly that and made it look easy. Show-off, he thought to himself. If it were his decision, he would have sat on his front stoop in the flush of morning and enjoyed the cup of coffee, but Russo was in a hurry. Sure, he thought, it's easy to be in a hurry when you can sip coffee and walk at the same time. So as they walked, he held the cup far enough away from his body to avoid the inevitable coffee splash, and when they reached the corner, he dropped it into an overflowing trash basket.

Professor Peter Gradinsky lived on the third floor of a five-story brownstone. Whoever was in his apartment buzzed O'Brien and Russo into the building without asking them to identify themselves. O'Brien guessed the intercom was broken. The turn-of-the-century building was well kept. As they climbed the stairs, O'Brien noted that someone had put flowers in vases inside each of the coffin corners—recesses in the walls on the landings to allow mourners carrying a coffin to complete the turn. There were expensively framed oil paintings—real oil paintings rather than the tacky reproductions commonly used for decoration—on the walls, so O'Brien figured the tenants probably knew and trusted each other. That meant there wasn't a lot of turnover in the building.

Gradinsky's door was opened by a tall, thin woman, wearing modest glasses, whose long, narrow face was framed by sensible light brown hair. O'Brien guessed fifty-two but was pretty sure she would claim she was forty-five if anybody asked but nobody ever did. Russo noticed that her prim white cotton blouse was wrinkled and suspected she'd slept in it. "Yes?" she asked.

O'Brien had learned a lesson with Geri Simon. This time he let Russo speak first. Obviously there was some kind of woman-to-woman communication he hadn't been aware of previously. "Mrs. Gradinsky?" Russo guessed correctly. Russo then introduced herself and O'Brien.

Grace Gradinsky looked at her quizzically. "Yes?"

"We'd like to speak with you about your husband," Russo continued, "Peter Gradinsky?"

Grace Gradinsky's face remained impassive. Neither agent could read anything into it. "Is he all right?" she asked calmly. "Has something happened to him?"

"No, we don't think so," O'Brien said. "Mind if we come in for a couple of minutes?"

She stepped back and allowed them to come into the apartment. They stood under the graceful arch separating the entrance foyer from the living room. Russo said bluntly, "Mrs. Gradinsky, we got a report that your husband is missing. Is that true?"

Gees Louise, Russo, O'Brien thought, take it easy there, partner. You're using all the charm of a truck.

But in response Grace Gradinsky showed her first trace of emotion. She closed her eyes and swallowed while pushing back a nonexistent curl. Then she caught herself. Looking directly at Russo, she demanded somewhat defensively, "Who told you that?"

The manner in which she asked that question made it pretty clear to O'Brien that she thought she already knew the answer. The fact that she asked "who" rather than "how" or "where" told him a lot.

"Let me explain something to you," he said in the most confidential tone he could muster. "Sometimes, when we're in the middle of one investigation, we come across information about something totally different. So, unfortunately, I can't . . . you understand, I can't really tell you how we found out about this. Obviously we did, though. So now what we're trying to do is make sure everybody's okay."

As most people did, she responded in a tone mirroring the tone he used when asking the question. "And then you want to ask him some questions, right?"

He nodded. "Honestly it's nothing that big." Then he said it again for emphasis. "Honest."

"All right," she decided. "Come in." She led them into the living room. A plush sofa and two comfortable-looking wingback chairs were arranged around a large oak armoire, which O'Brien assumed contained the TV set. Bookshelves covered the far wall from floor to ceiling. There were two additional rooms and a bathroom beyond the living room. Their doors were closed, but, O'Brien thought, one of those rooms was probably used as an office. The apartment was tastefully immaculate. Every object seemed to be precisely where Ralph Lauren might have placed it. Even the books were perfectly aligned; not a single book was laid casually on top of other books or pushed against the wall. Nothing in the apartment looked new, but everything appeared well cared for. This was the type of apartment, he decided, that you could just move right into and you'd know exactly where the laundered and folded towels would be found.

The two agents sat side by side on the sofa. There was a highly polished wooden coffee table in front of them. Grace Gradinsky took the easy chair to their right, in front of the windows. She sat almost perfectly upright, as if balancing an invisible book on her head, and asked O'Brien, "Could you tell me again what is it you found out?"

"It's not that much," he admitted. "Just that he was supposed to meet some people and didn't show up. Now they can't find him. The people up at Columbia told us he hadn't been there the last few days." He didn't mind that she was questioning him. Answering questions was an effective way of establishing a relationship with a subject. Make the interview as conversational as possible. Give up a little in hopes of getting a lot.

She closed her eyes and nodded slightly. "He hasn't been home in three days," she said evenly. "I don't know what to do, Detective . . ."

"Agent," he corrected. "We're FBI, not NYPD."

Three nights earlier, she began, Peter had been working at home early in the evening when the phone rang. It was about seven-thirty, maybe a little later. She had answered it and a man whose voice she didn't recognize asked to speak to him. "They were only on the phone for a few seconds. Then Peter told me he had to go somewhere. He didn't tell me where, he didn't tell me who he was meeting. He didn't tell me anything. He just said he'd be back in a little while, gathered up some papers, and left. That was it." She looked away and whispered, "That was it."

As gently as possible, Russo asked her why she hadn't called the police.

"I don't . . . I mean, I don't know," she said, fumbling for the right words. "Peter is such a . . . he's such a shy man. I was certain he was going to come back any minute. And I knew if I made a big fuss about him, he would just . . . he wouldn't understand. I know it doesn't make sense, but I promise you, it would if you knew him."

"The man who called," O'Brien asked. "You remember anything different, anything unusual about his voice?"

She considered that. "Well, he did have a pretty strong Russian accent. I mean, all that he said to me was, like . . ." In a bad parody of a Russian accent she said in a masculine voice, " 'I speak please to Professor Peter.' That was all he said."

Russo asked, "Did Peter talk to him in English or Russian?"

"Russian. I couldn't tell what they were talking about. I only know the tourist words. You know, *nyet, dos vadanya* . . ."

For the next hour Grace Gradinsky seemingly did her best to answer all their questions. Peter Gradinsky had been born in Cleveland, Ohio. His parents had settled there after immigrating from the

Ukraine. His father worked in the paint box at a General Motors plant. His parents primarily spoke Russian at home, which is where he had learned the language, and then he majored in it at Colgate. They had met at Colgate and had been married for twenty-eight years. They'd lived in this apartment for more than twenty years; it was rent-controlled and the landlord really wanted them to move out. They did not own a car. They had no children. No, Peter had not been acting any differently recently. Organized crime? No, that's ridiculous, Peter didn't know people like that. No, he didn't seem un-usually nervous when he left the apartment that night. No, he'd never just disappeared like this before. The longest he'd ever been gone without an explanation was a few hours. As far as she knew, he was not in contact with Soviet government officials. No, he was not spending any more money than usual—she actually laughed out loud at that question—and there certainly had not been any unex-plained deposits made to their bank account. Yes, she always held on to both their passports; Peter didn't even know where she kept them. She thought it might be important that on occasion he worked as a translator for the State Department. She didn't really know what level security clearance he had; Secret, she thought. At least that's what was stamped on those folders he brought home.

"Excuse me?" Russo asked somewhat incredulously. "You're telling us that Peter brought home folders that were marked Secret?"

Grace appeared unsettled. "That isn't all right?" She looked at Connor. "He told me he had a clearance for all those papers. He just translated them, that's all. He wouldn't even let *me* look at them." She smiled at the memory. "I used to say to him, 'Who am I going to tell, Peter? My mother the big famous spy?'"

O'Brien could hear the tremor in Laura's voice as she asked, "Mrs. Gradinsky, are any of those folders here now?"

"Oh no, I'm sure of that. It didn't happen that often. I mean, he only brought them home a few times. He just isn't doing much work for the government anymore."

"Those times that he did bring them home, where'd he keep them?"

"In his desk. In his office." She pointed toward the closed doors. Behind one of them, obviously, was the professor's office. "He put a little lock thing on the drawer. He didn't tell me the combination, but that's where he kept them."

Connor O'Brien leaned forward and listened intently to her answers. As always, he took copious notes, but within minutes of beginning this questioning he was certain of one thing: Her answers were total bullshit. This woman knew substantially more than she intended to reveal, and nothing short of pulling out her badly chewed fingernails with a pair of pliers would make her tell them the truth.

An experienced agent can tell pretty quickly whether or not a subject is being truthful. Answers consist of a lot more than words; what's important is the pauses between those words, the attempt to inject phony emotion into them, body language—unusually egotistical or arrogant people like to lock eyes when lying to you as a means of proving their intellectual superiority—and even demonstrating extreme concern by being overly cooperative. People telling the truth just tell the truth, whereas people who are lying try to act like they're telling the truth, usually with about the same success as a drunk trying to act sober.

So to O'Brien the first question to be answered was why she was lying. Everything else flowed from that. When Russo had finished compiling a list of the professor's co-workers who would know his normal routine, O'Brien asked, "How is his health, Mrs. Gradinsky? Blood pressure, cholesterol, things like that?"

She actually laughed at that question. Peter Gradinsky was the most health conscious human being she had ever known. Obsessive. Fanatical. That's why she laughed, she explained. "He thinks there's a vitamin that can cure anything. You wouldn't believe how many pills he swallows every day. Red ones, green ones, you just name it, he takes it."

O'Brien smiled as if in recognition. "I know. I know exactly what you mean. My father was very much like that. There must have been a thousand of those little bottles all over the place." That was a complete lie, of course, and even he was amazed how easily the words slid off his tongue. But then he made his point: "So where'd Professor Gradinsky keep all those bottles? If you don't mind, I'd like to take a look at them."

Surprisingly this was the question that stopped her. She coughed nervously, then recovered her balance and explained that he kept his pills locked in the same desk drawer in which he kept the documents he brought home.

She waited expectantly for Connor's next question. But he just sat there, looking right at her, as if waiting for her to continue her response. That was an interviewing technique he often used. Silence makes most people uncomfortable, creating a vacuum that they invariably fill with additional details. "I mean, I don't know the combination," she finally added. "You know Peter," she said, then caught herself. "Well, you don't. But as I told you, he's a very private man. He doesn't like anyone touching his things. Even me. You should just see how upset he gets if I look in his pants pockets when I do the laundry."

Rather than being upset that her husband was missing, O'Brien realized, she was furious. He could feel her anger swelling as she continued, "It's like I committed a federal crime. Days'll go by and he won't talk to me. And for what?" She looked to Laura for support. "For looking in his pockets?" Just as suddenly as the outburst began, she caught herself. "I'm sorry," she said, deflated, "I'm just . . . I'm upset is all."

She composed herself, brushing off her blouse as if it were covered with crumbs. She brushed too hard and too long. Russo saw the tears forming in her eyes. "I love Peter," she said finally, and added emphatically, "Really I do. But sometimes . . . sometimes I don't understand why he does the things he does."

They understood, Russo said supportively.

"Would you do me a favor, Mrs. Gradinsky?" O'Brien asked

politely, handing her his notebook. "Would you write down for me the medicines he takes, and maybe the name and phone number of his doctor and the drugstore where he fills his prescriptions?"

While Grace provided that information, Connor excused himself and used the bathroom. When Grace finished, Russo asked her for a recent photograph of her husband that she could keep. The best Grace could offer was a picture of the Gradinskys with another couple taken in a crowded restaurant. "That's him on my right," she said, pointing to him, "the shorter man."

When Connor returned, she gave him back his notebook, in which she had listed all his pills and vitamins. In return, both agents handed her their business cards, the expensive ones with the full-color raised FBI seal and the New York headquarters phone number. They asked her to contact them the moment he returned, promised to keep her informed of any progress they made in their search, and finally Russo suggested, "Mrs. Gradinsky, don't you think it would make sense for you to file a missing persons report with the NYPD?"

"Oh no no, not yet," she responded instantly. "Peter's all right, I'm sure of it. Really, you just don't know how angry he'd be with me when he found out I went to the police. Please don't do anything. Just . . . just give him a few more days, please. If he isn't back, I'll do it. I will, honest I will."

"Wow, that was a strange one," Laura said as they walked to his garage to pick up his car. "I've seen people get more upset about their cat getting loose. She's a tough one, isn't she?"

"I think she knows where he is," O'Brien responded, "or at least she has a pretty good idea. She knows he's safe too. That's why she doesn't want to get the cops involved. And wherever he is, he took off on his own. If he was running, he was running real slow. Anybody who takes the time to pack all his pills isn't in a big hurry to leave."

"I thought she said they were locked in his desk."

"Sure they were. Except that when I was in the bathroom, I checked the medicine cabinet. Three of the shelves were crammed with pill bottles, aspirin, all kinds of cold crap—some of it expired two years ago—hair spray, all the usual stuff. You couldn't fit one more thing on any of those shelves. But the bottom shelf was empty. Obviously the professor cleaned it out."

As they walked along, occasionally their shoulders touched. It was casual, accidental, natural, and neither of them said anything about it and moved farther away.

"So what are you thinking?" she asked.

He shook his head. "I don't know exactly. I mean, let's look at it: We got a missing college professor that the mob's more interested in finding than his own wife. And after meeting her I'm wondering that if I was Gradinsky, who would I rather have find me?"

Driving downtown, they debated their next move. Officially this was the end of their investigation. Unless they could come up with a compelling reason to continue, it was back to the Country Club. Slattery couldn't justify giving them any additional time without opening up the great gates of the bureaucracy and letting loose the flood of paperwork that would inevitably flow through.

If there is a single aspect of the job despised by just about every agent, it is the paper trail. Every aspect of every investigation has to be reported and recorded, every plan has to be approved, every dollar has to be accounted for with receipts, and every additional request has to be put on paper. People often ask me how difficult it was for me to work undercover inside the mob for six years. It was real tough, I tell them, real tough, but it did have at least one wonderful benefit: For six beautiful years I didn't have to fill out a single form. Except for the fact that I could have been uncovered and whacked at any minute, I was in agent heaven. I rarely took any notes—I couldn't risk the wiseguys finding them in my apartment—and I wore a wire fewer than a dozen times. I remembered as much as I possibly could about every day, every conversation, and as often as was safe and necessary I spoke with my case agent and gave him all the details. The case agents with whom I worked were responsible for generating the mountains of paperwork.

The fact that the mob was looking for a Columbia University Russian professor was interesting, but certainly not of sufficient importance to justify a commitment of substantial government resources. Simply stated, no one was going to make a federal case out of it. But for Russo, and only slightly less so for O'Brien, it offered the lure of opportunity. For at least the next few months they were stuck in the Country Club. While they were part of a potentially important investigation, laying the foundation for an attack on the entire structure of organized crime in New York City, their role was little more than record-keeper. They spent their days and nights noting who came to the social club and when they left and who farted into the microphone and laughed about it. After perhaps another six months spent listening to the same people telling the same jokes they would testify at numerous trials that the official transcriptions were true and accurate reports of legal wiretaps.

It was a necessary assignment in the building of a successful career, but Laura Russo was just too ambitious to sit back and let the bureaucracy control her destiny. There had to be a way to convince Slattery that there was substantially more to this case than what had thus far surfaced.

O'Brien listened politely as she laid out the arguments she would use with Slattery. He had already decided to support her, but his reasons were less professional than personal. Things do happen that way on the job. Simply put, he was having a good time working with her.

If asked, O'Brien would have claimed that he firmly supported the relatively new movement for women's equality, but it was still very hard for him to completely overcome the evolutionary process that had created the American male. He would definitely have objected to being called a male chauvinist pig—he was thrilled to be in the women's camp—but the undeniable fact was that when she was working intently, she really was cute. Even during the long interview with Grace Gradinsky, even after sitting through the four-hour mandatory sensitivity training course, even after competing against female agents at Quantico, he just couldn't help appreciating the way her white silk blouse followed the contours of her lovely breasts. As much as he tried to resist, several times that afternoon he found himself stealing looks at her, trying hard to make it appear as if he were looking at the books behind her. "Look," he told her as they parked in the bureau's underground garage, "I think I got a good idea about how we can get this case going."

"Tell me," she said, and her face brightened.

Several minutes later they were sitting in Slattery's office. "National security," he said to Slattery, invoking the holy phrase.

Slattery sighed deeply. That was just about the last thing he wanted to hear that afternoon. The good news for O'Brien and Russo was that Slattery was having a very bad day. Some clerk in Human Resources was giving him a hard time about his 67-E, his personnel file. Slattery was just beginning to think about retiring—he had his years in—so he wanted to make sure his records were in good order. That way if he made the decision, he would have no difficulty getting his pension and health insurance benefits. As it turned out, it was a very good thing he'd initiated the process.

According to the bureau, Special Agent James Slattery did not exist. His 67-E was gone. The clerk had assured him that this was not really a problem, that almost definitely his records had been taken upstairs to be transferred to a computer disk, and that whoever took the file just forgot to leave a red slip in its place. Nothing to worry about, the clerk said.

"Let me make sure I've got this right. You're telling me that officially I don't exist and that I shouldn't worry about it," Slattery had asked incredulously.

"Oh, come on, of course you exist," the clerk replied. "Just not on paper."

Slattery was furious. He wanted to know exactly what he had to do to make sure the problem was solved. Actually, the clerk told him, that was sort of the tricky part. Because officially he didn't exist, he couldn't make any requests to Human Resources. Somebody else would have to make that request for him.

Slattery had slammed down the phone without resolving the problem. He hated himself for yelling at clerks, but how the hell could they lose his entire career? It was embarrassing. Americans throughout the world were relying on the efficiency of the FBI to fight crime and protect them from domestic upheaval. Or whatever they were calling the fight against communism. But according to the bureau, he had officially become the man who never was. Real efficient.

And then O'Brien and Russo were sitting across from him suggesting they open up a major new investigation. "What are you talking about?" he asked.

That's when O'Brien invoked the magic words "national security."

Slattery buried his face in his hands and just couldn't help laughing. What else could happen to him today? National fucking security. The two words that throughout the forty-year cold war opened the vault. "Oh, please," he practically pleaded, "don't do this to me today."

O'Brien knew that he had him on the run. "C'mon, Jim, look at what we got. There's something going on here. One, a Russian-language professor who occasionally translates secret documents for Uncle Sam suddenly turns up missing. We don't know what kind of documents, we don't know the last time he worked. We don't know if he owed anything to anybody or what he might have had in his possession. We know diddly-squat is what we know. Two, we do know that the mob is looking for him, but we don't know why. Three, his wife says that the night he disappeared he got a phone call from a man speaking with a Russian accent and responded by putting on his coat and walking out the door. Certainly sounds a little *Manchurian Candidate* to me. Four, he's been gone at least three days and she still hasn't reported it to the cops. It doesn't even look like she called the college to find out if he was showing up to teach his classes. Which he isn't, by the way. And we're pretty sure she knows a lot more than she told us . . ."

"She definitely wasn't too upset that he was gone," Russo added.

"Five, we're guessing now, but it is possible somebody warned her not to make a big deal out of it and he'd be fine." He paused and looked at Russo. "Anything else?"

"He left on his own, we know that," she added. "He took time to pack all his pills, so he had to know he was going to be gone for at least a few days. And he's definitely connected."

Slattery had really tried to pay attention, but one thought kept flashing in his mind, bright as one of those neon signs in Times Square: I'm the fucking invisible FBI agent! But still he managed to hear enough of O'Brien's earnest pitch to know there was very little there. Put it all together and it sounded an awful lot like a guy who owed something to somebody had just taken off. Only a few years earlier Slattery had worked with the NYPD on a joint task force investigating the Michele Sindona case. Sindona, the pope's banker who had been indicted for looting the Franklin National Bank, had been kidnapped on 42nd Street in the middle of the afternoon, about a week before his bank fraud trial was set to begin. It turned out that Sindona had fled to Sicily to avoid the trial until the chief witness against him could be murdered. He was hidden by the Gambino family.

That kind of convenient disappearance happened pretty often, although maybe not on that level, and the hideout was usually in a place like Red Hook in Brooklyn or Flushing, Queens, rather than Naples. But Slattery knew that the mob only searched for people with whom it did business. If forced to guess about this guy, Jim Slattery would have put his chips on gambling losses.

But he listened to O'Brien and Russo with as much enthusiasm as he could fake. The relationship between agents in the field and their supervisors can be more complicated than a large family with an inherited fortune. Often it is symbiotic. The agent in the field is dependent on his or her support team. A supervisor can get up on the wrong side of the bed one morning and end a six-month investigation on a whim. But the career of the street agent or supervisor might also hinge on an agent's work. If an agent screws up, the support team might sink with him. So for a case agent it's a balancing act between the bureau's rules and the needs of his people.

There are good and bad supervisors, case agents, and support teams. It really is the luck of the schedule. There are wimps afraid to take a step outside the box without permission from Washington in triplicate. But there are just as many people who would take a bullet to protect their operation. Well, maybe an administrative bullet, but if it came down to it, they would risk their careers to give the agents in the field the support they needed to succeed.

Generally the agents who worked with Slattery respected him. O'Brien knew that Slattery got all the punch lines. In this situation, for example, he knew that they didn't even have enough evidence to interest the Mayberry PD, much less convince the bureau to commit time and resources to the investigation. And he had no doubt Slattery knew it too. But he was also pretty confident Slattery would get the real message: Trust me on this one.

His timing was perfect. Today was the day on which Slattery semi-officially stopped giving a damn. Spend the bureau's money? Sure, the taxpayers can afford it. Bend the rules? Break them? Okay, break them in fucking half. Just make sure nobody gets hurt and remember the golden rule: Cover thy ass.

Slattery grabbed a yellow legal pad and a government-issue Bic pen. "National security, huh? That's pretty serious stuff." Each of them played the game superbly. By the time Slattery finished covering the long sheet of yellow paper with his notes, the pieces seemed to fit together neatly. Officially Slattery determined that there was not even hard evidence that national security had been compromised for him to go through the whole rigmarole of informing Washington. Instead, the best he could do—and he said this to O'Brien and Russo with a straight face—was provide limited support for an additional week. That way, if this did turn out to have serious implications, no one could accuse him of allowing national security to be compromised. And if it turned out to be something as benign as the mob trying to collect a debt, he could still defend his actions. It was all right there on the sheet of yellow paper.

Slattery would designate this a "preliminary investigation," meaning they would be investigating to determine if there was anything worth investigating. It would cut down substantially on the initial paperwork. But limited support from the FBI is still quite impressive. Consider it the silver standard rather than the gold. In an effort to locate Columbia University Professor of Slavic Languages Peter Gradinsky before the mob found him, and determine why he had taken a hike, government resources would be employed on an "as available" basis. This wasn't a full-court press; the bureau wasn't going to take any agents off their current assignments to work this one. There were probably eleven hundred agents working in the New York office, and they were already busy conducting probably ten times their number of investigations, just about every one of which was deemed more important than this one. But memos would be circulated stating the basic facts with an enlargement of the yearbook photo. Support facilities would be available for transcriptions, translations, and basic research. Agents with downtime might be recruited to do some grunt work. O'Brien and Russo were satisfied. Thrilled, actually.

Obviously this was not a "Priority." Not a whole lot was going to happen in a hurry. But normal investigative procedures would be taken: With the permission of a friendly federal judge, which would be easy to obtain once the catchall term "national security" was invoked, the Gradinskys' telephone would be tapped. Based on available manpower, for at least part of each day—exactly which hours would be determined based on Grace Gradinsky's patterns—there would be visual surveillance on the apartment, and when she left, she would be tailed. Another subpoena would be obtained, this one for a record of the telephone calls Gradinsky had made from both his apartment and his office; the numbers would be run through a reverse phone book to try to determine whom he'd called. All his recent credit card purchases would be examined and his accounts marked to ensure that the FBI would be notified immediately if his cards were used. Hotels and motels in the New York metropolitan area, with an emphasis on the lower-priced places where he might pay with cash, would be checked to determine if he had registered using his own name. His bank records would be subpoenaed to determine if he had made any sizable transactions, either deposits or withdrawals, within the past month. Car rental agencies would be contacted to see if he had rented a car. The professor's photograph and a brief descriptor would be circulated throughout the NYPD, transit police, housing police, and all other local law enforcement agencies with a request to contact the bureau with any information about this missing person.

Accomplishing all of this could take several weeks, and Slattery felt confident that long before it was completed, Professor whoever would show up somewhere. Most probably alive.

The first action was getting a tap on his home and office telephones. Unlike bugging a social club or a mob hangout, this was pretty simple. Judge Margot Sklar signed a warrant that same afternoon. That night FBI technicians went into the basement of the Gradinskys' building and located the telephone box. It was an old one, a rusting gunmetal-gray box overflowing with a rainbow of wires. It was the kind of mess that installers and repairmen referred to as "an electric circus." Normally, unless a technician gets lucky, in a box crammed with as many wires as this one it would take more than an hour to locate and isolate the Gradinskys' phone. But in this case the technician picked out the wire seconds after he'd opened the box.

It was the one with the tap already on it.

FIVE

This is no fucking way to treat me," Bobby Blue Eyes complained.

"You still breathing?" Fast Lenny asked.

"Yeah, so?"

"So shut the fuck up and keep breathing. Fucking skinny marink like you, you should be happy we even take you along, all the good you can do if we get jammed up."

"He's got a point there, Bobby," Jackie Keys agreed sympathetically. "What the fuck we need you for? We wanted comic fucking relief, we woulda brought Robin fucking Williams."

There was no way of predicting how people would act on the way to a job. Even a setup like this was supposed to be. Crime is a dangerous business: If things go wrong, people could end up dead or spending years in a ten-by-twelve cage. There were probably as many ways to prepare for a job as there were people doing them. I knew people you couldn't shut up with a lead pipe when they were on the way to do some work, while there were other people who wouldn't make a sound. Some people always ate a big meal; other people got so nervous they couldn't eat one bite. One man I knew quite well was a singer, so to relieve tension on the way to a job, he would sing Broadway show tunes; another guy talked sports. Just as in this particular situation humor and bravado were used to lighten the very somber mood.

Five men were squeezed into Fast Lenny's Chevy as they headed uptown to the Garment District. Lenny was driving. Jackie Keys was in the death seat next to him. Bobby was sitting in the back, squashed between Little Eddie and Tony Cupcakes like a doughnut between two boulders. Bobby's nose was itching, but there wasn't anything he could do about it. Both his arms were pinned against his sides, and if he wrestled them free, he would have to sit uncomfortably with his arms out in front of him for the remainder of the ride.

Everybody had an assigned role in the heist. Fast Lenny was driving the backup car. If the truck got tailed, he would use this car to slow down the pursuit. Jackie Keys would open up the truck door if it was locked and get the engine started. Bobby would drive the truck. Eddie and Tony would provide whatever muscle was necessary. A job this simple could have probably been handled by a couple fewer people. The only people absolutely necessary were Lenny, Keys, and Bobby. But Lenny knew that Tony was having some trouble earning and wanted to throw something his way, and Eddie he owed for bringing him into an exotic car job right off a lot in Scarsdale six months earlier. Besides, extra muscle was never a bad thing to have along.

In those days after six o'clock in the evening the Garment District emptied faster than a bus full of geriatrics at a turnpike service area. Nobody actually lived in the area and there were no restaurants to draw a crowd. So after dark it really was possible to hijack a delivery truck right off the street without too much difficulty.

Fast Lenny Matriano, who less than a year earlier had completed a four-year stay in Dannemora for assault with a deadly weapon, the weapon being a thirty-eight-ounce Dave Winfield model Louisville Slugger—although Lenny swore in court that he'd checked his swing—parked the car on 29th just off Broadway about forty minutes before the truck was scheduled to get there. From that spot they had a nice clear view of the electronics store. The store's outside lights were turned off, meaning it was pretty dark under the opened awning, and the interior lights were dimmed. Bobby assumed that the owner had also forgotten to put a decent tape in the exterior security camera. Lenny was conservative. He liked to take a good long look at the neighborhood before going to work. He liked to get the feel of it.

Meanwhile, Bobby was still locked between Eddie and Tony tighter than a champagne cork. He was trying to squirm free, but the more he moved, the harder Eddie and Tony pressed against him. They thought it was hysterical.

While waiting for the truck to get there they traded Garment District tales. Everybody had at least one. There isn't a connected guy in New York who hasn't done some work in the Garment District. Since they sewed the first *schmatteh,* there has always been some manufacturer who needed cash to pay for his next season or settle a gambling debt or get his pregnant girlfriend fixed and no bank would give him toilet paper. So he was willing to pay the going interest rate. Plus. Or maybe one of the union locals was having problems. Or a furrier had a walk-in box with good minks and bad locks. Or a designer who needed some arm to help him get the money he was owed. There was always something. But all Little Eddie wanted to talk about was what he was going to do to Benny Rags the next time he came around. "Ever see a guy shit velvet?" he asked rhetorically.

The truck got there about twenty minutes late. It was one of those big U-Hauls. The driver parked next to the hydrant directly in front of the store. Jackie Keys was out of the car and halfway down the block even before the driver left his cab. Bobby, Eddie, and Cupcakes were only a few steps behind him. The adrenaline was flowing. Bobby noticed that the driver didn't bother locking the cab. As they approached the store, Bobby saw the driver knocking on the glass door, then cupping his hands and peering inside. He was looking for somebody. Ah gees, Bobby thought, now where the fuck is the owner?

The driver was a black guy, middle-aged, wearing glasses. His black leather coat was unzipped and he was wearing one of those T-shirts that boasted "I'm with Stupid," with an arrow under it. When he heard them coming, he turned around and the arrow pointed directly at Little Eddie. Eddie reached him first. "What's going on?" Eddie asked as friendly as he could manage.

"I'm looking for the owner here," the driver explained. He pointed to a hand-printed sign taped on the inside of the door. "He went somewhere for a sandwich." It was then the driver spotted Jackie Keys climbing up into the cab. "Hey," he shouted, and ran protectively toward his truck.

Little Eddie grabbed him by the shirt and pushed him against the truck, which shielded him from the view of passing cars. Bobby knew he had about thirty seconds to get the truck rolling before the odds of being spotted increased dramatically.

Eddie lifted the driver off the ground and half shoved, half tossed him into the cab. Unfortunately Jackie Keys was in the driver's seat, trying to get the truck started. The driver slammed into Jackie, knocking off his glasses. They landed under the brake pedal. Jackie reached for them, but they were stuck under something. "Fuck!" Jackie shouted.

The driver was too terrified to scream. Over and over he repeated, "Don't hurt me, don't hurt me."

"Shut the fuck up, fuckhead," Cupcakes snapped at him. "Nobody wants to fucking hurt you."

The driver scrambled over Jackie and into the passenger seat and pressed up against the door, holding up his hands protectively in front of him. He glanced at the handle, clearly wondering if he could get the door open and make a break for it.

"Don't even fucking think about it," Cupcakes warned him. Before the driver could make a decision, Little Eddie had moved to the passenger side of the truck and was standing outside the door. The driver relaxed into a ball, leaning against the door. "That's a good boy," Tony said.

Jackie was reaching under the brake pedal, struggling to get his glasses loose. Bobby said to him evenly, without any sense of panic, "Forget it, Keys. Just get the truck started now."

Jackie relaxed. "Yeah." He started to pop out the ignition, then stopped abruptly, as if smacked in the face by a sudden realization.

"What?" Bobby asked.

Jackie turned to the driver. "Give me the key." The driver handed it to him. "Thank you." Jackie slipped the key in the ignition and the engine ka-ka-chunked into life. Jackie got out and Bobby slid behind the wheel.

On the passenger side Little Eddie opened the door and got in, squeezing the driver into the middle. "Don't say one fucking word," Eddie warned him. The driver nodded.

Bobby checked the rearview mirror. Lenny was right behind him. Bobby put the truck in gear and took off. He stopped at the first traffic light, hitting the brake pretty hard, and as he did, he heard Jackie Keys' glasses crunching under his foot. He headed for the East Side Drive. He'd planned a route on which there were no tolls and little chance of traffic at that hour. He took the drive south and got off at the Williamsburg Bridge exit. Fast Lenny followed several car lengths behind until he was sure they'd gotten away clean, then he took off.

Bobby drove down through the Lower East Side, finally stopping next to a vacant lot littered with all kinds of garbage in the shadows of the bridge. Little Eddie got out of the truck first, dragging the driver with him. Holding his shirt collar with his right hand and sticking him with the pointing finger of his left hand, he told him, "I ain't got time to fuck with you, so listen good. You say one word to the cops, I swear to God I'll find you and cut your motherfucking balls off. Okay? Got it?"

The driver nodded. "I won't say nothing. I swear. Just don't hurt me," he pleaded once again. "I got kids." Bobby smelled something familiar, then saw the stain spreading in the driver's crotch. That didn't surprise him. He'd seen lots of guys pee in their pants. He'd seen guys so scared they shit themselves.

"All right," Eddie continued, releasing the driver's shirt and putting a comforting hand on his shoulder. "But I gotta do this or they're gonna be over you like oil on Arabs. They're gonna think you gave up your load to us." And with that he punched the driver in the face. It was a short but powerful blast. The driver staggered backward, blood pouring out of his smashed nose, trying desperately to maintain his balance. "Hey. Asshole," Eddie instructed him, "fall down. Don't be no fucking hero." Without taking his eyes off Eddie the driver half sat, half stumbled onto the ground. "Good boy, now you just sit there for a while," Eddie said, then got back into the truck. "Let's get outta here," he told Bobby, shaking his head and sighing. "Fucking guy."

Bobby drove to a warehouse near the Fulton Fish Market, under the West Side Highway extension. Fast Lenny was waiting there with Cupcakes and Jackie. They were already laughing about the store owner. "Fucking guy goes out for fucking dinner? What the fuck was he thinking? Fucking asshole."

The truck had a roll-up rear door, which was padlocked. The key was on the same chain as the ignition key. Bobby opened the lock and lifted the door. Then he just stood there, stunned, staring into the empty truck bed. "Holy fucking shit," Cupcakes said with awe when he realized what had happened, "we been robbed."

The five of them stood there staring at nothing for a few minutes. They couldn't believe it. Somebody had had the balls to hijack the load from the hijackers. "I'm gonna fucking kill that fuck," Little Eddie promised, deciding instantly that the thief had to be the owner of the store. "That no-good motherfucker set us up."

Eddie figured the owner had to be double-dipping. By stealing the merchandise off the truck before it could be stolen, the owner could sell it hot for a substantial amount of money, then after the truck was hijacked, he could get the total value of the load from his insurance company. Even to Eddie it seemed like a smart plan, except for the fact that Eddie intended to personally rip out the guy's lungs and feed them to the lions in the Bronx Zoo.

Bobby didn't see things quite that clearly. At heart he was an optimist. He couldn't believe that anyone could be stupid enough to believe they could get away with stealing from the mob. That just didn't happen. And after *The Godfather* movies it happened even less. "Just cool it, Eddie," he said. "We're gonna take care of this, don't worry 'bout it."

There really was nothing else to be done that night except dumping the truck. After wiping it down to get rid of the fingerprints and picking out the remains of Jackie's glasses Bobby drove it over to the big U-Haul parking lot in Hunts Point. This was the main holding lot for the entire metropolitan area. Trucks, vans, and trailers of all sizes were kept here until they were needed. There had to be at least three hundred vehicles parked there. The security guard had done business with the families for a long time, allowing trucks to come and go without keeping any records. Bobby drove the truck onto the lot, parked it somewhere in the middle, and wiped off the steering wheel one last time. This was the best possible place in the world to hide a U-Haul truck, right in the middle of three hundred other U-Haul trucks. It would be weeks before it was found.

Bobby had the hustler's mentality: Throw a dozen balls into the air and hope you catch a couple of them when they came down. And if you didn't, then throw up a dozen more and take another shot. So he was able to accept this fiasco—at least temporarily—better than a man like Little Eddie, who lived and died with every deal. Bobby lived his life on pretty level ground, while Eddie's life was a series of peaks and valleys, peaks and valleys. For Eddie this was one deep valley.

But because this was Fast Lenny's deal, it was up to him to make it right. He said he'd go see the store owner first thing the next morning and, unless he got the right answers, "The fucking funeral's gonna be in the afternoon."

Eddie was still fuming the next morning, like a volcano cooling down after the eruption, as Bobby leaned on the buzzer marked "Gradinsky." A few seconds later, without asking who was there, whoever was in the apartment buzzed the door open. The professor lived on the third floor of a five-story walk-up on the Upper West Side, and by the time they climbed to the third floor, Eddie was sweating worse than a poster boy for global warming. "Jesus," he wheezed, breathing heavily as he banged a fist on the door, "they gotta air-condition this fucking world."

A muffled woman's voice asked from behind the locked door, "Who is it?"

"Some friends of the professor," Eddie replied gruffly. "Just open the goddamn door."

Bobby let out a low, appreciative whistle. "Nice manners."

Members of organized crime don't conduct formal interviews. Things don't work that way. My experience has been that whenever a connected guy wants information from a civilian, all he has to do is ask the right questions. Generally. Sometimes you ask nicely, sometimes it's necessary to ask less than nicely, but most of the time it isn't necessary to ask more than once. And for that a great debt is owed to the motion picture, television, and publishing industries. Most often people have been so terrified by everything they've read about organized crime that when a real live wiseguy shows up at the door, they won't hesitate to tell him everything they know.

The fact is that when your last name is Bonanno or Gambino or Genovese, people are intimidated before you say hello. As with just about all wiseguys, the threat is implied. It isn't just the fear quotient either; there is also the celebrity aspect. For a lot of civilians, talking to a real live gangster is as exciting as meeting a major movie star. It gives them status: They are so important that the mob needs to talk to them. When I was active, at times I spoke with people who could hardly wait for me to leave so they could call their friends to brag, "Guess who I was just talking to." Some of them would have been thrilled if I'd hit them. "Hey, guess who just broke my nose."

So Bobby and Little Eddie were confident that whoever opened the door would not hesitate to speak with them. A nicely dressed older woman with a long, narrow face opened it. Looking at her, Bobby was reminded of the chess piece the horse, except with long hair.

Looking at Bobby, overdressed for the morning in a well-tailored dark gray suit, white tie on white shirt, and a Brooks Brothers camel coat, the woman was reminded of the most recent Charlie Bronson mob film. But if she had any doubt about the identity of the two men standing before her, one glance at Little Eddie, dressed as usual in a blue track suit with white piping, the zippered top half-opened to reveal a tight white T-shirt, settled it. "Come in, please," the woman said politely, "I've been waiting for you." As she led them into the living room, she told them, "The FBI was here yesterday but don't worry, I didn't tell them a thing. I told them he was talking to the Russians and they believed me."

"Good," Bobby said, then looked at Eddie and shrugged. He did not have the slightest idea what she was talking about. The fact that the FBI had already been there did not upset him; actually he sort of expected it. Bobby, who liked things orderly, was impressed by the living room. It was impeccably neat. Not even the dust was out of place. Mostly out of habit he checked the place out. The living room windows looked out onto a checkerboard of backyards, some with gardens, others paved. There was a fire escape landing out the windows, which were double-locked. As he sat down on the long sofa, Bobby said evenly, "Look, lady . . ."

"Grace," she said pleasantly. "Okay, please, tell me. Where is he?"

Almost simultaneously Eddie asked, "Where's who?" and Bobby wondered, "What are you talking about?"

She looked at both of them and said, as if the answer to that question were obvious, "My husband. Peter. You people are with the Mafia, aren't you?"

It was a simple question impossible to answer. This woman was either smart, stupid, or simply naïve. And without knowing anything at all about it, it certainly was possible that the apartment was bugged. Bobby explained, "See, Grace. It's Grace, right?" She nodded. "See, Grace, that's not something we talk about, you know. I mean . . ." He searched for a polite way of saying it.

Little Eddie helped him. "Like who the fuck you think you are asking a question like that?"

Grace was not intimidated. "What are you trying to say?"

Eddie shot a warning finger at her. "Don't fuck with me, lady. I'm not having a good day, okay? What I am is none of your business. You understand?"

Grace cleared her throat. "All right," she agreed. "I do understand. I won't ask you any more of those kind of questions. All I want to know is, where is my husband?"

"Jesus fucking Christ," Eddie blurted out in frustration, "you're worse than my old lady. What is this bullshit about your husband? How the fuck should . . ." Eddie's voice grew louder and louder.

"Eddie! C'mon, man, calm down. Just cool it." Bobby knew what happened when Eddie's volcanic temper erupted. Movie people portrayed men like Little Eddie as sort of cuddly lugs, big strong guys who weren't too bright, but who really meant well and would never hurt a civilian. That wasn't Little Eddie LaRocca. Eddie was a legitimate tough guy. His pride was invested in his strength and his brutality. When Eddie's rage was let loose, there were no rules and no one could control him. People got hurt. So smart people feared him. This woman, this Grace, had absolutely no idea how close she was to that eruption. "Just relax, man, it's okay."

Bobby took a deep breath, and as he turned back to Grace, he forced a pleasant smile. "All right, help me out here. We just want to know one thing. Where is your husband?"

Bobby saw the fear growing in her eyes. "You mean he's not with you? I mean, really not with you?"

Eddie responded, "What the fuck are you talking about, lady? What's this 'with us' bullshit? I never met the guy in my life, and if I knew where the fuck he was, you think I'd be sitting here?"

Her head began shaking nervously as the realization settled in. "I thought . . . ," she began. "I mean . . . sometimes he tells me that he does things. For you people, for the Mafia. He comes home and shows me a big roll of cash. They pay him in cash. That's why I thought . . . I don't understand. If he's not with you, then where . . ."

Bobby grasped both her hands as if to keep her rooted to the moment. "Hey! Grace! Stay with me. What are you talking about?"

She was having trouble catching her breath. "Peter. Sometimes he just goes away for a few days. Like now. And then . . . and then . . ." And then she began losing control. "Oh God, oh dear God . . ."

"Shhh . . . ," Bobby said softly, "it's okay. Honest."

Little Eddie couldn't believe this was happening. "This is total bullshit."

Bobby turned on him, steel in his voice. "Stop. Now." In response Eddie settled back into the deep cushions and disdainfully waved him away, mumbling something under his breath. Although it had not been planned, Bobby and Eddie were playing their variation of the old cop game—call it good crook, bad crook. Bobby went back to Grace. "And then what? What happens?"

She began sobbing. "When he comes back, he tells me . . . I mean, he doesn't tell me any of the details. I don't know anything, I swear . . ." She looked to Bobby for reassurance.

"That's okay, don't worry about it. So? Tell me, what does he tell you?"

Grace continued. Occasionally, and always without warning, Peter Gradinsky would simply disappear for two or three days. During that period he would make no contact with her. The first time it happened she had been frantic. But a day after she had reported him missing to the police department he walked into the apartment, perfectly fine. He couldn't tell her any of the details, she told Bobby. "He said that for my safety it was better if I didn't know too much. And then he admitted he'd been doing secret work for the Mafia.

"When he came back, he always had a lot of money with him. Two thousand, three thousand dollars. In cash. He loved to keep it in his pocket." When he left this time, she continued, he told her he'd be back in a couple of days. So she assumed he was working for the Mafia again. And, to be completely honest, she admitted, she was happy about it. It'd be nice to have some extra money during the holidays. That's why she hadn't called the police. It was only after those

FBI agents showed up that she began getting nervous. And it was why she didn't give those agents any information that might help them.

Bobby wondered aloud why the FBI would be interested in a college teacher—unless they knew considerably more about the situation than he did. "You got any idea how they found out he was gone? Who'd you talk to about this?"

"Nobody, I swear. Peter told me not to tell anybody about any of it." She wiped the tears from her eyes with the back of her hand.

Bobby pulled the handkerchief from the breast pocket of his jacket and handed it to her. He smiled. "Don't worry about it, it's clean." When she had better composed herself, he asked, "Lemme guess. It was a guy and a girl, right? She was sort of nice-looking?" Grace nodded. Bobby took a deep breath and frowned. "Yeah, we know them. All right, now just answer me this: You're telling me your husband never told you what kind of work he was doing? I mean, come on, Grace, you know that's a hard thing for a guy like me to believe."

Eddie answered, "Now, wait a minute there, Bobby. I don't tell my wife nothing either."

Grace shook her head. "No, he didn't. Really."

"But like didn't you ever wonder? Just one time, didn't you ever think, what the fuck do those guys want with my husband?"

"Of course I did. I just thought, you know . . . I mean, Peter's very smart. He really is. A lot of people don't realize how smart he is. I mean, you should hear him speak Russian. We went to Moscow four years ago and it was like he was born there. We'd be walking on the street and . . ."

And then Bobby got it. It all made sense. The guy could speak Russian. The guy could speak fucking Russian. That had to be the reason the wiseguys were looking for him. What else could it be? His good looks? Bobby was angry that he hadn't made the connection right away. During the previous few years an entire Russian mob had come out of nowhere. The Soviet Union had emptied its prisons and allowed thousands of people to emigrate to America. Many of them had settled in Brooklyn, an area on the water called Brighton Beach. Moscow on the Hudson they began referring to it. The five families never had much of a presence in the neighborhood; nobody spoke the language or knew the traditions. So Russian wiseguys filled that need. They came to New York and established their roots. They set up their businesses and took care of anybody who got in their face. Bobby assumed there was a name for them, for the members of Russian organized crime, but he had no idea what it might be. He didn't know the Russian word for wiseguy.

So the Russian-speaking professor had been working for the Italian wiseguys. This was truly an amazing piece of information. Bobby had heard the rumors that some of the families were starting to do business with the commies, but without any real evidence he'd figured it was just people flapping their mouths. The immigrants brought some money with them to Brighton Beach. Anybody who could grab a piece could become a wealthy man.

Bobby could feel his heart pounding like Gene Krupa was in there banging away. He cleared his throat. "Lemme ask you this, then. You ever hear your husband talk about anybody he was working with? Anybody come around here maybe?"

She thought about it for a few seconds, then started nodding. "There was one man he did mention. I know this is someone who drove him to the meetings sometimes. It used to make him laugh. He told me this man was huge, that he had to weigh at least three hundred pounds." She was looking directly at Bobby, and the memory of Peter Gradinsky's joke was making her smile. "And they called him Skinny Al."

Eddie sat up. "Holy fucking shit," he said, carefully enunciating each word.

"What?" Grace asked, alarmed at his reaction. "What?"

"It's nothing," Bobby said. "That's just a guy we know is all." Actually it was a guy they used to know, a guy who only hours earlier had had all his organs neatly put back inside his body cavity and had been sewn up by an assistant coroner in preparation for his funeral.

As Bobby and Eddie left the apartment, Bobby told Grace Gradinsky he would contact her as soon as he got any valid information. "Honest," he lied earnestly, "you can trust me."

Eddie started laughing out loud as they walked down the three flights. "Poor fucking guy," he said, finding the whole situation hysterical. "All he's trying to do is make a few bucks and next thing you know he gets himself caught up between us and the fucking commies. Now, that's funny."

"We don't know for sure that they got him," Bobby said seriously, trying to get his mind around the problem. "You know, there's lots of other things could have happened to him."

"Yeah? Like what? Like maybe he got eaten by one of them sewer alligators?"

Bobby thought about it for a few seconds, then shrugged. "Like a lot of things." But even to himself Bobby had to admit that the professor's situation didn't look too promising. He disappeared right about the same time as the guy who usually drove him to the meetings, and then that guy turned up deader than a brick. There was a pretty good chance the professor had been with him the night he got whacked. For whoever did the work he would have been just a slight complication.

But until they found some evidence, say a body or at least part of a body, there was always hope. Stranger things had happened. Besides, the professor's fate was not his concern. For him the thing that was most interesting was this connection between the family and the commies. The professor's wife had said he'd worked for the mob "several times," meaning that whatever they were doing was an ongoing arrangement. And it had to be pretty important, meaning lucrative; otherwise the Russians would never risk a confrontation with the family. Maybe the professor didn't belong to anyone, but definitely he was working for them.

When they got outside, they found it had started raining and the wind had kicked up. By the time they got back to the car, they were soaked. "Man, give me a fucking break, huh?" Eddie complained, turning up the volume on the radio. If there was a bug planted in the car, nobody was going to be able to overhear a word he said. The theme from *Ghostbusters* was playing and Eddie started singing along loudly, "I ain't afraid of no ghost, I ain't afraid—"

"Gees, Eddie," Bobby interrupted, "a voice like that, you should be in Vegas."

Eddie knew he was kidding. "C'mon," he said.

"No, I'm being serious," Bobby said, " 'cause if you were in Vegas, you wouldn't be here and I wouldn't have to listen to that screeching." Then he laughed.

"You're some funny guy," Eddie said seriously, adding, "I loved that picture. 'Specially the part where the girl turns into like this monster, 'member that part?" He didn't wait for an answer. "Made me think about my wife." When Bobby didn't respond, Eddie pointed out to him, "Get it? I was saying my wife is a monster. See, *that's* funny."

Bobby made a big deal about considering Eddie's joke. "I don't think it's so funny. She's pretty tough. Like how do you think she's gonna react when I tell her your joke?"

Eddie chuckled. "Don't you fucking dare. Then I'll have to call the Ghostbusters." Both of them laughed at the thought of Eddie's wife responding to being compared to a monster. Finally Eddie asked, "What are we doing now?"

"Beats the hell outta me. It doesn't look like we're going to be finding this professor any time soon." Bobby took off his wet hat and placed it on the backseat. "I guess we see what Franzone wants to do."

Traffic in New York City, which was terrible under good conditions, got a lot worse when it rained. It took them more than ten minutes to go a single block. Some song Bobby had never heard was blasting from the radio. "Can't you turn it down?" he asked.

Eddie looked at him with surprise. "I'm like you, I like it loud," Eddie told him. "So nobody can hear us talking."

Bobby leaned closer to the dashboard. "FUCK YOU!" he screamed. "See what those cops make me go through?"

They were not the only members of the crew trying to figure out what was going on. At just about that same time Henry Franzone was sitting in the back room of Popi's Place, a bar on Seventh Avenue off Bleecker known mostly in the neighborhood for its greasy hamburgers and less well for the high-interest loans that actually kept the place in business. The back room at Popi's was very popular with the crew because not too many people ever sat there. It provided the privacy necessary to conduct a lot of different types of business. Franzone was there to meet a man named Frank Weimann, whom he'd known for five years. Weimann was a recruiter at an executive placement firm, but what mattered most about him was that his wife, Lisa, worked as a secretary-stenographer at FBI headquarters in the city.

Organized crime got information in two ways. Most of the time, like Bobby Blue Eyes and Little Eddie, people just asked nicely. That, and the unstated threat of ending up in a trash compactor, was often enough. But sometimes they got it the old-fashioned way: They paid for it. Just as law enforcement has traditionally used paid informants, so has organized crime. And like law enforcement, the payoff wasn't always in cash. It might also be a reduction in debt or the return of a favor, but it was something of real value. Weimann, however, always wanted cash, with the amount depending on the value of his information.

Organized crime is a cash business. There are not a lot of people who take checks or credit cards to settle gambling debts or loan payments or for drugs or cut-rate merchandise. It's cash and carry. Or, as some people used to joke, cash *or* carry—either you pay the cash or we carry you out.

Some people make a lot of money; being able to spend it is the problem. In order to spend money, you have to be able to prove to the government that it came from a legitimate source—a job, for example, or from a legitimate business operation—and that you've paid taxes on it. If the government can show you've spent more than you've legally earned, they can make a case against you. That's the main reason so many wiseguys show up on union payrolls. They get a weekly paycheck, and they pay the taxes and the Social Security. There was the story of a guy out on Long Island named Matty Glenn who came out of prison and immediately started dealing drugs. He made a fortune. In less than a year he'd bought a million-dollar house, a Cadillac, a big boat, he'd bought beautiful clothes for his wife and jewelry for his girlfriend. He paid taxes, not exactly every dollar he owed, and claimed he was a jewelry salesman. One night he pulled into his driveway and DEA agents leaped all over his car with their guns pointed at him. "What are you guys doing?" he screamed. "I'm a salesman."

"Matty," one of the agents told him, "you been on the street ten months and you got a million-dollar house, a big boat, an expensive car, you've bought clothes and jewelry. How could you afford all that?"

"Easy," Matty replied, "I'm a *good* salesman."

Most connected guys carry rolls of cash with them, and they're not shy about flashing it. Some of them I knew would put big bills on top and make the roll thick with singles and fives. Not Franzone, though. Franzone never walked out his front door with less than $5,000 in his pocket. And, as people said about him, he rarely walked *in* that door without the same $5,000 in his pocket. Henry Franzone had what is known in the business as "short arms," meaning they just couldn't reach the bill. Every bill. Like a lot of captains, he expected his crew to provide for him. Usually they did.

"Good afternoon," Weimann said respectfully as he joined Franzone at the table, "it's good to see you." Within seconds a pot of espresso and the proper cups had appeared on the table. Franzone believed completely in the old traditions. Business was done as gentlemen, with respect for each other and the world in which they lived, although it was difficult for him to respect the man sitting opposite him. There is nobody hated more by the wiseguys than a snitch, a rat, a traitor, stoolie, whatever you wanted to call him. A person who betrays his own people for personal gain.

Technically Weimann didn't fit this description. Lisa Weimann was doing the actual work, and all he was doing was negotiating the terms. Franzone recognized the distinction but still found Weimann coarse and dull and despised him. But as long as their business interests coincided, he would be cordial to the man and treat him properly. *"Salute,"* he said, raising his cup and nodding. He was careful not to call Weimann by name, in case the walls were listening.

Weimann carried a leather briefcase with him, which he held on his lap. "*Salute* to you," he replied, tapping the briefcase with his free hand. "I got most of those . . . um, items, I guess, that you asked me for."

Franzone noticed that Weimann's voice was a little higher-pitched than normal, evidence that his nerves were constricting his vocal cords. "Thank you very much. That's a good thing. But maybe there's something else you wanna tell me?"

Weimann sipped his espresso but never took his eyes off Franzone. Frank Weimann was absolutely thrilled to be there, sitting at the same table as a real mafioso. Weimann was a true Mafia buff. He'd seen *The Godfather* in the theater seven times and at just about every opportunity would imitate Brando making an offer that couldn't be refused. He also had read all the popular crime literature. What set him apart from the many other Mafia groupies was his access to real information. Franzone owned him. No one else even knew his identity. He was a gift from a friend of the family's at the MGM Grand in Las Vegas. Lisa Weimann, it turned out, loved the blackjack tables. Loved them to the ring of $21,000 more than she had. In return for forgiving her debt, in addition to cash payments, the Weimanns agreed to provide information on occasion.

Franzone used this resource sparingly. Twice a year, at most, and then only if the matter was important enough to risk blowing the connection. This seemed like one of those times. Franzone needed more information about what was really going on. A college professor didn't come home a few nights, why was that important? Why was the FBI interested? Why was Tony Cosentino asking him for help rather than using his own crew, which was something he had never done before?

Frank Weimann leaned forward conspiratorially and said, "The bureau is real interested in this professor. They're putting a lot of people on it."

No shit, asshole, Franzone thought. Why the fuck you think you're sitting here? But what he said aloud was, "Really? No fucking way."

Weimann nodded earnestly. He glanced nervously around the room.

There was a part of Franzone that wanted to reach across the table and strangle him right there. They were the only two people in a back room only slightly larger than a storage closet. Who the fuck did he think was going to be watching, Eliot Ness?

Satisfied they were alone, Weimann slid the briefcase off his lap and passed it under the table to Franzone. He did not seem to notice that there was no tablecloth covering the table, so that if anybody was watching, they would be able to see this handoff. Obviously, in a back room with the door closed, no one was watching. "Whattya got in here?"

Weimann swallowed hard. "The names and addresses of the agents running the operation," he said. "Plus I got a transcript of the interview they did with the wife and a couple of authorization forms."

Franzone played the game well. He tried to be everything Weimann needed him to be. Leaning forward, he asked in a low voice, "You find out why they're looking for this fucking guy?"

"It's really weird. Nobody's saying anything about it. Whatever they want him for, it's got to be real important, because they're keeping it supersecret."

Franzone exhaled thoughtfully. Normally he discounted whatever Weimann said by at least a third, based on his conclusion that the guy was a major jerkoff and often exaggerated the facts to try to impress him. But this was the first time Weimann had admitted that even his wife couldn't break through security. Whatever was going on, obviously it was real important to the bureau. That was interesting. "All right," Franzone said, pulling out his roll and peeling off five one-hundred-dollar bills. "Here. Now, you listen to me good. You hear one word, you get in touch with me. You call the number. *Capisce?*"

Weimann held the money tightly in his fist and nodded in obeisance. "You can depend on me."

Continuing to play his role to perfection, Franzone playfully tapped Weimann on his cheek just as he had seen an actor playing Meyer Lansky in some film do, then told him, "Youse a good kid. Don't you ever fuck up with me."

Weimann beamed.

Franzone did not return to the Freemont Avenue Social Club that afternoon, which was probably a good thing. Fast Lenny knew only one way to express his feelings: loudly. And so he was screaming angrily at everyone about everything—even Duke, who couldn't hear a word he was screeching. First thing that morning Lenny had walked into the electronics store, grabbed the owner by the throat, and, ignoring his assistant completely, literally dragged him into the back. The owner was predictably terrified; too terrified, in fact, to scream for help. "I swear to God," he pleaded with Lenny. "I don't know what happened. I swear."

"You no-good motherfucker. Where the fuck is that shit at?"

"I don't know, I swear," he swore. "I swear." Tears were rolling down his face. "The truck never got here. I stayed here all night waiting for him, he never got here. I swear."

Lenny loosened his grip. The man stumbled backward and fell. He was too scared to even try to get up. "What are you talking? You telling me you don't know what went down?"

"Yes." He hesitated. "No." He paused again. "I don't know nothing, I swear. Honest to God, Lenny, the warehouse told me the driver

left, but he never showed. I don't know what the hell happened to
him."

"You want to know what fucking happened," Lenny yelled, "I'll
fucking tell you what happened." Lenny kicked him in his kidney as
hard as he could. "The fucking truck was empty, that's what fucking
happened. What do you think, I'm stupid? That what you think?
You think you can get over on me?" He reared back and kicked him
again. And then again. And again. The owner desperately tried to roll
away from him, but Lenny walked right after him. His rage was
fueling his rage.

The owner was trying desperately to shield his head with his arms.
"I don't know, I swear. It was the driver. It had to be the driver."

Over and over he screamed it, the driver, the driver, until Lenny
finally heard him. "Don't fuck with me," Lenny warned him.
"Whattya saying?"

Still cowering, the owner pleaded, "I ain't crazy, Lenny. Gimme a
break. I swear to God I'm not stupid enough to cheat you. I know
what happens to me."

He babbled on, and eventually he started making sense to Lenny.
He knew the guy and the guy definitely wasn't crazy. They'd done
several scams together and the guy had always been honest with him.
He'd always split the take fairly. But the driver? That fucking wimp
cowardly bastard driver? Who would've guessed that guy had the
balls to pull off a job like this one? That prick unloaded the merchandise somewhere between the warehouse and the store. He was
going to open the back of the truck when he got to the store and be
shocked, shocked, when he discovered he'd been robbed at a rest stop
on the Jersey Turnpike.

Fast Lenny kicked the owner a couple more times for being stupid
enough to leave the store rather than wait for the delivery, then
helped him up. He informed the owner that there was going to be a
change in the deal. Instead of the owner keeping the insurance
money and Lenny keeping the merchandise, Lenny was going to get
all the insurance money. Every penny. The job now was to find the

driver. Allowing people to scam the mob and get away with it would only encourage more people to try it. Obviously it had to be stopped dead.

Later, at the social club, Fast Lenny was still so upset he couldn't stay in his seat. He couldn't sit there even to eat, which proved he was definitely upset. He was all over the place, complaining to everybody that he had been robbed, explaining in detail what he was going to do to the driver when he found him. Apparently, though, finding him wasn't going to be that simple. The guy had disappeared. And it turned out his driver's license was a complete fugazi. The name on it was Franklin Washington. Nobody even knew his real name.

Bobby listened to Fast Lenny screaming. He wouldn't dare smile—he wasn't stupid enough to provoke Lenny—but it was pretty funny.

SIX

Connor slid one of the surveillance photographs across the table to Laura Russo. "Here's a good one of the happy couple." The photograph, taken the previous afternoon, showed Bobby Blue Eyes and Little Eddie leaving the Gradinsky apartment. As seen from the roof of the five-story brownstone diagonally across the street, the two mobsters cast long, thin shadows as they walked briskly down the steps.

Laura was slowly working her way through a pile of photographs, carefully examining each one with the large rectangular magnifying glass that she had received as a graduation gift from her mother. She glanced casually at the picture and forced a smile. "Nice hat," she said. Then went back to work.

Connor frowned. "Boy, even his shadow's better dressed than I am."

She looked up, and this time her smile was real. "Oh, come on, Connor, you dress fine. You just have your own style, that's all."

"Yeah. Moe Ginsberg chic," he said, referring to the cut-rate clothier on Fifth and 21st Street where he bought most of his clothes. Unlike his father, Connor did not have a "wardrobe." Rather he had "clothes." In his case it was usually "a pile of clothes." When it came to dressing, he followed one strict rule: Socks had to match. Everything else was fair game.

His lack of interest in dressing properly used to drive his mother crazy. "I guess the good news is that you can't dress down for this occasion," she said sarcastically as he got ready for a high school dance, "because you're already there."

Connor was one of those few people whose closets improved significantly when they joined the bureau. Agents were expected to dress appropriately for their assignment, which most often meant a blue suit, white shirt, and neutral tie. The day he graduated from Quantico he bought three blue sports jackets and three pairs of slacks, a blue suit and a gray suit. He had yet to wear the gray one. Fortunately for him, agents working organized crime in New York were allowed to dress casually so as not to stick out in Little Italy and other mob hangouts.

O'Brien was wearing what he called his "comfort clothes": khakis, a white shirt, and cordovan moccasins. Not only wouldn't he stand out in a crowd, no one would notice him if he was all alone—which was exactly how he preferred it. He took a good long look at another surveillance photo before spinning it across the table, and stated firmly, "Maybe it's just me, but personally I never trust people who wear hats that don't have writing on them."

Beginning an investigation is like trying to follow a road map on which the roads and the towns are not identified. No matter how long you stare at it, you don't know where you are, where you're going, or how you're going to get there. O'Brien and Russo had bits of intriguing information that seemingly led nowhere. They had spent the entire morning reviewing everything they had, trying without success to fit some of the pieces together. Russo called this kind of work "a strategy review session," while O'Brien referred to it as "the usual bullshit."

At the beginning of their careers most FBI agents dressed alike and worked alike. They followed the standard procedures taught at Quantico. They didn't take the side roads or look for shortcuts. But as they gained experience, each agent developed his or her own methods for working a case. O'Brien preferred covering as much ground as possible, talking to people, making himself visible, figuring he'd eventually shake loose some information. Russo was more of a plodder, much like her favorite detective, Agatha Christie. She liked taking the time necessary to examine each piece of evidence, believing without any doubt that there was always just a little more information to be squeezed out of it if she were just smart enough. She would literally spend hours bent over a single photograph with that magnifying glass. Early in her career, to perfect her skills, she had attempted to identify every book seen in the background in a photograph of John Kennedy sitting at his desk in his Hyannis Port library. She'd managed to list 256 titles.

The boredom was beginning to get to O'Brien. "Hey, I got an idea," he said brightly. "If we're gonna spend all day in here looking at pictures, why don't I go out and get us the new *Playboy*?"

Without even bothering to look up from the photograph she was examining she told him, "You're not funny, Connor."

Connor pulled down the skin under both eyes as far as possible with his forefinger and middle finger, then rolled his eyes as far up into his head as possible. "How 'bout this, then?" he asked. "This any funnier?"

This time she leaned back in her chair and looked at him. And frowned. "What are you gonna do next? Fart jokes?"

"C'mon, Russo," he practically begged, "this isn't getting us anywhere. We gotta find this guy, and unless he's hiding under this table, he's not in here."

"Just give me a couple more minutes," she said in what definitely was not a couple-more-minutes voice. The only good news, as far as O'Brien was concerned, was that they just didn't have too much more to examine. Russo had gone through most of the surveillance photos. Both of them had read the most recent transcripts from the taps in the social club and Gradinsky's apartment. The Gradinsky apartment had picked up seven personal calls in which the professor was not mentioned and one order for Chinese food. About all they learned from the pile of material was that Grace Gradinsky was still not discussing her husband's absence with anyone, which O'Brien believed reinforced his theory that she knew where he was, and that she preferred hot-and-sour over wonton.

O'Brien had just started making a list in his notebook of lists he intended to compile when Russo hummmmmmed in interest. "This is interesting," she said. "Look at this."

He walked around the table and leaned over her left shoulder. And the extraordinarily fresh scent of whatever it was she was using in her hair hit him hard in his gender. It took him a couple of seconds to refocus on his professionalism. Russo was looking at the photograph given to her by Grace Gradinsky. It pictured Grace and the professor with another couple, sitting at a table in a restaurant. They had obviously finished dinner, as empty coffee cups and the remains of dessert littered the table. Grace and the other woman were holding cigarettes and smiling directly into the camera. From the cut of her hair and up-to-date dress it was apparent to Russo that the photograph had been taken within the past couple of years. "Who are those other people?" he asked.

She glanced over her shoulder at him. "Now, how do you expect me to know that? I got an idea. Why don't we ask her?" She shook her head and returned to the photograph.

"Well, then, what's so interesting?"

"Look." She held the magnifying glass over an area of the table directly in front of the professor.

Connor leaned forward to get a better look. "Whoa," he said, stepping back, "you're right. That's the biggest damn glass of water I've ever seen." She took one very deep "how long do I have to put up with this?" breath, and Connor suddenly became serious. "All right, okay, what? What've you got?" He looked at the picture again. Framed by the magnifying glass were a glass of water, part of a knife, a saucer with two cigarette stubs drowned in a spill of coffee, a little pillbox holding what he guessed were saccharin pills, a pack of Marlboro, and a book of matches. "Yeah? And?"

"Check out the matches, Sherlock."

He looked again. In an elegant Palace Bold Script typeface the name "Gino's" was clearly embossed on the matchbook cover. Below it, in a much smaller type partially hidden beneath the scratch strip, were the words "Maspeth, N.Y." Connor guessed there was a phone number on the back. He stood up straight. "Okay. So what am I missing here?"

"Don't you know who Gino is?"

"Lemme guess. Gino?"

"Uh-oh, somebody hasn't done his homework, has he? See what it says, Maspeth? Maspeth, Queens? Ring any bells?"

He got it. Louder than the Liberty Bell. "Tony Cosentino," he said with admiration. "Of course. Tony's gotta be Gino, right? Damn, if I wore a hat, I'd tip it to you." He picked up her magnifying glass and held it high in the air, carefully examining it. "I got to get me one of these."

The first connection had been made. Admittedly it was pretty thin, but it made complete sense. They had known from the day they overheard Bobby and Little Eddie in the social club that the professor was in some way connected to the mob. What they didn't know was who or why. The body of Skinny Al D'Angelo had been found in a car trunk the day after the professor went missing. D'Angelo was a member of Cosentino's crew. And here was evidence that the professor had been at Cosentino's restaurant. Either it was a truly amazing coincidence or these men had something in common. It was the beginning of "who."

Searching for a loophole in her reasoning, Connor pointed out, "Well, first of all, we don't even know for sure that this picture was taken at Gino's. They could've gotten the matches some other time."

"Big deal. Doesn't make any difference. I mean, we can find out easy enough where this was taken, but the fact that he's got the matches is what matters. It's a connection. Remember what his wife said, that they didn't own a car? Then what the hell were they doing going all the way out to Queens for dinner?"

"Maybe they couldn't resist that wonderful Queens cuisine." Connor couldn't argue with Laura's assessment. He'd lived in the city most of his life—and never once had he gone out to Queens for dinner. Not counting the Bridge Diner, of course, but nobody who'd ever eaten there would count it.

"And second of all?" she asked.

"Just kidding about that," he admitted. Assuming Russo was right, and at this point in the investigation they had nothing else, Professor G and Skinny Al had Tony Cosentino in common. Two-Gun Tony Cosentino had been elevated to captain in the bloodletting after the sudden and expected death of Carmine Galante, who died with his lit cigar in his mouth when a shotgun was fired into his chest from about six feet away. Cosentino was considered a real heavyweight. Nobody knew for sure, but the bureau estimated he had participated in at least twelve hits. Possibly more. Thus far, though, the bureau had been unable to get anywhere near him.

Tying together the professor and the victim, Skinny Al, opened up all kinds of possibilities. Identifying Skinny Al's killer, or even finding out why he was killed, might lead them to the professor or, more likely—considering the players—whatever was left of the professor. Conversely, finding the professor might lead them directly to Skinny Al's killer.

Admittedly there were many questions this scenario didn't begin to answer. Like who was the Russian on the telephone with the professor? And why were Skinny Al's arms and leg practically crushed before his killers bled him to death? But it was a beginning. Connor figured it was sort of like the first words on a map, words that supposedly gave you important information but in fact told you absolutely nothing you didn't already know: "You are here."

Connor was waiting with anticipation and impatience as Laura slowly worked her way through the pile of surveillance photographs. Three more pictures and they'd be out of that room. Two more . . .

Meanwhile, he brought all the necessary paperwork right up to the minute. The primary purpose of all these reports, which when read carefully confirmed that they knew almost nothing about the "disappearance of Gradinsky, Peter NMI, Professor of Slavic Languages, Columbia University," was to provide Jim Slattery with the official cover he needed. Few supervisors played the paper game better than Jim Slattery. Inundate headquarters with paperwork, he knew from experience, and it'd be a long time before anybody bothered looking at all of it. Long enough, he was betting, for this investigation to be concluded.

. . . and just as Russo reached for the last photograph, a clerk walked into the room carrying a large manila envelope. Placing it on the desk, he said to her, "Here are those pictures you wanted."

O'Brien felt like somebody had punched him in the stomach. "Ah, Russo, c'mon. Please. This is bullshit."

Her elbows resting on the table, she spread her hands in supplication. "Hey, nobody's making you stay here. Go. Please. You got something to do, go do it. Meanwhile . . ." she indicated the new pile—"I've got work to do."

He leaned way back in his chair and clasped his hands behind his head. In a controlled voice he asked, "Okay, let's try it your way. What've we got there?"

She held up the first photograph for him to see. It was black-and-white and pictured the body of an obese man squeezed into the trunk of a car. The lid was up as if to display the contents of the trunk. The body was lying on its left side, facing outward. His head was pushed down into his chest, probably to enable the trunk to be closed, making it impossible to see the final expression on his face—although shoving his head down into his chest had caused the skin from his fleshy neck to swell outward, much like what happens when someone sits on a water bed, forming a collar of fat into which his chin had sunk. His light-colored shirt was almost completely stained dark with blood. His left arm was under his body, and his right arm from the elbow down was bent straight backward over his hip at an impossible angle, folded back like a jacket sleeve being packed, making it obvious it had been snapped.

A crime scene photograph is not intended to be a piece of art. Its only purpose is to record all possible details of an event at a specific time and place. Just about every violent crime scene or fatal accident is photographed from every conceivable angle. These photographs are admissible as evidence during a trial. I couldn't begin to estimate how many crime scene photographs I've looked at during my career, how many bodies I've seen pictured bloody and bent, broken and cut up. And whatever their intended purpose, these photographs never fail to stimulate the senses. It's macabre, I know, but for me, at least, it's impossible to look at a photograph of a corpse—usually bloodied—and not wonder about the person and how he got there. And maybe wonder what he was feeling at the last moment of his life. Having been in situations that I thought could end up with me being in one of these pictures, I remembered my own feelings. It was as much practical—how the fuck did I get here and what can I do to get out of it?—as it was nervousness, fear, or apprehension.

O'Brien stared at the photograph of the late Alphonse D'Angelo and wondered what the hell Skinny Al had done to end up stuffed in that trunk. "Very nice," he said finally, putting his thumbs and forefingers together to form a rectangle, then pretending to look through it at the photograph as a director might look through a lens, "although I'm not crazy about the composition. And the model ain't so beautiful either."

"Look at all the blood. Old Al must've bled eight buckets."

"Gee, I'm sorry the poor man's death affected you so terribly. Try to hold yourself together."

Laying down the picture, she began examining it by quadrants. She didn't spend a lot of time looking at D'Angelo's body. The forensic pathologist would determine what the body had to say. As she worked, she asked O'Brien, "You ever hear of anybody burning out the eardrums? What do you think that's all about?"

Surprisingly O'Brien hadn't seen that many real bodies in his career. Contrary to the general belief, the bureau didn't work many homicides. Murder is a federal crime only under very specific circumstances, for example when it is committed on federal property or across state lines. Your everyday murder isn't something that agents can legally investigate, although the resources of the legendary FBI crime lab are always available to local law enforcement agencies. And the burned-out eardrums were completely new to him. There is a widespread belief that the mob uses some sort of code to make clear to everyone the reasons a person was killed. Leaving dimes on his closed eyes means the guy was an informer. I've heard of victims found with a canary in their mouth, obviously meaning they talked too much. Chopping off a victim's hands meant he somehow violated the family's security; he allowed someone or something to get too close. Cutting off a guy's prick and stuffing it in his mouth meant that he had some sexual problems and maybe messed with the wrong man or woman or man's woman. But Connor had never heard of anyone's eardrums being burned out.

The meaning appeared to be pretty obvious: Skinny Al had heard something he wasn't supposed to hear and therefore had to be killed. But when dealing with the mob, Connor knew that what seems obvious may be quite different. "Hear too much evil, I guess. I mean, with these guys who knows?" He glanced through the pile of photographs of D'Angelo's corpse in the trunk. He looked just as dead in all of them. Having seen more than enough of Skinny Al, he sighed loudly. "Russo, please," he said, "that's enough. Let's get out of here." And then, without having planned it, he added, "C'mon, I'll buy you some dinner."

"Why, Agent O'Brien," she responded, "that'd be very nice. But I think they roll the stand away at five o'clock." As soon as she heard the words come out of her mouth, she regretted them. If she could have grabbed them out of the air and stuffed them back in, she would have done so. Laura Russo would never admit it, but she was flattered. While they'd shared many meals in the weeks they'd been working together—mostly takeout at the Country Club and in O'Brien's car—this was the first time that O'Brien had made what sounded suspiciously like an invitation for a real dinner. Before O'Brien could respond, she tried to cover for herself. "I'd like to but I can't. I got plans tonight."

Plans tonight? she thought. Plans tonight? What a poor excuse for an excuse. But having said it, she was committed to it.

Plans tonight? O'Brien knew exactly what that meant: plans tonight was the ultimate "I can't think fast enough to make up a believable excuse" turndown. Like every single man trapped in New York's dating jungle, Connor had heard it before. And like pretty much every single man in New York lacking Donald Trump's ego, he interpreted that to mean: I'd rather wax my entire body three times a week than spend one minute more with you than absolutely necessary. "That's fine," he stammered, "no big deal. There's just a few things I wanted to go over. We can do it tomorrow."

"Great." She sat there pretending to examine a photograph of the car trunk after Skinny Al's body had been removed, but that was a prop to cover her embarrassment. Why, she wondered, why, why, why?

Both O'Brien and Russo, two highly professional law enforcement officers, were desperate to get out of that room without further embarrassing themselves. Their egos were saved by the ringing telephone. Connor grabbed it. After listening for a few seconds he said, "Right away," and hung up. "Slattery," he told her. "He wants to see us for a minute."

"Let me grab my stuff," she said, so incredibly grateful for that phone call that she had to constrain herself to pack up her belongings at a natural pace.

Slattery was beaming when they walked into his office, but for reasons having nothing to do with the case. Minutes before, an administrative clerk in Washington had called to tell him that they were confident they knew what had happened to his personnel folder, although they had not yet found it. Until it was located, however, whenever necessary they would accept his stipulation in lieu of the proper support paperwork.

"In other words," he'd told the clerk, "I am, therefore I exist."

It was a weak joke—Slattery accepted that—but even then the officious clerk had absolutely no idea what he was talking about. Instead, he cautioned him, "You really shouldn't let something like this happen. It creates a great deal of difficulty for us."

He was still smiling when they sat down. "Here," he said, handing a memo across his desk to O'Brien. "Somebody's been using your guy's credit card."

According to the National Bank of North America, which had been officially requested by the bureau to report all transactions involving this card, Peter Gradinsky's Visa had been used the previous night to pay a $75.00 bill at the Morningside Heights Tavern, a restaurant on 118th Street. The fact that the card had been used was interesting, but it was hardly proof that the professor was alive. Slattery had used exactly the right terminology: "Somebody" had used the card. It could have been anybody. But they also knew the chances that a thief—or a killer—would risk using a victim's credit card in the area in which the victim might be known were pretty slim. Generally, stolen credit cards are used within hours of being grabbed—before the owner can report them missing or before the owner can be reported missing—and usually a long distance from the owner's neighborhood. So there was at least a slight reason for optimism.

Russo also found it curious that exactly seventy-five dollars had been charged to the card. She had seven credit cards that she used too often—including J. C. Penney and Macy's—and she could not recall a single time her total bill had come out exactly anything. Particularly such a nice round number. More likely, she figured, he was getting some cash. There was only one way to find out. "Hey, sailor," she said to O'Brien, "still wanna take a dame to dinner?"

The words "What happened to your plans?" had formed in his mind and were racing toward his mouth, but he caught them at the last second. "Sure," he said. "There's this nice little place I know on 118th Street."

Only after O'Brien and Russo had left his office did it occur to Slattery that somebody should inform the professor's wife. That wasn't his job, he knew that, and this type of information was supposed to be kept confidential. But he figured that by this time the woman would be absolutely frantic. He opened up the case file and dug through it until he found O'Brien's report of his interview with . . . Slattery checked the wife's name. Grace Gradinsky. No harm done, he decided, and picked up the telephone.

The Morningside Heights Tavern had been carefully decorated to look as if it hadn't been decorated. It would probably best be described as studied casual. As you entered, a long bar faced the door, stretching the width of the room almost from wall to wall. There were cash registers at both ends of the bar and large television sets suspended almost directly above them. Only one of them was on, turned to the local news. On the wall to the left a five-dollar football pool sign-up sheet announced that the Giants were three-and-a-half-point favorites over the Redskins. It was still five days before the game and most of the boxes were already filled in. Columbia University's football schedule, cheaply framed photographs of old Columbia athletes, Ivy League pennants, and several fraternity banners were hung evenly spaced on the other walls. Booths covered with powder-blue vinyl lined the three remaining walls, and several small wooden tables were set up next to the booths, leaving the area in front of the bar empty for the meet-and-greet crowd. Connor couldn't quite see for sure, but he would have bet his inheritance that names and political slogans had been carved into every table in the place and that there were chunks of ice at the bottom of the urinals. Connor had spent four years in campus bars exactly like this one. He decided the only thing missing from this one was the sawdust on the floor.

There were about a dozen people in the place. Two dark corner booths were occupied by couples, a knot of coeds was gathered at one end of the bar, and at the other end one man was sitting alone, hunched over a book and a beer. The bartender was wiping glasses and hanging them mouth-down in an overhead rack, and the single waitress was serving the couples in the booths. O'Brien and Russo sat at the bar.

The bartender was big enough to double as a bouncer. Early thirties, Connor guessed, popular with the coeds. The kind of bartender who might accurately be described as "a big lug of a guy." "Hey," he said pleasantly, smiling confidently, "what can I get for you?"

Bureau regulations strictly prohibited agents from drinking on duty, but in those situations in which it would be inappropriate not to have a drink agents have been known to imbibe. Unofficially you do what you have to do and the system looks the other way. Connor ordered a beer, Laura a glass of white wine. As the bartender served their drinks, Connor introduced himself and Russo as FBI agents.

"For real?" the bartender asked Connor. "Her too. Really?" When Connor confirmed that, he looked at Russo and smiled. His name was Billy Garvey, he said smoothly, "But people call me Gravy." Sure, he'd be delighted to answer their questions. In fact, he decided, it was more than that—he'd be *privileged* to answer their questions. He was a bartender—answering questions was an important part of the job. Yes, he had been working the previous night. No, he didn't know Professor Gradinsky by name, but that didn't mean anything—lots of people whose names he didn't know came in regularly. One reason people go to dimly lit bars, he pointed out, was to protect their privacy.

Russo showed him the professor's picture. Garvey stared at it hard, then frowned. "Maybe? I don't know." He took a deep, thoughtful breath, really focusing on the photograph. "You know, he looks sort of familiar, but it's not like he's a regular. Guarantee you that. Why, what happened to him?"

Finding the answer to that question, Laura explained, was precisely the reason they were asking these questions. "So, Gravy," she asked, "you see him last night? It's important."

Continuing to look at the picture, Garvey shook his head while inhaling, to emphasize the fact that he really was trying to place the face. "It was real busy. It was ladies' night. You know, girls drink free. And then one of the frats had a thing for some pledges. Man, I was humping all night."

O'Brien repeated the question. "So? Did you see him or not?"

"I don't know. I don't think so. But I mean, who knows? It's possible. What can I tell you?" As Garvey returned the professor's picture to Russo, he snapped a well-practiced "aw shucks golly-gee" grin at her.

She ignored it, then told him, "Well, apparently he used his credit card in here last night."

Garvey pushed back from the bar. "Hey, what do you want me to tell you? If he did, he did. I'd like to help you out, swear to God, but I don't remember seeing him and I was here the whole night."

O'Brien asked about the waitresses. Three girls had worked the floor the previous night, Garvey said. He knew their first names, but not their last names or telephone numbers. He had nothing to do with scheduling, he explained, that was the manager's job. "And when will he be here?"

"He's the *manager*," Garvey said, flashing a big smile at his very own cleverness. "He manages himself."

O'Brien handed him his card. "Ask him to give me a call when he comes in, okay?" And then he flashed him his biggest and phoniest smile in return.

Back out on the street O'Brien did a passable imitation of the bartender. "He's the manager"—big smile—"he manages himself."

Laura Russo laughed easily.

"Let's go," he said, jerking his head, "I got a place."

His place was *El Polo Loco* on West End between 98th and 99th. Even that early in the evening it was crowded and noisy. "Hey, Mr. Connor," a chunky hostess greeted them, "how you doing? Come. Come."

They were seated against a wall. Their conversation was carefully professional. When you'd go through Quantico? Who were your instructors? Where'd you go from there? You know so-and-so? Russo was surprised how comfortable she was with him. If he was coming on to her, she decided, he was amazingly good at hiding it. She tried to identify the strange feeling in her chest. It took a while, but finally she realized that it wasn't what she was feeling, but rather what she wasn't feeling. And that was anxiety. Connor wasn't treating her like this was a date; instead, it was just the guys out for a pleasant dinner after a long day.

He did everything right as far as she was concerned: He didn't put his hand on her back and try to direct her, he didn't help her with her coat, he barely even held open doors to allow her to proceed him, and at the end of the meal he accepted her share of the bill without protest. He was the perfect nongentleman, which Laura appreciated and naturally interpreted to mean that he wasn't the slightest bit interested in her.

That pleased her. It was exactly what she wanted: to be treated as an equal. One complication in her life that she definitely did not need was another relationship with an agent. Another agent? She didn't need any type of romantic relationship at all. None. And just to make sure she didn't forget it, she repeated that thought to herself.

As they left the restaurant, she made a point of holding the door open for him. He didn't seem to notice. The temperature had fallen several degrees. They stood in front of the restaurant and Laura began listing the things she wanted to accomplish the following morning. He noticed that every word she said was punctuated with a white puff of breath, almost as if she were speaking in cartoon speech balloons. He wondered if it was possible to blow breath rings, remembering his grandfather's amazing ability to blow concentric smoke rings. He decided to test it, puckering his lips and exhaling slowly. The result was a steady white stream of visible breath. "You know," he said, cutting her off in midsentence, "there's something I want to show you."

"Excuse me," she corrected him curtly, "but I was in the middle of a sentence."

"Sorry," he apologized with considerably less sincerity than she would have liked. "But I promise, this is something good."

She stared at him, wondering what it might be. Oh, please, she thought, don't let him screw it up by doing something stupid. "What is it?"

"Hey, c'mon, gimme a little break here."

Reluctantly she nodded in agreement. "Okay," and then added a bit more lightly, "Legally I have to warn you, though, these hands are registered weapons. Don't make me use them."

As O'Brien drove over the Brooklyn Bridge, he asked if she had ever been to Brooklyn. Once, she said, and only very briefly. Since arriving in New York she hadn't even had time to explore Manhattan, much less the other boroughs. "Then you're in for a real treat," he said, morphing into a tour guide. "They built this bridge in the 1870s 'cause Brooklyn was ready to declare itself an independent city. New York didn't want the competition. When it opened, the toll was a penny." There was an old legend, he continued, that if you tossed a penny off the bridge, you would receive an abundance of success.

"So what do you get for a dollar?" she asked. There was surprisingly little traffic. The views from the bridge enchanted her. She looked over her right shoulder at the brightly lit Lower Manhattan skyline. "Wow," she said, "double wow."

"And when the Mafia expanded out of Little Italy, Brooklyn was right there waiting. There were probably a million Italian immigrants living there who didn't trust banks. It had the docks, it had trucking, swamps, unions, everything the aspiring mobster needs." The Mafia, he explained as he drove through Brooklyn Heights and down Flatbush Avenue into Prospect Park, found its home in Brooklyn.

Brooklyn surprised her. From everything she'd read, even after her brief visit, she'd believed Brooklyn to be one massive drug-ravaged decaying city. She had imagined acres of burned-out and abandoned buildings, filthy streets, and gangs camped on just about every corner. Instead, Brooklyn appeared to be a series of small neighborhoods, some better maintained than others, but almost none of them fitting her apocalyptic vision.

Almost as if O'Brien were reading her mind, he continued, "Don't let this fool you. There are pretty rough parts too, just not around here." He turned onto President Street.

"Why's that?"

He stopped across from 561 President. "Money and Mafia," he said. "Nobody screws with either one." He pointed at a well-kept brownstone with a large front stoop. "That's it."

The building had a long, narrow front yard with two rectangles of grass separated by a cement walk. The front of the property was protected by a six-foot-high chain-link fence. A small sign warned that the premises were protected by the Silent Guardian, presumably an electronic monitoring service. Unlike similar houses on either side, she noticed, this house had no bushes in front. The entire yard was well lit. Every window in the house was covered with curtains. "What are we looking at?"

In his best tour guide voice he said, "To your left, ladies and gentlemen, is the home of Robert San Filippo, better known to his fans as Bobby Blue Eyes and Bobby Hats. Mr. San Filippo has lived there with his wife, Veronica, and their ten-year-old daughter, Angela, for nine years." He looked at her and smiled. "And people say I don't have an exciting social life."

The stakeout is second only to working a listening post when rating the most boring law enforcement assignments. A stakeout consists almost entirely of sitting or standing and watching. Some of the time it means watching an inanimate object, a building, a restaurant, maybe a car. Only if the person you're watching moves do you move. In the winter it's too cold, in the summer it's too hot. If you're standing outside, you get really tired; if you're in a car, you get cramped. In the car you can't keep the engine running because you can't waste gas. You can't drink too much coffee to stay awake because then you have to go to the bathroom. Same thing with eating. You definitely can't read. About the only thing you can do is listen to a transistor radio.

"What are we doing here?" Russo asked.

"Nothing really," he admitted, without taking his eyes from the house. "I just like to know as much as possible about the people I'm investigating." He glanced at her. "Looks pretty normal, right? I mean, you know, for a mafioso."

"Yeah, very." She watched as O'Brien took his notebook from a jacket pocket and wrote a few sentences. "What happens if they spot us?"

"Doesn't matter. What's he gonna do? Quit the Mafia? These guys already assume we're everywhere. It's probably a good thing that they see us every once in a while." He stopped writing. "In the old days each of the bosses had at least one agent assigned only to them. Some agents spent most of their career watching one person."

They sat there for almost an hour, mostly in silence. There were a lot of questions Russo would have liked to ask him, but knowing that in response she'd have to answer similar questions, she kept quiet. O'Brien let her lead. Several lights were on in the house when they got there. After the first twenty minutes a light went off in one room and seconds later a light was turned on in another room. Maybe ten minutes after that, a curtain was pulled back and some-body peered outside for a few seconds, then released the curtain. At that distance it was impossible to see who it was. Several cars passed. One car parked and the driver got out and went into a brownstone farther down the block. Eleven people walked by: four singles, two couples—one of them walking a golden retriever—and a group of three teenage boys. About every four minutes a plane roared over-head, causing Connor to explain, "This is a secondary flight path to Kennedy. They use it when they get backed up." And that was it, that was all the action. There had been no sign of Robert San Filippo, a.k.a. Bobby Blue Eyes, a.k.a. Bobby Hats.

"Had enough?" he asked finally.

"That's enough for me." As they started back to Manhattan, she wondered, "Think that was him looking out?"

"No way," O'Brien said. "He's not gonna be sitting home this early. This is business hours. He's out there somewhere doing his thing."

For a few minutes Russo tried to imagine what it might be like to be married to a hood like San Filippo. Not real good, she decided. And for an instant she flashed on her mother, remembering her standing stoically at the kitchen window, waiting hopefully for her husband to come home.

Connor dropped her off in front of her apartment. "See you in the morning," he said easily.

"You got it." She gave a little wave over her shoulder as she went up the steps. She was pleased that there had been none of that end-of-date uneasiness. But she did notice that he waited in front, watching her, until she was safely inside.

It was exactly eleven o'clock when he got home. Connor melted into the deep pillows on his couch and turned on the local news. Wind-down time. Well, well, well, he thought, this is an interesting development. He'd had a good time, no doubt about that. And he had the feeling, as in one of the B movies in which the plain-looking secretary takes off her glasses and is transformed into a beautiful woman, that if Russo took off her officious personality, she would be pretty damned interesting.

His phone rang. "Hey, Con," Diana Thomas said with a happy bounce in her voice, "whatcha doing?"

After a momentary hesitation he replied, "Nothing."

Laura Russo was luxuriating in her bathtub. She finally had proof that this indeed was a special night: For the first time since she'd been in New York she'd managed to find the elusive balance between hot running water and cold draining water that kept the tub perfectly warm. It was close to a perfect time. The only light in her apartment came from candles scattered around the bathroom. Vivaldi's *Four Seasons,* which she loved although she seemed constitutionally unable to match the correct season to the music, was playing softly on her cassette radio. And her cat, Buck, was stretched across the closed toilet lid keeping her company.

The night had confused her. Connor O'Brien had turned out to be both less and more than she had originally pegged him. Russo was just beginning to explore her reactions when she heard the unmistakable sound of someone trying to open her front door.

One of the first things she'd done after moving into the apartment was screw a thin piece of metal to the door frame. It didn't prevent the door from being used, but when the door was opened or closed, it scratched against it. Anyone who didn't know it was there would assume the sound was ordinary wear and tear, the settling sounds a house makes, and wouldn't even notice it. But to anyone listening for it, the sound was unmistakable. The cat, Buck, had heard it first. His ears suddenly cupped with curiosity, then he sat up. That had gotten Laura's attention. She turned off the water and the music and heard it too.

The apartment was a floor-through. The front door opened onto a narrow hallway. To the left, after entering the apartment, were the kitchen and living room. To the right was her bedroom. And almost directly across the hallway was the bathroom.

Whoever was at the door was having great difficulty getting it open. That was obvious from the ticking sound the plate made each time the door was pushed or pulled. She had installed a Medeco lock and a security chain the day she moved in, and she had also replaced the existing tumbler, so it would require extraordinary smithy skills to break in. Either that or simple brute force. She wasn't sure she had remembered to chain the door; usually she did, but not always. That didn't really matter. If someone wanted to get in badly enough, they could get in.

There was no one who could help her. The building had only two apartments on each floor and her neighbor, Ginger Snaps as she referred to herself, loved to party. She was out every night. Not that Ginger could provide any real help if she were home. In fact, it was probably better she wasn't home. That way she couldn't get hurt.

Laura moved deliberately. She got out of the tub and blew out all the candles. Then she stood still for several seconds, letting her eyes become accustomed to the darkness. She took several deep, calming breaths. Laura Russo took great pride in her ability to maintain her composure in stressful situations. Not many things frightened her. But even she would have to admit that her heart was pumping big-time.

She focused on her primary objective, her only objective, which was to get hold of her weapon. She knew exactly where it was: in its holster under her bed, where she'd kicked it out of view when she'd stripped for her bath. She grabbed a large bath towel and wrapped it around her body. Then she let the towel drop onto the floor, deciding if she had to move quickly, it might inhibit her. And if it fell, she didn't want to be distracted when automatically grabbing for it.

She felt around the bathroom sink. As she did, she almost knocked over her toothbrush holder, a ceramic mug from San Jose that she'd bought to commemorate a successful job working undercover in a Medicare fraud investigation. But she caught it, preventing it from crashing to the floor. She placed it gently on the sink counter, then continued feeling around until she found the large bottle of mouthwash she knew was there. She unscrewed the cap and put it in the sink. Mouthwash wasn't much of a weapon, but if necessary, she'd splash it in the intruder's eyes, which would buy her a few precious seconds. Then, purposefully, she walked out of the bathroom.

As she passed the front door the intruder pushed hard against it. She heard him grunt with the effort. She stopped and waited. A few seconds later she heard a slight scratching sound she recognized instantly—he was trying to pick the lock. Her eyes were adjusting to the dark now and she could move around a lot more easily. She went back into the bathroom and retrieved the towel, then laid it on the floor next to the front door. Anyone coming into the apartment wouldn't notice it; they'd trip or their feet would get entangled in it. That would give her a little more time.

She reached under her bed and grasped her weapon, the standard-issue 9mm SIG. It fired sixteen shots—fifteen in the clip, one in the chamber—rapid, accurate, and deadly. She slid it out of its holster and switched off the safety. The moment she wrapped her palm around its handle she knew she had control of the night. The telephone was on the far side of her bed. She started to move around the bed, intending to call 911, then stopped. Fuck you, she thought, I got my gun and the darkness. Fuck you. You're trying to bust into my house. I win.

She was freezing. She had cracked open a window in her bedroom when she got home, and now she was standing there naked and wet. That's fine, she decided, cold keeps you alert. Holding the gun with both hands, she eased her way along the wall, moving toward the door. If possible, she wanted to get a look at the intruder through the peephole. He was still there—she could hear him muttering as he worked the lock. She leaned against the door and with her left hand reached for the peephole.

"Fuck," he snapped angrily. "Fuck—" His words sliced through the door. He was inches away from her. The width of the door. Two, three inches at most. She held her breath. "—This bullshit." His voice had a meanness to it. It was gruff, threatening. Dirty. She thought she recognized it from the Country Club sessions but couldn't be certain.

She exhaled. She took another deep, soothing breath and slid open the peephole—just in time to see the muscular back and shiny long black hair of a tall man disappear down the stairs. She leaned against the door and put on the safety. She relaxed. The sound of the exterior door slamming shocked her back into action. She moved quickly through the living room to the front windows. As she pulled back the blinds, she heard a car door slam. She scanned the street, but it took her several seconds to find the car. It was a dark sedan. From that height she couldn't identify the make or model. It looked like some type of sports model, but she couldn't even be certain of that. The driver pulled out from the curb and took off down the block. The car was already moving before he turned on the lights.

The traffic signal on the corner had just turned red when the car reached the end of the block. The driver paused to check traffic, then made a left turn through the red light. And was gone.

It was several minutes before she turned on a light. And then she turned on all the lights in the apartment and picked up the phone to call O'Brien.

SEVEN

The day had not started well for Bobby Blue Eyes. He had about four million things that needed to get done and instead he found himself sitting in a headmaster's office listening to this guy blabbing about the many benefits of Manhattan Poly's enrichment program. Yeah, Bobby thought, and I bet I know who gets the main benefit. You get my $15,000 to teach a ten-year-old which fork to use on the salad. Personally he thought the whole thing was ridiculous. They were going to be studying the same gravity he'd studied back at St. Margaret's, and no matter how much tuition you paid, what went up still came right down. Enrichment program? Enpoorment program was more like it. As far as he was concerned, it was just more of that liberal bullshit.

But there he was, sitting quietly and looking happy about paying $15,000 tuition. He was there because Ronnie insisted he be there. She made very few demands on him, but about this she was adamant: Whatever it cost, Angela was going to get the best possible education. That was the price of peace in his home and he knew he had to pay it.

He didn't like being judged, though, and that was exactly what it felt like this headmaster was doing. "We're a national product transportation company," he'd explained when asked about his job as the vice president of A&I Trucking, adding, "I think it's fair to say that we're well known all over the country for moving hazardous materials." That statement was totally accurate, if perhaps a bit short on the details. A&I was known by prosecutors in eight states primarily for moving steel drums containing chemical waste products into toxic dumps.

Mostly they discussed Angela, who was sitting between Bobby and Ronnie chewing on a straw. While her grades in her previous school, St. Mary's of Brooklyn, were slightly below average, when Bobby casually mentioned a few of the right names and promised they would call him directly, the headmaster complimented Angela's consistency. As the meeting ended, the headmaster explained that while he couldn't make any promises, pointing out that there were a limited number of places available for new students, Angela would receive every possible consideration.

As they drove home, Bobby asked Ronnie, "You want her going there?" She did, she said. "Okay, then. She's in. Case closed."

"Yeah, right, Mr. Magician," she said sarcastically. "Like you know."

Bobby shrugged a "what do you want from me?" shrug. It was a pretty amazing thing: Fourteen years they'd been together and Ronnie still did not fully appreciate the power generated by the organized crime families of New York City. Bobby didn't care, let her be in the dark. But the fact was that nothing that happened in the city was beyond the reach of the families. Nothing. Unions, cops, politicians, tables at exclusive restaurants, publishing, admission to exclusive schools, tickets for anything from Broadway to Yankee Stadium, all of them were for sale. The city worked because the people whose responsibility it was to make it work understood this and made the proper accommodations. Bobby didn't fool himself into believing that he himself had the power to get Angela into Manhattan Poly—that important he wasn't—but as a respected individual he could ask that the necessary telephone calls be made and they would be made.

He put Ronnie and Angela in a cab and headed out to Queens to pay his respects to Skinny Al's family. Franzone had asked him to represent the crew at the funeral. Franzone had also sent enough flowers to bury a battalion. This was still pretty early in the day for

Bobby; in his life mornings generally weren't considered prime time. As Little Eddie once explained to him, "Late nights and mornings go together like homos and hookers."

Bobby was through the Midtown Tunnel and on the Expressway before he picked up the tail. What surprised him was not that he was being followed, but rather that whoever it was, was driving a great car. Usually the feds drove "vehicles," boring boxes on wheels with all the excitement of a dark green Dodge sedan. But this tail was driving a charcoal-gray Firebird. That was a really nice car, really nice. Bobby'd looked at buying one himself when they introduced the sloping nose design in 1983, but the elegant design just made it too easy to pick out of a getaway race. He was actually angry with himself that he hadn't spotted the tail sooner, as he made it a habit to regularly check his mirrors. He didn't know when they'd got on his ass; he guessed it had to be when he dropped off the wife and kid at the house, but there was no question they were there. He sped up, slowed down, changed lanes, played ticky-tack with his signals, but no matter what he did, they stayed comfortably in their slot, three cars back and—when possible—one lane to the right.

Bobby waited until the last possible minute, then sliced through two lanes to get over to the Van Wyck ramp. The Firebird stayed with him. Jerks. One thing for sure, they weren't trying to hide their presence. It took him a little while to figure out the ploy: Only after they'd followed him through several turns did he realize that the Firebird was the decoy. He was supposed to spot it. A third car, the traditional dark sedan, was trailing the Firebird. That was the real tail he was dragging along. It's a fucking wagon train, he thought. After the Firebird dropped back, the dark sedan would take its position. That was supposed to fool him? That was a pretty funny idea. Two cars, that definitely appealed to his ego: He was so important that they assigned two cars—actually a car and a "vehicle"—to track him to a funeral.

Bobby had been tailed several times previously. He'd play the game depending on how he felt at that moment. Sometimes he tried to lose them, sometimes he'd let them come along for the ride. It didn't seem to make any difference in the outcome. He figured they did it because that's the way they had always done it. It was like moving clockwise in Monopoly: It didn't actually make any difference which way you moved around the board, but the rules of the game had to be respected and followed. But these people tailing him were an embarrassment to the whole cops. They didn't even have enough respect for the rules to pretend they weren't following him.

Actually it was a pretty funny thing. The funeral was being held at the Linden Brothers Funeral Home off Grand Avenue. Bobby had been to Maspeth maybe five times in his entire life and didn't really know his way around there. He knew the funeral parlor was off 62nd Street and figured he could find it. How hard could it be? He found 54th Street and turned right, watching the street numbers get higher. Unfortunately he turned left on 62nd *Road* by mistake. He figured the sign was making the mistake. How could they be stupid enough to have a street and a road with the same number that weren't the same one? But they did. He tried to correct his mistake by doubling back and he got lost. And then he got angry because he was lost, so he drove faster, which caused him to get even more lost. He started cursing the bastard *cafone* who figured out they should name the street and the road the same number just to confuse people. Within a few minutes he was completely lost in Queens, mad at everybody.

And the two cars tailing him followed as he made every single wrong turn. He kept going. They kept going. There was no way he was going to stop and ask for directions. He never asked for directions. He wasn't an ask-for-directions kind of guy. He could find his own way. He didn't care how long it took—Skinny Al could be Skeleton Al by the time he found it, but he would find it.

Suddenly the dark sedan sped up, passed the Firebird, and, finally, passed Bobby. He didn't get a clean look at who was driving, he just saw two people in the front. The sedan cut into his lane about thirty feet in front of him. The driver slowed down and put on his blinker. Bobby figured out what they were doing and smiled. Then he put on his blinker. Then the Firebird put on its blinker. Obviously the FBI knew where he was heading. That was not much of a surprise— where else would he be going at eleven o'clock on a Thursday morning? More important at that particular moment, they knew how to get there.

The sedan led them right to the Linden Brothers. When they got there, the driver of the sedan parked at a hydrant directly across the street from the funeral parlor. Bobby pulled into the parking lot, which was filling up fast. The Firebird followed him but parked in the back of the lot. Bobby watched as two men, both neatly dressed in tailored dark suits, got out of the car and went inside. The driver was tall and dark, well tanned; his passenger was considerably smaller, with very short blond hair and extremely broad shoulders. Who the fuck are those guys? he wondered.

The Linden Brothers was crowded. As Bobby walked in, he respectfully took off his white hat. There were two funerals, but only a few elderly people were there for the Schwartz service. The second chapel was packed for Skinny Al.

A mob funeral is a social occasion at which at least some business is conducted. There are rules to be followed. Certain people are required to be present, among them his boss, members of his crew, his family and friends. As Skinny Al wasn't a boss, Henry Franzone was not required to be there. While Bobby didn't fit into any of those categories—he wasn't with Cosentino and wasn't friends with the victim—he was welcomed as the official representative of Franzone's crew. An ambassador of respect.

Two large men wearing sunglasses flanked the entrance to the chapel. Bobby recognized one of them as Jackie Fats, whom he'd known casually for maybe ten years. Fats was bouncing up and down nervously. Bobby walked over and shook his hand. "Jackie," he said.

"Good to see youse," Fats responded. "Go 'head in."

The room was buzzing. Men were gathered in small groups at the back of the chapel. A closed mahogany coffin covered with flowers stood on two trestles at the front of the room. Bobby went forward,

bowed, and paid his respects, then joined the mourners in the back
of the room.

Bobby looked around, spotting several familiar faces. He saw
Cosentino in the middle of the side aisle and started walking toward
him. This was protocol; he would convey the deep sympathy of
Henry Franzone and his people at the untimely death of Al D'Angelo. But as he got closer, he saw that Cosentino was talking to two
men—the two men from the Firebird. Cosentino was facing the rear
doors, looking toward Bobby, so their backs were to him. But their
suits were unmistakable. Whoever those guys are, Bobby decided,
definitely they're not FBI. Another guy, a soldier Bobby had met a
couple of times named Jimmy or Johnny something, was watching
over the group. Bobby stopped, waiting for permission from him to
proceed. He was standing only a few feet away from them, close
enough to overhear bits and pieces of conversation. So he didn't even
have to strain to hear their heavy Russian accents.

He looked down and cleared his throat, trying to hide his surprise.
Russian? Bobby didn't know Russian, but he'd seen enough movies
and watched enough television to recognize the accent. Whatever
was going on, it was now officially crazy. Why were there Russians at
Skinny Al's funeral? And why were those Russians following him? He
kept his eyes averted, not wanting Cosentino to think he was listening to a private conversation.

After standing there for several minutes he was beginning to feel
uncomfortably exposed and maybe just a little bit insulted when
Cosentino and the two Russians laughed loudly and shook hands.
The Russians turned and started walking right toward him. As they
passed him, one of them, the stocky guy with a blond buzz cut and
a pockmarked face, glanced at him and immediately looked away. It
happened much too quickly for Bobby to even guess whether or not
the guy had recognized him. As he turned to take another look at the
Russians, he heard a deep voice commanding, "Mr. Cosentino is
ready for ya."

Bobby pasted on a disarming smile and moved forward. As he did,

Jimmy or Johnny whispered something in Cosentino's ear, probably Bobby's pedigree. Cosentino grasped Bobby's hand firmly and accepted his condolences and, still holding Bobby's hand, pulled him closer. "How's it going?" he whispered. "That thing you're doing?"

"It's okay," Bobby told him. "We got some interest."

"That's good. But see, don't take too long. This thing, it's gotta be done by next Thursday night. You unnerstand what I mean, right? It's gotta be done by then."

"I understand, Mr. Cosentino," Bobby said.

Cosentino released Bobby's hand and took a step backward. "Maybe you need some more help, huh?"

"No, we're doing okay," he said. Thursday? That was a week, not a lot of time. But for some reason next Thursday was a big day.

"That's good, that's good," Cosentino said, tapping him lightly on the cheek to indicate their brief conversation was finished.

Bobby sat through the service. According to the priest, Skinny Al was a pillar of respectability. He gave to the church, he was nice to his friends, and he worked hard to earn a living for his family. It was a speech long on platitudes, short on details. Skinny Al's brother, a civilian, gave a nice little talk, telling a funny story about the Thanksgiving when Skinny Al almost choked to death. Al was so big, the brother explained, that no one could get their arms far enough around him to give him the Heimlich, so instead, they punched him in the solar plexus, dislodging a chunk of bread. By the time he was finished speaking, he was laughing so hard at the memory that tears were rolling down his face. Bobby noticed the Russians leaving early, but at least 150 other people stayed. It was not the kind of room in which you spent a lot of time looking around, but the day did have the feeling of a team reunion to it. People in this business may not become close friends, but through the years they do business with a lot of different people.

As the service droned on—several cousins felt it was necessary to tell not-so-funny Skinny Al stories—Bobby sat there trying to figure out what the hell was going on: With all the heavyweights in this room why did Cosentino farm out the work to another crew? What was going on that he didn't want his own people involved? Why were those Russians following him? And why did they make themselves so visible at Skinny Al's funeral? Things like that didn't just happen. Their showing up at the funeral had a motive and had to have been approved by Cosentino himself. And where did the FBI fit into the whole thing?

Like theme music running softly in the background of a movie, the reality against which everything in the world of organized crime takes place is the possibility of sudden death. Just like what happened to Skinny Al, although based on the damage done, it had to be semi-sudden. It's always there, always bubbling just below the events of the day. So Bobby carefully measured all of these questions to determine if they added up to some type of threat against him.

It didn't seem like it. If somebody wanted to whack him, they would try to get permission to whack him, and if they did, then they would whack him. It wasn't any more complicated than that. There was no reason to go through all these shenanigans. But as he reviewed the last six months of his life, the last year even, he couldn't think of a single thing he'd done—to anybody—that would put his life in jeopardy.

In fact, it was pretty much a time of peace in the mob. There were always certain beefs, there were always some people ready to complain that they weren't being treated fairly, there were always disputes about territory or splits, that was the natural order of things. But overall the families were doing well; business was good, people were earning, and nobody more than necessary was getting hurt. Even the recent recession that the whole country had stumbled through hadn't put a dent in business. People always want to gamble. They always want girls. They always want bargains. They want to drink, they want drugs, they want what they want when they want it. And when the national economy is bad, people always need to borrow money. It was simple economics: demand and supply. What the people demanded the mob supplied.

As Bobby walked out of Linden Brothers, he noticed that the dark sedan was still parked across the street. By this time several other nondescript sedans were also parked there. Law enforcement always turns out for a mob funeral. As Bobby walked toward his car, he put on his sunglasses—then suddenly changed direction and walked directly across the street to the dark sedan. Even from a distance he could see two men sitting in the front seat. One of them was black, which was still somewhat of a novelty in this part of the crime world. Hey, Bobby thought, it's pin-the-tail-on-the-honky time, and laughed to himself.

Both men were wearing reflective sunglasses. FBI putzes, Bobby thought. As he got within a couple of feet, the driver kicked over the engine, enabling the black guy in the passenger seat to roll down his window. He and Bobby locked sunglasses. Bobby wasn't shy. Leaning into the car, he casually rested an arm on the window frame. Smiling confidently, he said, "Hey, thanks a lot, guys. I'd hate to have them bury him without me."

The driver leaned forward so Bobby could see him. "Professional courtesy, Bobby," he said,

"Listen, I'm heading downtown. Any chance you guys could pick up some doughnuts on the way and meet me there?"

"Gee, sorry," the passenger said, "but after this you're on your own. You know, sometimes they give us important work to do."

Bobby banged his fist on the window frame. "Good for you. I like to see guys get ahead." He stood up. "See you tomorrow?"

"We never know, Bobby, we never know."

When Bobby drove out of the parking lot, they followed him to the first traffic light and, as promised, dropped him.

Canal Street was backed up for blocks. Caught in the gridlocked traffic, Bobby was fuming. Now, this really is a fucking crime, he thought. Where the fuck are the cops when you really need them? Fucking Ed Koch. You want to help people? It doesn't take a genius to figure out that you got to put cops at the major intersections and make them give out tickets to those bastards who block them.

It took him forty minutes to go four blocks. He double-parked in front of a double-parked truck, put his PBA card in the windshield, and left his blinkers on. He was only going to be a few minutes. Three Guys Plumbing Supply was crowded, at least ten men standing in front of the counter talking pipes. Bobby walked right past them, right into the back room. As he did, a small black guy was coming out carrying a clipboard under his arm. The guy looked familiar, and his nose was bandaged pretty good, but Bobby couldn't place him.

"Jesus fucking Christ, Tommy," Bobby said loudly as he walked into the office, "why don't you clean this fucking place up?"

"Hey, big guy," So Solly Tommy said, genuinely happy to see him. "Now my fucking life is complete." The top of his desk was buried under layers of paperwork. Tommy got up and came around the desk to greet Bobby. He gave him a big hug. "What's a matter with you? You don't like my filing system?"

Bobby shook his head. "How do you keep track of shit? Boy, I don't get it."

Tommy tapped the side of his head with his forefinger. "It's all up here. You heard of Einstein, right? I'm a fucking Crimestein." They both laughed easily. The two men had been doing business for twenty years, since Bobby was a crazy teenager, without a bad word ever passing between them. Tommy had fenced the first heist Bobby had ever planned, two dozen new tires taken from a gas station near the Lincoln Tunnel. He indicated the chair in front of his desk. "Sit. Sit. You want a cup?"

Two sugars, Bobby told him.

"Carol," Tommy yelled, "get in here."

"What do you want from me?" Carol shouted right back at him. She was an attractive middle-aged woman who was wearing a tight black skirt, a white blouse that hugged her chest—the top two buttons were open—and a big, brassy smile. With the right casting director she could have easily played a moll.

Tommy gave her the order for coffee and Danish, and after she had gone, he turned back to Bobby. "So what do you got for me?"

"You ever heard about Cabbage Patch dolls?"

"Fuck, yeah. You kidding me? Those things are tougher to get than pussy in the Vatican. Why? You got some?" Bobby smiled broadly. "No shit," Solly Tommy said happily. "You fucking prick. Those things are fucking gold mines. You got the real thing or the fugazis?"

"Hey, Tommy, please. What do I look like to you?"

"It don't matter to me, kid. As far as I'm concerned, a fucking doll is a fucking doll. But some of the crapola, they stuffed them with kerosene rags. Those fucking dolls are more dangerous than you are. So now the cops are going around collecting them."

"Fugetaboutit, Tommy, this is primo shit." Actually Bobby had no idea if these dolls were real or counterfeit. But he had nothing to lose by taking a shot. Tommy was nobody's fool. He could take care of himself. If he got jammed up, Bobby would settle with him. No problem.

"Whatever you got I'll take." They negotiated a fair price and made arrangements for delivery. It had been a while since they'd seen each other, so they spent some coffee time catching up, then, as Bobby was getting ready to leave, Tommy asked him, "So, Bobby, answer me this. Think any of your guys want some VCRs? I got this whole fucking truckload come in last night . . ."

"Holy fucking shit," Bobby said, remembering suddenly where he had seen that little black fuck with the clipboard. He started to run outside but knew it was much too late to catch him. The driver was long gone. "That guy . . ." He was so angry he couldn't even get the words out. "That little fucking guy with the clipboard?" He pointed outside. "That's the fucking guy who ripped us off the other night."

It was obvious from Tommy's reaction that he knew nothing about it. "Whattya talking about? That little guy? No fucking way. He was scared shitless doing business with me."

"I don't fucking believe it. That no-good little fucker." Bobby told

Tommy the whole story—admittedly with some appreciation for the little guy's huge gonads. "Fucking guy ripped us off before we could heist the load. I mean, what kind of bullshit is that?" Both men were laughing by the time Bobby finished telling the story. "When I tell this to Lenny, there's no way he's gonna believe it. I swear to God, what he's gonna do to him you wouldn't wish on your first wife's divorce lawyer. You got his name, right?"

"Course." The deal had been concluded no more than an hour earlier, yet in one of those mysteries of life the paperwork had already been buried on Tommy's desk. He searched through the pile until he found it. "Here. Here it is." He handed Bobby a Xerox copy of a standard business form. It included the man's name and address. All the blanks had been filled in. And at the bottom of the form Tommy had made a copy of the guy's driver's license.

"Fucking guy," Bobby said, laughing at the audacity of Mr. Benjamin Franklin Washington.

In Tommy's business, identities were flexible. Nobody did much checking; all people cared about was the merchandise. Either you came recommended by a good person or you bought pipes at the front counter. Either you had the goods or you didn't. Nobody ever got a dime from Tommy based on his name. Naturally Tommy had paid him in cash. The merchandise was good, it had all been checked. The guy had come to Tommy from a guy who knew a guy. Tommy agreed to make the phone calls but didn't offer much hope in finding him. There wasn't too much that could be done—and it was highly unlikely that, after seeing Bobby walking in, the driver would ever again avail himself of Tommy's services.

Bobby was laughing all the way back to the social club. Tommy had promised to spread the word, and Bobby had no doubt that if the guy stayed around New York, eventually they would catch up with him. He'd have to tell the story to Fast Lenny, which would definitely piss Lenny off even more, but he thought he'd better forget to mention the fact that he'd walked right by the guy and hadn't recognized him.

Mickey Fists was holding court when Bobby got there. "Hey, Bobby," Mickey greeted him, "I got a good one for you. How do you make a hormone?"

There were four men at the table, all looking at him expectantly. He knew he couldn't let them down. So as he turned up the volume on the radio, he shook his head. "I don't know, Mick. How do you make a hormone?"

"You don't pay her the two hundred bucks you owe her!"

Everybody laughed, even Bobby, who'd heard the joke two hundred times. Actually it was a lot better than most of Mickey's jokes. The kid, Vito V, handed him a message. Normally a person in Duke's position would be the one to take messages, but his condition made that impossible. So that job fell to the youngest person in the club. "Mrs. Grada-insky called you," he said. "She wants you to call her soon as possible."

Ah shit, Bobby thought, just when I was sitting down to get comfortable. There was no possible way he would use the telephone in the club, might as well use a party line. He got up, waved off the Duke, who was carrying a hot cuppa toward him, and went to return the call.

He walked across Canal Street into Chinatown and found one of those cute little pagoda phone booths. The cops couldn't tap every pay phone in New York, and this one was far enough outside Little Italy to have a reasonably good chance of being secure.

Grace Gradinsky answered on the third ring. "You called me," he said, seeing no reason to identify himself. "What's going on?"

"They found him," she said.

A chill ran through Bobby's body. "Dead or alive?" was the right question, but he didn't know how to ask it. He settled for "Who found him?"

She corrected herself. "I mean, they didn't exactly find him. They just found out he's okay. He used a credit card the other night to get some cash. He does that sometimes. I didn't tell them that, though." There was a sense of urgency in her voice as she gave him the details precisely as she'd gotten them from James Slattery. "So," she asked when she finished, "what does that mean?"

"It means what it means. What else could it mean?" Naturally she agreed. Bobby told her he'd go to the restaurant and speak to the people. See if anybody had any information. But given his wide knowledge concerning the fraudulent use of credit cards, he wasn't particularly optimistic. "Don't go getting your hopes up," he warned her. "The feds were probably there already. They're pretty good. So if there was anything worth knowing about, they probably found it out already."

By the time he got back to the social club, the group at the card table was in the middle of a somewhat heated discussion about sports. Georgie One-Time had insisted that the easiest sport to fix, with the obvious exceptions of boxing and horse racing, was football. The real beauty of fixing a football game, he pointed out, was that you didn't need to change the outcome of the game—the winning team could still win—just the point spread. "All you need's one official. He throws two flags at the right time, fugetaboutit. It's over. All she wrote."

Vito V was adamant that baseball was the easiest game to fix. "You just gotta buy the home plate umpire." The kid's real name was Vito Valentine, which he had changed from Valentino. When Fast Lenny wondered how Vito V could get to an umpire, the kid told him, "It's not that hard. Umpires got human foibles too, you know."

The table was completely silent for several seconds, and then Georgie started laughing. "What are you, shitting me? That's fucking bullshit. I been a baseball fan my whole life and I never heard of an umpire getting a fur ball."

Vito was smart enough to understand how careful he had to be with his response. He was not in a position to make fun of a wiseguy. "Oh man, I'm sorry. See, that's not . . . Like what I meant to say was . . ." and this time he pronounced it very distinctly—"foible. You know, like a weakness. Like he likes women. Not fur ball."

Georgie glared at him. "Then learn to speak fucking English, why don't you?" Georgie laughed again. "Fucking guy thinks umpires get fur balls."

"Hey, Vito," Mickey Fists asked, "I don't get one thing. Why's it a weakness to like women? You saying it's strong to like men?"

Mickey had him there, everybody knew that. "No," the kid explained. "See, what I mean is if the umpire likes the broads, you can get to him that way. A broad and a camera, that's a combination that can get a guy rich."

Bobby turned up the volume on the radio and joined the card players. As he sat down, Silent Sammy Mastrianno asked his opinion. "Fuck," Bobby shrugged, "how the hell do I know? Guarantee you I know who loses, though. The guy who collects on the bet if the thing ever gets known."

In reality, fixing a team sport is probably not that difficult to do. All you have to get is a couple of key players or officials. Vito V was absolutely right: Everybody does have a foible, and usually they're not that difficult to find. Or satisfy. Think umpires don't gamble? Think they don't play cards for high stakes during the World Series, for example? Think football officials don't like the ladies? But the actual fixing might well be the easiest part. To make it worthwhile, you need to lay down a lot of money, and you can't bet a large sum on an unimportant game without somebody noticing. So it has to be a big game, the play-offs or World Series, the Super Bowl, meaning it gets a lot of attention. But in this world winning is only the beginning. You got to live to spend it. Bobby was absolutely right. If the bookies find out somebody is stealing their money, they will go after him. And they'll keep going after him until that debt is settled. That really is the primary reason most games are legitimate.

"Any you guys ever do business with the Russkies?" Bobby asked. Fast Eddie looked at him curiously but didn't say anything.

Nobody leaped to answer. Finally Fast Lenny said, examining his palm, "Yeah, I did a couple things with a Russian. He was all right, you know. Smart. Why, whattya need?"

Bobby banged his foot on the floor three times to get the Duke's attention. The Duke felt the vibration and turned around. Gimme one, Bobby signaled. "Nothing big," he told Lenny. "It's just that missing teacher thing Henry's got me working. You know, I figure Russky teacher, I should talk to the Russkies. So I thought if you got a name, maybe I could ask him some questions."

Fast Lenny took a few seconds to calculate the various ways he could profit by making this introduction. But without knowing specifically what Bobby had in mind there was no way to solve that equation. He was safe, though. Bobby was a player, and if things worked out, he would take care of Lenny. "I don't know. Lemme put the word out for you. See what happens. How soon?"

The much sooner, the much better, Bobby told him. Then he took a deep breath and suddenly remembered. "Hey, Lenny. You're not gonna believe who I almost ran into this afternoon." As Bobby suspected, Lenny couldn't guess—but hearing how close Bobby had been to grabbing the bastard got his boiler started once again. He went through the whole story, explaining in great detail what he was going to do to the little fuck when he caught up with him.

The rest of the afternoon went pretty quickly for Bobby. After leaving the club he went directly to Pam's apartment. Whatever else was going on in his world, Pam made him feel good about himself. Sometimes he thought she could read his mind; or more accurately, his prick. She had even given it a name: Mr. Upright Citizen. He laughed every time she said it. Ronnie had a name for it too: She called it "that thing a yours." He could hear her saying it. "Keep that thing a yours in your pants."

The truth is that in his whole life, from the time he was fourteen years old getting his first blow job on the playground, no woman had ever pleased him as Pam did. She did these things with her hands and her mouth that he had never even seen in the pornos. She touched him in places no woman had ever touched him before, and to his great surprise one of them—although he would never admit this to anyone—was his heart.

Pamela Fox was the woman he so wished Ronnie would be. He

really wanted to desire Ronnie the way he did Pam. But Ronnie wasn't that person. He was certain Ronnie had never slept with another man. Sex with another guy? Ronnie thought *Playboy* was risky. The nuns would have been proud of her. Ronnie doing the things to him that Pam did? He almost laughed at that thought. He couldn't talk to Ronnie about doing the things he did with Pam in her next lifetime. Fuck that, her next two lifetimes.

He spent almost two hours at the apartment with Pam. It was getting dark outside when they finally got out of bed. And for the first time since they started seeing each other, she complained when he got ready to leave. "You know, baby, I hate it when you come and go."

He made a joke out of it. "What are you talking? I came three times. I'm only going once." But he hoped she meant it the good way. For an instant he thought about taking her uptown with him. He could go up to the Heights Tavern and take care of business, then they could have a nice, quiet dinner at Patsy's. Oh, he'd love to walk into Patsy's with Pam. Fucking tongues would be hanging on the floor. Then afterward they would go to bed and he would go home. But that was one fantasy that wasn't going to come true. He didn't kid himself. Too often men who mixed pleasure with business ended up sorry.

Bobby was feeling so warm inside when he left the apartment that he neglected to take even the most basic precautions. He didn't even bother checking the block up and down to see if anything unusual caught his attention. He just got in his car and drove away. If he had taken just a few extra seconds, he might have spotted the charcoal Firebird parked at a hydrant about halfway down the block. And maybe he would have seen the two men sitting in the front seat, who watched with interest as Bobby got into his car and drove away.

Bobby picked up Little Eddie at the club. As they headed uptown, Eddie described in detail "Mount Lenny's eruption." He was laughing so hard as he told the story that he had difficulty catching his breath. "Oh man, you shoulda seen the fucking guy after you left. He's screaming for had to be twenty minutes." Eddie did a poor imitation of Lenny's nasal voice. " 'I can't fucking believe it. The guy peed his pants. What an actor. He should be on TV. No, better, I tell you what, he should *pee* on TV. I mean, the guy pees his pants, you gotta believe it when a guy does that, right? That's fucking sick, to fake something like that.' He goes on and on like this, then finally he sits down and shuts up. 'I'm done,' he said. 'That's it.' And then, I swear to God, four seconds later he stands up and starts screaming again. 'That no-good fucking this, fucking that. How can a guy pee his pants and not mean it? You gotta trust a guy who does that.' I swear to God, Bobby, I thought I was gonna die."

Little Eddie had been brought up properly in the mob, so he would never think about asking Bobby where he'd been that afternoon. With a broad, he hoped. He knew that fucking Ronnie was driving him nuts. Eddie's own philosophy of life and love was pretty simple: Every guy needed somebody to love, and as long as he could keep that broad from meeting his wife, everybody would be happy. But truthfully in his own life he rarely went out on his wife, Joyce. And then usually only when he was with the other guys and the situation demanded it. Eddie always told people that there were a lot of things he loved about Joyce: her pasta, her pork ribs, her shrimp marinara, her banana cream pie. But the fact was that he loved all of her. And, as he also joked, there was more of Joyce to love every week.

The Morningside Heights Tavern was just starting to get crowded when they walked in. The Knicks-Lakers were on the TV. The Knicks were so awful that a bar was about the only place any intelligent person could bear to watch them. At least the Lakers had Lew Alcindor, as Little Eddie insisted on referring to him. None of that African name Kareem Karoom Kaboom or whatever it was he was calling himself. The guy was an American, a New Yorker, and he should have an American name.

Bobby and Little Eddie stood at the bar, which ran parallel to the rear wall stretching from side to side. Several coeds noticed Bobby and drifted toward him. There wasn't another man in the place wearing a sports jacket, much less an obviously expensive tailored Italian suit. And none of the other men in the bar could match his cool. He smiled back at the girls and took the time to appreciate the flow of their tight sweaters around their taut young titties. Now, that is truly great advertising, he thought, but did nothing more than think about it. He was working.

He and Eddie had a couple of drinks and picked up the rhythm of the place. There was a nice vibe going. There were two television sets above the bar and both of them were showing the game, although the sound was off and Bruce Springsteen was blasting out of the wall speakers. The two bartenders were working hard, so Bobby waited patiently. He noticed that the bartenders were the only people who handled the cash register, so they would have processed the professor's credit card. When the second round was delivered, he gave one of them a twenty-dollar tip, without doubt the largest single tip he was going to get out of the crowd that night. The bartender smiled at him. "When you got a minute," Bobby said pleasantly. The bartender nodded.

Getting that one minute took most of the next hour. By that time the crowd noise was killing Eddie. "Why ain't they home studying?" he yelled at Bobby, who could barely hear him.

Finally the bartender returned, casually wiping the bar with his wet rag as he spoke. He said something about questions, but Bobby pointed to his ears and shrugged. The bartender nodded and yelled, "Give me one more minute."

Ten minutes later he tossed down his rag and pointed to a doorway filled with long strings of colored beads. Bobby and Eddie followed him into a corridor about thirty feet long. Small signs on two doors identified both of them as restrooms. That confused Eddie, who asked the bartender, "Which one's the men's room?"

"They're unisex," the bartender told him. "They're for both."

Eddie just shook his head sadly. He'd never heard of any such thing. Fucking Democrats, he thought.

The bartender introduced himself as Billy Garvey, then added that everybody called him Gravy. "Good to meet you," Bobby said, shaking his hand but not even bothering to make up some phony name. "Anyplace a little more quiet maybe?"

The door to the rear restroom opened and a girl walked out, sniffling two or three times as she passed. "Sure," Garvey said, a friendly smile on his face, "step into my office." The three men went into the restroom. It was a real tight fit. Only if Eddie turned sideways could the three of them be in there without his stomach pressing against one of the other men.

"Fuck this," Eddie decided. He squeezed outside and stood directly in front of the door.

Inside, Bobby suggested to Garvey, "Take a seat." He indicated the toilet.

"That's okay," Garvey said, waving his hand dismissively, "I'm on my feet all night."

"Hey, pal," Bobby coldly informed him, "that wasn't a fucking request."

"Now, wait a second," Garvey said, still smiling. "I don't know what you're thinking, but . . ."

"I'm thinking you better fucking sit down right now, that's what I'm thinking. Okay, now you know."

Garvey sat down on the toilet seat. His smile disappeared.

Bobby read people well. This Garvey had an ego; he probably spent the whole night having the girls sucking up to him, so the quicker he was reminded of his impotence in this situation, the more cooperative he would be. "Now, this isn't going to take long, I promise you that. I just got a few questions you can answer for me. First question, how long you been working at this place?"

"I don't know, eighteen months, twenty months maybe."

"Good. See how easy this is? Next question, were you working two nights ago?"

Garvey thought about it, then nodded. "Uh-huh, I was. Look, if you're gonna ask me about that guy, the professor? Two people were in last night . . ."

Bobby placed his index finger to his lips and shushed him. "Listen up. I don't really care if the whole Royal fucking Mounted Police came in with their horses. You just answer the questions I ask you. Third question, did this Professor Gradinsky come in here?"

With a rolling chuckle Garvey said, "Honest, I'm telling you just like I told them—"

Bobby smacked him across the face with the back of his hand. It wouldn't mark him, but it would communicate the proper message. Unfortunately Bobby hit him a little harder than he'd intended and Garvey's head bounced against the tile wall.

Bobby recognized the fear in the bartender's eyes. And for just an instant he remembered that the fucking truck driver had reacted the very same way—while he was busy ripping them off. Garvey said emphatically, "No, I don't—"

Bobby lifted his foot about three inches off the ground and slammed his heel down on the tip of Garvey's toes. Garvey screamed and involuntarily started to get up—but Bobby put his palm on the bartender's forehead and shoved him back onto the seat. He warned him, "Don't be an asshole, kid. Don't fucking lie to me. I know he used his credit card in here."

The only person in the corridor who heard Garvey scream was Little Eddie, and he was very busy trying to deal with the fact that a boy and a girl had gone into the second bathroom together. Together! It was the first time in his life he had ever seen anything like that, and he couldn't figure out if they were having sex or doing drugs in there. There was only one other thing they could be doing in a bathroom, and he refused to accept that possibility. Sex or drugs, those were the options. And as much as he hated everything about drugs—except for the profit margins—that's actually what he hoped they were doing. The thought of them having sex in the bathroom was just too disgusting for him.

He thought about the places that he and Joyce had had sex. The bed in the bedroom, that was it. The two of them have sex in a bathroom? The two of them couldn't fit into a bathroom together.

Bobby took out the photograph of Gradinsky and held it up. "Look here." He pointed to the professor. "This guy. You ever see him in here?"

"I don't know him, I swear," Garvey said, then covered his head with his arms. "He might have had dinner here once in a while, but I don't know him. Please don't hit me in my face anymore." He looked up and said completely seriously, as if it explained everything, "I'm an actor."

"Yeah, right, you're John fucking Wayne." When Bobby again raised his hand, the bartender recoiled fearfully, lifting both feet off the ground and cowering against the wall. There was a long scrape over the guy's left eye where Bobby's ring had smacked him and a good-sized welt on the right side of his forehead compliments of the wall. The welt was swelling rapidly. Putting down his hand, Bobby said, "Okay, lemme ask you this. You ever hear of the soap *One Fucking Life to Live If You Know What's Good for You?*"

Billy Garvey closed his eyes and nodded.

"Good. So lemme ask you one more time. Tell me about this professor."

"I swear I'd tell you if I knew him. I swear to God. You gotta believe me."

Bobby sighed. "You know what, I believe you. You ain't that good an actor. But lemme tell you one thing. I find out you're lying to me—and believe me, if you're lying to me, I will find out, even a little tiny lie—I'm gonna find you and I'm gonna reach down your throat till I grab hold of your motherfucking nuts and I'm gonna turn you inside out. We understand each other?"

"Honest, I don't know the guy."

"I said, we understand each other?"

Garvey nodded. "Yes, sir."

"Good." He turned to leave the bathroom but stopped. "And good luck with the acting."

Bobby didn't waste his time questioning the manager on his way out. A bartender working in the same place for eighteen months gets to know his customers better than any manager. If Gradinsky was even a semiregular, Garvey, Gravy, whatever, would have known him. The professor was missing either by choice or by force, but either way it was difficult to believe he would wander into a local joint for dinner. If he wanted to stay missing, he wouldn't risk bumping into people he knew; if he was being held by other people, they wouldn't take him out in the old neighborhood for a nice, friendly dinner. There are no time-outs in missing.

Bobby didn't doubt the credit card had been used. But he was certain of one thing: It hadn't been used by Professor G.

As they left the tavern, Eddie glanced back at the hanging beads. The couple was still in the bathroom. Gees, he thought, they've been in there more than fifteen minutes. They gotta be going for the Guinness record book.

EIGHT

An assault on an agent, whether successful or not, automatically triggers the highest-priority investigation. Before dawn agents from the New York office were swarming over Russo's building like ants on sugar, or better, like the mob on money. In addition, several forensic experts from the crime lab in Washington caught the 7 a.m. shuttle and by noon were scouring the building for any type of evidence. The crime lab people in particular are magicians at plucking dust from the air and somehow using it to link a specific individual to a specific event.

But even Theo Kojak couldn't have done much with Russo's place. Any fingerprints or palm prints that might have been left on the doorknob were smudged beyond recognition. There were too many years of prints on her door and the hallway walls to be useful. The downstairs foyer door had been opened with the same jeweler's pick that the intruder had used to try to jimmy the apartment door. It left a few scratches on the lock, and if the pick was ever found, the lab's Toolmarks Unit might be able to match it. The operative word being "might." But even that was a real long shot. A partial shoe print had been found in a small puddle of hardening pea soup that someone had dropped on one of the treads, but it had been made by a popular soft-soled shoe that could have belonged to just about anybody. A gum wrapper was found in a corner, but later that day agents confirmed it had been tossed there by Russo's neighbor, Ginger Sanchez. Russo thought it was pretty amusing that six different agents found it necessary to interview Ms. Sanchez about her gum wrapper toss. Laura speculated it was the most thoroughly investigated littering case in bureau history. And early in the afternoon, after the NYPD had been notified, two patrolmen and a sergeant also spent the necessary time with Ginger to completely corroborate her wrapper story. Collectively they spent more time with Ms. Sanchez than with Russo. And they found it more difficult to believe that Ginger was a second-grade teacher than that Russo was an FBI agent.

Russo did her best to stay out of their way. She answered every question but really could offer no valuable information. She had barely seen the back of the intruder's head. And while it was impossible to identify the person who tried to break into her apartment, she was pretty certain that she knew who sent him.

O'Brien brought it up first, suggesting, "Maybe your boyfriend's jealous."

"You think it was him?"

O'Brien looked at the impressive array of FBI agents and NYPD detectives elbowing each other for space. "Tell you what. If it was just some druggie trying to make a score, I'd say he picked the wrong place."

Connor had tried hard to be properly solicitous, but she made that difficult for him. Rather than being shaken by the attempt, she was actually excited. She was pumping adrenaline. "Don't you see?" she told him when they had a few minutes by themselves. "This proves we're bothering somebody. It's like you say you like to do, shake the bushes and see what drops on your head. The bureau's got to pay attention to this now."

Slattery was waiting expectantly for them. He was as animated as Russo had ever seen him, a big bag of nervous energy. She immediately assured him that she was perfectly all right.

"Great," he said distractedly, and never said another word about it. Instead, he waved a folder at them. "You two need to see this stuff right now."

They were seated in the conference room, at the far end of a long mahogany table. O'Brien was next to Russo, Slattery across from them. He handed them each a copy of the complete file. It contained three separate reports. "The first one's a transcript of a conversation that took place yesterday inside the club," he explained. "Apparently our boy San Filippo had met with Cosentino." Slattery turned to the second page and scanned down with his index finger. "Here, go to the second page. Right in the middle." He read aloud, " 'San Filippo: Two-Gun says we gotta find this guy by Thursday night.' LaRocca then says . . ."

"Who's that?" O'Brien wondered.

Russo told him. "Little Eddie."

"Oh, that's right. You never hear him called that."

" 'LaRocca,' " Slattery repeated, returning to the transcript. " 'What the fuck's so important about then? San Filippo: (Unintelligible) says that (unintelligible) doesn't tell me anything. But he was pretty fucking serious about it. LaRocca: Yeah, well, shit.' " Slattery looked up from the transcript. "So what's happening Thursday night?"

O'Brien took a shot. "The Mad Mongol's wrestling Don 'Demon Seed' Stevens?"

Slattery ignored him and looked at Russo. She shook her head, then said, "Whatever it is, the professor's part of it." She bit down on her lower lip, a habit she'd developed many years earlier. "I just don't get it. Where's the connection?"

"Here," Slattery said, turning to the second report. "Look at this."

O'Brien laid his forearms on the table and began reading what appeared to be a toxicology report.

Slattery continued, "It's the report from the crime lab. They made it a priority." Specifically it was from the Chemistry Unit. As O'Brien and Russo read through the technical jargon, Slattery interpreted it for them. "Before they killed Skinny Al, they burned out both his eardrums with cigarettes . . ."

Russo winced involuntarily. It was difficult to hear that without imagining it. The pain must have been extraordinary.

". . . and so what happened, and this is actually pretty interesting, when they pushed the lit cigarette into his ear, they knocked off the ash, but they also knocked off a few fragments of unburned tobacco. And the ear, the ear's sort of like a cup holder. When something that small gets inside there, it stays there. The coroner found a minuscule amount of unburned tobacco . . ." Slattery couldn't help editorializing. "This guy did a great job. And then he sent it along to the lab.

"It got sent to the Chem-Tox Unit. The agent there . . ." He searched the report for a name. "Martz, this Martz, he analyzed the tobacco sample. The mass spec, fluoroscope, whatever thingamajigs he had, he got a profile for the tobacco. Then he sent somebody out to buy packs of every brand of cigarettes they could find and profiled that tobacco. First thing they discovered . . ." He paused. "Either you guys want to guess?"

Once again O'Brien couldn't resist a straight line. "Smoking's bad for your health?"

"It wasn't an American brand. The tobacco was much too strong."

Russo was beginning to make the connection in her mind.

"So they went up to the foreign tobacco and newspaper store on M Street and bought out the place. I think it was . . ." Once again he searched the report. "Yeah, here it is, seventy-two different brands from around the world. And they made a match." He frowned. "I can't read this name, but it's Russian."

"Shit," O'Brien said with admiration, truly impressed. The implications were enormous.

"Are they sure?" Laura asked.

"Positive. They ran every test they could think of. It's one of the most popular Russian brands. Apparently it was pretty easy to make the match. We got nothing like it here. You guys understand what this means, right?"

"It means we got trouble in River City," O'Brien said. The evidence strongly indicated that Skinny Alphonse D'Angelo, a made member of organized crime, had been killed by a Russian. Not just killed. This wasn't a mugging or a robbery, it wasn't any accident, this was slow, torturous murder. There was obviously a reason he was killed, and that he was tortured, meaning that there had to have been some prior interaction between Skinny Al and the Russians that didn't go well.

Russo said it out loud. "So we got the Italians and the Russians in the same ballpark, don't we?"

"Yep," Slattery said evenly, "that we do."

This was the match made in hell that law enforcement had long been dreading. The good news was that whatever happened between them, the result had been Skinny Al squashed into the trunk of a car. The bad news was that the Italians and the Russians were doing some kind of business. "Now, just wait a second," Russo interjected. "I don't want to burst any bubbles, but this is a pretty big leap we're making here. We don't have the slightest idea what this was about. There's a pretty good chance it didn't have anything to do with the families. Maybe it was just two guys fighting over a woman or something. Maybe it was territorial or a bad loan, maybe it was about the cold war. I mean, it could be absolutely anything. It doesn't need to be the Apocalypse."

"Yeah, you might be right," O'Brien agreed. "It doesn't need to be, except for the fact that on the same day they found Skinny Al doing his Hunchback imitation a Russian professor who had worked with him goes missing and hasn't been seen since. There's gotta be a connection there."

"That's what I think too," Slattery agreed. "So now the question becomes, where does our professor fit into the whole picture?" He paused and glanced at Russo. "Russo, could you go get us some..."

Her incredulous look cut him off at his ego.

"I'll get it," O'Brien said quickly. "How do you want it?" There was a hot plate in the corner and on it was the perpetual pot of coffee. Slattery wanted his regular. O'Brien poured one regular, one with milk and no sugar for himself, and one for Russo—black and strong.

"Let's look at this logically," Russo said, rising. A blackboard on wheels had been pushed against a side wall. She picked up a stub of yellow chalk and started writing. "Whatta we got? We got an Italian who speaks English. We got a professor who speaks English and Russian. And we got a Russian who may or may not speak English, but definitely speaks Russian." She drew a lot of arrows. "To me it looks like Gradinsky's interpreting Russian for the Italians. I don't know what else it could be."

When stressed, Slattery gnawed at the ridge of skin bordering his fingernails. It was a habit that had long ago proved impossible to break. He'd tried everything, from bandages to Mercurochrome, but nothing had worked. It's easy to stop doing it, Slattery liked to tell people, paraphrasing Mark Twain on smoking—in fact, I've already done it fifty or sixty times. So as he sat there watching Russo write down her equation, he started biting his skin. "Let's just say you're right, okay?" he said when she finished. "That still doesn't get us any closer to the professor."

O'Brien was slowly stirring his coffee with his finger. "Here's the thing that I don't get. What do the Italians need the Russians for? They already control pretty much every place except Brighton Beach, and they sure as hell ain't going to the mattresses for that. So? What?" They were stuck at the intersection of Mafia and Russian Mob without any idea which way to go. He picked up the third report in the file, asking, "What's this one?"

Russo ignored his questions. "At least we got some idea how the professor fits into the whole picture." She drew an arc from Italian to Russian. "It turns out the professor is the missing link."

O'Brien just couldn't resist. "And all this time I thought that was Arnold Schwarzenegger." After pausing briefly for the laugh that never came, he repeated his question to Slattery. "What else we got here?"

What they had were the initial results of the expanded investigation Slattery had initiated. The FBI's New York field office was second in size and budget only to the Washington, D.C., headquarters. Approximately twelve hundred agents were assigned to New York, and at any point they would be working about 25,000 different cases, ranging in importance from interstate car theft to national security. These agents had about five thousand regularly paid informants and maybe another five thousand who would drop a dime when necessary. In addition to O'Brien and Russo, four agents had been assigned temporarily to this case, which for administrative purposes had been designated MisPro, obviously meaning "missing professor."

An actual FBI investigation isn't nearly as intricate as usually dramatized by television or in the movies. There isn't a whole lot of trickery or cleverness involved. Mostly it's just a lot of hard work. Almost every investigation begins with the collection of a massive amount of readily available information. Telephone numbers to middle names. These four agents were doing the basic background work, gathering all the material necessary to create a snapshot of Professor Peter Gradinsky at this moment in his life. The material included his personal data provided by the university, transcripts of interviews conducted a day earlier with four of his colleagues in the Slavic Studies Department, a graduate assistant, and two West End Avenue neighbors, telephone and credit card records and canceled checks for the previous three months. Among the receipts was a copy of the seventy-five-dollar charge from the Heights Tavern.

O'Brien and Russo spent several minutes reading the summary: Peter Edmund Gradinsky was born in Cleveland, Ohio. His father, George, had emigrated to America from what was then the Ukraine prior to World War II. He settled in Cleveland, sponsored by a distant cousin. It was there he met and married Beatrice Miller of Shaker Heights. Three years after Peter was born they had a second child, a daughter they named Diana. Diana was currently living in Chicago with her husband, Charles Berkow, a commodities trader. The family had lived on Chicago's West Side. Peter attended public elementary and secondary schools, graduating from the High School for the Humanities. He earned his undergraduate degree in 1960 from Colgate University, a highly competitive liberal arts college in upstate New York, where he majored in political science. It was at

Colgate, in the midst of the cold war, that he became fascinated by Russian culture. He received his postgraduate degree in Russian language studies from Columbia, intending to work as a translator for a multinational corporation doing business with the Soviet Union, but instead accepted an offer to stay at the university and teach. He supplemented his income as a freelance translator for corporations, among them U.S. Steel and IBM, as well as the State Department, and had earned a minor literary reputation for his acclaimed translation of Alexander Solzhenitsyn's *The Gulag Archipelago*. After a perfunctory FBI investigation nine years earlier he had received a *Secret* clearance, enabling him to work for the government. There was no indication that he had had access to any sensitive government materials, nothing that might be of interest to a foreign government. Most of his work had been done for the Department of Commerce involving trade agreements . . .

This went on for another page, listing more details of his life, including his degrees, honors, and a long list of clubs and organizations to which he belonged, ranging from *Who's Who Among American Professors* to the American Society of Professional Translators to AAA. Using the shorthand he'd invented, COB, O'Brien copied much of this information into his notebook.

As they read the material, Slattery excused himself to return to his office, telling them, "I got to call Washington. Apparently they didn't find my folder where it was supposed to be lost, so I'm still persona nonexistent."

From the interviews with the other members of his department, it became clear that Gradinsky was well respected and reasonably well liked, but that he had no close friends among his peers. He was considered an excellent teacher and was popular with his students. While no one considered him to be the star of the department, he was described as "reliable," "dependable," "extremely hardworking," and "solid, a rock." His teaching style was described as "the usual," "without any real flair," and "appropriate." No one knew anything about his tastes in music, movies, or even television. He was considered "extremely supportive" of his students and was known for spending hours of his free time working with students who needed additional help. In fact, his graduate assistants liked to hang out in his office, which was described by the one graduate student who had been interviewed as "overflowing with piles of paperwork that he would put on the floor if somebody really needed a place to sit down."

Without exception everyone described him as passionate about his work and a very private person. Only a few of his colleagues had ever met his wife, and none of them had ever been to his home, or even knew of anyone else in the department who had been. The exception was Geraldine Simon. Her duties as departmental secretary included answering his phone when he wasn't in the office and scheduling his appointments. The professor paid her a little extra to take care of the scheduling and billing for his freelance work. Simon spoke to Grace Gradinsky regularly, mostly about such matters. She had been to the Gradinsky apartment several times, usually to drop off materials, but she had been invited to dinner on two occasions. In her interview she referred to him as "a true gentleman."

Geri Simon also mentioned that she had noticed minor changes in him the past few months. He seemed somewhat distracted, she said, occasionally missing appointments and misplacing personal items. He had also been doing a lot more freelance work, which kept him out of the office more often than usual. And for the first time, he insisted on personally handling the billing and payments for this work. Simon remembered that among the companies for which he'd worked were Random House, Time Inc., McDonnell Douglas, and Pan Am. There were several more that she could not remember, and she did not recall him working for any private clients. He didn't seem to be spending more money than usual—in fact, she'd laughed at that question, responding, "*More* money than usual?"—but she did point out that she was probably not the right person to ask about that.

It took them much of the afternoon to dig through all the material. They drank lunch, bottled water for Russo, Coke and coffee for

O'Brien. And from time to time, as they worked, Russo found herself sneaking glances at him, as if she were back in the library at Ohio State being very careful not to get caught peeking at the Buckeyes' star running back. She noticed that O'Brien would occasionally leaf back through his notebook, sometimes spending several minutes searching until he found what he was looking for. "Anything?" she asked once.

He responded with a half-shrug, which she interpreted as a good strong maybe. "I don't know yet. Tell you later."

Slattery returned later that afternoon, still officially lost. "All right, here's what's going on," he said, still charged with enthusiasm. "This Russian connection has gotten the assistant director's attention. He's calling out the cavalry. He wants to know what's the big deal about Thursday night. So for the next six days this gets a Priority designation, meaning we pretty much get whatever support we need."

A Priority designation. That was a big deal. Washington was watching. This case definitely had the potential to move their careers—but depending on the outcome, that move could be either up or down. Slattery helped them lay out a strategy. All the agents in the city working either organized crime or counterintelligence would be asked to squeeze their informants for rumors as well as facts. As all three of them knew, within organized crime rumors tended to be the shadows of facts. Transcripts of conversations that had taken place in the Freemont Avenue Social Club over the past six weeks would be reviewed to see if any leads might have been overlooked, as would all surveillance reports covering members of both Franzone's and Cosentino's crews.

The bureau liaison to the NYPD's Intelligence Unit would reach out to his counterpart to see if they'd felt this particular breeze, although Slattery agreed with O'Brien and Russo that at least for the present the cops would not be brought into the case. Personally none of them had anything against the cops—there were some fine detectives in the NYPD—but the reality was that the 25,000-cop force leaked information worse than a roof made of old newspapers.

As the afternoon began easing into evening, and they finally began collecting all the paperwork and cleaning up the conference room, Slattery remembered to ask Laura Russo, "That thing last night, you sure you're okay?"

Fine, she told him.

Even after all these years Slattery was still not entirely comfortable treating male and female agents equally. "You know, if you'd feel more comfortable staying in a hotel tonight, the office'll pick up the tab."

She flashed him her most demure look. "Why, you old softie you."

Slattery actually blushed. He averted his face so she wouldn't see it, but she did. "Anyway," he continued, "we're gonna keep the watchers outside your place for a few days. But I doubt whoever it was is coming back."

When they finally got outside, Russo glanced at her watch. It was still much too early for it to have been such a long day. They walked around the corner to the Mountway Deli. O'Brien preferred it because its booths offered at least a hint of privacy. The city was in the midst of its daily transition from day to play. The streets were jammed with people on their way home or to restaurants, movies, concerts, sports events—the many million places for fun in New York—where they would resume the lives they'd left behind that morning.

To Russo it just seemed like everybody was racing somewhere important. Like the whole world was on the way to an exciting party to which she hadn't been invited. Her life seemed stuck in one gear: Special Agent Laura Russo. She was her job; her job was her. Lately the only differences between day and night in her life were the light and the temperature. The only male in her life was Buck, and he had four legs, a tail, and slept on her head. It's my choice, she reminded herself, my choice, my choice, my choice.

As they settled into a booth, O'Brien took his notebook from his jacket pocket. Folded sheets of paper he'd stuffed between specific pages started falling out. When he tried to catch them, other papers did the same. Then the book seemed to leap out of his hand, and as he grabbed for it, still more papers fell out. Russo started laughing and didn't stop even when she realized the whole thing was an act performed for her benefit.

"Don't give up your day job," she advised him, patting his hand with mock sympathy. And then she added, "Or your night job."

He collected all his papers, unfolded them, put them in a pile, and ironed them flat with his hand. "There," he said, beaming proudly like a little kid.

That was part of his act too, she knew. But still it was cute. "What?"

"There," he said, pointing at the papers. "There's your real Professor Gradinsky."

"I'm all ears."

He made an exaggerated show of letting his eyes roam slowly up and down her body. Then, holding up his palms in protest, he said, "Boy, that is definitely not true."

This time it was Russo who felt the rising warmth of embarrassment—and cut it off. "Ha, ha, ha," she said as sarcastically as possible. "Okay, Agent O'Brien, let's see what you got."

"Okay. What I got is a whole lot of right angles that don't make a square." A waiter stood silently by the table, his order book poised for action. O'Brien looked up at him. "Look, we're a little busy right now saving the world. Give us a few minutes." The waiter nodded seriously and retreated. Connor continued, "Here, look at this. This is the list of clubs that he belongs to. Notice anything a little strange?"

She read down the list but nothing popped out. "What?"

"Remember how Grace told us they didn't own a car? There was no reason for her to lie about that. It's too easy to check. So now you tell me, how many guys you know who don't own a car belong to the American Automobile Association?" He grinned proudly, showing her his teeth. "First thing we need to do is get somebody at Triple A to pull his membership card and get the plate number and model of the car he's got registered with them."

"Let me have some paper," she said. He pulled a clean sheet from his notebook and handed it to her. She began making her own notes.

He continued, "So we know he's not exactly the guy his wife told us he was. Then this next thing. Look how people described him." He quoted from the reports: plain, mostly; nothing spectacular. "Now look at this." He dug out several canceled checks from his paper pile. "So how come he's spending $640 here, $235 here, here's one for almost $400, all in Bloomingdale's men's department?"

Russo still didn't get it. "He's buying clothes, I guess."

"Well, yeah," he said, "I guess so too. Russo, you're a woman, so let me ask you this. Why would a man who for his whole life apparently has shown no interest in clothes suddenly start shopping for a new wardrobe at Bloomies?"

She got it. "You think he's got a girlfriend, don't you?"

"There you go. It all fits. Remember what that secretary, Simon, said in her statement? He's been acting differently lately, missing appointments, misplacing things." He paused, then said emphatically, "Taking care of his own finances at the office, because if good old Grace doesn't know how much comes in, then she sure as hell doesn't know how much goes out. And notice that he's paying by check instead of using his credit card. I'll bet I know who sees the credit card bill and who gets his canceled checks." He started humming the first bars of "On the Street Where You Live," trusting that Laura would know that in *My Fair Lady* that song was sung by a love-crazed character.

While Russo had a lot of faith in mankind, her experiences had taught her to have a lot less faith in individual men. She had learned from her former husband that married men do have affairs. In that situation apparently the only thing the other woman had that she didn't was a criminal record, which made it even tougher to understand. In so many ways that experience had shaped every day thereafter. But the Professor Peter Gradinsky who had been created in her mind just didn't seem like that type. That Gradinsky had been solid, a bit of a nerd. He didn't seem real desirable. She frowned and thought, they fool you.

The waiter returned. "Excuse me," he said. "You people finished saving the world?" Once again his pen was poised for business against his order book.

Russo found herself anticipating O'Brien's response to that straight line. It was like throwing a slow ball to Babe Ruth. "Yeah," he said, handing over the menu, "I'll have a burger, please. Medium."

"That's it?" she said to him, actually disappointed.

"I'm not that hungry," he explained, then added, "And give me a cherry Coke too, please."

After Laura had ordered her tuna on whole wheat hold the coleslaw, she picked up the thread. "There's another thing I noticed," she said. She leafed through O'Brien's papers until she found the transcript of the interview with his graduate assistant. "See what she says about his office, that she had to take piles of papers off the chairs to sit down?" She closed her eyes and shook her head. "You saw the apartment. It looked like the soup cans were alphabetized. He's obviously a totally different person in his office than he is at home. I have this theory that being messy is genetic. There's no such thing as being half-neat. Either you are or you aren't."

O'Brien considered that. After several years spent believing that one day he really was going to clean out his closet and all the drawers in his bureau, desk, and file cabinet, and feeling guilty every time he looked at them, he had come to the realization that that day was never going to come. He had accepted the fact that on the day he died his apartment was going to be a mess. And after that epiphany he had never felt guilty about it again. Russo was absolutely right. He is who he is. And he is messy.

Russo reached for her conclusion. "Believe me, if Grace had followed him around with a vacuum cleaner and a hatchet, it wouldn't have made any difference. He couldn't help himself. But that apartment was immaculate. I mean, come on, the mail was perfectly stacked, the magazines were squared. She was putting on a show for us that everything was fine."

"You think she knows, then?"

That could easily have been the beginning of a long and heartfelt discussion, in which she would have explained womankind to him. Instead, she said flatly, "Women always know."

To show his appreciation for her good work, he lifted the bread basket and offered, "You want another roll?"

She pushed it away. "Okay, let's look at this again." She picked up the pen and got ready to take some notes. "Assuming we're right, assuming he's got a girlfriend, how does that help us?" She put down the pen and sighed. "This thing keeps getting more and more complicated. I mean, at this point about the only thing we know for sure is that at least he's breathing well enough to use his credit card."

O'Brien cleared his throat and said softly, "There's one more thing I have to tell you. He didn't sign that credit card receipt."

"Tuna on whole wheat?" the waiter said.

Not one thing in the Gradinskys' apartment had been moved an inch since their last visit; including, O'Brien noted, Grace Gradinsky's hair. It looked as if it had been frozen in place by Captain Kirk's phaser. She had greeted them nervously, assuming they had wanted to deliver some news in person. Laura explained quickly that they just needed to ask her a few more questions. Once again they sat on the couch and she sat on the edge of the chair opposite them. O'Brien took the credit card receipt from his notebook and handed it to her. "Do you recognize this, Mrs. Gradinsky?"

She was not wearing her glasses. She held it an arm's length away, obviously so she could read it, but it made it appear as if she were keeping her distance from something distasteful. She shook her head emphatically. "No, no, I don't think so." She handed it back to him. "Why?"

"That's funny, that was my question to you." There was a directness in his voice that Russo had not heard before. And all the warmth was gone.

Grace stood up. "I don't know what you think you're doing . . ."

"Mrs. Gradinsky, misleading a federal agent is a serious crime. Don't make us do something about it." Russo glanced at him. There was absolutely no such crime, serious or frivolous. But obviously Grace Gradinsky didn't know that. "Remember this," he said, laying his notebook down in front of her. It was open to the page on which she had written her husband's medical information. Next to it he laid down the credit card slip. Even at a glance it was obvious that the handwriting in his notebook and the signature on the bottom of the slip were the same. It was quite florid; handwriting experts might describe it as "lyrical." The bowls were unusually rounded and several letters were made with additional loops. It was unique. Clearly Grace Gradinsky had gone to the restaurant and paid the bill with her husband's credit card, signing his name. "Now, why don't you just sit down and tell me why you did this?"

She sat down gracefully. Laura noticed that her lips were tensed almost white, evidence that her anger was fighting to get out. "If you're such a good detective," she said evenly, "then where's my husband?"

Laura tried to calm the situation. "Mrs. Gradinsky, we're doing everything possible . . ."

O'Brien was having none of it. "I asked you why you did it," he repeated.

She looked down at the extremely clean carpet, defeated. "I didn't plan it," she began. "I just . . . I was looking for him. We've eaten dinner there several times. I thought there was a chance he might be there." She paused to steady herself, clinging desperately to the remains of her dignity. "I guess I stayed a little longer than I expected." She looked at Russo. "You know how you watch the door, and you have the feeling that the next time it opens he's going to walk in?"

"Yeah," Russo agreed, "yeah, I do." And that was true, it was a feeling she knew well.

"So while I waited I had something to eat. I really haven't had much of an appetite lately, I'm sure you understand. Then I had a few drinks. It made the night pass. I didn't even know I had Peter's credit card with me until I went to pay. So I used it; they didn't even look at it. They let me put a few dollars extra on it for cash for a cab. I forgot all about it until you . . . until you two showed up. I was so worried that you were going to forget about him. I mean, it's not like it's some big case, he's just a college professor . . ." She looked away.

Russo was sympathetic. "So you figured the receipt would keep us interested?"

O'Brien didn't wait for a response. "And there was no phone call from any Russian, was there?"

"Yes," she said, responding to Russo's question, "because that way you'd believe he was still alive."

When she said that, Laura Russo literally felt a chill wash over her body.

Grace Gradinsky's answer was true if less than complete. She saw no reason to tell them that after Slattery had called her so excitedly, she'd contacted Bobby San Filippo for exactly the same reason: to make sure that the Mafia continued to search for her husband.

O'Brien didn't even change his tone. "That phone call," he said, making what he thought was a pretty good guess, "there was no Russian, was there?"

His question seemed to momentarily confuse her. "Yes," she said. "No. I mean, somebody called and he went right out. But I don't know who it was." She sighed deeply. "It could have been anybody. I don't know, really I don't."

"All right," O'Brien agreed. "But just one more thing." He searched through his overstuffed notebook until he found the sloppily folded surveillance photograph of Bobby Blue Eyes and Little Eddie on the steps of the Gradinskys' brownstone. He laid it down in front of her. "Who are these guys?"

She shook her head. "I can't."

He tapped the photo. "This is why you didn't call the cops, right?"

"Please." She looked to Russo for help.

"Hey, it's your life," O'Brien said almost flippantly. "Either you want to find your husband or you don't. But I got to tell you something, Mrs. Gradinsky. I'm getting a little tired of your bullshit. Now, here's the reality of this situation: Russo and I, we're civil service employees. Pretty much whatever happens our jobs are protected; so are our pensions. You don't want to help us, that's fine, I got a big pile of cases sitting on my desk. I'll just go back to the office and put this one on the bottom and work another one. It doesn't make any difference to me. I'm gonna get the same paycheck."

Russo reached across the table and took Grace Gradinsky's hand. She squeezed it reassuringly. Civil service? she thought. He really is out of his mind.

Grace Gradinsky told them all she knew about her husband's disappearance. She knew only the first names of the two men in the photograph, Bobby and Eddie—at least she believed the heavyset man's name was Eddie. They had come to the apartment the day after Russo and O'Brien's first visit and had asked a lot of the same questions. Several times in the past, she admitted, her husband had done some work for "the boys," as he mysteriously referred to them. When she had asked him if he meant the Mafia, he'd smiled but did not deny it. The only person he had ever mentioned by name was a "Skinny Al," and then only because he supposedly weighed three hundred pounds. Grace specifically remembered that this Skinny man's name was Al because she really loved Bill Cosby's character Fat Albert.

O'Brien was surprised. Grace Gradinsky was a talking avalanche: Once she started talking, pretty much nothing slowed her down. Occasionally, she continued, without any warning her husband wouldn't come home for two or three days. The first time it happened she was frantic, but just as she was about to call the police, he came home. He told her firmly that when he was working "for the boys," she was not, under any circumstances, to contact the police. If the police found out what he was doing, he warned her, it could put his life in jeopardy.

No, she didn't know what he was doing for them. He never told her. Obviously, though, it involved translating of some kind because, she explained, "There really isn't anything else Peter could do for the Mafia."

When he disappeared this time, she assumed he was with them. O'Brien was correct, that's why she didn't file a report with the police. But when "these two," she said, indicating the men in the photograph, told her they didn't know where he was, she didn't know what to do. "You see the problem that I had," she pleaded with Connor. "I couldn't exactly tell the police that I was worried because my husband might not be with the Mafia."

That photograph of the two couples had been taken on their anniversary, at a restaurant named Gino's. They were with their friends George and Pearl Zelma. Peter had suggested the restaurant, telling them he'd met the owner, and they had a lovely evening. "You two should try it one day," she said. Neither agent responded to that suggestion. At the beginning of the meal the waiter had delivered a bottle of champagne to their table, which he said was compliments of the owner. No one ever referred to him as "Gino," only as "the owner," which she thought was a little pretentious.

That was it. She pleaded with them to continue looking for her husband, and O'Brien informed her that "the entire New York office is looking for him. But anything else you think of, you got to call us right away. And if those two *schmegegis* show up"—he pointed at her for emphasis—"you call us right away."

She agreed to do that.

O'Brien and Russo walked up West End Avenue in contemplative silence. Russo finally said with sadness, "She doesn't have the slightest idea, does she?"

"No," he agreed, and Laura heard the resignation in his voice as he finished, "she doesn't."

O'Brien suggested stopping by the Heights Tavern one more time just to see how fast Gravy could run, but she told him that neither the joke nor the idea was very funny. He offered to drive her downtown but she refused, as he was certain she would. They stood on the corner of West End and 76th Street for several minutes waiting for a cab. "You don't have to wait," she told him. "I'm fine."

"It's a habit," he said as an empty cab stopped across the street. Connor spotted it at almost exactly the same time as a man with a briefcase who was waiting with a woman, about halfway down the block on the west side of West End Avenue. Connor and the man locked eyes for an instant, which was all it took for both of them to recognize the New Yorker in the other, and then they took off after the prize. The other man had the advantage of being on the same side of the street as the cab, but Connor didn't even hesitate. He prided himself on being an expert at the city shuffle. He dived right into the traffic, one eye on the oncoming cars, the other on his competition. Connor figured the guy would be slowed by his briefcase, but the man was swinging it hard enough to give him some forward momentum. Connor was forced to hesitate in the middle of the street for an ambulance, and it looked certain that the cab would be lost. He considered using the going-to-the-hospital ploy, a New York gambit that carried with it absolutely no guarantee of success. Once he'd actually heard someone respond to that line, "Too bad, I've got tickets to *Cats!*"

It turned out not to be necessary. The guy stepped out of his shoe—and actually stopped to retrieve it! Losing a cab just because a shoe came off? Out-of-towner, Connor thought smugly.

He had his hand on the door handle seconds before his opponent limped up. Connor smiled at him. "I need this cab," the guy said urgently. "I got to get my wife to the hospital."

O'Brien looked down the block. A woman was standing on the curb, holding her coat closed with her left hand, seemingly slightly bent over. It was impossible to determine anything about her from that distance. It was a cab-or-*Cats* moment: Connor relented. There was nothing else he could do. "Sure," he said, opening the door and stepping aside.

"Thanks," the man said, slipping into the backseat. Connor closed the door and watched as the cab shot forward to the woman and stopped. The rear door was pushed open and she got in. A little too sprightly, he thought suspiciously. It was at least five minutes before another empty cab appeared. When it stopped, Laura opened the door for herself. And O'Brien realized he didn't have the slightest idea how to say good night to her. If she were a man, he would shake her hand, but after all the time they'd spent together the past few days, he would have felt ridiculous shaking her hand. And he certainly would have felt awkward giving her a light kiss. So he ran for the high ground and did neither. "You're all right?" he asked.

She solved the problem for him. "I'm fine," she said, and then gave him a friendly kiss on his cheek as she got into the cab.

O'Brien stood in the street watching her cab drive away.

All the way home Laura Russo thought about the investigation. It was being run like a game of checkers, she decided. They were moving forward very slowly across the entire width of the board, taking advantage of whatever openings they spotted rather than committing to a single strategy. We're not going to get there in time, she thought.

Most of the time agents live surprisingly normal lives—punctuated by occasional bursts of frenzied activity. About the only personal things O'Brien had gotten done the past few days were buy fresh orange juice, replenish his supply of Mallomars, then flip through his mail, throwing away the junk and tossing the bills on his desk.

There were twenty-six messages waiting for him on his answering machine: He had won a three-day vacation to Disneyland that entitled him to participate in "an extraordinary real estate opportunity." He had been selected to receive a financial newsletter available to only "a few insiders." There were three beeping attempts to send him a fax, there was a wrong number from someone speaking rapidly in Spanish, and all the rest were the bits and pieces of the life of an attractive single man with several close friends in New York City: What are you doing Friday night? *Beep.* Just checking in. *Beep.* I think I met somebody you might like. *Beep.* It's Fred, what do you know about the Rappoport case? *Beep.* Hey, Con, you still have Nancy's phone number, the one we met at Marty's? *Beep*. Hey, pal, you'll never guess what happened. *Beep*. Did I leave my compact, a little gold one with my initials on it, in your apartment? *Beep*. I got three tickets for the Knicks next Tuesday, you interested? *Beep*. You see that piece about organized crime moving down to Wall Street in the Week in Review? *Beep*. I got a funny story to tell you. *Beep*. And finally, three increasingly desperate calls from Mops, wondering where he was, asking why he hadn't returned her phone calls, and reminding him once again that she was "the only mother you have." As he sifted through his bills, he called her back. She told him, "I was calling you because Belle was missing and I was frantic."

Belle was her Chihuahua. "She's under your bed," Connor told her, having had this conversation several times before. "Behind the shoe boxes." Mops admitted she'd found her sleeping there an hour earlier, then segued into other topics, among them getting together for dinner, going to his nephew's soccer game, and by the way, how was the rest of his life? "The rest of his life" was Mops-speak for are you dating someone I should know about and why aren't you married yet and why do you do this to me?

Connor marveled at her ability to so easily reduce him to his simplest parts. In a single phone call he traveled the vast distance between a well-respected FBI agent heading a significant investigation and being his mother's son. When he finally got off the phone, it took him considerable time to bounce back. During any investigation it's vitally important that the investigators take time away from the case just to step back and get a little perspective both on the case and on their lives. Connor's plans to catch up with his life evaporated with that phone call. Instead, he opened his notebook and started reading through it from front to back, trying to find the connections that were always there.

He was finishing his second cup of coffee when Diana Thomas called. "What are you doing right now?" she asked.

He thought seriously about it. Diana was a very attractive woman who obviously had a thing for him. "You know," he decided, "I got all this work I need to get done. Give me a few days."

After hanging up he stared at the telephone for a few minutes, then picked it up again and dialed Russo's number. She answered curtly, on the first ring. "Hello?"

"It's me. I'm just going through my notes and there're a couple of things I'm curious about," he said. And then he remembered, "Hey, excuse me. Are you okay?"

She was sitting on the floor in front of her fireplace, dressed in flannel pajamas, rereading Slattery's documents as she enjoyed her one glass of wine. An artificial log was providing just enough light and warmth for her needs. She leaned back against the couch and picked up her wineglass. The log was made of compressed paper, but it could have been real.

NINE

Fast Lenny had them laughing good. "I swear to God, I used to knock him crazy with them fucking phone calls. That Vinny, he's a scary guy, you know what I mean. But he don't scare me, ever. I used to find out from his brother Sal, Sal shit-for-brains they shoulda named him, 'Where's your brother gonna meet tonight?'

"And this guy would tell me, 'He's going to the Casa D.' So then I would call up there and say, 'Gimme Vinny DiSanto,' and then I would hang up. Vinny would go to the phone, no answer. Then I would do it again. I was driving him nuts. So then he tells Funzi, Funzi told me this later, 'Funzi,' he's saying, 'the fucking agents are on us.' So Funzi, who don't know nothing, asks, 'Why you say that?' And he tells him, 'I just got two calls, no answer. They're checking to see if we're here.'"

Naturally everybody thought this story was hysterical. "You gotta understand, I do this all the time to him. 'Sal, where's your brother going tonight?' Another time it was the Cockeyed Crow up on 85th Street. I called him there three times. I swear to God the third time he was swearing at the phone. Louie told me he turned white. I'll knock him fucking crazy."

As funny as Fast Lenny was, that's how funny Georgie One-Time wasn't. Whatever anybody else was talking about, he brought it back to money. That's where the "One-Time" came from: There was only one time that anybody saw Georgie reach for a check. Georgie had a good piece of a profitable concrete business. His connections inside the union enabled him to bid low and still turn a pretty good profit. His connections inside the construction industry often got him inside information about competitors' bids—and on occasion they were able to change his bid after the submission deadline. So when the laughter over Lenny's story died down, he said to Little Eddie, "I got a call yesterday from Mike Delves, the boss up at Colonial, and he says to me, 'I'd like to do business with you, but you gotta help me with the number. So I tell him I can drop my number without any embarrassment, but if I do, the job's gotta be mine.'"

Bobby raised the volume on the radio and tossed his hat neatly onto the middle of the table, as if gently landing a flying saucer. "Hey, Georgie, maybe you wanna get me a job on one of those sites," he said. "I can be, like, Superforeman. You know, like Superman? I can get concrete laid without even being there."

Tony Cupcakes shouted above the laughter, "Then that must make me Superforeplayman. I can get laid without my wife even being there!"

"Hey, Lenny," Bobby asked, sitting down, "you talk to your commie friend for me?" Duke put a steaming cup of cappuccino in front of him.

As Lenny replied, the one phone in the club started ringing. "First of all, he's not my friend. He's my business associate. I don't got commie friends. I got commie business associates. You understand the difference?"

"Hey," Bobby said, raising his hands defensively, "no offense."

"Okay. But the guy's getting a little goosey on me. There's something going on that I don't know. He's putting me off on things like he never did before. Give me a little more time . . ."

Vito V had answered the phone. "Hey, Lenny," he shouted, holding up the receiver.

"Excuse me."

Bobby sipped his cappuccino, listening to Eddie complain how he wasn't getting his right piece of the weekly payments from a loansharking deal. "We figured out how much everybody got coming,

you know what I mean? Who gets $150, who gets $175. It's supposed to be according to how much money each person put on the
street. It was broke down so that everybody gets even at the same
time. But the guy wasn't paying regular, and Tommy, who brought
the guy around, says all of a sudden that he ain't responsible for the
money. Well, fuck that prick, I says to him, then what do we need
him for? And this fucking guy, he—"

Lenny sat down and said casually, "They got that fucking driver."

"No shit," Little Eddie said, laughing.

"Where is he?" Bobby asked.

"He's s'posed to be picking up a payment from Jerry the Jeweler."
Half his face was a smile. "Fucking guy."

In the world of organized crime, people communicate just like
they've done it since the first creature stood up on two legs and said,
"Give me two rocks on the green dinosaur to win." They talked to
each other. The so-called underworld might be the most tangled, extensive grapevine in history. But somehow it works. The word
spreads. Somehow people find out what they need to find out. In
this case the word was that Henry Franzone's crew, especially Fast
Lenny, was looking for "a little wimpy-acting colored guy, probably
wearing glasses, with a banged-up nose," probably trying to fence
some merchandise. Pretty much every fence who worked with the
mob on a regular basis got the word.

So it wasn't exactly luck that they found him. A guy fitting his description had been trying to sell some loose diamonds to a friend of
the family's on the Bowery that everybody knew as Jerry the Jeweler.
Jerry the Jeweler would buy precious stones without asking questions
or requiring documentation. And considering the potential legal
consequences of that policy, he paid out a fair price. The truck driver
had approached Jerry with a sack of diamonds two weeks earlier.
That was no problem. They had done business twice before, and the
seller had been a stand-up guy. In this case the man, who said his
name was Franklin Jefferson, claimed to be representing the owner
of the stones. Provenance was not an issue with the Jeweler. If any-

body asked him where they came from, he had a standard answer: "From the earth. You want them or don't you?" The only thing the Jeweler cared about was whether the stones were real or fugazis. He had taken Mr. Jefferson's diamonds on consignment. The sale would have been completed several days earlier and Jefferson would have been history, but Jerry's associate had gone to Israel for business and stayed longer than expected. He had just come back with cash, and Jerry had arranged for the suddenly very nervous Mr. Jefferson to be paid his money that afternoon.

When the Jeweler got the word, he didn't hesitate to contact a friend of the family's. The Jeweler was a smart guy, he knew it was in his future interest to cooperate. And if maybe he got to keep some of the cash as a reward, just a taste, who would notice?

Franklin Jefferson was late for the meet. An hour, two hours, no phone call, no nothing. That didn't surprise Bobby. If he were that guy, he'd be late too. At least five years late easy. And even then only if he felt completely secure. There was no doubt in Bobby's mind that Franklin fucking Jefferson had gotten to the Bowery early and was hiding there, watching, waiting.

The jewelry market on the Bowery, which consists of dozens of individually owned stalls crammed side by side in a large ground-floor space, is actually in Chinatown. Mostly Jews and Chinese work there. In this situation a person like Franklin Jefferson would prefer to do business down on the Bowery rather than on 47th Street because it was such a public space. To do business on 47th Street, in the Diamond District, sometimes you had to go upstairs, into offices, into back rooms, inside walk-in safes, and there was nobody to hear you shout if you needed help. Downtown there were always civilians around. You yelled, somebody would hear you. You did business in the light.

By five-thirty, just as the after-work lookers were drifting in, Little Eddie spotted the truck driver. The guy's decision to wait until the place got crowded seemed sensible but actually worked against him. Crowds provided the cover of a forest rather than the visibility of a

few thin trees. It made it real difficult for Jefferson to spot Little
Eddie, who was sitting behind the counter of an antique watch
dealer halfway down the row from the Jeweler's stall just watching;
or Lenny, who had been standing at the pay phone, mostly hidden
by its privacy walls, for more than three hours and was totally pissed
off. It also made it harder for the truck driver to move quickly if he
had to get out of there. Jefferson was approaching from the back of
the place. Apparently he'd come in through a side door and been
working his way around, trying to determine if the Jeweler had been
straight with him. Evidently he was satisfied, because he cautiously
approached Jerry's booth. Even from a distance Little Eddie could see
the guy's face was banged up pretty good from the shot Lenny had
given him.

"Hey, what's happening?" Franklin Jefferson asked Jerry.

"You," Jerry replied, looking happy to see him. Jerry had the salesman's gift, a natural smile that was wide and shallow. He reached
across the counter and shook hands. The man is cool, Bobby
thought. Bobby was watching from the back of Jerry's booth, hidden
behind a curtain. Jerry was blocking part of his view, but he could
see the guy well enough to remove any doubts about his identity.
Bobby had a tremendous desire to walk out from behind the curtain
and just level the guy. He really couldn't wait to see the look on the
guy's face when he realized he was a dead man.

"You got my money?" the little guy asked, continuing to scan the
room like a breathing lighthouse. Bobby noted he was wearing a
down jacket, which was much too warm for the mild fall weather. So
Bobby guessed he had a piece on him, hidden beneath the coat.

"Sure do," Jerry said, opening a small counter safe. "You get any
more like that, you let me know, okay? I can handle whatever you
get." He took a manila envelope out of the safe and handed it to Jefferson. "You want to come in the back and count it?"

Jefferson opened the envelope and peered inside. Satisfied that the
cash was there, he closed the clasp, folded it in half lengthwise, and
jammed it into his pants pocket. Whoa, Bobby thought, the guy

must be completely freaked out. He had never seen a man accept a large payment for a deal without counting the money slowly and carefully. Twice.

As Jefferson turned to leave, he ran smack into an old man wearing a navy peacoat, sunglasses, and a woolen cap pulled all the way down to his eyebrows. Mickey Fists had his right hand in his coat pocket. If Bobby hadn't known who it was, even he would have had a tough time recognizing him. Jefferson had never met Mickey, so he had no idea he was bumping into his fate. "Excuse me," he said.

Bobby watched the old man work. Supposedly, when Crazy Joey Gallo was just getting started in the rackets, he was in the passenger seat of a car, on his way to see a man about a late payment on a debt. He was looking into the rearview mirror scrunching up his face. When the driver asked him what he was doing, Gallo told him, "Practicing to look mean."

Mickey Fists looked very much in control. He had a faint smile on his face. Bobby figured his pacemaker had to be racing. For an instant, as Franklin Washington Jefferson, whatever the hell his name was, took his first step away from the counter, the two men were chest-to-chest. Mickey didn't hesitate. He put his left hand on the guy's shoulder to hold him in place and sort of thrust his right hand, hidden in his jacket pocket, into his stomach. The old man was smooth, Bobby thought, fully aware he was watching a real pro in action. Jefferson's whole body drooped, as if the soul that had held it rigid had evaporated. His eyes darted rapidly around the place, searching desperately for an escape route. The Jeweler had turned around and gone into the back. He didn't want to witness nothing. Mickey was so cool that when Jefferson started looking around, Mickey responded by pushing harder into his chest.

Any hopes that Jefferson might have optimistically harbored that this was a simple stickup disappeared within seconds. Bobby stepped out from behind the curtain, Little Eddie walked down the aisle in front of him, and Fast Lenny came from behind. Before Jefferson could take a breath, he was surrounded. It was done so casually that no one in the place paid any attention to them. Mickey pushed harder into Jefferson's stomach and said something Bobby couldn't hear, but he was pretty sure it was a warning not to make any noise. They walked out of the place together.

Tony Cupcakes' new Cadillac was waiting right in front. He'd had the car only three months and definitely did not want to use it on this kind of job. But they needed a car right away and the water pump in Lenny's car was leaking, Eddie's Chrysler was a piece of crapola, and Bobby's car wasn't big enough for all of them. So Tony reluctantly threw an old sheet and some blankets over the seats and pleaded with everybody not to get blood all over the car. "It's a bitch getting it out," he explained, "particularly those cloth seats I got."

Bobby half pushed the guy into the backseat and climbed in after him. Lenny got in on the other side. Eddie sat in the front with Tony. Mickey stood on the sidewalk, the proud father watching his brood. This was not the kind of work he did too much anymore, being semiretired, but he was clearly pleased the job had gone as well as it had. He gave a little wave, turned, and walked proudly down the block as Tony drove away.

The truck driver—nobody cared enough to ask him his real name—was not a moron. When he saw the backseat covered up, he knew that this was a bad ride to be taking. Tony headed north on the FDR. Nobody said a word for several minutes, but then the truck driver broke the silence. "Am I allowed to ask where I'm going?"

"Shut the fuck up," Lenny warned him. His voice was bristling with anger.

"Hey, c'mon, Lenny, huh?" Tony Cupcakes reminded him. "I'm asking you nice, watch the seats."

"Fucking guy," Lenny sighed. Once again everyone was quiet— this was serious business they were doing—but the silence made Lenny too uncomfortable. "Answer me this, you asshole. What the fuck were you thinking? I mean, did you really fucking think you were gonna get over on us?"

The truck driver was trying hard to control himself, but he was having a tough time of it. "I swear to God, I didn't know nothing about you guys coming," he said. There was a quiver in his voice. "Nobody was s'posed to get hurt. Honest, I swear, I figured the store's insurance would cover the missing load. And then when you guys were all over me, what was I gonna say?" He paused. "I'm begging you guys, gimme a break." He waited, looking first at Lenny, then turning to Bobby. But the only answer was the loudest silence he had ever heard. "C'mon, please, listen to me. I know shit that's going down. I can tell you a lot of things."

There really is no way of predicting how people will act when they believe they're negotiating for their lives. They cry, they beg, they threaten reprisals, often they try a bribe: "Whatever you're getting paid I'll double it." They're brave, they're cowardly, they pray, they curse their killers, they just can't believe that this is actually happening to them. And a few people are unbelievably stoic: They understand the rules of the society and accept their fate without a murmur of protest.

Each of the four of them had been on rides like this one before. It was part of the job. So they pretty much knew what to expect. The truck driver was a negotiator. He wanted to trade information for his life. He spoke rapidly, knowing he didn't have much time left to save himself. "I know stuff," he kept telling them. "I can give you a truckload that's worth $15,000 easy." He turned to Bobby again. "I'm supposed to drive it. Just me, no security. I'll just hand it to you, swear to God."

Bobby listened to the guy's tales all the way up the FDR into the Bronx. Tony had decided on upstate. Finally Bobby said to the driver, "All right, lemme hear what you got to say."

The truck driver took his first good breath since being shoved into the car. He had a shot. "Look, I drive trucks, right?" He didn't wait for an answer. "I'm supposed to drive one of those big gasoline tankers tomorrow night. There's like ten thousand gallons of gas in one of those tanks, and just about any gas station in New York will buy it all."

Hijack a gasoline truck? Why not? Bobby thought. Actually he liked the concept. The gas stations had been ripping him off ever since the fuel shortage during Carter; this was his chance to get even with Mobil or Shell, Amoco, Cities Service, Gulf, get even with them all. "Who you driving this truck for?" he asked.

The driver shrugged. "I don't know their names. Some Russian guys. Igor, Boris, I don't know. They pay me off when I park the truck. Five hundred cash for the night."

"Jesus Christ, Bobby," Eddie said, glancing back at him, "what the fuck's going on with all these Russkies?"

Bobby turned and looked right at the truck driver. It was something that he tried to avoid. Looking at men caught in this situation always made him uncomfortable. "Now, just what are the commies doing with a gas truck?"

The truck driver's mouth was racing now. He'd hooked someone, now he needed to pull them in. Carefully. "I don't know, really, I don't know. Selling it, I guess. All I know is I'm supposed to pick up a full load at the Staten Island Terminal and deliver the gas to two stations on Queens Boulevard. Then I drive it up to the Bronx and park it there, in that big parking lot they got near the stadium."

Bobby was curious. "You ever drive for these guys before?"

Few people have ever been more enthusiastically cooperative than this driver in this car at this time. "Oh yeah, a few times. It's always the same thing. Deliver the gas to the gas stations, then go park the truck. Honest, all you gotta do is tell me where to meet you. I'll hand you that truck on a platter." As they crossed over onto the Hutch and then onto the Taconic Parkway, Bobby asked the same question several different ways. But no matter how he phrased it, the answer was always the same: The driver did not know why the Russians were selling gas to gas stations.

"Let me ask you this, then," Bobby said. "What about these Russians? Just what do you think they're gonna do to you when they find out you gave up their truck? Think they're gonna give you a nice present maybe?"

The driver was pretty blunt about it. "They gotta catch me first. I'm gonna go so far so fast they're gonna start calling me Hurricane."

Bobby had to laugh. Maybe this wasn't such a bad guy. Too bad you fucked up so badly, he thought to himself.

Lenny wasn't happy with all this conversation. It was too much talk, as far as he was concerned. "Selling gas to gas stations?" he said. "That's bullshit. Lemme tell you this. You want gas for free, just come to my house when my wife is making her spaghetti sauce."

Bobby had almost no doubt the driver was telling the truth. People taking this ride rarely held back information or told lies. Their only hope was that something they said might keep them alive until they could figure out a next move. The driver didn't have much else to offer. The truck and the cash in his pocket, that was it. He gave Bobby all the details: when and where he was supposed to pick up the truck, make his deliveries, drop the truck. This was a sweet deal, the driver swore; all they had to do was let him show up.

He offered all the information he had, beginning with complete descriptions of the Russians. They were young guys, both of them real muscular. One of them, the taller one, had a deep ugly scar stretching from the corner of his eye right down his cheek. The shorter guy had a modified Mohawk; he'd shaved the sides of his head but left his blond hair on top. The driver had seen their car and was pretty sure it was a Chevy Camaro, a silver Z28. And then he began talking about other jobs he'd done, mentioning as many names as possible, trying desperately to catch a miracle. At one point he even offered to help Lenny with directions, explaining that he'd been driving trucks for fifteen years and knew every shortcut and back road in the region.

Lenny paid absolutely no attention to him. But every once in a while he would suddenly drive off the parkway, just to make certain they weren't being followed. The FBI and the NYPD just couldn't be trusted. Fast Lenny was an experienced driver. He knew how to spot a tail and how to shake it. No one was tailing them, though, he was sure of it.

Bobby was starting to feel sorry for the truck driver. Personally he didn't have anything against the guy. He seemed like a decent small-time crook. His real crime was stupidity. He hadn't set out to beat the mob; things just happened that way. The mistake he made was that when he had the opportunity to make things right simply by explaining what happened, in which case he wouldn't have had a problem, he walked away with the load. Cheating the family out of a score was a capital offense. Maybe if he had a rabbi, a made man to speak up for him, his situation might have been mitigated. But nobody knew him, nobody would miss him, nobody cared. And if he was allowed to walk away from his situation without punishment, other people would get the wrong message.

The guy just wouldn't shut up. Lenny was about to bust a lung, but there wasn't too much he could do about it. He didn't want to slug the guy in Tony's car. He respected Tony too much to get blood all over his new cloth seats. And given the circumstances, it would have been pretty ridiculous to threaten to kill him.

The truck driver was also beginning to get under Bobby's skin by the time they turned onto the road up to Swan Lake. The road weaved several miles through a heavily wooded area. There were several summer resort communities around the lake, but except for a caretaker or two, they would be deserted this time of year. Bobby had been up there two years earlier. Georgie One-Time's brother-in-law had rented a place on the lake for a month and Georgie had thrown a party there for the entire crew.

When Lenny made the left turn into the darkness, the truck driver knew he was a dead man. He started screaming. For the first time he started fighting to get out of the car. He clawed at Bobby, screeching like the cornered animal he was. Tony started screaming at everybody, "Watch my car! Watch my car!" Lenny had taken off his coat when it got too warm for him in the back. He picked it up and threw it over the truck driver's head, then started bashing him in the head with his elbow.

Finally the truck driver quieted down and started crying.

"I knew it," Lenny said. "Fucking wimp." And slugged him again in the side of his head, just for the pleasure of it. The truth is that there are people who enjoy the violence, who love pulling the trigger. Bobby wasn't like that. For him a hit was never pleasurable; it wasn't like he really enjoyed it—although admittedly it was always thrilling. He couldn't help feeling that way. The adrenaline just raced through his body, making him acutely aware of everything going on around him, stretching every second into forever.

Two miles off the highway Tony stopped the car and turned out all the lights. Lenny snapped the plastic cover off the dome light and unscrewed the bulb so the light wouldn't go on when the door was opened. Then they sat silently in the darkness and waited. They waited for their eyes to adjust to the darkness, for a car to come down the road, for a flashlight in the forest, for an unusual sound. They waited for anything unexpected. The truck driver was sobbing, mumbling something Bobby couldn't understand, gulping air. As they sat there, Bobby looked into the woods. It was like looking into death.

The woods were a good place for this type of work. Isolated and dark. Ironically, whacking the driver wasn't necessarily the difficult part—there were a lot of men who loved the rush that came with that—the troublesome part was getting rid of the body. The body was the strongest evidence that could be used to connect the killer to the victim. Without a body detectives had nothing to detect. But sometimes getting rid of a body turned out to be a hassle. There were a lot of different options: Saw it into pieces and drop the pieces in various sewers or other bodies of water or bury them. A lot of bodies have been buried under tons of concrete in construction sites of basements. A body can be weighed down and dropped out in the ocean as a fish gift. On occasion some people used a double coffin, a coffin with a false bottom that allowed two bodies to be buried together. And then sometimes people buried a body in a field and relied on wild animals.

Lenny got out of the car, then leaned back in and grabbed the truck driver by the neck of his shirt and literally pulled him out of the car. The guy was much too terrified to put up any real resistance. Bobby got out the other side and quietly closed his door. It was freezing. Bobby had forgotten to bring an overcoat, so he turned up the collar of his sports jacket and pulled the lapels together. Then he reached around his back and pulled his gun out of his waistband. It was a Remington .38 Special. Bobby didn't have a silencer with him, but with any luck it wouldn't matter. He was working backup. Lenny was the shooter. Unless there was some kind of screwup, he would not have to fire his gun.

A layer of decaying leaves covered the ground. Bobby felt like he was walking on a damp sponge. Lenny was carrying a throwaway, but he did have a silencer for it. Lenny, Bobby, and the driver walked into the woods, Lenny never letting go of the driver. The little guy was shivering, and whimpering, pleading, promising. And then he let loose in his pants. "Oh Christ," Lenny said softly, "that's fucking disgusting."

If the driver responded, Bobby didn't hear him. They were moving down the side of a sloping hill. Bobby walked a few steps behind them, constantly turning and looking around. Nobody was going to make a big deal over the fact that some two-bit hustler disappeared—unless they could pin his disappearance on a made man. Doing that successfully would make some cop's Christmas very merry. It was a trade law enforcement would make every day of the week and twice on Super Bowl Sunday.

It was nearly pitch-black in the woods and Bobby could barely see the two men walking only a few feet in front of him. Mostly he was looking down at the ground, watching his steps. He heard Lenny order the guy, "Walk over there." And an instant later he heard the unmistakable *pop! pop!* of a silenced weapon being fired twice. It sounded more like a kid stomping on an overturned paper cup than bullets being fired into a man's head, although the gunshot probably wasn't as loud as the pop of air. The truck driver grunted involuntarily as his life burst free of his body, and that was the last sound he made. The leaves pretty much absorbed the sound of his body hitting the ground. Then, a couple of seconds later, *pop! pop!* That was Lenny again, Bobby knew, putting two more slugs into the truck driver's brain, just to make sure he was forever dead.

"That's it," Lenny said without emotion. Lenny was holding on to the manila envelope filled with cash and the guy's wallet when Bobby came up to him. "Watch yourself," Lenny warned. The truck driver's body was lying on its side, his blood pooling on the leaves, and Lenny didn't want Bobby stepping in it.

Lenny took the cash out of the envelope and put it in his pants pocket. He'd split it up later. He put the driver's wallet in his jacket pocket. Without that wallet no one would be able to identify the truck driver, even if all it contained was phony IDs.

"What do you want to do with him?" Bobby asked. It didn't make sense to bury him. Unless they were willing to dig a really deep hole, within a few days hungry animals would dig him up. This was a feast for them. They'd carry parts of his body throughout the woods. Chances were that no matter what Lenny and Bobby did with the body, no one would find it for a long, long time. If ever. The only people wandering this deep into the woods this time of year were hunters, and most of the land around the lake was posted.

Lenny thought about it. The land rolled downhill into a narrow ravine. "Gimme a hand," he said, grabbing one of the driver's arms. Bobby grabbed the other arm and they began dragging the corpse. It slid along the slick surface a lot more easily than Bobby expected, like shit on silk, he thought, and it took only a few minutes to roll it into the ravine. Then they covered the body with leaves. In the dark it looked like it was completely covered, but it was impossible to be certain. "Fuck it," Lenny decided, "that's good enough. Let's get out of here." Bobby turned around to return to the car, but suddenly Lenny spit at the corpse. "Fuck me again, you fucking bastard," he said, and that would be the truck driver's epitaph.

Bobby reached down and grabbed a handful of leaves, then began wiping the touch of death off his hands. As best as he could, he checked his pants, shoes, and socks for bloodstains. Lenny did the same thing. They were both clean, but they would get rid of the clothes they were wearing as soon as they got back to the city. That probably wasn't really necessary, but this was a business in which the price of simple mistakes is measured in years. For Lenny that was nothing, a pair of slacks, a T-shirt, and old sneakers. For Bobby it meant throwing out a $700 suit, $175 shoes, and a $3 pair of socks. It didn't thrill him, but he accepted it as the cost of doing business.

By the time they climbed back up the hill and got to the car, Lenny was breathing hard. He had to pause a couple of times to catch his breath. Nobody said a word as they got into the car. Tony turned around and drove about a mile up the road. "This is good," Lenny said. Tony stopped the car and Lenny got out. He walked a few steps into the woods and then heaved the silencer as far as he could in one direction, then he turned and threw the wallet in the opposite direction. Neither the silencer nor the wallet would ever be found.

Nobody said a word for several minutes as they headed back to the city. Finally Little Eddie decided, "I guess that's one way to christen this car." Tony was the only one who didn't laugh.

This was an unremarkable murder, a simple hit. It was without complications or high risk. Each of the four men in the car had been involved in hits before. The complete absence of remorse was a tribute to their professionalism. This had all been done according to the rules. Anyone who felt bad about it was simply in the wrong business.

That didn't mean it had no impact on them. It was a solemn undertaking. Literally and figuratively. Bobby had participated in five other hits, although he'd pulled the trigger himself only twice. None of these men were afraid of death, but each of them greatly respected it. So while this job remained a monster in their minds, they didn't say a single word about it on the drive home.

Halfway down the Taconic, at a place where trees closely bordered the parkway, Tony slowed down. When he was certain there were no cars behind him, he pulled over to the side. "Okay," he told Lenny, "this is good." Lenny had unloaded the gun and wiped his fingerprints off it with a handkerchief. He got out of the car and walked several feet to the tree line. Anybody driving past would assume he was relieving himself. A car sped by, he waited. Another car. He waited. And then he heaved the gun into the woods. A minute later Tony eased back onto the parkway and kept going. The job was done.

They were just about back in the city when Eddie asked, "Any you guys interested in that gasoline truck?"

Bobby had been thinking about that for most of the drive, but not for the $15,000 reason. As a teenager Bobby had practically rebuilt his first car, a 1960 Plymouth Fury with a 425 Hemi. One time the car had two very distinct problems, a banging coming from the rear right side and a bad oil leak. It didn't seem possible the two problems were related, but they were. The banging in the back was caused by a loose exhaust pipe hitting the underside of the car. Occasionally the pipe brushed against the oil line, which eventually started leaking. That experience had taught Bobby to at least consider the possibility that two seemingly unconnected events happening at the same time might have a common root.

In his whole life the only Russian he'd ever known was a really stacked young brunette named Irena who worked for a furrier on 37th Street and loved having sex in cars with stick shifts. A lot of wonderful memories were made in that '60 Fury. Actually she'd played an important role in his life. This was just after he'd graduated from college, before he was tied up to Ronnie, when there was still a chance he might try the straight world. He was a smart kid; he could have been successful at many different things. But Irena helped him make the decision: Not only did he get laid regularly—although somewhat uncomfortably—Irena also told him exactly where the security cameras were hidden and when the most valuable furs were left out of the vault for the night. The result had been the first substantial score of his life. The choice was made.

But until the last couple of weeks that had been his only real contact with a Russian. He knew all about the Russian mobs, he admired their success at organizing so quickly, but he didn't know any of them. Now it seemed like they were coming out of the Kremlin in waves: The professor wasn't technically Russian, but he taught the language. Two Russians had trailed him to Skinny Al's funeral and had business with Cosentino. According to Grace Gradinsky, the professor had worked with Skinny Al—which made sense because Cosentino was the boss searching for the professor. And now this truck driver had been working for the Russians. Somehow the pieces fit together like a banging exhaust pipe and an oil leak. "Yeah, I'm in," Bobby replied to Eddie's question. He intended to learn a little more about these Russians.

No one ever again mentioned the truck driver. From that night on, he had never existed.

The next morning Bobby and Little Eddie planned the heist. Tony Cupcakes wanted in; so did the kid, Vito V. Joey Scars, a tough little guy who had been down in Florida meeting some people who claimed to be able to deliver as much as 140 pounds of marijuana a week, was in the club and heard about it and asked in. Legally this job belonged to Fast Lenny because the information came from his source, but he was okay with sharing equally. There really was no logical reason for Bobby to believe that this job might lead to the professor—there are thousands of Russians doing business in New York—but Bobby had a feeling he wasn't about to ignore. Besides, the worst thing that would happen is that he would end up with a share of an oil tanker heist.

He spent the rest of the afternoon with Little Eddie chasing the professor. To Eddie's absolute delight, they went back up to Columbia. Bobby had no plan, but there wasn't much else for him to do. The clock was running down and he was pretty much out of options. He needed a break, so why not just take a shot? You never know who's waiting around the next corner, he figured, you just never know.

Identifying themselves as private detectives hired by the professor's relatives, they spoke with two of his colleagues and his graduate assistant. Neither of the teachers had the slightest idea what might have happened to him, but both of them acknowledged that this sort of behavior was completely out of character for Professor Gradinsky and they were quite worried about him. "He's a good man," one of them said. "He's got a fine accent."

The graduate student had just wandered into the administration office as Bobby and Eddie were getting ready to leave. When she overheard them asking Geri Simon more questions about Gradinsky, she introduced herself. She was a tall, attractive coed named Natalie something, who to Eddie's disappointment was wearing very loose pants and a bulky knit sweater. She looked like she had a figure underneath all that cover.

She was extremely concerned about the professor, she explained. She'd been coming to the office every day since he'd disappeared, desperate for any news. She'd even gone out searching for him herself, going to all the local places where previously she'd been able to find him. She was so frustrated at the fact that no one seemed to be doing very much about this—no one had even hung up a notice on the departmental bulletin board, she pointed out—that she had called the police department.

Great, Bobby thought to himself, that's definitely what we need. More people looking for this guy. Next thing the Coast Guard's going to be searching for him.

Natalie something sighed. "They weren't any help at all. They told me they couldn't do anything until he was reported missing by a member of his immediate family. And I don't think she's going to do that." She hesitated, obviously making a decision, then decided to confide in Bobby and Eddie. "I'm assuming that Gra—his wife, she didn't hire you, but you should know that his marriage isn't so great. Sometimes he complained to me about her. Personally? I think she's glad he's gone."

"You know him pretty good, huh?" Eddie said in his best detective voice. Bobby couldn't believe what he was hearing. Who would've guessed? That randy old professor.

"I've been working with him more than a year. He is truly an enchanting man," she said brightly. This was the first time Bobby had heard Gradinsky described as anything but plodding and ordinary. "You should hear him when he reads the great Russian poets. He's . . ." Bobby watched as her eyes searched the air for a meaningful description. ". . . a man given to grand feats of verbal ecstasy." She leaned back, satisfied with that tribute.

"Wow," Eddie said aloud, impressed if not certain he understood her meaning, and wondering if they were talking about the same guy.

Verbal ecstasy? Bobby thought. Nice try. "Lemme ask you this, Natalie," he said. "Did you see a lot of the professor?"

She nodded and, completely missing the intended humor in his question, replied seriously, "Oh yes, at least three or four days a week. Peter was my mentor so we worked together very closely. He was helping me write my thesis."

Peter? That's pretty good, Bobby thought to himself, practically feeling the pain on his knuckles that would have resulted if he had dared refer to Sister Mary Margaret, his fifth-grade teacher, as just plain Mary. This Natalie certainly knew a lot about the professor's life; she knew the people on the faculty he respected, she knew the places he liked to eat and what he ordered, that he was reading *Gorky Park* when he disappeared, even his secret strategy for finding a parking spot on campus. But she knew nothing at all about his relationship with Skinny Al or, most important, just where he might be at that very moment. "I need to talk to him," she said. "If you find him, tell him it's very important." She would not confide in them, even when pushed, but emphasized, "It really is important."

Later, as Bobby and Eddie walked back to their car, Eddie asked, "You think he's boffing her?"

Bobby laughed at him. "Do I *think* he's boffing her? Do I think he's boffing her? Is the pope Catholic? Fuck yes, I think he's boffing her. You heard her, four times a week."

"Man, that's really something," Eddie said, astonished by the thought. "What the fuck is a piece of ass like that doing with that schmuck?"

"You heard her. He's got verbal ecstasy."

"Sure he does. And I got a fifteen-inch schlong. What does that mean, verbal ecstasy?" Eddie asked.

"It means he can talk her into giving him blow jobs," Bobby explained.

On the way back they stopped at Charlie DaSilva's place on Mac-Dougal Street in the Village for a cannoli. They sat at a table in the window. It was a gloomy day, dark and blustery, the perfect harmony for Bobby's mood. He had read that after Mickey Mantle retired, he used to dream that he was locked outside Yankee Stadium and kept running around the place desperately trying to find an open door. That's sort of the way he felt about this search, like he was running around in a big circle unable to find the key to get inside. He had gathered some decent information, but it didn't lead anywhere. It was like trying to find the words in a bowl of alphabet soup: The letters were all there but they were floating around aimlessly.

He wondered if those two FBI agents working the case were doing any better. Franzone had given him their names and home addresses, but there wasn't too much he could do with that information. What was he going to do, bug the feds? The FBI had a lot of advantages, no question about it, but they also had one big problem: They were restricted by the law. They needed the bullshit search warrants, they weren't allowed to use the family methods to encourage people to give up information, and they didn't have access to the same range of people.

His own involvement with the bureau had been sporadic. Two different times he'd been picked up by members of the joint FBI-NYPD Organized Crime Task Force and questioned about specific killings, but in both cases they had nothing more than a hunch. Those were obviously fishing expeditions and they didn't catch anything. He'd been tailed many times, too many times to count up. Sometimes the

tail was obvious, sometimes it was supposed to be covert, and he figured there were times when he had been followed without knowing
it, but the only crimes he'd ever been charged with were a conspiracy
rap that never even got to court and a wire fraud charge for working
for a bookie during the '78 World Series. He'd been convicted in the
bookmaking case and received a six-month suspended sentence. A
couple of times bureau agents had approached him on the street to
feel him out about cooperating with them, just answering a few questions from time to time. "Building up some credit for when you're
gonna need it," one of them had called it. He'd laughed them away.

He respected the bureau. They had some smart guys working
there. And they played by the rules. He was reminded of that every
day by the precautions their shadows caused him to take. And those
agents he'd met . . .

"I just can't fucking believe it," Eddie whined, interrupting his
thoughts.

"What's that?"

"That fucking professor. Where's he get off banging a cute little
cunt like that? I swear to God, sometimes this world just isn't fair."

Bobby chuckled at that thought. Eddie was right about that one.
"C'mon," he said finally, "let's go get some gas."

TEN

Numbers can't lie. Dig deep enough into the numbers and the answer is there. Most people never think about it, but almost all of their daily transactions generate numbers, and those numbers can often be attached to them and can then be used to create the legendary paper trail. Law enforcement agencies not only think about it, they rely on it. The foundation of pretty much all intelligence-gathering is built of numbers.

The FBI's information-gathering machine was finally operating at close to full strength, collecting those raw numbers from banks, credit card agencies, the telephone company, even the Motor Vehicle Bureau, any numbers that might be used to track the professor. But as always, it was up to the agents to turn those numbers into facts.

O'Brien got to the office almost an hour earlier than usual the following morning. He walked into the conference room just as Russo was taking a big bite out of a lightly buttered bagel. Two empty coffee cups and an opened folder were in front of her. Another pile of reports was sitting in the middle of the conference table. "Morning," she said midbite.

"Don't you ever sleep?" he asked incredulously as he hung his wet trench coat over the back of a chair.

"Sure I do," she said. "I think I did it last year."

He took his own bagel and two cups of coffee from a white paper bag. "Here you go," he said, placing one of those cups and two packs of Sweet'n Low in front of her. "So?" He indicated the pile of reports: "What do we got?"

"Thanks," she said. She tore the sipping triangle off the plastic lid. "Some of this stuff is pretty interesting." She flipped through several pages until she found what she was looking for. "Look at this. These are his phone records. Remember, his wife told us that the phone call that got him moving came in at about seven-thirty? There were only two calls to his number around that time, give or take what, fifteen minutes, say. One was from his office, the other one was"—she searched for a different sheet of paper and found it almost immediately—"from a phone in a place called Off Limits. It lasted"—she checked the first sheet—"one minute and twenty-eight seconds."

"What's Off Limits?"

She smiled. "Nothing, apparently. That's the joke."

"I don't get it."

"It's a strip club. That's their slogan, '*Nothing* is Off Limits!' "

O'Brien squared his shoulders, stood up ramrod straight, and in the most officious tone he could muster said nobly, "Perhaps it would be better if I take this interview on my own."

"Down, boy," she commanded. "Down, boy."

His shoulders deflated. "You never let me have any fun."

Ignoring him, she continued reading from her notes. "The morning after he disappeared somebody used his ATM card at three different banks for a total of $650. He still has in his possession a Visa, a MasterCard, a Macy's charge card, a discount card from something called Diner's Delight, a few more things like that, but except for the bank card and the Visa at the Heights restaurant, none of them have been used."

O'Brien confirmed the obvious. "I guess that's the good news. If somebody else had them, you figure they would've used them at least once, right? Before getting rid of them?"

She picked up the coffee cup and swiveled to face him. "Not the mob. They don't take those kinds of chances."

The bright red polish on her nails stood out against the stark white

Styrofoam cup. He'd never noticed that color before and wondered if she was doing something new or whether he was simply paying closer attention. "Yeah, you're right. Anything else?"

"Yeah, one more thing," she said, imitating Slattery's understated sense of drama. "This." She handed him two sheets of paper stapled together.

The logo at the top of the first page identified it as an official communication from the New York State Department of Motor Vehicles. He glanced at the numbers. "Whoa," he said, impressed, "double whoa."

In response to a subpoena issued by Judge Margo Sklar the DMV had provided information concerning two vehicles registered in the state of New York. Asked to identify any vehicles registered to Peter Gradinsky—both his home and his office addresses had been provided, as well as his Social Security number—the DMV reported that seven months earlier Gradinsky had registered a light brown 1981 Datsun 280Z to his office address. Motor Vehicles provided a license plate number and a copy of an unpaid ticket issued to that vehicle for parking at an expired meter six weeks earlier. "Who'da thunk it, huh?" Russo said. "New women, fast cars. Our guy's leading a whole secret life."

"Least we know what he's doing with the mob's money," O'Brien replied, somewhat distracted. It was the second part of the report that most intrigued him. It was a copy of a report filed by two agents O'Brien did not know, Richard Soll and William Madden, "concerning the surveillance of a known member of Henry 'the Hammer' Franzone's organized crime family, Robert San Filippo, a.k.a. Bobby Blue Eyes, a.k.a. Bobby Hats." This was a bit of information that had been lying there unnoticed for a couple of days, lost in a blizzard of paper, but to Connor it stood out like an elephant in a game of musical chairs.

As a normal part of the investigation into the murder of Alphonse "Skinny Al" D'Angelo, surveillance teams had been assigned to several different crews. There was some speculation that this killing might be the first shot in what was potentially a major family war over disputed territories. In fact, when O'Brien and Russo were working at the Country Club, they had been alerted to pay particular attention to any mention of this killing.

Skinny Al's funeral had been as much of an event for the bureau as it was for the mob. Strict mob protocol is observed at funerals, which allows the FBI to keep track of winners and losers in the ongoing power struggle inside organized crime. It was learned from an informant inside the Freemont Avenue Social Club that San Filippo had been asked to represent Franzone's crew at the funeral. The morning of that funeral Special Agents Soll and Madden had been assigned to follow San Filippo. This was a "bright light" operation, meaning the bureau wanted Bobby Blue Eyes to know he was being tailed. The bureau wanted him to know that it had taken a special interest in his future. That's standard operating procedure. It tends to make people nervous—specifically the person being followed and all the others deemed not important enough to earn a tail. It makes all those others wonder what the FBI knows that they don't know.

According to Soll's report, when he and Madden arrived outside San Filippo's home early on the morning of D'Angelo's funeral, they discovered another vehicle already waiting there. Initially they had assumed that the two men in the car were also members of Franzone's crew. Probably security. At first the occupants of this vehicle did not appear to be aware of the FBI's presence, but even after they realized a second car was tailing San Filippo, they made no move to respond. In fact, they did absolutely nothing to interfere with the tail. When this three-car motorcade reached the funeral parlor, the two men in this car were welcomed inside, making it highly likely they were mobsters. Soll and Madden dutifully recorded the license plate number of this vehicle, a 1983 charcoal Pontiac Firebird, and submitted it as part of their report. Just another piece of basic information. A straw in a haystack. Nobody bothered to check the plates.

Until Jim Slattery found it. Slattery knew that Bobby San Filippo was also searching for the missing professor, so he'd requested Bobby

Blue Eyes's file on the slight chance there might be something there that could assist the bureau's investigation. The presence of the second car caught his attention. Years of experience had taught him that San Filippo was simply not important enough to merit an escort. He was security, he didn't get his own security. So who were the guys in the second car? He ran the plate through the DMV.

"You see this?" O'Brien asked. The car was registered to the G&C Corporation, 1405 Brighton Beach Boulevard, in Brooklyn. Brighton Beach. Little Odessa. The Russians were finally in play. He let out an appreciative whistle.

It wasn't just that two Russians were tailing San Filippo. What made it even more interesting was that the two men in the car also attended the funeral. This was mourning by invitation only. The fact that these two Russians had been invited guests at the funeral of the month raised all kinds of unpleasant possibilities.

Russo asked, "You have any idea what G&C might be?"

"Just some bullshit dummy corporation," O'Brien guessed. "They use them all the time for cover. Use 'em and lose 'em. If there's any kind of problem, they just evaporate. This is probably just a mail drop." He picked up the phone and dialed Brooklyn information. "Let's find out."

"It's unlisted," she told him.

He hung up the phone. "You ever had a blintz?"

She looked at him suspiciously. "A what?"

"A blintz. You know."

"You sure you don't mean a Blimpie?"

"No, I don't. I mean a blintz." He tried to describe it. "It's like a pancake, except it's not. Put your coat on."

Before leaving the office they requested copies of the corporate records of the G&C Corporation, located at 1405 Brighton Beach Boulevard. O'Brien figured a dummy corporation would probably have dummy directors, but you never know. It was worth the five minutes it took. They also called Jeff McElnea, the bureau's liaison with the NYPD, gave him the plate number of the professor's car, and asked him to request a soft alert. If the car was spotted, they wanted to be notified immediately, but they did not want the car stopped.

One bagel into the day, they were on their way to Brighton Beach. Even with light traffic on the Belt Parkway it took them a full hour to get there. Actually that was not a long time, Russo realized as she looked around, to get to another country. Brighton Beach could have been a small Russian village on the Black Sea. There were more signs in Russian than English. Many of the women were wearing scarves and heavy black coats. As they looked for 1405 Brighton Beach Boulevard, O'Brien gave her the two-minute tour: Brighton Beach was a small village wedged between the much more upscale Manhattan Beach and world-famous Coney Island. Historically it had been a fishing community, but eventually it had become a popular haven for mostly Eastern European immigrants. In the years following World War II, survivors of the Holocaust had settled there, and the area had become largely Jewish. A second wave of immigrants, this time from the Soviet Union, began settling there in the mid-1970s. New Yorkers knew it mostly for the large restaurants near the beach that served huge platters of every known type of fattening food. "See, you don't even have to fool around with the meat," he explained to Laura. "There's no pretense here. You can just order your fat straight." She looked extremely dubious. "Hey, I'm not kidding. It's true. You can order it boiled, fried, well-done, however you want it. Believe me, Russo, you like fat, this is the place to get it."

"That's gotta be it," she said, ignoring him. "There's your mail drop."

He followed her gaze across the street. She was looking at a large, somewhat run-down Gulf station. In front were two cement islands in parallel, with two sets of pumps on each island. Behind them was a garage with two repair bays. The door to one of the bays was raised and two men were working underneath a car on a lift. Above the garage doors the nearly faded remnants of the name Albie's Service Center, which had once been spelled out in blue block letters, was barely visible. O'Brien looked around for the current name but couldn't find it. Then, in gold letters on the inside of the glass door to the office, he saw the name G&C Corp. The owners weren't exactly hiding the name, but they certainly weren't advertising it either.

He pulled up to one of the pumps and got out of the car. The attendant, a ruggedly handsome square-jawed man, approached him. "I help you," the attendant said in a thick Russian accent.

He's thirty-four, O'Brien guessed, tells the girls he's twenty-eight. "Fill it, please," O'Brien told him, "the cheap stuff." He glanced around the gas station. He could see a half-filled candy and gum rack and a soda machine inside the office. "Where's your men's room?" he asked.

"In back," the attendant told him, pointing with his thumb. "Key in the office."

"Thanks." As Connor walked toward the office, he glanced back at the car. Russo was half-turned in the passenger seat, looking back over the seat at the attendant. Not her type, he thought. A second man, an older man, thin and dark and cold, was sitting behind an old wooden desk, reading a Russian-language newspaper. The man handed him the key, which was attached to a metal ring obviously made to fit around a wrist. A metal tag indicated it had been stolen from the Surf Motel of Brighton Beach.

Connor's first thought when he opened the door to the men's room was that it had seen better times. The Civil War, for example. Filthy did not begin to describe it. The whole place stunk. The toilet seat had lost a bolt and was askew on the bowl. A corner of the porcelain lid had been broken off. The cloth towel had been ripped off the dispenser winding mechanism and hung straight down, covered with dirt and grease. In the sink a thin stream of water ran from the cold water handle, while the hot water handle was missing. There was graffiti written in black marker on the walls. On the mirror someone had scratched the words "Suck my big dike" and provided a phone number. Some of the tiles were missing from the floor, revealing the cement subfloor.

It was the kind of place that made O'Brien decide to throw out his shoes because they touched the floor. He stayed in there just long enough to be convincing, careful not to touch anything, and returned to the office. "It's beautiful," he said to the older attendant, putting down the key. "Who did your decorating?"

The man obviously didn't have the slightest idea what O'Brien was talking about, and just as clearly did not care. He didn't even bother putting down his newspaper. Connor continued, "Is the manager around? The temperature gauge in my car is way up, maybe somebody could take a look at it?"

"No manager," the man grunted. "Not here now."

"Well, then, you think maybe one of those mechanics might take a look at it?"

"Busy." He finally looked up from the newspaper. "Everybody very busy today. Tomorrow good time for you come back. Hokay? Tomorrow?"

"How about you? Is this your place?"

The man shrugged proudly. A good firm "maybe." "Tomorrow, come back," he repeated. "We take good care of you."

For an instant O'Brien considered identifying himself as a special agent of the Federal Bureau of Investigation. But the most this might have accomplished in this situation, he knew quite well, was that the guy would put down his newspaper to be polite. Contrary to how members of the Efrem Zimbalist Jr. fan club felt, the badge wasn't all magic. It would not make the owner or the manager suddenly appear. And it would definitely make his interest in the gas station known to people he didn't necessarily want to know about it. "I'm sure you will," he said pleasantly as he left.

The first attendant was still hanging around the car, drying his hands on a filthy rag. "Three dollars ninety-five cents," he said. "Even."

"I guess I must've had more gas than I thought," Connor replied, handing the guy four dollars. "Keep the change." The man smiled good-naturedly at the joke, revealing two large gold teeth in the front of his mouth. Seeing that, O'Brien smiled broadly in return.

There were several cars parked on the side and in the rear of the station. O'Brien drove around the side, but the charcoal Firebird was not there. "I didn't think it'd be here," he told Russo. "You know what this place is, right?"

"A gas station?" she guessed.

He nodded. "Either that or the biggest mailbox in the world. Okay, I admit it, I was wrong. Happy? So now all we gotta do is figure out the connection between a Russian-owned gas station and organized crime. It just doesn't make sense to me."

"Let's ask Slattery to put some surveillance on it," she suggested.

"Right." O'Brien was one of those agents who liked to absorb the entire scene and then focus on the details later. After leaving a place he'd sit down and list in his notebook everything that caught his attention. His theory was that the things he remembered would most likely be the important things. He had the same theory about women.

One of the things he did remember was the way Russo looked at the husky attendant. So when they stopped at a red light, he turned to her and asked, "I want you to tell me the truth. Do you think I'd look better if I had gold teeth?" He bared his teeth in the rearview mirror. "Just like a couple."

She laughed. "Gold teeth?" She looked at his reflection in the mirror. "Let me see." She looked carefully and thought about it. Nodding her head, she decided, "Maybe a gold tooth." As he eased into traffic on the Belt Parkway, she said, "Hey, O'Brien, what happened? I thought you were taking me to a Blintzie's?"

"Next time." He skillfully moved into the fast lane. "Let me ask you this, Russo. What do you think? You think he's still alive?"

She stared straight ahead. The most significant difference between being in the middle of a real criminal investigation and the stories you see on TV is that in the stories the good guys always win at the end. Going in, you know Brad Pitt isn't going to be killed in the last fifteen minutes. The killer is going to get caught. And all the scars are makeup. Unfortunately that's not the way the real world works. Cops do get killed. Killers do get away with murder. Scars last a lifetime. And when you're in the middle of a case, you never know if the next step you take will break it wide open or cost you your life.

Speculating doesn't do you any good. Any time I spent while working undercover trying to figure out where the operation was going proved to be a colossal waste. I never knew what was going to happen in the next five minutes, much less at some indeterminate time in the future. The only thing that really matters is facts. What happens next.

Sometimes during an investigation agents get to know people they will never meet. They learn secrets about them that have been carefully hidden from the world, hidden even from those people closest to them. And when an agent focuses on one person, it becomes difficult not to wonder about them. To wonder where they might be at some particular moment, to wonder about their fate. To wonder why they took a particular action or what they were thinking when they did it. Laura Russo was too good an agent to admit that she had spent considerable time wondering about the professor. "Sure, sometimes I do," was the most she would tell O'Brien. "I don't know. I just can't think of any reason they'd want to get rid of him. I hope so. You?"

"You ever see *The Man Who Knew Too Much*? The Hitchcock picture?"

"No."

"Well, it's about this really nice guy, that's James Stewart, who the bad guys are after because they think he knows something, but he doesn't know he knows it. All he knows is that to save his family he's got to find out what it is that he doesn't know that they think he knows. It's a great picture."

She looked at him curiously, trying to decide just how serious he was. With O'Brien that was always a difficult question to answer. "All right," she surrendered, "what happened at the end?"

"James Stewart found out what he didn't know that he knew. Doris Day sang 'Que Sera, Sera, Whatever Will Be, Will Be,' and they got their child back safely."

"Good. Now that that's cleared up, I don't have to see it. And your point is exactly . . . ?"

"Whatever it is that the mob and the Russkies are doing together, we can assume it's not a nice thing. And it has to be really lucrative, because it would take a small fortune to keep these guys from killing each other." As always, he was thinking out loud, almost as curious as Russo to hear if he stumbled onto anything important. "We know for a fact that the Italians don't know where the professor is, so obviously they didn't take him. And I just don't believe the commies would jeopardize this alliance by holding him. If I'm right, he's more important to us than he is to them, because he can put the Italians and the Russians in business together."

She was confused. "So what is it that we know that we don't know we know?"

"That's our real problem," he said earnestly. "We don't know." He shrugged. "But that might be why the Italians are looking for him."

About a half hour later, as they approached the city, the radio staticked to life. As O'Brien preferred to use his own car, a car on which he lavished pennies, this CD radio was arguably the slum of the art. "O'Brien," he acknowledged.

"Hey, O'Brien, it's Freiberg." Agent Mickey Freiberg ran the Special Operations Group in New York. He was the go-to guy for just about all technical matters. "I got some news for you. The cops have spotted that car you were looking for, the Z."

Peter Gradinsky's car. "Where is it?"

Freiberg rustled some papers. "I got it right here . . . somewhere. Here. Like five minutes ago he was driving downtown on West End Avenue. A squad car picked up on him on 96th Street. They're waiting to hear what you want to do."

He glanced at Russo. She gave him the thumbs-up, then leaned over the seat and picked up the emergency beacon he kept in the back. It attached to the dashboard with a big suction cup. O'Brien keyed the mike. "Okay, it's gonna take us at least twenty minutes to get there. Tell the cops to stay with him, but lay back. Don't lose him. Thanks." Laying down the mike, he guessed, "Maybe he's going home."

"Right," she said doubtfully, "in a sports car his wife doesn't know he has? I don't think so." Laura took the cigarette lighter out of its socket and laid it in the ashtray, then plugged the emergency beacon into the socket. "Here we go," she said, and turned it on.

For the most part the drivers in front of them ignored the flashing red light. Begrudgingly they would eventually move to the side so the agents could pass. O'Brien knew what they were thinking, the same thing any real New Yorker would think: I wonder where he bought that red light? Maybe I should get one.

The beacon helped, not tremendously, but it helped. When they reached the Manhattan Bridge, a cop held up traffic for them, which enabled them to race across the bridge at speeds approaching twenty-five miles an hour. O'Brien went up the East Side. Freiberg continued to report the Z's position. The car had not even slowed down when it passed the professor's building. It had turned onto Broadway and was still heading downtown.

By the time O'Brien was able to intersect the Z on Park Avenue and 58th Street, rush hour had begun. Traffic was barely moving. The two cars passed heading in opposite directions, O'Brien going north, the Z moving south. The Z was in the inside lane. "There he is," O'Brien said, but the Z's tinted windows made it impossible to see the driver. The NYPD squad car, alerted by radio that O'Brien had finally reached the area, spotted his beacon and hit his siren very briefly to attract his attention.

Unfortunately that siren also got the attention of the person driving the Z. The car edged over two lanes, into the turning lane. "He's moving over," Russo said. "I'll bet he saw our light."

At the next corner O'Brien made a U-turn and began heading downtown. Slowly, very slowly. He shut off the beacon. He was a full block behind the Z. Traffic was moving forward by the inch. "You see him?" O'Brien asked.

"He's all the way over on the right."

O'Brien keyed the mike. "Okay, we see him. Looks like he knows we're here." The NYPD dispatched several unmarked cars to the area. They were told to block the intersections when they got to that stretch of Park Avenue. The problem was that normal rush-hour traffic was already blocking several of those intersections, making it extremely difficult for the police cars to get there.

Like an ancient sailing ship in pursuit on a windless sea, O'Brien drifted forward inches at a time. He was using all his New York City driving skills. The instant he saw the slightest opening, he went for it. Once he sliced in front of a woman driving a station wagon, getting a blocking bumper in front of her before she could cover—and in response she flashed her middle finger at him. The car to his left switched lanes, unexpectedly vacating several valuable feet of space. A cabdriver spotted the gap at the same instant O'Brien did and challenged him to it. It was a game of hard-core bumper chicken, of who would brake first. O'Brien knew he had the edge, because he cared nothing about adding another dent or scratch to his car. He played the game with expertise, refusing to look at the cabbie, thus avoiding the often critical mistake made by amateurs in this game. The cabbie hesitated, suddenly uncertain O'Brien knew he was there, and braked at the last second—allowing O'Brien to slide in and fill the traffic vacuum. "God, I love these people," he said.

Block after block, irritated drivers banged on their horns, battling for every precious foot of rush-hour road. The Z was moving too, but O'Brien saw right away that its driver was considerably more cautious than him—a fatal vehicular weakness after three o'clock on a weekday afternoon. The agents moved almost a full block in less than fifteen minutes, gaining almost two full car lengths on the Z.

Suddenly O'Brien screamed, "Hold on!" and darted forward about eight feet. He looked at Russo and took a relieved breath. "You okay?"

She could see how much he was enjoying this. She frowned. "Not funny."

He knew it *was* funny. "Hey, partner, think of it this way. We're making history here. This has got to be the slowest chase in history. Can't you just feel the tension building?"

"Oh. Oh," she said in the monotone delivery of a really poor actor. "Be still, my heart. I can hardly bear it. This is even more exciting than bumper cars."

"Well, if that's the way you feel about it," he said, opening his door, "you drive." O'Brien got out of the car. A pizza deliveryman was bicycling down Park, skillfully slaloming between cars. As Russo watched incredulously, O'Brien took out his badge and held it up high as a highwayman stopping a stagecoach. The pizza deliveryman walked his bike to a halt. Russo could see O'Brien say something to the teenager, who nodded and got off his bike, taking his pizza with him. O'Brien mounted the bike and began pedaling down Park Avenue.

She sat there in stunned disbelief. But one very long threatening horn blast from the big Buick inches behind her knocked her back to reality. The car directly in front of her had moved forward almost three feet and she had remained in place. Through some osmotic process she understood that this was a grave violation of traffic jam etiquette. She scrambled into the driver's seat and rolled forward.

During their career almost every agent does at least one thing that one day causes them to wonder, what the hell was I thinking? Why in the world would I do something like that? But few of them ever do anything as ridiculous as Connor O'Brien, who had appropriated a pizza delivery bicycle and was pedaling it down Park Avenue in pursuit of Professor Peter Gradinsky's Datsun 280Z.

Initially O'Brien had stayed as close to the curb as possible, but even that path was blocked. He had the option of dashing through the stalled traffic, but he knew there is a vast difference between exhibiting a good sense of humor and a death wish. So he made a decision, lifting the front tire over the curb and onto the sidewalk.

Seconds later he was madly pedaling down the sidewalk, bending forward over the handlebars, elbows flared, yelling, "Out of the way. FBI! FBI! Coming through."

He could have easily walked or jogged up to the Z. It was caught in traffic, it wasn't going anywhere, fast or slow. He would never admit his real reason for taking the bike, but at least a little part of it came from a childish urge to impress the girl. Within a minute he had caught up to the car. As he got off the bike, a fashionably dressed couple was walking past him. "Here," he said to the man, "hold my horse." The man reflexively accepted the bike and stood there holding it.

As O'Brien started moving toward the car, he heard the man's wife telling him, "Put that bike down right now, Marty. Why are you always doing things like this to me?"

The Z's tinted windows prevented O'Brien from seeing inside. Normally this would have made him very wary. Tinted car windows are the hallmark of drug dealers, and drug dealers often carry large guns. But this car belonged to a college professor. What could he be packing? A thesaurus? O'Brien had no idea who was behind the wheel. It was entirely possible he was about to meet the elusive Professor Gradinsky. Somehow, though, he didn't believe that was about to happen.

O'Brien remained cautious. You never know. In textbook fashion he approached the car on the driver's side, cutting down the driver's angle of sight by brushing against the car. He stopped before reaching the driver's window. Anybody feeling the need to take a shot at him would have to twist almost completely around to get a clean shot, which was very difficult to do while sitting in the driver's seat. He reached under his jacket and grasped the butt of his own gun. Just in case.

Russo was five car lengths behind him. She watched him ease carefully alongside of the car—and when she saw him reach into his jacket for his weapon, she decided to move. Screw this, she said to herself, turning off the engine and dropping the keys on the floor mat. She grabbed her handbag and put it over her shoulder. And then she got out of the car and started walking rapidly toward the Z.

There is a story New York cops like to tell about the rookie detective who was investigating a Manhattan robbery. He asked the victim, "Have you seen anybody around here acting strange lately?" Twenty-four hours later he was still writing. So New Yorkers are used to seeing some pretty unusual things. But even the experienced New York drivers behind and next to Russo were completely shocked to see a woman get out of her car right in the middle of rush hour and simply walk away, abandoning it on Park Avenue. They responded instinctively, like great animals in distress, crying out with their horns.

O'Brien kept his right hand on his gun. With his left hand he reached over and tried to open the car door. It was locked. He tightened his grip on his weapon and again tried to open the door, at the same time screaming loud and clear, "FBI! FBI!" The door remained locked.

Russo was darting between cars, banging hard on their hoods as she walked in front of them to make certain the drivers saw her. She assumed most of the drivers would figure she was insane, which was not necessarily a bad thing in this situation. They weren't going to interfere with her. Her bag was open and her hand was holding her gun, but she didn't show it. Finally she took a position by the passenger-side window of the Z. She was blocking a white sports car, and its driver was practically apoplectic, leaning out the window to scream at her, "What the hell's a matter with you, lady? You can't stand there. This is Park Avenue!"

O'Brien banged on the car window. A second later the window smoothly slid down. Again he shouted, "FBI! FBI!"

An attractive young woman leaned out the window and turned to look at him. "I'm . . . I'm sorry," she said, obviously confused. "I don't know . . . Was I doing something wrong?"

Both agents took their hands off their weapons. Park Avenue had become a band of a thousand car horns. Drivers who could not possibly see what was taking place had picked up the cry and were leaning on their horns. Over the racket O'Brien pointed to the curb and told the young woman, "Pull the car over there."

Russo shouted to him, "I'm going to get your car."

The woman edged the car to the curb. O'Brien noticed that the ends of her medium-length light brown hair were curled in that brainy coed style. He couldn't see her body but ventured a guess anyway: twenty-three and tells the truth about her age to the day.

Russo completely ignored the venom other drivers were hurling at her. Instead, she felt liberated. She was an extremely responsible person, an FBI agent, sensitive to the needs of other people. No one who knew her would believe she was capable of abandoning a car in the middle of rush hour. But she'd done exactly that. She'd done it. As she slid back into the driver's seat, she glanced into the rearview mirror. She could see the driver of the car directly behind her. His face was scrunched up and his mouth was moving rapidly. She couldn't hear him, but she had a really good idea what he was saying. Or, actually, screeching. She watched him for a few seconds, then opened the window and stuck her middle finger victoriously into the air, feeling very much like she was on her way to becoming a true New Yorker.

"Special Agent O'Brien. FBI," he told the young woman, flashing his badge. "Can I see the registration for this car, please?"

"Really?" she said. "FBI?"

"Really," he told her. "Now, let me see the registration, please."

"Why? Was I doing something wrong?" she asked, fumbling through her thick wallet. She smiled at him. "I mean, I couldn't exactly have been speeding, right?"

"No." He smiled back. "Just let me—"

"I know, I didn't signal when I changed lanes, did I?" She continued searching the compartments of her wallet, which seemed to be leaking slips of paper from every pocket. "It's got to be here," she said, almost to herself. Then she stopped and looked right at him. "Are you really FBI?"

"Yeah, really. C'mon, show me the registration." She was quite attractive in a youthfully exuberant way, Connor decided. He knew the type: a young woman certain of her abilities and confident that success and recognition were only a few years away.

Meanwhile, Russo had taken one very big breath and cut over to the curb. As she got out of O'Brien's car, the driver of the Buick that had been caught behind her put down his passenger window and screamed at her, "You bitch."

She didn't hesitate, shouting right back at him, "You prick!" and feeling very good about it.

The young woman driving the professor's car sighed, snapped closed the purse on her lap, looked sheepishly at O'Brien, and, as he described such behavior, tried to "cute her way" out of a problem. "It's not really my car," she admitted. "I don't have the registration."

He did have to admit that she was sort of cute—in a confrontational way. "All right, then, whose car is it?"

She averted her eyes. "Well, he's sort of my boyfriend."

O'Brien locked a pleasant expression on his face. He had no intention of providing any information to her. He wanted to create a vacuum of information and let her rush in to fill it. "Okay, what's your boyfriend's name?"

Russo joined them at the car window and identified herself as an FBI agent. The young woman smiled at her too, seemingly impressed.

O'Brien told Russo, "She doesn't have the registration with her. Says it's her boyfriend's car, not hers."

Russo asked the young woman, "What's your name?"

"Natalie Speakman."

"And what's your boyfriend's name?"

In an instant Natalie Speakman's attention shifted from O'Brien to Russo. Abandoning cute, she went directly for sisterhood. "I think you know that already. That's obviously why you stopped me, isn't it?

See, here's my problem," she appealed to Russo. "His wife doesn't know about . . . you know, about us. He said he was going to tell her, but if she finds out and—"

Russo was coldly professional. "Stop. Please. I have no idea what you're talking about. All I asked you for was his name. I don't care about the details, I just want a name."

"You know who it is. Peter Gradinsky," Natalie admitted. "Look, this is really embarrassing for me. He's my mentor at Columbia, and if his wife finds out about us, she'll . . . This is ridiculous. I mean, you're his . . ." She sobbed two, three, four times, then burst into tears.

"Look, Natalie," O'Brien began sympathetically.

Russo gently pushed him aside. She leaned into the car, inches from the young girl's face. "Stop it right now," she ordered. "We don't have time for it. We need some answers from you, you got it?" When the girl failed to respond, Russo repeated firmly, "Got it?"

Natalie gulped, then looked at Russo and nodded.

"Let me explain the situation to you," she told Speakman. "You're driving a car that belongs to a missing person. You don't have the registration. Believe me, we can cause you some serious problems. But I'm going to offer you a choice. You can either come back to the office with us and call your lawyer from there, or you can come with me right now and answer a few questions."

"But I need to talk to you," she insisted. "I want to."

"Fine. Good." Russo stood up and looked around. She spotted a parking garage just around the next corner. She told O'Brien to get in the Z and park it in that lot.

O'Brien did as directed. He was quite impressed at Russo's ability to play good cop, bad cop. Or, as he decided would be more accurate in this instance, good cop, bad copess. Russo and Speakman followed him into the garage in his car. Minutes later the three of them were sitting in a booth in a coffee shop.

"Okay, now," Russo said, "let's hear it. What are you doing with Gradinsky's car?"

"I just want you to find him," Speakman said.

"Then answer my questions," Russo told her. She reached across the table and put a reassuring hand on Natalie's, and in a much softer voice added, "We want to find him too. But we've got to have your help."

If O'Brien hadn't seen Russo do almost exactly the same thing with Grace Gradinsky, taking her hand and holding it, he would have sworn it was heartfelt. Coughing into his cupped hands to hide an appreciative smile, he opened his notebook.

Speakman surrendered. She was working toward her master's in Russian literature, she explained, and had been Gradinsky's graduate assistant for almost a year. They had started dating a month after they'd met. "You know what I mean," she said to Russo, making quotation marks in the air. "Dating?"

Both agents acknowledged that they understood.

Absolutely no one knew about their relationship, Natalie continued, especially his wife. At least once a month, sometimes more, he'd told his wife that he had to go to some secret meeting, which would allow them to spend a night or two together in her apartment. He'd bought the car several months earlier, paying for it in cash, but that was a big secret too. She kept it for him. That's why she had the keys and was driving it. He was such an extraordinary man, she rhapsodized, sensitive, caring, open. His passion, she explained, was the Russian language.

O'Brien studied her as she rambled on about Peter Gradinsky. Yeah, right, he thought, the Russian language and a few other things. Her description of Gradinsky had about as much resemblance to anything O'Brien and Russo knew about him as would his portrait painted by Jackson Pollock.

"You want to tell us where he is?" Russo asked gently. An interesting way to ask that question, O'Brien noted, as it assumed she knew the answer.

"I don't know, honest," the young woman claimed. "The last time I spoke to him was more than a week ago. I called him and told him

I needed to see him. We were supposed to meet for lunch." She exhaled. "He never showed up. That's the last time I spoke to him."

O'Brien was surprised. "You called him at home?"

Her answer seemed obvious. "Sure, I called him there all the time. I'm his assistant. I mean, if I hadn't called him at home sometimes, Grace . . . his wife?"

"We know," Russo affirmed.

Natalie continued, "She definitely would have suspected something was going on. Don't you think? Like when I talked to her, I would make up this boyfriend I supposedly was going out with and I'd make up all these details." She smiled demurely. "His name is Simon and he was . . . he is a carpenter. I didn't want him to be one of those intellectual types."

Russo laughed, a little too hard to be natural, O'Brien thought, then she said, "I can't believe it. I did the same thing when I was in college. I made up a boyfriend just to get my mother off my back. Only mine was a crusading journalist, a muckraker."

"You remember his name?" Natalie asked.

"Sure I do." Russo blushed. "Alex Newman." She chuckled at the memory, then repeated his name. Russo then asked Natalie if she believed those secret meetings actually took place. "Oh yeah," Natalie said firmly. "Absolutely. Peter told me everything. You mean you don't know?"

"Know what?" O'Brien asked.

"Wow, that's weird," she continued. "Peter told me he was working for you guys. For the FBI, as an interpreter. He said he went to meetings that the FBI had with Russians. He was interpreting for you guys."

"And you believed him?" Russo asked.

She nodded vigorously. "Oh, absolutely. Peter never lied to me. Never," she insisted. "Why? You don't think it's true?" She smiled knowingly at both of them. "I mean, come on, let's look at the facts here. Why else would you people be trying to find a missing college professor?"

O'Brien answered, "Well, Natalie, the bureau's a big place. We don't know everybody who works for us. I'm sure it's possible." He looked to Russo for support. "Right?"

"Of course it is," she agreed. She explained to Speakman, "They just told us to find him. They didn't tell us why."

"Well, I've known Peter for almost a year. And he's not the kind of person to lie." She caught herself, then added, "Except, you know, when it's absolutely necessary. Like to Grace. But I'm absolutely positive everything he told me is true."

O'Brien asked, "Let me ask you this, then. Did he ever tell you anything about these meetings with the Russians?"

Connor really hadn't expected much of an answer, so he was quite surprised when he got a good one. "Uh-huh, yeah, he told me all about them. He even described some of the Russians who were there. There were like these two Russians. What was his name?" As she scanned her memory, neither Connor nor Laura dared move. "Vasily," she finally remembered, "Vasily something. Peter always called him Vaseline because that's how smooth he was. Peter told me about his accent. Peter's very good with accents, you know. Vaseline wasn't from Moscow, he said. He said he was probably from somewhere in the Ukraine."

O'Brien was writing furiously. "He say anything about the other guy?"

"Barney Ruble?" She laughed at that thought. "That's what Peter called him, Barney Ruble because he said he looked just like that character in *The Flintstones,* Barney Rubble. He said he had blond hair, a real big nose, and he didn't have a neck. The big difference, he said, was that Barney Rubble was smarter."

Russo chuckled pleasantly. "Peter sounds like quite a guy," she said, sounding so sincere that O'Brien almost believed her.

"Oh, he is, he is." In response to another question from Russo, with whom she was clearly bonding, she said that Peter told her the meetings were held in a lot of different places. "Like one night he went to this diner on Route 3 in New Jersey, a couple of times he had to go all the way out to Brighton Beach, once they met in this big room in the back of an old gas station. Then there was"—she grimaced, trying to remember—"Little Italy, I think, one night . . ."

Watching Natalie open up so completely to Laura Russo, Connor couldn't help but admire the younger woman's complete loyalty to Gradinsky. The fact was that during his own undergraduate years he'd known a dozen Natalie Speakmans, girls who maintained a fierce faith in their own vision of the world. In that world he usually played the part of the mirthful cynic, but a cynic who just might possibly be converted by the love of a nubile young woman. It worked for everyone involved. No hard feelings. Nobody got hurt. He looked at Natalie and considered it: Yep, he decided, under very different circumstances he could definitely play in her world.

And then he glanced at Laura Russo, leaning forward, intense, operating simultaneously on three, maybe four different levels. Doing so well exactly what they had been taught—she had become the person the subject needed her to be.

Russo glanced at him, indicating that it was his turn to ask a question. In his reverie he'd lost his connection to the interview. He had no idea what Russo had just asked. "Okay, good," he said, hoping that made some sense. "Did he ever tell you what they discussed at these meetings?"

Natalie nodded. "Yes, definitely. But he told me I couldn't discuss it with anyone. It was mostly economic negotiations, he said. They were talking about selling *billions* of dollars' worth of oil." She emphasized the word "billions," to ensure that it would not be mistaken for "millions."

"Billions," O'Brien repeated. "Wow, that's a lot." Russo kicked his calf with her foot under the table.

But the young woman agreed with him. "He used to joke about borrowing a few million. He said they'd never miss it."

"Natalie"—it was Russo's turn—"did Peter ever claim he was involved with the Mafia?"

She laughed. "Oh yeah, I forgot all about that. Yes, yes, he did. He told me he knew some of the boys." She put her index finger against the side of her nose and pushed it to the side. "If I knew what he meant." She waived the possibility away. "That was the one thing I really wondered about, Peter and the Mafia? What did he need them for?" She said the "them" with disdain.

They asked her several more questions, but that was pretty much the extent of her knowledge. It was likely she was telling the truth, that she didn't know where he was. They traded telephone numbers, and O'Brien and Russo walked her back to the garage.

Later, as they drove uptown, Russo asked, "You hear that thing she said? About borrowing a few million? You don't think he really did something that stupid, do you?"

O'Brien considered that. "Well, he might have considered it, but I don't think he was ever in a position to get his hands on that kind of money." They drove in silence for a few minutes, then O'Brien started laughing.

"What?" she asked.

"Newman? New man? That was the best you could do?"

"Well, it could've been true," Russo responded. "So now let me ask you a question. You think she's cute?"

He made a face. "She's all right, I guess." He wondered if there could possibly be a right answer to that question.

Russo agreed. "Well, I thought she was attractive." She cleared her throat. "Did you notice anything . . . you know, special or different about her?"

He thought about that. "No, I don't think so. Why?"

It was Russo's turn to laugh at men's insensitivity. At least this specific man. "Are you telling me you didn't even notice she was pregnant?"

ELEVEN

Benny Rags was hanging on the wall, screaming loudly for help, when Bobby walked into the Freemont Avenue Social Club. He was making so much noise that it wasn't even necessary for Bobby to turn up the volume on the radio. "Jesus H.," Bobby said, cringing at his yelling. "Please. Somebody turn that guy down."

Little Eddie put two fingers in his mouth and whistled, a loud, shrill bolt of sound. "Benny! Shut the fuck up or I swear to God, I'll leave you hanging there all day."

"Bobby, help me out here," Benny pleaded, trying desperately to maintain his dignity. "Guy's fucking crazy. Hey, get me down and I got a great shirt for you, no kidding."

"I don't know, Benny. I thought you liked hanging around with all of us." Bobby took off his hat and handed it to him. Instinctively Benny took it. "Here. Make yourself useful. And don't go getting it dirty."

Over the laughter Benny said, "That ain't funny. I swear to God I ain't never coming around here with clothes again. Go ahead, pay full price for all I care."

It turned out Benny had come around with a carton of velour zip-up tops. When Little Eddie demanded his money back for the cheap Banlon shirts he'd bought, Benny had the *cojones* to tell him that his business was strictly cash-and-carry. To which Little Eddie responded that if Benny didn't refund his cash, they were going to have to carry him out.

That forced Benny to gently remind Little Eddie that he had never actually paid cash for the shirts, so technically he wasn't entitled to a refund. Little Eddie told him that he wasn't interested in all that technical bullshit, he just wanted his money back. That was when Eddie picked up Benny and hung him by his shirt on the coat hook. For a short time Benny had flailed around like Road Runner just after discovering he'd run off a cliff into midair, but then he'd given up until Bobby walked in.

Bobby had been really surprised. Until that moment he hadn't believed that a coat hook was strong enough to support a person, even a skinny guy like Benny. But there he was, hanging there.

When Benny finally shut up, Georgie continued the story he'd been telling. "So like I was saying, Frankie Pits started a superstructure job. Gees, this is going back gotta be fifteen years ago, with all these guys from the union. I went on the job and I knocked them all off. I got my own guys, am I right? So Frankie says to me, 'You can't knock my men off.' I said to him, 'I can't knock your men off. Fucking watch me.' I forget who was delivering the concrete. Mileto maybe."

An old-timer, Nick Nunzio, who didn't come around that often, said, "Had to be Mileto or Amato fifteen years ago. Had to be."

"Whatever," Georgie continued. "Sos I called him up and I told him, 'No concrete.' Then I called Frankie and I tole him, 'Don't bother ordering no concrete for tomorrow, 'cause you ain't getting any.' That was the end of that. He seen I had a fucking stranglehold on him, so what the fuck could he do? I mean, you know what I mean?"

Bobby sat down next to Mickey Fists, who was using the butt of his cigarette to light his next one. "Don't you know that shit's bad for you?" Bobby said. "You trying to kill us all?"

"I'm a fucking attic, Bobby," Mickey agreed. "I can't help it."

"Addict, you mean," Bobby corrected him. "You're a fucking addict."

The Duke picked up Mickey's full ashtray and replaced it with a clean one on permanent loan from Rao's. "No, I'm an attic. When I was coming up, we all used to go up into my attic to smoke," he explained. "I swear to God, the smoke was so thick up there the motherfucking rats just rolled over and suffocated, that's how bad it was. That's what my lungs are like now, so that makes me a fucking attic."

Lenny showed his approval by punching him in the shoulder. "Fucking guy," he said, impressed. And then he imitated him: "I'm an attic." Finally he pointed at Mickey's Camels. "Gimme one a those."

The Duke returned with the cappuccino. "Who's in?" Tony Cupcakes asked, desperate for a card game. Vito V wanted in, and Georgie, Eddie, Mickey. "Bobby, you in?"

He shook his head. "Later." Bobby sat there quietly, sipping his cappuccino, leaning over to look at Mickey's hand, laughing at the right times, occasionally throwing a funny line into the conversation—once he glanced over his shoulder to ask, "So, Benny, how they hanging?"—but mostly savoring the comfort of this place and the companionship of these people. There was a level of friendship and trust, honor and pride, that he had never experienced before in his life. Bobby had been a good athlete, he'd been second-team all-Catholic league in baseball and lettered in baseball, basketball, and soccer at St. Mac's, so he had experienced the euphoria of being part of a successful, winning group, but this was much more than that. Much more. He was surrounded by people who had made it in a tough, tough world. People who were not afraid to break rules or heads. These were the kind of people you trusted with your freedom and your life. A bunch of very good guys going through life together. Even the Duke and crazy Benny Rags played their roles perfectly.

Fast Lenny spun a card into the middle of the table. "Stick that baby up your behind," he said to the table, laying down his winning hand. And then he asked Bobby, "So whattya want to do about that thing?"

That thing to which Lenny was referring was the ten thousand gallons of fuel. Bobby didn't have an answer yet. "I don't know, open a gas station maybe." He was definitely going to have to do something, there was no question about that. When Franklin Washington Jefferson Lincoln Roosevelt whatever didn't show up to drive the truck, there was a pretty good chance that the delivery would be canceled. But Bobby doubted that. There was just too much money involved to leave it in somebody else's hands. And it was real easy to hire another driver.

Grabbing the truck would be simple, but then what? What do you do with ten thousand gallons of gasoline? You just couldn't drive into a gas station and ask if they needed ten thousand gallons of high-test. You couldn't use it yourself—even if you and all your friends were driving '58 Cadillacs, it would take years to use all that gas. And it wasn't the kind of merchandise So Solly could stick in his back room until he found a customer.

But Bobby suspected that he might be able to get more out of that load than gasoline. Potentially that truck was a direct connection to the Russians. What he needed more than cash were some answers—which then might be turned into a lot more cash. There was no question in Bobby's mind that Cosentino was doing business with them. It certainly seemed possible that the Russians had the professor. And nobody wanted to talk about it. Even Lenny's Russian connection had faded big-time. These might be completely different Russians, but they spoke the language—money—so they knew the right people.

Cooperation was the wave of the future, and people like him were either going to rise with it or get drowned by it. The one thing he knew for sure was that this load was owned by the Russians. If he was smart enough, it could be his passport into their world. He had nothing to lose, and the least he would gain was ten thousand gallons of gas. And it had occurred to him that the first sound of "dollar" was *da.*

When the hand ended, Little Eddie had gone to the bathroom. On his way back to the table he had this great idea. Hanging on the back of the bathroom door was a dartboard with six long-nosed darts embedded in it. Grabbing those darts, Little Eddie stood eight feet in front of Benny Rags and warned him, "Don't fucking move!"

"You're fucking crazy, Eddie!" Benny screamed at him. "That ain't funny. C'mon, somebody help me."

Eddie's first throw bounced off the wall about a foot to the right of Benny's head. His second throw was short and again off to the right. "Shit," Eddie muttered disgustedly, then ordered, "Hey, Benny, spread your legs wide as you can."

Benny's eyes opened wider than a hooker's purse on Christmas Eve. "Hey! Hey!"

Lenny was laughing so hard he was having trouble breathing. Bobby yelled above the laughter, "Hey, I get it. I know, I know. You're William Don't Tell 'em Nothing!"

Lenny suggested loudly, "I'd spread 'em if I were you, Benny."

Eddie closed one eye and reached back with the dart two, three, four times. The tip of his tongue poked out of his mouth. He aimed right between Benny's legs and . . .

Benny Rags was pushing against the wall with his hands and feet as hard as he could. He was screaming, "Don't you fucking dare." Finally his shirt ripped open and he dropped straight to the ground. He covered his head with his hands as the dart kind of drooped way over his head, bounced off the wall, and landed right in his lap. He grabbed it and angrily heaved it sideways at Eddie, who was laughing so hard he had to rest his hands on his knees. The dart flew well wide of its target.

Benny was terrified. He scrambled to his feet and took out his wallet. "Here's your fucking money," he said, throwing two twenties at Eddie.

"Oh man, I can't breathe," Eddie gasped, trying to stop laughing long enough to catch a breath.

"It ain't that funny," Benny Rags said, picking up his carton of velour tops and heading for the door. "Fucking bastard ruined a good shirt."

Eddie picked a dart off the floor to throw at Benny, but he was

laughing too hard. The laughter continued for a long time, reinforced two or three times by people imitating Eddie telling Benny to
spread his legs. "I swear, Eddie," Mickey said, "I thought that was it
for me. I couldn't fucking breathe. I thought I was going to die."

When the laughter finally ended, Bobby carefully laid out his plan
for the night. He went through it in detail. Who was going to do
what when. And while there was some complaining, eventually
everyone went along with it. A few of the people didn't exactly understand Bobby's reasoning, but Bobby was Bobby, and that was
good enough for them.

According to the truck driver, who was lying in a ditch under a
blanket of leaves and now covered by the first snowfall of the season,
the load was scheduled to leave the Staten Island storage terminal at
about nine o'clock. That would get the truck to the first gas station
in Queens after it closed at eleven, which was the way the owner
wanted it. Bobby figured that by the time the dispatcher realized that
the driver wasn't showing up and found a replacement, it would be a
whole lot later than that. But just to be certain, they got to the terminal a little after eight.

Lenny was driving the car. Tony would drive the truck. Bobby
would close the deal and Eddie was there just in case. Just in case of
anything. Vito followed them in the backup car.

None of them had ever been near an oil storage depot before, so
they didn't know what to expect. That was okay. Bobby's plan did
not require gaining access to the tank farm. With millions of gallons
of highly flammable fuel and valuable equipment just sitting there,
he assumed the front gate would be heavily guarded. And if the side
gates weren't manned, at least they would be locked and security
cameras would be scanning the entire area. Knowing the route that
the truck was going to follow, he planned to wait until it got clear of
the depot before making a move.

He assumed wrong. The facility was surrounded by a six-foot-high
chain-link fence that was not even topped with barbed wire. The
light posts were set about twenty-five yards apart, but they were the

old type; they still used dull incandescent bulbs rather than the much brighter neon. Even then several of the lights weren't working, having either been broken or simply burned out and not been replaced. Rather than illuminating the yard, about the only purpose these lights served was to make themselves visible. The front entrance was open wider than a bookie on Super Bowl Sunday. The gate itself was tied back. There was a guardhouse, but there was a light on inside, so it was easy to see that there was no one there. It was unbelievable, there wasn't a guard in sight. And if there were any surveillance cameras, no one could spot them. And these were people used to finding the cameras. "How could this be?" Lenny wondered. "These people must be nuts."

"Well, big guy," Cupcakes pointed out, "it ain't like people are coming in off the street to steal five gallons of gas. How many people you know got their own tank truck?"

Bobby wasn't comfortable with the situation. If there was a Bible of organized crime, the First Commandment would probably be "Nothing is that easy." Deals, women, life, everything has a price. And to his experienced eye this looked way too easy. So while Tony and Lenny waited in the car, Bobby and Little Eddie strolled through the front gate, easy as tourists walking into a theme restaurant.

They walked into a world of shadows. It was as if they were moving across a checkerboard, from light square to dark square. Long fingers of light from the posts on the perimeter poked between the tanks to illuminate dull gray rectangles of gravel. When they stepped into that light, they cast their own long shadows that faded into the darkness. And when they moved into the shadows, they might just as easily have been walking in a cave. But even in that darkness it was difficult not to be awed by the size of the tanks. Walls of steel towered above them. "Gees," Bobby said, "I feel like fucking Gulliver."

"What's that?" Eddie asked, looking around. "Tell you what, these things are pretty fucking big," he added, greatly impressed. Then, always the consummate professional, he decided, "You know, you could drop a stiff into one of these things and nobody'd ever find it."

The storage facility was laid out in a grid. The tanks were aligned in long rows, front to back, side to side, equidistant from each other. In the darkness it was sort of like being in a maze; no matter which way they walked, everything looked pretty much the same. It was a world almost completely devoid of color. All of the tanks were painted the same pedestrian white, the ground was covered with blue-gray gravel. Those patches of night sky visible between the tanks were as grim as the bottom of a burned pot. The only actual color in the whole place was the red airplane warning lights on the top of the tanks in the distance, blinking as brightly as Rudolph's nose.

Bobby's jobs had taken him to a great variety of places, from the back room of a run-down strip club on 42nd Street to the sixty-fifth-floor suite of the CEO of one of America's most successful brokerage houses. He'd been on a yacht in the Caribbean and inside a tenement in Spanish Harlem. He'd been in hospital rooms and locker rooms, factories and showrooms; he knew how to move around the private rooms in the terminals at JFK as easily as the stalls at the Fulton Fish Market. Wherever it was, he'd been there, from the Top of the Sixes to Calvary Cemetery out in Queens. But this was one of the most unusual places Bobby had ever been. It felt like he was out for a stroll on some distant, mostly deserted planet.

The tank farm appeared to be completely unguarded. At one point they saw a man about seventy yards away walking purposefully between two storage tanks. He was wearing a yellow hard hat. The man spotted them, but rather than being alarmed or even curious, he waved pleasantly to them with the clipboard he was carrying and continued on his way.

"This place gives me the creeps," Eddie decided. "Come on, Bobby, let's get the fuck outta here."

Bobby ignored him. With the excitement of an explorer who had just discovered a world of potential riches, Bobby was simply taking it all in. Later, when he had more time, he would try to figure out how to exploit it. Where there was money to be made, there was a way. Suddenly, though, as they moved into a patch of dim light, they heard people talking. Then laughing. They stopped and listened. But the voices were much too far away to be intelligible. "Come on," Bobby said.

They walked toward the voices. As they rounded a storage tank, three rows over they saw the spotlight illuminating a tanker truck being filled. The truck that brings the gas to the gas station was getting gas. Bobby smiled at that thought. They stood in the shadows and watched. Two men were standing next to the tanker, both of them holding clipboards. One of them was wearing a baseball cap, the other one a yellow hard hat. "That's got to be our truck," Bobby said.

After standing there for several more minutes watching absolutely nothing happen, Eddie decided, "This is certainly a big thrill."

They returned to Lenny's car and waited. Bobby actually closed his eyes and caught a few minutes' sleep. Finally, at about eleven o'clock, preceded by two long blasts from the air horn, the fully loaded tanker barreled through the front gate. Lenny gave the truck a big jump—there was only one good road out of the storage yard—then took off after him. Vito V followed close behind.

It took less than a minute to grab the truck. *Ba-da-bing* . . . The driver stopped at a traffic light. Before he realized what was happening, much less had the chance to get on his radio to call for help, Bobby was standing on the step pointing a gun at his head . . . *ba-da-boom*. The driver immediately put up his hands and yelled to Bobby, "Whatever you say." He wasn't about to risk his life for a load of gas.

Tony slid behind the wheel. If it had an engine and tires, Tony could drive it. Eddie tied the compliant trucker's hands behind his back and put him in Vito's car. The only thing the guy said was, "I haven't seen nothing and I don't know nothing." Vito would ride around for a while, then drop him. Tony was going to park the truck up in Hunts Point, near Yankee Stadium.

Bobby's first stop was the gas station on Queens Boulevard. Lenny stayed in the car, parking around a corner to make sure that nobody in the station could identify his car. The station was closed. Bobby banged on the front door. Eventually an inside door opened and a shining bald head appeared. "I'm closed," the bald head yelled.

"You expecting a fuel delivery?" Bobby yelled right back.

The bald man was yawning as he unlocked the front door. By the time it dawned on him that there was no tanker sitting outside waiting to be unloaded, it was too late: Bobby was inside, one hand deep in his jacket pocket. The bald guy had been in the business long enough to know what was going on. "Hey, pally," he explained calmly, "I don't keep much cash around here." He started moving toward his desk.

One summer in high school Bobby had pumped gas for dating money. He knew how it all worked. Customers paid mostly by credit card. If the guy was lucky, there was two hundred bucks in the register. He would pay for the delivery by check—no way he was going to keep that much cash around. It didn't matter what brand of gas he put in his tanks, whatever the sign out front said; nobody knows the difference, and it was all pretty much the same product anyway. And he also knew that the owner kept a baseball bat, a steel rod, or maybe even a gun behind his desk for just such nighttime visits as this one. Running a gas station that stayed open at night was a tough business that attracted tough guys. "Hey," he ordered sharply, "stay the fuck away from the desk. Just stand right there. I want you to answer me some questions."

The bald guy took a deep breath. He was prepared to be robbed, not answer questions. "What?" he asked. He seemed a lot more angry than frightened.

Bobby was holding loosely to the butt of his pistol, but he saw no reason to show it. The guy was cooperating, there wasn't any reason to escalate the situation. For the first time Bobby got a real good look at the guy. There was something strange about him, something weird, besides the fact that a ball of fat hung limp under his chin like a suspended flowerpot, but Bobby couldn't figure out precisely what it was. "You the owner?"

He nodded, his several chins slightly trailing the rest of his head up and down. "Yeah, so?"

That answer surprised him. Not necessarily what he said, just the way he said it. He'd pretty much figured the owner had to be Russian, but this guy was pure New York. His accent came right off the city streets. That just didn't fit. Bobby was still trying to figure out the scam the Russians were running; his best guess was that they were stealing gas from the terminal and delivering it to gas stations they owned, or selling it to other Russians. It was basic economics: get free, sell high. One hundred percent profit. That scenario made a lot of sense to him.

But this guy wasn't Russian, and back at the terminal it didn't look like they were busting anybody's balls. "Who are you buying this load from?"

The guy smiled at that question. "Who the fuck you think you are to ask me that?"

Bobby took his hand out of his pocket and let his gun hang at his side. "Well, see, actually it isn't just me that's asking the questions. I got my friends with me." He held up the gun for inspection, purposefully not aiming it at the guy. "You know, Mr. Smith and Mr. Wesson. So you tell me, who do you want to talk to? Me or my friends?"

The man ran his hand thoughtfully over his impressively bald head. Bobby couldn't remember ever seeing such a perfectly bald head, with the possible exception of Mr. Clean on the commercials. The guy's skin was stretched tautly over his skull, and Bobby guessed it was being pulled tight by the weight of the fat under his chin. He looked really carefully at the guy's head: There wasn't one single dot of stubble fighting through. And then he realized what was so strange about him: The guy had a glass eye. His left eyeball didn't move. It was locked in place, precisely in the middle of his eye socket, staring straight ahead. The guy's right eyeball was darting from side to side, maybe looking for an advantage, but that left eye just bored into Bobby. He'd heard stories about people putting an informer's head in a vise and tightening it until his eyes popped out of his head, and he knew that Sammy Davis Jr. had a glass eye, but he had never seen one this close. It was almost mesmerizing. "You the law?" the bald guy with the one glass eye asked.

It was Bobby's turn to smile. "Do I look like the law?"

"Legally, if I ask you, you gotta tell me. Otherwise nothing I say counts. You know that, right?"

Bobby was getting bored with this game. "What are you, Perry fucking Mason? I gotta tell you, you're starting to piss me off now." He waved a cautionary finger. The guy's right eye followed it. The left eye didn't move. It just kept staring. That was disconcerting. "I promise you, you don't want to do that. So I'm asking you nice, who you buying this load from?"

The guy shrugged. "Some Russians. They come around with the product and they give me a good price. That's the whole deal."

"What do you mean 'some Russians'? Gimme some names."

"You're kidding me, right? Boris and Morris. What the fuck do I know names? They're selling gas, I'm buying gas. What else do I got to know?"

"So they give you a real good deal?"

"Fuck yes, they do." The bald guy sighed in frustration. "So is this a robbery or what?"

Bobby was honest with him. "I haven't decided yet. So how do they afford to do it? What kind of scam they running?"

"This is fucking bullshit," the bald guy said, moving toward his desk.

Bobby reached him in two steps and shoved the barrel of his gun under the guy's chin, pushing his head backward. "You wouldn't be the first," he warned.

The bald guy with one glass eye finally got the message. "Oh, wait a second. Who you with?" he asked.

"I told you, Smith and Wesson." Bobby held the gun there. For the first time he saw fear in the man's eye. "No names, remember? The next time you open your mouth it better be answers coming out. Got it?" He pushed the barrel so deep into the guy's chin that the front sight disappeared completely into layers of fat, like a rock sinking into quicksand. "Got it?" he repeated.

The man nodded. Gently he grasped the gun with his thumb and forefinger and moved it away.

"Now, tell me the story."

"Don't flatter me, there's no big story. I mind my own business. Guy comes in here one day and wants to sell me a few thousand gallons thirty cents cheaper than I can get anywhere else. Pay after delivery. You don't got to be no fucking genius to know that's a good deal. I'm an independent. I don't have no contract with a brand. I buy on the open market. The truck shows up, the gas is good, I pay him, everybody's happy. He comes by every couple of weeks for like a year now."

"What's your name?"

"Beck. Mike Beck."

Bobby lowered his gun and took a couple of steps backward. He moved to Beck's left, partially out of his eyesight. "Okay, so let me ask you this, Mike. How the fuck can they afford to do that?"

"Hey, I don't need to look a gift horse up the ass to know there's some shit there. Truth is I don't give a flying fuck. Maybe it's my good looks. I don't ask them no questions, they don't give me no answers. Everybody goes home happy."

"Yeah, but Mikey, just between you, me, Smith, and Wesson, you got to have an idea. A bright guy like you, you didn't get all this"— he indicated the gas station—"by not paying attention. So come on, what do you think?"

Beck eyed Bobby, trying to figure the upside. "I don't know for sure, I'm telling you this straight up. But if they ain't draining it out of the tanks, then the only thing I can figure is that they're not paying no taxes on it. I mean, figure it out, what else could it be? People don't know it, but there's like seventy cents taxes on every gallon you put in your car. If you don't got to pay that"—he exhaled in admiration—"that's a lot of fucking moolah."

Cheating the government? Now, there was a concept Bobby could appreciate. "Those fucking commies," he said with great respect. "Didn't take them long to figure out capitalism, did it?" He actually laughed at the thought. Waving his gun casually, he asked, "So how do they do it?"

"Magic. How the fuck should I know?"

While listening to the guy, Bobby was running numbers in his head. Without knowing the details—how many gallons times how much per gallon they were putting in their pocket—it was impossible to reach any kind of valid conclusion. But if the Russians really did have access to a substantial amount of gasoline and had figured out a way to sell it without paying taxes on it, then they had discovered the mother lode. Whatever the number was, it had a lot of zeroes backing it up. Millions of dollars, easy. Tens of millions. "Sorry to have to tell you this, Mike, but tonight's delivery is going to be a little late."

"Like how late is late?"

"Probably never." These were potentially the kinds of numbers that mob guys only dreamed about on Christmas Eve. This is incredible, Bobby thought. We're busting our humps to earn a few thousand bucks, while these commie motherfuckers are making millions. Things were beginning to make sense.

"Shit," Beck muttered. "You're killing me here, pal. You're making me buy from those legitimate bastards. Those no-good fucking thieves."

Bobby laughed. "Hey, don't blame me. You lay down with hookers, you're gonna get fucked." Beck did not appreciate the joke. "One more thing I want to know," Bobby continued. "Those Russians who show up to get paid? Tell me about them."

"Ugly fuckers," he said, shrugging. "A big guy and a small guy. The big guy's got this scarred-up face . . ."

"Yeah, I know," Bobby said. "I know. Lemme guess. I bet they're driving like a gray Firebird too, right?" Small world, small fucking world.

"You got 'em."

Bobby shook his head. If all this was true, it was no fucking wonder why Cosentino went outside his crew for this job. He didn't want people to know what he was doing. It was amazing. When it comes to a couple thousand dollars, he does the right thing: He shares like a good guy, the way he's supposed to. But when there's millions of dollars up for grabs, he wants to keep it for himself. Maybe he'd share a few bucks with his people. Unfuckingbelievable.

One thing he still couldn't figure out was exactly how the professor fit into the whole operation. But he figured he must be getting close. Cosentino was doing business with the Russians, it made sense for him to have a Russian speaker he could trust. So what happened to make the professor disappear? Maybe the Russians happened.

Bobby put his gun back in his pocket. "Hey, Mike," he asked nicely, "you know my name?"

Beck shook his head from side to side, his chin swaying gently.

"Know where I live?"

Again Beck shook his head.

"Think about that before you go shooting off your mouth to anybody. Know what I mean?" For an instant he considered cleaning out the cash register, then just as quickly decided against it. Holding up gas stations wasn't his style. He didn't see any reason to make the bald guy with one glass eye and the hanging chin of Babylon's life any tougher. So he backed out the door, being careful to stay to Mike's blind side. He watched Beck watching him through the front window. Now, that's funny, he thought, he's keeping an eye on me—which, considering his condition, was the very best he was capable of doing.

No question, that glass eye creeped him out. Walking back rapidly to Lenny's car, he ran through as many applicable phrases as he could think of: Keep your eye on the ball. The eye has it. Eye eye, sir. Well, that was two eyes. She's the apple of my eye. By the time he got back to the car, he was stuck on An eye for an eye.

Back in the car, all he told Lenny was that the Russians were running some kind of gas scam. That was absolutely true, if not complete. Not telling Lenny wasn't a business decision—he wasn't trying to get over on him—but until he knew a lot more, he decided to keep quiet. He didn't need people talking. They drove straight up to the parking lot in the North Bronx where the tanker was supposed to be dropped. It was after 1 a.m. by the time they got there.

The lot was packed with trucks of all types, although only a few of the cabs were rigged to trailers. It was pretty much a transit station, a secure place for independent truckers to park for a couple of days while waiting for their load. But unlike the fuel terminal, this place had extensive security. It was surrounded by an eight-foot-high chain-link fence topped with the new kind of razor wire. Nobody was going to climb over that fence without leaving a large slab of skin as a souvenir. High-intensity neon lights spaced on poles about twenty-five feet apart were directed inside the lot, and scanning cameras were mounted on every third pole. The front gate was locked and manned by a security guard, who responded to Bobby's shouts for some help.

Again Lenny had parked out of sight.

Bobby saw immediately that this guard took his job seriously. He was a young, good-looking black kid. His rent-a-cop uniform was immaculate, down to the sharp crease in his pants. The guard approached the gate with a professional smile on his face and a steel club in his hand. "Yes, sir?"

Standing in shadows outside the locked gate, Bobby informed the guard that the tanker scheduled to arrive about that time wasn't coming. "So you just hold on to that money," he said, assuming the guard was supposed to pay the driver. The guard wasn't sure what was going on. Without making a big show of it, he took a couple of steps backward, spread his legs a comfortable distance apart, and began gently tapping the club into the palm of his left hand. There wasn't too much Bobby could do to change the situation. They were on *Candid Camera;* he wasn't about to pull a gun on the guy just to get a few answers. "Now, calm down, okay? There's just a couple of things I want to ask you."

The guard stood there impassively.

Bobby reached into his back pocket. The guard tensed but did not make a move. Bobby pulled out his wallet and took a fifty-dollar bill out of it. He curled it up and stuck it in the fence. The guard didn't move to take it. "Whattya need?" he asked.

"Like I said, just a little information. These people who own this truck. How many deliveries like this do they do every week?" Bobby was just trying to get some idea of the scope of the operation. He was guessing two or three runs a week.

The guard considered the question. "I'm not supposed to give out that kind of information," he said, but he said it with a lack of conviction.

"Yeah, I know," Bobby said, holding high a second fifty-dollar bill. "But I figure you can go back inside and rewind this tape so nobody sees this." He curled the second fifty and stuck it in the gate. They were standing about fifteen feet apart, separated by the fence. From a distance it might have looked a bit like an Old West shoot-out— except it was negotiations at ten paces.

"They run three trucks out of here," the guard finally blurted out. "Every truck makes at least four or five runs a week." Then he volunteered, "They use a lot of different drivers. They don't want anybody knowing too much about their business."

"You got a phone number for them, don't you? I mean, you're supposed to call them when the trucks show up."

The guard shook his head. "I can't give that to you."

Bobby stuck another fifty in the fence.

"I can't," the guard said.

"All right," Bobby agreed, "that's okay." He made no move to take back his money. "Here's what I want you to do. I want you to call that number and tell them somebody took their truck. Tell them the delivery didn't get made tonight. Then you tell them that if they want their truck back, they should call this number tomorrow around noon." Bobby always carried a pen and scrap paper in his pocket. He wrote down the number of the phone in the social club. There was no way the Russians could trace the location of that number. It was bootstrapped, meaning the calls to that number were relayed from the original phone listed in the name of an old Chinese lady who lived on Doyers Street in Chinatown. It was the same system used by every bookmaking operation. "Now, you sure you got that?" Bobby was always careful to make sure his messages were clearly understood.

The guard repeated the message.

"That's good," Bobby said, sticking a last fifty in the fence. Bobby turned to leave, then paused. The guard hadn't moved. Bobby pointed to the security cameras. The guard nodded. "It's all good," Bobby said to himself as he walked away, "all good."

It was almost four o'clock in the morning when Bobby finally got home. Ronnie and Angela were long asleep. He looked in on his daughter, who was lost in dreamland. Ronnie stirred when he sat on the side of the bed and started getting undressed, but said nothing. She'd stopped asking him about his days, and more pointedly his nights, years earlier. She had pretty much figured out his pattern: If he took a shower before getting into bed, he'd been with another woman. If he simply undressed and got into bed, he'd been working. The truth was that in either case she was no longer curious about the details.

He sort of shimmied across the bed and curled himself up against her body. She barely moved. She was wearing flannel pajamas, which he really hated. The feel of a woman's skin still thrilled him, even his wife's. He cupped his hand over her flannel-covered breast and wrestled with sleep, wondering how it was possible to be so close to a person yet feel so far away.

Most civilians probably have some difficulty blending their work life and home life, but usually there is some overlap and they can talk about it with their wife or husband, and that person can at least relate to some aspects of it. But in this business—and this is equally true for people working in law enforcement—people have to live two completely different lives. There is no overlap between life with the Family and life with the family, and there was very little about life outside the home that a wiseguy could discuss with his wife. There was a real sense of discordance when either world intruded upon the other.

Bobby lay there with his eyes closed, but his mind was doing laps at Indianapolis. He knew he'd grabbed something big by the tail, but he couldn't be certain exactly what it was he was holding on to. Whatever it was, it was definitely a lot bigger than he had originally believed. And it was a lot more important than finding some missing teacher. The problem was that the bigger things were, the more dangerous they tended to be. The one thing he knew for sure was that he needed to be careful, real careful, that this thing didn't suddenly turn around and bite him.

Somehow, though, the professor was in the middle of all of this. And the fact that Cosentino needed him to be found by Thursday night was pretty strong evidence that something important was going down that night. He wondered, how would his life be affected if he woke up Friday morning and the professor hadn't been found? Or maybe, what would it cost him if he didn't find the guy? That was only one of the many questions it was impossible to answer without knowing a lot more facts, like the value of a friendship when a million dollars is involved.

Sometimes it seemed to Bobby that the bed must have no right side, because whichever side Ronnie got up on, it was always like it was the wrong one. But she was in a particularly surly mood the next morning, which was just about the last thing he needed. He paid the minimal attention necessary to know when to agree and nod his head, which he did convincingly. Something about visiting his parents on the holidays, problems with her car, play dates for Angela. He caught some of the familiar phrases—"the things I do for you," "no consideration for anyone else," "have to do everything around here myself," "don't know what it means to give," and the big one, "she's your daughter too!"—and resisted the urge to respond. He was smart enough to know that there were some battles he couldn't win if he had George S. Patton and the entire fucking U.S. Army on his side.

He still kissed her good-bye when he left, though, and most of the time he still meant it. Comfort counted.

The Duke, Little Eddie, and the kid, Vito V, were the only people in the club when he walked in. He rarely got there that early, and the thin shafts of sunlight angling through the exposed top of the front windows gave the place an unusually cold feeling, but it still had that warm familiarity about it. The *Daily News* and the *Post* were lying on the card table, and as he waited for the phone call, he read both of them. It was a slow news day; even the regular bullshit was bullshit. That was one of the things he loved so much about New York: It was always the same but constantly different.

Every few minutes he glanced at the clock. When the Russians called, he intended to set up a meet for later that day at some public place. Probably the Tic Toc. Eddie would be his backup, Lenny the outside man. He wasn't going to play tough guy, no threats, no demands. The thing that these guys had that he wanted was information. In return he could offer them their fuel truck—and his cooperation. He knew the streets and he had hooks into some people who knew some people.

Eddie was trying to figure out the Jumble in the *News* when the phone rang. It was a few minutes after noon. Mostly out of habit now, the moment it rang he immediately looked at the Duke to see if he responded. Just a little quiver was all the evidence he needed. But as always, the Duke didn't move.

Bobby answered it. "Yeah?"

In a thick Russian accent a voice asked, "Bobby?"

Bobby froze. In an instant it seemed like every nerve in his body was vibrating. They knew his name. They knew his motherfucking name. "What?" he asked.

The Russian said calmly, "So listen, we got your fucking message."

"So?"

The Russian laughed. "So now we send you our message." There was a brief pause, and then he heard a single, long, and desperately tortured scream. It seemed to last forever, and the sound ripped through his body. It was beyond a cry for help, beyond anything he'd ever heard before. This was a plea for a quick death.

When it subsided, the Russian spoke again. "Hey, Bobby, you go fuck yourself, hokay?" And then he hung up.

Bobby stood there holding on to the phone until Eddie took it from his hand and gently put it back on the hook. "What the fuck was that?" he asked.

TWELVE

Hey, hey, come on in here," Slattery shouted to O'Brien and Russo as they walked past his office. "You guys gotta hear this." Even before they'd settled on his couch, he hit the play button on the reel-to-reel.

"Jesus H.," a familiar voice said. "Please. Somebody turn that guy down."

Connor smiled at Laura. "Sounds like your boyfriend." He started to ask Slattery, "How come you—"

He was interrupted by a loud, shrill whistle, then somebody shouting, "Benny! Shut the fuck up or I swear to God I'll leave you hanging there all day."

Slattery was sitting on the top of the desk, next to the recorder. "That's Eddie LaRocca," he said. "Sounds like they had some guy hanging up on something."

Then an unfamiliar voice. "Bobby, help me out here. Guy's fucking crazy. Hey, get me down and I got a great shirt for you, no kidding."

"I guess that's Benny," Russo said.

Two other agents passing the office heard the recorded whistle and stuck their heads in the door to listen. One of them looked questioningly at Slattery and pointed at the recorder. "Bobby Blue Eyes," Slattery replied loudly, "over at the Freemont. Come on in here. Listen."

Bobby's voice was heard again. "I don't know, Benny. I thought you liked hanging around with all of us." And after a brief pause, once again, "Here. Make yourself useful. And don't go getting it dirty." Then the social club erupted in laughter.

Slattery guessed at the action. "He must've given him something."

To O'Brien most of this sounded more like it was taking place inside a college fraternity house than in an organized crime social club. Boys will be killers, he thought. In that ever-important category of level of maturity, it reminded him of the time they'd hidden one of his frat brothers inside a folded convertible sofa, then ordered a pledge to open it up. When that brother jumped out, they were afraid the pledge was going to die from shock. That was funny; but what these guys were doing was just cruel.

He eased back deep into Slattery's comfortable couch and stretched, stifling a yawn by biting down hard on the inside of his cheek. You never want the boss to see you falling asleep at the office. But he had to admit it, he was tired; tired and frustrated as hell. And his eardrums were still vibrating from the night before.

He and Russo had spent the night at Off Limits. Ironically O'Brien had never been inside a strip club, but Russo had spent considerable time in the clubs while working undercover. *Visiting* them, as she had forcefully pointed out. At the time, the strip clubs in New York had not yet become socially acceptable. For the most part they were still exactly what they were intended to be: the place where money went to meet sex. O'Brien had just never felt comfortable being ripped off to watch women take off their clothes. He preferred the pleasures of his own apartment.

But Russo knew her way around clubs in Chicago, Florida, and Vegas. Strip clubs and the mob went together like rock stars and supermodels. It was the perfect business for organized crime: mostly cash—and even better, many of the men paying that cash did not want anyone to know they had been there. So all of the rules could be relaxed a little. Actually, a lot.

Off Limits was one of the first upscale clubs in New York. The bouncers wore tuxedos. The show room itself was dark, with pin spots lighting the semicircular stage in front. There were two poles on the stage, and as O'Brien and Russo walked in, two girls were riding them to the sound track of *Urban Cowboy,* which was blasting out of the two huge speakers on either side of the stage. The entire room was vibrating. O'Brien knew that one of the performers was undressed as a cowgirl because she was still wearing a ten-gallon hat and a quarter-inch rhinestone G-string, while the other girl had apparently been a nurse, as she had on a white G-string and a long stethoscope which seemed to disappear between her breasts. Watching them perform, O'Brien whispered to Russo, "Wow, I think I saw them on *Star Search.*" And then he corrected himself. "Or maybe it was *Police Search.*"

There were several doors around the room. Russo said into his ear, "They go to private rooms."

O'Brien was gamely trying to keep his eyes off the stage, but losing. "Who does?" he asked.

"The doors," she said emphatically. "Hey, stay with me, Agent O'Brien. Playtime later."

He heard the irritation in her voice. For one of the few times in his life he really didn't know what to say. Connor O'Brien was not a shy man. He had dated a lot of lovely women, but in all his travels he had never encountered a woman with the mountainous, perfectly sculpted breasts of the nurse. He was in awe of her physical geography. When he finally looked at Russo, he was very careful to look directly into her eyes, never letting his gaze fall any lower than her nose.

It suddenly occurred to him that she might be feeling somewhat intimidated by the girls on the stage. Trying to find something supportive to say to her, he whispered, in retrospect quite foolishly, "That's a great blouse you're wearing."

Another thing he had never seen in all his travels was the look she gave him in response to that, which registered somewhere between "pathetic loser" and "immature moron." Russo just shook her head in disbelief and moved across the room. O'Brien sheepishly followed close behind.

Off Limits was a little more than half-full, with most of the customers as close to the stage as legally permitted. As the dancers moved to the foot of the stage, these men slipped bills into the cowgirl's hatband and the nurse's G-string. In the dimly lit back of the room other strategically dressed women were socializing with customers and occasionally would escort one of the men through one of those doors. The bar was to the left, and it was being tended by two pneumatically breasted women wearing low-cut lacy bras. The waitresses, dressed out of the Frederick's of Hollywood catalog, moved around the room carrying drinks and bottles on trays balanced on their bare shoulders. Properly chastened, O'Brien made a great effort to keep his eyes on the bottles, and for the first time in his life he noticed the undeniably erotic shape of a champagne bottle.

They went through a set of black double doors under an exit sign into a corridor. The corridor was about as bright as dusk. "Boy," Connor said softly to Russo, "they must save a bundle on their electric bill." A door on the right was the men's room, indicated by the silhouette of a cherub peeing, while the door facing it bore the outline of two pendulous breasts. There were four pay phones on the wall to their right. As O'Brien suspected, there were no numbers on these phones. Taped to the wall around the phones and on the privacy screens were numerous business cards, some of them featuring photographs of women in seductive poses, most of them having only one name—O'Brien counted three Monas—but all of them boasting "out calls."

Both agents, armed with several dollars in quarters, picked up pay phone handsets and dialed a special number at AT&T. This service was used primarily by installers and repairmen to check their work, but when necessary, law enforcement agencies also used it. After a series of clicks and switches their calls were answered automatically. Within seconds a computerized voice reported the number of the phone from which they were calling. According to Bell Telephone's records, six telephones connected to eight lines had been installed in Off Limits. One of them had been used to call the professor, causing him to leave his apartment and disappear. That call had not been made from either of the first two pay phones. O'Brien and Russo hung up and moved to the next pair of phones.

One of those phones was in use by a large man wearing what was obviously a cheap blond wig. He was whispering into the receiver, but O'Brien could hear him negotiating. The man sensed O'Brien behind him, turned, and looked at him with real disgust. O'Brien took a few steps backward and leaned against the opposite wall, waiting while Russo finished checking the other phone.

She was leaning forward into the booth waiting for a response from the phone company. Two men came out of the restroom and walked between O'Brien and Russo. Almost compulsively they examined Russo's form. She'd spent enough time in these clubs to know exactly how to dress on the proper side of the line without making any kind of obvious statement. She was wearing a tastefully short skirt which showed off just enough of her well-shaped legs to be fashionable rather than provocative, ending slightly south of mid-calf, sheer stockings or panty hose—O'Brien couldn't be certain, but his bet was on stockings—and a cream satin blouse. The top three buttons of the blouse were opened to reveal the swell of her own cute breasts. She was carrying a trendy black purse, and O'Brien wondered if any of the men looking at her had any concept of the firepower inside that bag.

O'Brien watched the men watching Russo, while trying to project an attitude of protective independence. Admittedly he found himself following their eyes to her body. Within the realm of reality, he decided, she was fine.

The bewigged man hung up, hitched up his pants, and walked back into the club without looking at O'Brien. As Russo stepped back from the phone and shook her head, he picked up the fourth phone and dialed the service number. It took only a few seconds to confirm that the professor had not been called from this phone. So whoever had called him had not used a public phone, meaning most likely it was not a customer who had called him.

Russo guessed the other phones were in the office—that one probably had several lines—and in the strippers' dressing room. O'Brien raised his eyebrows playfully and smirked when she mentioned the dressing room. She dismissed him coldly: "I got it the first time."

The office was the more likely location, although considering how much they'd learned about the professor, it was not impossible the call had come from the dressing room. The office was behind a set of deep purple velvet curtains, which were almost hidden by a bouncer O'Brien estimated to be about the size of the New York Giants' offensive line. As they approached him, he whispered to Russo, "Use your charm."

"Excuse me," she said pleasantly to the giant, who looked down upon her. The bouncer was a dark-skinned Asian; Korean of one of the northern Japanese islands, O'Brien guessed.

"Can I help you?" he asked politely.

She took her badge from her purse and showed it to him. "Yes, you can. I'm Agent Russo, this is Agent O'Brien, FBI. We'd like to speak with the manager."

The bouncer looked from the badge to Russo, from Russo back to the badge. "Really?" he asked, surprised and impressed. "You're an FBI agent? Like on TV?" She nodded. "Just wait right here," he said, and slipped through the curtains.

O'Brien leaned forward and said quietly to Russo, "I'll take it from here." Even Laura couldn't help laughing at him.

The bouncer quickly reappeared, holding open the curtain for them and revealing the first brightly lit area they'd found in the club. "This way, please." As O'Brien followed three steps behind Russo, the bouncer winked at him.

It took his eyes several moments to adjust to the bright lights. At the end of another short corridor a middle-aged white man was standing in front of a half-opened gray steel door. The door had a peephole drilled into it about two inches below a store-bought Private sign and a Medeco lock. But it was the manager who caught O'Brien's attention. The man's thinning jet-black hair appeared to have been glued in place, and several very long strands were combed directly over the top, sort of like a thin shadow trying to cover the entire north pole. Connor guessed forty-eight, desperate for thirty-nine. He was of medium height and his upper body bore the last traces of once-serious muscles. He was wearing a black-and-white-checked sports jacket over a tightly stretched gray V-neck T-shirt. The T-shirt accentuated those muscles, while the single-button jacket was an obvious attempt to hide his paunch. The perfunctory gold chain hung loosely around his neck, matched by the equally perfunctory diamond pinkie ring. A large unlit half-chewed cigar was poked firmly into the corner of his mouth. Looking at him, O'Brien was absolutely thrilled. Thrilled! Standing before him was the living, breathing proof that clichés were indeed born of reality. He would have staked his inheritance that the man's name was Sid. And he would have given great odds that he had at least one tattoo. "What's the problem?" he asked.

Russo introduced herself and O'Brien, then paused to allow him to respond. "Okay," he said, failing to identify himself, "so what's the problem?"

"Are you the manager?" she asked.

O'Brien was practically mesmerized by the chewed cigar, which bobbed with every word.

"The owner." He corrected himself. "Co-owner. Ike Jones. I'll ask you again, we got a problem here?"

Sure it is, O'Brien thought, refusing to accept the name Ike for an answer.

"It's really simple," Russo explained. "I can get a warrant if I need one, but I'd rather not have to do that."

Ike Jones held out his hands together prayerfully. "Please, I'm not looking for trouble. Just tell me. What? What?"

"We need to know the numbers of your telephones," she told him.

He squinched up his face, tilting the end of his cigar almost straight upward. "What?"

"The phone numbers," O'Brien repeated strongly. "Of your phone."

Jones was wary. "That's it? Really?" They both nodded. "You're the FBI and you were going to get a search warrant for that?" He laughed at the thought. "Let me ask you this. Why didn't you call information? We're listed." He didn't wait for an answer. "Sure, come on in."

He led them into the office and closed the door. The room was obviously soundproof, as the thunderous music was reduced to a distant thump. There was a single three-line phone sitting on a coffee-cup-stained glass-top desk. While Russo checked the phone numbers, O'Brien surveyed the room. In addition to the desk, the office contained a high-back leather executive chair, two straight-back chairs, and a black leather couch. Notebooks dated by months lined the two shelves behind the desk. Obviously ledgers. There were three photographs in cheap black plastic frames hanging on the wall, all of them picturing Sid holding large fish. That was no surprise to Connor. Unlike a deli, this was not the type of place in which celebrities wanted to have photographs of themselves with the owner—or the entertainers—on the wall. "Nice," O'Brien said admiringly, "nice."

"Look," Ike asked O'Brien, "what's going on here?"

Here it comes, Connor thought hopefully.

Ike continued, "I run a clean place here . . ."

Yessss! O'Brien thought. There is a God in cliché heaven. "Of course you do," he agreed.

"This is it," Russo said, standing behind the desk and holding high the telephone receiver.

"This what?" Ike asked. For the first time he grasped the cigar stub and took it out of his mouth. Waving it to make his point, he declared, "This is bullshit is what it is, you ask me."

"Why don't you sit down, Mr. Jones?" Russo suggested, pointing to one of the straight-back chairs.

Defiantly Ike walked around the desk, settled into his desk chair, and leaned back. He picked up a tiger-shaped cigarette lighter and pressed down twice on the tail. The tiger's red eyes lit up and a flame shot out of his mouth. As Ike lit the stub, he asked, "You want to tell me what's going on?"

"Ike? Right?" Russo replied. He nodded.

O'Brien took out his notebook. Sid, he thought. And I'll bet he has a whole collection of Hawaiian shirts for his trips to Florida.

"Okay, Ike," she continued. "Do you recognize this guy?" Like a magician reaching into his top hat, she again reached into her purse, this time pulling out the photograph of the professor.

Ike examined it, then frowned. He shook his head slowly. "No, sorry. Doesn't look familiar."

A lot of guys come in here, O'Brien guessed he would add.

He handed back the picture and shrugged. "With all the guys who come in here . . ."

Placing it back in her purse, Russo asked, "So then, that wouldn't have been you who called him from this phone last Monday night about eight o'clock?"

"From this phone? That's interesting. Nah, wasn't me."

"You have any idea who might have made that call?"

Ike watched a single long strand of smoke spiral into the air. "Last Monday? Could've been anybody. Everybody uses this phone, the girls, the bouncers, friends drop by."

Figures, O'Brien thought, all Monas all the time.

Ike shrugged again. "I wish I could help you, but it's impossible."

Without looking up from his notebook O'Brien took a shot. "Skinny Al ever use it?"

Ike looked at him curiously. "Skinny who?"

"Skinny Al. Al D'Angelo. Big fat guy comes in here sometimes."

"Nah, I don't know him. Skinny Mike, maybe. He's this big fat black guy works here couple nights a week. But I don't know any Skinny Als."

"No Skinny Al," O'Brien repeated, writing it firmly in his notebook. He looked up. "Any other Skinnys? Besides this Mike?"

Ike shot him a challenging look. "That s'posed to be funny?"

O'Brien had at least a dozen completely unprofessional responses to that very question he had been using since he was a teenager, ranging from a goofy expression to classic punch lines like, "Not as funny as your face." The shame was that he couldn't use any of them while on the job. But before he could respond, a young woman poked her head in the door. "Ike, can I use the—" She stopped. "Oops, sorry. Didn't know you had company." By the time O'Brien turned around, she was gone.

Russo answered for him. "Ike, were you here Monday night?"

He considered it. "I'm always here." He beamed. "Hey, FBI, take a look around. Well, excuuuuussse me," he said, doing a truly awful Steve Martin impersonation. "But name me one place any red-blooded American guy would rather be than right here."

"Okay. Then you tell me, who made the call?"

He sighed. "Beats me. I'm telling you, your guess is as good as mine. I spent a lot of time out on the floor and this door's open . . ."

Russo nodded agreement. "Sure. Yeah. So let me ask you this one, Ike. Who are your partners in this place?"

The bank, mostly, he said, laughing. Then he named several other men; the only one whose name was familiar to either O'Brien or Russo was a well-known Manhattan real estate developer. Two of them were Wall Street guys, Ike explained, who used the place to impress investors. Another one was the executive VP of an ad agency, and the last partner was "the faggot son of this rich guy who bought in trying to convince everybody that he's straight."

"Oh, Ikey," O'Brien said doubtfully, "come on. A cash cow like this place? T&A, maybe a little hooking on the side, watered-down overpriced booze. Smack, snow, weed, whatever the fuck else. Just who the fuck do you think you're kidding? You really expect us to believe nobody has hooks in here?"

Ike rolled his cigar stub around his mouth as he glared at O'Brien.

Turning to Russo, he said, "Too bad Ed Sullivan's off the TV. 'Cause your partner's got some funny act." Then to O'Brien he repeated coldly, "I said I run a clean place here."

O'Brien stood up, knowing he was on the verge of becoming the cliché. "Well, I guess we're gonna have to find out about that now, aren't we?"

Russo also stood. "If we have any more questions, Ike, we'll be back. And, just one more thing. Your liquor license? Is that in your name? Your real name?"

As they walked out, Ike was standing behind his desk, glaring at them, muttering to himself. O'Brien paused at the door. "And you know what else?" he said defiantly. "I don't believe your name really is Ike." He paused for emphasis, then snarled, "Is it?" Then he practically spit out, "Sid!" He marched out.

They had just about reached the velvet curtain when Ike shouted after them, "Hey, FBI!" They turned around. He was standing in the doorway, frowning. "Come on back." When they were again settled in the room, he laid it out for them. "You hear this from me, I'm a fucking dead man, you know that, right?"

"Okay," Russo agreed, "it's a deal."

He looked at O'Brien. "How 'bout Bob Hope there?"

O'Brien nodded. "Whattya got?"

"It's mostly like I said, I run a clean place here." He paused. "You know, considering."

"Considering," O'Brien agreed.

"No drugs in here, period. The customers or my girls, I'm real strict about that. That other thing, there's nothing official going on, you know what I mean? But you're a smart guy, you know the facts of life, you gonna operate in the city you gotta have a name."

Russo held her breath. "Of course."

Once again Ike rolled his cigar stub around his mouth, closed his eyes, and wiped his forehead with his hand. "I didn't have much choice." He inhaled deeply and explained, "Two-Gun Tony comes around pretty much every week. If not him, one of his people. I give him whatever I give him, usually between four and five Gs. I've never had one problem." He paused, waiting.

Neither O'Brien nor Russo made a sound. Within seconds Ike leaped into the silence. "He was around Monday night with a few of his people. They come in the office, I go out on the floor. If somebody made a phone call, it was one of them." He finally took the cold stub out of his mouth and squashed it into an Off Limits ashtray. "Anything else?"

"No," Russo told him, "I think that's it." She looked at O'Brien. "You?"

He shook his head. "Nothing."

As they stood up, Russo promised, "We got your back."

Ike chuckled ruefully. "I sure hope so."

Once again they had just about reached the velvet curtain when Ike shouted for their attention. "Hey!" And once again they stopped and turned. "It's Arthur," he said, and stepped back inside.

They ended up in a booth against the back wall at Odeon, making lists and diagrams on a paper tablecloth, drawing lines between names, constructing timelines, reviewing O'Brien's notes, trying to find the pattern they just knew had to be there. They had added one really important piece of information earlier that night: The phone call from Cosentino had caused Gradinsky to pack a bag and get out quick. They now had pretty solid evidence that their original theory was right: Columbia University Slavic Languages Professor Peter Gradinsky was the connection between Two-Gun Tony Cosentino's Bath Street crew and the Russian mob, at least Vaseline and Barney Ruble. Natalie Speakman put him with the Russians, Ike/Arthur tied him to Cosentino. The obvious assumption had to be that he was working as an interpreter for the Italians. It certainly couldn't be the other way around, O'Brien pointed out over the Death by Chocolate, since Gradinsky didn't speak Italian and it didn't seem likely the Russians would need a Russian translator.

The fact that Cosentino was putting pressure on San Filippo to find the professor before Thursday night was a pretty good indication the two groups were planning to meet later in the week. Natalie had even given them some vague idea of where these meetings generally took place. The big questions were why: Why were they meeting and why was the professor on the run?

That's pretty much what Connor was still trying to figure out as he sat in Slattery's office the next morning with his eyes closed. Why and why?

But he snapped back to attention the moment he heard Bobby Blue Eyes' voice on the recorder respond to some question, "I don't know, open a gas station maybe."

He glanced at Russo, who was looking at him, and saw the beginning of a smile forming on her lips. Either she was thinking about her Russian gas jockey or she was beginning to see the pattern too. "Open a gas station" is not the punch line of too many jokes.

All the friendly banter and the laughter in the office subsided as they listened to Bobby laying out his plan to hijack a fuel delivery truck. Organized crime at work. Slattery informed them, "This is all yesterday. The hijacking was supposed to take place last night. We're trying to track it down, we're talking to all the companies, but so far we haven't got anything." When Bobby finished describing the job, Slattery shut off the tape recorder. "That's pretty much it."

"Boy oh boy," one of the other agents joked about Benny Rags as he left Slattery's office, "I've heard of the Wailing Wall, but that was the first time I ever actually heard it."

When the other agents were gone, Slattery closed his door. O'Brien and Russo had remained on the couch. He sat down across the coffee table from them. And smiled knowingly. "I know something you two don't," he said.

O'Brien took a guess. "You found Judge Crater?"

"Better," Slattery promised, "much better."

"Who's Judge Crater?" Russo asked, looking from O'Brien to Slattery. Her whole body sagged. "Please. Don't tell me somebody else is missing now?"

Connor explained, "He's this New York legend. Joseph Force

Crater. He was a state supreme court justice who walked out of his office one afternoon in 1930 and nobody ever saw him again."

"That's the legend," Slattery agreed, "but the fact is that ole Judge Crater ended up in a herring barrel tossed into the East River. A mobster, Red something, killed him for beating up the guy's sister, who was a hooker."

"That for real?" O'Brien asked, impressed.

Slattery nodded. "Scout's honor. They worked it in this office for fun about forty years ago. There's a file around here somewhere. But I got something a lot better than that for you." He stood up and returned to the security of his own desk. When you work on an investigation, you never know which single piece of the puzzle is going to make all the difference. So, like Connor O'Brien, you collect everything and you just keep hoping you get lucky. "Remember when they went to put the tap on Gradinsky's phone, they found out somebody was already listening to him?"

"Cosentino?" O'Brien figured.

Slattery slowly and knowingly shook his head from side to side. "That's what I figured too. Or at least somebody from the family. But I was wrong." One of the least-known departments in the Federal Bureau of Investigation is ERF, Engineering Research Facilities. Through the years it's had several different names and been moved around a lot in the organizational structure, but it's always done an extraordinary job providing technical services to agents in the field. These are the guys who plant the microphones and the surveillance cameras and all the other devices the bureau uses in its investigations. "I'll tell you what, I didn't even know they could do this, but they traced it backwards. They found out where it was . . . um . . ." Slattery had never been particularly adept at technical descriptions, gravitating toward "whatchamacallits" and "whoozits" rather than the correct terminology. He waved his hands through the air. "Whatever it is they do, that's what they did."

It was not a particularly difficult feat of engineering, but it was very clever. The technicians traced the wire back to its point of origin, put a wire on that wire, and called the telephone company service number to find out that number. This was long before the availability of Google or any of the other search engines that allow you to type in a phone number to find out to whom it belongs and where it's located. Law enforcement has long relied on the extremely limited-circulation reverse phone book, a phone book arranged numerically, to track a phone number. Slattery picked up a sheet of paper and asked, "Ever hear of the G&C Corporation?"

"Son of a bitch," Russo said.

"The fucking Russians," O'Brien said, disbelieving. "They were on to Gradinsky the whole time."

Russo was trying to sort out the details in her mind. "How did they find him? I don't get it."

"Who knows?" Slattery replied. "There's a million ways. These people have money, they have resources, and apparently they've got a lot to protect. When someone they can't identify starts showing up at important meetings, they're going to be curious. They got a lot at stake. You figure they'll do whatever's necessary to find out who he is. You ask me, I think there's a pretty good chance that's the Skinny Al connection."

O'Brien just couldn't believe it. "We were right there, at G&C. It's a gas station in Brighton Beach. We were there."

Slattery picked up a copy of their report. "I know, I read about it." He paused and licked his lips and said very quietly, "There's something else I want you people to hear." He walked around his desk and handed them copies of a six-page document. "The techies went a little further for us. They tapped the tappers." He chuckled. "Don't ask me how. I still think it's a miracle when I flip a switch and a light goes on, but those guys put a reverse wire on the Russians' phone. This is a translation of a conversation that took place last night. Hot off the old Xerox."

When the bureau chooses to focus its resources on a specific investigation or individual, extraordinary progress can be made very quickly. Even with all its well-publicized flaws, the FBI remains the finest crime-fighting agency in the world. Apparently the bureau had had a freelance Russian translator provide a translation. Actually the document consisted of transcriptions of three separate telephone conversations. The first and third conversations were in English, the middle conversation in Russian.

"This first call was made from the office of a parking lot in the Bronx," Slattery continued. "It's a place for truckers to leave their rigs for a few days till they get a load. We've got it under surveillance now." He locked a large plastic reel onto the recorder and turned it on. A male caller identified himself as "Sean from the parking lot." The recipient of the call was an unidentified male. It was obvious from his thick accent that he was an Eastern European, presumably Russian. Sean said he was afraid he had some bad news. "The truck didn't show up," he explained. Instead, he said, a "real nice-dressed guy" had appeared at the front gate and told him the truck was being held, and if the owners wanted it back, they had to call a phone number—Sean slowly repeated the number for emphasis—at noon the following day.

"That's the Freemont," Russo said when she heard the number.

"Hats," O'Brien added. "You heard the guy say he was well dressed. It's got to be him."

Sean reported that the man had given him two hundred dollars to pass along the message and wondered if there was any assistance he could offer. The Russian asked fewer questions than either O'Brien or Russo might have anticipated, leading them to conclude that he had a pretty good idea who had hijacked his truck. He didn't even seem to be particularly upset or angry. When asked for a description of the man, Sean was somewhat vague, explaining that it was pretty dark and there was a gate between them. But the few things he mentioned accurately described Bobby San Filippo. The Russian ended the conversation dispassionately, reminding Sean that a driver would be there later that evening to pick up the second truck.

"This next one's all in Russian," Slattery told them as he snapped on the second reel. "It was placed from the G&C office to a rental apartment in Brighton Beach currently occupied by a man named"—he searched the document for a name and found it— "Vasily Kuz . . . Kuznetzov."

"Vaseline," Russo said to O'Brien. Then to Slattery, "We know him. That's one of the people Gradinsky was meeting with."

This conversation was quite brief. According to the transcription, the as-yet-unidentified caller asked Kuznetzov if he was awake. "Yes," he said, "very much." Calmly the caller explained that "a big truck has been taken (hijacked)." He then told Kuznetzov to "go to the apartment and get the (UNI)," meaning unintelligible. He was then to "bring her to the company."

Kuznetzov asked if this had to be done immediately. "Yes, right now," he was told. Kuznetzov could then be heard telling someone that he "must leave to do some work." In response an unidentified female in the background shouted something in Russian, which was indicated on the transcription as unintelligible.

Slattery took a deep breath as he took the second tape off the reel and put on the third tape. "This next one's pretty rough," he warned. "We know who this call's to. We got it from both places." It is not uncommon for someone to use a tapped phone to call someone who is also speaking on a tapped phone. In this instance the call was made to the social club, which itself was bugged. "This is from the Russian phone." Slattery hit the play button. "Bobby?" the Russian said.

Bobby's voice: "What?"

"So listen, we got your fucking message."

"Jesus," Russo said. She looked at Slattery, who nodded.

"Look at that, Bobby grabbed their truck," O'Brien said. "Unbeliev—"

He was cut off by a long, seemingly inhuman scream, preserved crisply and forever by the most sophisticated recording equipment then available. According to FBI lore, there is a repository of tapes designated "sensitive," which are never to be made available to the general public. Supposedly this collection includes a recording made by the serial killer on whom Thomas Harris' memorable Hannibal

"The Cannibal" Lecter was based, describing in detail each of his actions while skinning a living human being; a tape made by an individual who hides patiently outside his former home while waiting for his ex-wife to get there, then records when the woman arrives and is beaten to death; and several recordings made by people in the process of committing suicide. This Russian tape would surely end up in this repository.

The scream lasted less than five seconds. When Slattery turned off the tape recorder, the silence in the room lasted much longer than that. "Jesus," Russo said again, this time almost a whisper.

"We haven't identified the victim yet," Slattery said professionally, avoiding eye contact. He removed the tape. "The tape we got from the social club goes on several seconds longer."

"That's all right," O'Brien said, "I think we get the idea."

"Go ahead and play it," Russo said, then looked at O'Brien sternly. "I want to hear it."

"Suit yourself."

Using the tape recorder's time counter, Slattery fast-forwarded the fourth tape to a point several seconds from the end. Still long enough to feel the victim's agony. On this tape the scream seemed quite distant, muffled, but no less horrific. Then they heard the Russian hanging up, which was followed by several seconds of room tone, and finally someone asking, "What the fuck was that?" And then gently replacing the receiver.

This tape, made by the listeners in the Country Club, continued for several additional minutes. After the phone call had been completed, the voice asked again, "What the fuck was that?"

Bobby responded weakly, "That motherfucking Russian."

"The gas truck guy? I figured," the second man said, anxiety growing in his voice. "But I mean, what was that screaming? What the fuck was that all about? Bobby, tell me that wasn't Ronnie."

"I gotta go," Bobby said.

"Want me to come?"

"That's okay," Bobby said in a fading voice, followed by the sound of the front door closing.

The second man shouted after him, "Call me, okay? I'm there." And again, a second later, "I'm there."

Slattery turned off the tape recorder and sat down at his desk. "That's it."

O'Brien was incredulous. "What are you talking about, that's it?"

Slattery held up both his hands in restraint. "I mean, there's nothing we can do right now. By the time we got to a location for the Russians, the place was quiet. Just a gas station. Whatever they did there, it was over. There was nobody there. We didn't want to bust in and let them know we were there. The place is under twenty-four-hour surveillance. Anybody comes or goes we're tracking them."

"What are you, kidding me?" O'Brien said with frustration, indicating the tape. "You heard that. I mean, if there's the slightest chance . . ."

Slattery shook his head. "There's not. I'm telling you, we're all over it."

Russo spoke with more determination than O'Brien had ever heard. "When we go in, I want to be there."

Slattery agreed. "That's fair. Look, we need to get as much intelligence out of this place as possible before we take them down." O'Brien could hear every day of Slattery's long career in his voice as he continued, "I swear to God, Russo, if there was a chance we could make a difference, we wouldn't wait. And when we're done, somebody's gonna go for this. But we got a shot here to find out what the Russians and the Italians are up to. We've been trying to get here for a long time. So we're gonna wait and that's it."

"I'm outta here," Russo said. And seconds later she was gone.

O'Brien sighed deeply. "Well, partner," he said to Slattery, smiling wanly, "I think I'll be moseying along." And then he took off after his partner.

Being an FBI agent, a cop, a law enforcement officer of any kind, is a strange job. It requires you to put aside your normal human emotions while you're on the clock. On some levels it's a janitorial job, cleaning up the mess caused by exploding tempers and greed and accidents and pure stupidity. Responding to depravity, brutality, sadism, even death, is just part of the job. Destroyed lives aren't supposed to affect you when you're on the clock. From the first day of instruction you're taught to deal with it professionally, then move on to the next assignment.

Of course it isn't that easy. Changing gears abruptly is a really hard thing to do. For some people it's impossible. Sometimes the time you need to decompress just isn't there, so you just suck it up and keep moving forward.

Connor caught up with Laura Russo at the elevator bank. They rode down together without saying a word. Finally, as they walked briskly up Broadway, he asked, "What do you expect him to do?"

"Oh, it's not Slattery," she told him calmly. "I just need a little time, that's all."

He anticipated a long discussion about the job and responsibility and dealing with human suffering, after which she would have calmed down enough for them to get back to work. Truthfully he needed the cooling-off period too. Instead, she walked in thoughtful silence for several blocks. He stayed right with her. Eventually her pace slowed and she began glancing into shop windows. She stopped in front of a small lingerie boutique. Its single window was given to an elaborate display. Painted in lifelike detail onto a white paper screen which covered the entire back of the window was a black limousine with its rear door partially opened. And emerging from that door was a single long, slender mannequin's leg, wearing a sharply pointed black high heel and a silk stocking held up by a garter. Finally she asked O'Brien, "Nothing's changed, right? It's still all about finding Gradinsky?"

O'Brien was staring at the window display, his mind envisioning the nonexistent woman. "He's the mystery guest."

Laura was also focused on the titillating display and said knowingly, "But he's still a man, isn't he?" She looked at O'Brien, busy with his fantasy. "We really haven't thought too much about that, have we?"

Geri Simon had taken a "personal day." "Use 'em or lose 'em," was the way she described it. With the traffic on the Henry Hudson Parkway it took O'Brien and Russo almost an hour to find her small, neat house on Spencer Avenue in North Riverdale. It was the home in which she had grown up and lived in all her life, and there she still remained, single and resigned to it, sharing it with her elderly mother.

Russo dropped off O'Brien at Stromboli's Pizza Café on Riverdale Avenue where he devoured a meatball hero while she went alone to Simon's house. Certain conversations are easier just between women. Simon had initially claimed to be too busy for visitors when Russo phoned from the office, but reluctantly agreed to see her when Russo claimed it involved Gradinsky's life.

The house remained rooted firmly in the late 1950s, from the faded white doily on top of the RCA Victor TV to the three-way il-luminated log-set in the faux fireplace. Geri Simon had put on just enough makeup to try to make it appear that she wasn't wearing any at all. They sat at the kitchen table because, Simon explained, indi-cating the bedroom where her mother was resting, "She doesn't want me to smoke in the living room." She made a face. "She says the smell gets into her curtains." Simon lit a cigarette and savored a long puff. "You want something to drink? Some tea maybe?"

"No thanks," Laura said. "I just had some coffee."

"Sure." Simon leaned close to Russo and said in a subdued, husky voice, "Now, tell me about Peter. You found him?"

It was "Peter," Russo noticed. "Geri, I had a long conversation with Natalie Speakman," she said. Simon leaned back as if that name were a great wind. "She told me all about their relationship."

Simon pursed her lips and eyed Russo warily. "That's why it was so friggin' important for you to see me right away? To tell me that?"

Russo could feel Simon's anger rising. "This isn't easy for me either, believe me on that." She gently placed her hand on top of Simon's. "But I have to ask you this. Before Natalie were there other students . . . graduate assistants maybe?" Laura knew the answer; what she needed were the specifics.

She knew the answer because she had been in precisely the same situation. Larry Carty had been her first professor of forensic science. He was also her friend, her mentor, and eventually her lover. Unhappily married, misunderstood and unappreciated, burdened but brilliant, he had taken her under his wing and onto the convertible sofa in his office. Their romance lasted two semesters, which, she later discovered, tied his existing record. Their breakup was for her own good, he had explained to her. He was trapped at the university, and as much as he cared for her, he refused to hold her back from what he knew would be an outstanding career. There could be no greater proof of his love for her than the fact he would let her go. If she stayed and did not fulfill her potential, he would never forgive himself.

She had believed him right up until the day she met her replacement. Oddly enough, though, long after the storm had passed, she retained warm memories of him. And when she made her first arrest, she had called him with the news.

"What do you want me to say?" Simon asked. "Peter . . ." She waited for the right words. "Peter is a complicated man." She tapped the ash from her cigarette into a restaurant ashtray, then looked away. "I've known Peter a long time," she said, "a long time." She looked directly at Russo. "Do you understand what I'm saying?" She was fighting tears; she wiped her eyes. "The smoke," she explained.

"Of course."

"Everybody in the department knows about Peter and his . . . his friends. It's no secret, you know." She considered that. "I think Grace knows too. I mean, how could she not after all these years?"

Russo pushed gently. "Does he keep in contact with any of them?"

Geri was looking straight down now. "Oh, you know, a couple of them, I guess." It took some time for the meaning of that question to sink in. "You think?"

Russo nodded. "It makes sense. The special ones, the ones he trusts, I need their names and addresses."

Geri Simon nodded in agreement and stood up. "I've got them in the office. Give me a minute to tell her ladyship."

THIRTEEN

Control. That's the bottom line: Control your territory, control the people you do business with, control your personal life. Even control the times, the places, and the way you lose control. Do that successfully and you control your destiny. In this world everything counts. People are continually probing to find your weakness—and when they find it, they will exploit it. Maintaining your cool counts most. Cool is a lifestyle. It earns respect, and it is respect that makes all the difference.

Bobby Blue Eyes was cool his whole life. The Sinatra of the school yard. Nothing fazed him. He was always in control. Always focused. He earned respect. Out of control, out of sight was the way he described it. Or, sometimes, mind over everyday matters. And so he sat in his car, staring straight ahead but seeing nothing, both hands tightly gripping the steering wheel, desperately trying to regain control of his emotions.

Think, Bobby ordered his mind, think. Don't react. Be smart. Maintain control. It was hard, so damn hard. Pure, raw emotion was ripping apart his insides. No-good motherfucking Russians. Cocksucking bastards. Kill every fucking one of them. Tear out their lungs and feed them to the dogs. Get even, get even.

He smashed his right fist into the dashboard.

Think. Don't be stupid. Don't fuck up. Think. Don't do something you're gonna regret. Get control. He took several long, deep, calming breaths. He closed his eyes and tried to calm his emotions.

Fuckers! Long, deep breaths. Behind his eyes he felt the beginning of tears. He stopped that quick. No tears. There weren't going to be any tears. Not from him, not one. Maybe later, a long time later, after he'd taken care of business.

Long breaths. All right, first things first. He needed to be absolutely certain whose voice he'd heard on that phone. He knew, he just had to be sure. He drove several blocks into Chinatown, stopping next to a pagoda-like enclosure sheltering two pay phones. He took the roll of quarters from his glove compartment; his New York quarters, he called them, for pay phones and parking meters. While the phone was ringing he was struck by a horrendous thought—he wasn't sure that he wanted her to answer it.

Ronnie picked up on the third ring. "Hello?" She was out of breath.

He knew. He couldn't breathe. "It's me," he managed. "What are you breathing so hard about?"

"I was in the basement doing laundry. What's up?"

"There weren't any calls for me, were there?" Much better than "I was just calling to see if you were still alive."

"No. Why?" Normally Bobby called home only once a day, usually in the late afternoon to tell her if he would be home for dinner and what time to expect him. "Is something wrong?"

He sniffled. "No, nothing. Everything's fine. Listen, I'll call you later." He hung up the phone. Scratched into the reflective cover of the coin box were the words "Trust God." He'd seen the same two words scratched in the same scrawl on just about every pay phone in Manhattan, but they had never registered before. Bobby made church when he could, which admittedly was not on any regular basis, but always on Easter Sunday and Christmas Eve, plus the regular family and friend baptisms and first communions. But "Trust God"? For what? he wondered, and put another quarter in the pay phone.

His heart was pounding as he dialed Pam's number. The phone was answered after the second ring. He could hear the laughter in her recorded voice. "Hi, it's me. Either I'm here and I know it's you and don't want to talk to you, or I'm not home. Leave a message with your phone number and if I don't call you back, you'll know which one it is."

After the tone, as optimistically as he could manage, he said, "Hey, it's Bobby. Call me at the number soon as you get this message, okay?" "The number" being the phone at the club. He started to hang up, then added, just in case, "I miss you."

As he drove to the apartment on Sullivan Street, he tried to remember what she'd told him about her schedule. He was having a hard time focusing. She had said something about working a flight to Paris. That's why she wasn't answering her phone. Besides, how the fuck could the Russians even know about her? Hey, Ronnie knew everything, and if Ronnie didn't know about Pam, and she was living with him, there was no fucking way the commies could know about her. No way. The Russians were tough guys, not smart guys.

He drove at the speed limit, even stopping at a yellow light. Set a steady pace, he reminded himself, no need to race. When you moved too fast, when you did things without thinking through to the consequences, that's when you made mistakes. So it was keep moving forward, but set a pace. When he got to her apartment, though, he didn't waste time looking for a parking spot. He pulled right into a garage, the one thing every real New Yorker hates to do. "When'll you be back?" the attendant asked.

"When I'm back," he said. He reached under the floor mat in the back and grabbed the keys to the apartment. He wasn't stupid enough to keep them on his key chain where Ronnie might find them and wonder what doors they opened.

In the foyer he leaned on her buzzer hard and waited for a response. C'mon, baby, he thought, please. When his mind wandered to places he didn't want to go, he willed it to focus on the moment. Finally he gave up and used his key to open the door.

The apartment was on the third floor. He took the wooden steps two at a time, just as he did when he couldn't wait to see her. On the second floor he heard two people arguing in the rear apartment, the one directly beneath Pam's. When he got to her apartment, he rapped several times on the door. Habit, mostly, this time coupled with wild hope. He didn't wait very long, though, before unlocking the door. He took a couple of steps inside and quietly shut the door behind him. The place felt empty and very cold. Then he reached under his jacket and purposefully took out his gun.

He moved forward silently. He listened for any sound, searching for the slightest sign that something unusual had happened here. He walked past the bedroom, the bathroom, and the kitchen to the end of the hall and stepped into the living room. Sunlight was pouring through the window; specks of dust were floating through the light. But nothing was even slightly out of its place. He checked the window, which opened onto the fire escape landing. It was locked, and the wooden rod he'd jammed in there to prevent it from being opened was still in place. No one had gotten into this apartment from the fire escape.

Room by room he moved through the apartment. Everything was Pam-neat, where it was supposed to be. Where she'd put it. In fact, he had almost convinced himself that she really was working that flight to Paris when he slid open the door of her bedroom closet.

Her blue and white Pan Am overnight bag was sitting on the floor, hooked to the aluminum trolley she used to wheel it through airports. He stuck the gun back in his waistband and kneeled down in front of the bag and guided the zipper around two corners. Then he flipped open the lid. And took a deep, long breath. Ah fuck. Her travel kit was there, with all of her makeup inside. She always referred to the makeup kit as Dracula, because without it she wouldn't go out in the daylight. And she never traveled without it.

Bobby sat on the side of her bed. The message light on her answering machine was blinking. He hit the play button. There were four calls. The first call was from some girlfriend, a name he didn't know. Both the second and third calls were from a Pan Am dispatcher, the first call wondering where she was, the second call informing her they were bringing in a flight attendant on reserve. The fourth call was the call he'd made from Chinatown. It seemed like he'd made that call years earlier. He didn't bother listening to it. He erased all the messages.

He just sat there for a while, head bowed, hands clasped between his legs. Eventually he lay back on the bed, as he had done so often the past few months. This time, though, he buried his head in her pillow and inhaled her perfumed scent. He was so cold, so terribly cold, that still fully dressed he slipped beneath her heavy floral quilt and pulled it over him. She'd hate this, he thought. I'm lying in the bed with my shoes on. And he had never felt so empty and alone in his life.

He lay there for several hours, watching the afternoon move across the room and finally fade into twilight. She was dead, he knew that. He accepted it. And as much as he fought it, as much as he tried to push the awful thoughts out of his mind, he couldn't help wondering what they'd done to her. How had they tortured her before killing her? That scream, that hideous scream, would live in his mind forever. He would never be free of it.

What had happened in this apartment? Where'd they come from? Where'd they take her? He had so many questions and no answers. His mind played games, trying to grab hold of the day and yank it back into the past, trying to see what had happened hours earlier.

Not knowing was much worse than learning to deal with reality. It was possible, he understood, that he might never know what happened to her. Sometimes people just disappeared and were never seen again. That was a fact of his life. Oh gees, he thought; not knowing would definitely be the worst, having to live the rest of his life with the most terrifying nightmares his imagination could conjure up.

As the hours passed, his thoughts moved haltingly from despair to action. He couldn't just lie there, he had to do something. He had to respond to them. Anything. Finding her was impossible; there was no trick his mind could play to change that. He wouldn't even know where to start looking. Call the cops? No way. The only thing they could do was cause problems, and he couldn't give them any information. But finding the people who did this? He didn't know exactly how to do that. The parking lot attendant had their phone number. But getting it wouldn't do him any good unless he could crawl through the wire to find out where it ended. He could go back up to that lot and wait for one of their people to show up with the cash for the driver. That was a connection. It probably would get him into their organization, but they would certainly be looking out for him there.

Somehow, though, he would find them. There was no doubt in his mind about that. He would find them, no matter how long it took, and then he would kill them.

He'd made the worst mistake possible: He'd underestimated them. And the price was Pam's life. He just hadn't believed that these fuckers would be willing to walk away from a $50,000 truck filled with fuel to make their point. They didn't even try to negotiate. Whatever business they were doing, it had to be worth a fortune for them to make that decision. A fortune.

The question that kept bouncing around his mind was, how did they find out so quickly who took the truck? He'd left them a phone number, not a name. And that fucking Russian had called him by his name. And they knew where Pam lived. How? How?

Suddenly it was obvious. It was so fucking obvious that he hadn't paid any attention at the time. The Russians in that Firebird had tailed him to Skinny Al's funeral. At the funeral the Russians had been welcomed by Cosentino. He'd spoken with them. There was only one way to complete that circle—the Russians had learned all about him from Cosentino.

He let that thought float around in his head for a while, like a ball spinning wildly around a roulette wheel, just waiting to see where it dropped. It dropped right on Tony Cosentino's head. Fucking Two-Gun Tony Cosentino. There was no other answer. Cosentino gave him up early, that's why they were checking on him. They knew where he lived. Holy Mother, he thought. And if they tailed him to the funeral, they had to be on him at other times, no question, including those times he came to this apartment. Chances are Cosentino gave them the phone number from the Freemont too, so when they got the message from the parking lot guy, they recognized it. No wonder they knew it was him.

It all made beautiful sense. But there was one more thing that maybe they hadn't figured so good. Cosentino knew their names too. He knew where they lived too. And he was going to give them up too.

He couldn't just confront Cosentino. There were rules about the way these things had to be done. He was not permitted to speak directly to the boss of another crew. That meeting had to be arranged by another boss, an equal willing to accept responsibility for whatever happened at this meeting—by Franzone.

Reluctantly Bobby climbed out of the bed. He straightened the quilt and puffed up the pillow. He wanted the room to look perfect. For some reason, that was really important. He stood next to the bed. One more time he leaned over and put his face on her pillow and breathed in deeply. One more time, for just that instant, she was alive. He looked straight ahead as he walked down the hallway, knowing it would be the last time he would ever be in this apartment. He considered taking just one thing of hers with him, one little thing, anything, but he didn't. He couldn't. If Ronnie found it, there would be serious consequences.

He closed the door and locked it. Then he just stood in front of it, reluctant to leave. "Oh, baby," he whispered, "I'm so fucking sorry." As he walked down the stairs, he again found himself fighting tears. It was tougher than usual this time, and some of them slipped through his carefully constructed defenses.

Back at the Freemont, the first thing he did was reach out for Henry the Hammer. He's around, he was told. Sit tight, he'll find you. Bobby waited. The Duke kept the cappuccino hot. He leafed through a collection of magazines so old they would make a barbershop's seem current. The place was pretty empty. Vito was there,

trading boasts about women with Mickey. According to the kid, supermodels were lining up outside his bedroom waiting for their
chance. "Shit," he said, "if I was selling it, I'd be a rich man."

Mickey laughed. "Lemme tell you something, kid. You knock off
a piece of ass here, a piece of ass there, they all add up. Before you
know it, you got yourself a big fat ass."

Bobby said nothing. This conversation wasn't for him. Pam didn't
fit into that conversation. It wasn't like that at all. He couldn't stop
thinking about her, couldn't stop wondering. In another world they
might even have been together, for real. She was that kind of special
girl.

Franzone finally got back to him. When Bobby told him it was
important they talked right away, he agreed to a meet. He told
Bobby to go to the Chelsea Diner on 23rd and Ninth. The Hammer
liked their pies. For a little money, he said, they give you a nice big
slice.

"Was I right or was I right?" Franzone asked as they sat at an inside booth. "I mean, look at the size of this slice. C'mon,
fugetaboutit."

It was a nice slice, Bobby agreed. He didn't want to tell Franzone
too much, in case the situation with Cosentino got out of hand. The
only thing he told him was that he needed to meet with Tony
Cosentino as soon as possible. It was real important. "It's about this
thing with the professor. I gotta talk with him."

Franzone was noncommittal. Setting up a meet wasn't as simple as
making a phone call. Within the structure of the Mafia the line between a soldier and a boss was as real as a wall. Crossing the line carried with it great responsibility. For a time, for example, I served as a
liaison between my father and those people who wanted to see him.
It was my job to make certain those people asking to meet with him
had a legitimate reason. And then I would clear it with him. If Franzone made the call and the meet didn't go well, it could become a
problem for him.

At that moment Bobby just didn't give a fuck. Whatever happened, happened.

The Hammer finished his pie, then gathered the crumbs from the hard crust onto a spoon and ate them. "The best part," he said. "Most people don't know it, but that's where they put the protein."

Bobby did a good job not answering most of Franzone's questions. With all the competing agendas even within the same crew, at times a mob conversation was about as direct as a billiards ball. It had to bounce off two or three cushions before finally reaching its objective.

But Franzone asked one question that he could not avoid. Because Bobby belonged to him, Franzone was entitled to participate in all of Bobby's action. That was his piece of the money pie—and it was well known he liked big pieces. "That gas truck thing the other night," he asked. "You settle that thing up yet?"

"No, not yet," Bobby said. He left it at that. If there were problems when he was done, he would deal with them then. Franzone probably was going to be extremely pissed off. Too fucking bad. Everybody knows that a man has to do what a man has to do. Otherwise he isn't a man. The only valid argument he would be able to make was that if you let the Russians get away with this bullshit, you were giving them an open invitation to do the same thing, or a lot worse, in the future. But whatever punishment they decided he deserved, he was okay with it. Even if it became a problem for him, it would still be worth it.

Franzone agreed to speak with Cosentino. But guaranteed nothing. Cosentino would decide if he wanted the meeting to take place. The Hammer would then call Bobby with the answer. All according to protocol. "Thanks," Bobby said gratefully, and started to get up.

The Hammer handed him the bill. It was for $3.25. "You should leave a nice tip," Franzone suggested. "These people, they work hard here. Don't go insulting me."

Bobby did as he was told, and then he had to do one of the most difficult things in his whole life: go home. Go home to Ronnie and pretend his heart wasn't breaking. Go home and smile like nothing was wrong. Bringing home his work was one thing; Ronnie had accepted that necessity even if she hadn't embraced it—as long as he kept his guns locked away—but this was something very different. This wasn't business, this was sex. This was betrayal.

Driving to Brooklyn, Bobby tried to prepare himself. Pamela, this great woman he really cared about, this really special person, had been tortured and murdered. Because of him. Her body was probably lying in a hole somewhere. And now somehow he had to find it within himself to compliment his wife's meat loaf. Or her spaghetti or whatever the fuck she was making for him.

Turkey burgers. Ronnie was actually in a decent mood. During dinner she questioned him at length about the new blinds she intended to order. Mini-slats or traditional? Plastic or wood? A valance, yes or no? What color: cream, rose, or peach? Whatever, he told her, trying to focus, trying to force Pam out of his mind. "I want to order tomorrow," she said. "They're on sale."

"Blinds are always on sale," he explained to her. "It's like a gimmick. You couldn't buy them for full price if you wanted to. It's impossible."

What did he think, she was stupid? She knew that. But this was a special sale. A closeout, all the blinds in stock cut to order.

Whatever. Somehow he got through the meal. Ronnie knew something was wrong. "You're so quiet," she said. "You sick?"

"Just tired," he told her. After dinner he stayed put. The way he was feeling there was no place on earth good to be, so home with Ronnie and Angela was as good as any other place. Around midnight, when he was certain Ronnie was asleep, he got into bed. It was early for him, but he was emotionally exhausted. As soon as he settled down, though, Ronnie rolled over and shoved her body inside his. That was her signal that she was in the mood. These days it happened maybe once a month, sometimes less. That was fine with him. She was wearing her flannel pajamas. This is some great joke, he thought. Not tonight. I can't. He couldn't even bear to put his arm around her. He tried, he just couldn't do it. The thought of touching her while Pam . . . He couldn't. "I'm real tired, Ron," he said, turning his back on her.

He closed his eyes, feigning sleep. Eventually Ronnie squiggled away from him to her side of the bed. There are people who like to believe that most wiseguys eventually come to regret the life they picked. And mostly that's not true. Mostly the life picked us. It was my heritage, in my bones. I lived it. I went to prison. I left it. But regretting it would have meant turning my back on my father, and there was never a moment when I was capable of doing that.

Bobby and I were very much alike that way. While he may have regretted certain actions, it never occurred to him to question his allegiance to the traditions of the Black Hand, the Cosa Nostra, the organization, the Mafia. He could no more question his loyalty to the family than a bird could question its song. He was who he was.

He slept fitfully but dreamed he was still awake. He had no idea what time it was when the phone rang. Ronnie answered it and handed it to him. He glanced at the clock. It was 4:10 in the morning, either late or early depending on your life. "Yeah?"

"I'm real sorry, Mr. San Filippo, to call you so late. This is Joe Maresca." It took Bobby a few seconds to place him. Maresca was the owner of the brownstone on Sullivan Street. "You think maybe you could come over here now?"

Bobby's heart was pounding. "What's the problem?"

"See, I'm not exactly sure about that. The police are here and they want me to let them search your apartment."

Control. Control. He was actually happy about the phone call. Anything was better than nothing. "All right, gimme a little time."

Ronnie had learned early in their marriage not to bother asking questions he wasn't going to answer. "Want coffee?" she asked.

"That's okay."

She watched him dress. It was four o'clock in the morning and he put on a clean white shirt and a silk tie. She rolled over to go back to sleep. He was halfway out the door before he remembered to go back and kiss Ronnie good-bye. The price of peace. In response she flashed a smile.

Two NYPD detectives were waiting for him in an unmarked Chevy parked in front of Pam's building. They got out of the car to greet him and stood talking on the sidewalk. "What's up?" he asked.

The cops seemed pretty decent. "How well did you know the tenant of this apartment? Pamela Fox."

Did you know? *Did* you know? The last ember of the possible went cold. "A little," he said as casually as he could manage. "You know, she was a friend of a friend. I was just letting her stay here awhile. Why, what happened?"

One of the detectives had a thick black mustache and large black glasses. The guy was about a cigar short of Groucho. "I'm real sorry but I got some bad news. They found her body about four hours ago." He paused. "She was murdered."

He waited while Bobby absorbed that information. This was Bobby's greatest performance. That news might have sent other people reeling. He didn't even quiver. He swallowed a couple of times, and that was it. That was all the reaction he showed. Even at that moment he kept his cool. How much information could he ask for without sounding too interested? He bowed his head. "Wow." He took another breath. It was all about control. "You got any idea who did it?"

The second cop, who Bobby decided looked like a real thin Peter Lawford, explained, "Well, see, we were sort of hoping you might be able to help us out there."

Control. Deep breaths. "How do you mean?"

"You know, whatever you know about her. Her last address, who she was friendly with, that kind of stuff."

Groucho added, "It definitely wasn't a robbery. They left all her stuff with her, money, credit cards, everything. That's where we got this address from."

These two detectives worked together better than the '73 Knicks. The legal Lawford continued, "We're gonna tell you something completely off the record. This was personal, no question. She sure got somebody pissed off. Before they finally killed her—"

Groucho interrupted, "You don't want to know."

Lawford shook his head in disbelief. "Pretty girl like that."

"Fucking animals."

Bobby pinched at the corners of his eyes, as much to wipe away the sleep as the tears. "There's not too much I can tell you," he said, sighing. "She flew for Pan Am. They'll have all the personal details."

"How about this mutual friend who introduced you? You got a phone number?"

Bobby hesitated. The thing about good cops is that they know how to play the game right. "Well, let me tell you about that. Now that I think about it, maybe that wasn't exactly how we met." He sighed deeply and pretty believably. "Listen, you guys know how it is. I was just helping her out. It was no big deal."

"Sure," Groucho agreed.

"Of course," Lawford said. "Who wouldn't? Pretty young girl like that."

"Hey, Mr. San Filippo, I was just thinking," Groucho said. "When I heard your name, I knew I knew it from somewheres. You hang with the Hammer, right? That is you? I'm right, right?"

Bobby eyed him coldly. Here we go. "One and the same."

He smiled. "Say hello for us, okay? Tell him Popeye and Cloudy say hello. He'll know."

His partner continued, "Look, Bobby, me and Jack here, you know, we understand. About all this, I mean." He indicated the building, the apartment, Pam. The situation. "It's the kind of thing that the papers are gonna be all over. Maybe we can do something for you, you know, if you want."

Bobby understood. They were offering a deal. They would do as much as possible to keep his name out of the newspapers, which would keep Ronnie from finding out about it. Best effort, no promises. In return they wanted to establish a relationship similar to the one they had with Franzone. From time to time they would find him and ask him a few questions. Nothing about his own family, nothing they would ever use in a prosecution as evidence, nothing that would ever bounce back to him. Information that might put them on the right path. What's the word on the street? Who's up, who's down? "I'd appreciate that," Bobby said, accepting the offer.

"What about this?" Groucho asked. "Anything that might help?"

"No, nothing," Bobby told them. "I just saw her sometimes. It was just a . . . just a thing. She had her own life." He cleared his throat. "So what'd they do to her?"

"Oh man," Lawford sort of spit out. "It was brutal. Twenty-two years on the job and I swear to God, I've never seen anything like it. They crushed her. They dropped something heavy on her, but it looks like they did it limb by limb. Her feet, her hands, arms, and legs, then, you know, the rest."

"There's no way of knowing how much of it she lived through," Groucho added.

Bobby nodded his understanding. But he couldn't speak.

"We need to go on upstairs and take a look around," Groucho continued.

Bobby managed to reply weakly, "Yeah, okay. I got the keys in the car." He returned and gave them to Groucho. "Just give them to the landlord when you're done."

"You don't want to go with us?"

"No," he said. "There's nothing up there for me."

Bobby was growing beyond anger or grief. His focus was riveted on only one thing: retribution. In the end all things came to that. Revenge. The roots of the Mafia had been planted in Sicily hundreds of years earlier, when the poor had gathered together to strike back at the abusive landowners. And in all that time only the enemies had changed.

He gave no thought to the police investigation. Let them waste their time, nothing was going to come out of it. There really was only one place for him to go to wait to hear from Cosentino. He parked in front of the hydrant.

When he opened the door of the Freemont Avenue Social Club, every light in the place went on, the security system rigged to alert the Duke when someone came in late at night. Almost immediately the Duke came out of his room in the back, fully dressed and carrying a shotgun. Bobby raised his hands in mock surrender. The Duke smiled and pointed to the cappuccino machine. Bobby shook his head. Bobby then pointed to the Duke's room, clasped his hands together, and laid his head on them. Sleep. Sure, the Duke signaled.

Bobby lay down on the Duke's bed. A few hours' sleep, he figured, that's all I need. Mostly from habit, before closing his eyes he took a quick look around the converted closet. He wasn't looking for anything in particular, just something that didn't belong. He subscribed to the gambler's philosophy: Trust everybody, but cut the cards. He trusted the Duke, but he gave the room a fast sweep anyway.

Finally he settled down, closing his eyes—and within minutes the silence got on his nerves. Not that noise could bother the Duke, but the room was practically soundproof. Even if you could hear, there was nothing to hear. So Bobby lay there listening hard to the silence, and his mind began to wander. It was so fucking quiet he could hear his own thoughts. They crushed her, those cops had said. Crushed her. One limb at a time. Then . . . He didn't want to think about it, about her, about what they did to her, but that damned silence was driving him nuts. He slept. Fortunately he did not remember his dreams.

It seemed only minutes later that the Duke was shaking him awake, but it was late morning. The first person he saw when he came out of the back room was Little Eddie, prison-hunched protectively over a plate of bacon crisp and eggs. "Hey," Eddie welcomed him to the day, "it's Sleeping Ugly. What happened, kid, she find out you were cheating with the Amazon All-Stars?"

Bobby sat down at the table. Yesterday was about ten years ago. Lenny and Vito V were also there. He reached across and took two strips of bacon from Eddie's plate. "This shit's no good for you, Eddie. Clogs up your brain. Makes you think you got one."

"You're about as funny as a heart attack, Bobby." He tossed another strip across the table. "What was that all about yesterday? Where the fuck was you going so fast?"

The Duke put a cuppa down in front of him. Bobby stared into it, then replied, "Ah, just some shit that had to be taken care of."

"About the truck?" Vito V asked, putting down the newspaper he was reading.

"Nah," Bobby said, "nothing to do with that."

"Well, you heard from those guys or not?" Lenny asked. He was entitled to know, he owned a piece of the deal.

Bobby shook his head. "Not yet. Just leave it, okay? I'll figure it out."

Lenny wasn't a complainer, but he liked to cover his tracks. "Gees, Bobby, it ain't so easy keeping a tanker truck out of sight. I mean, you know . . ." He held his hands about a yard apart. "It's a fucking truck."

A little louder, Bobby repeated emphatically, "I said I'll figure it out. Now fucking drop it."

Lenny wagged a warning finger at him and chuckled sarcastically. "Hey, Bobby, I like you and all that, but don't you fucking talk to me like that. I don't know who the fuck you think you are, but nobody talks to me that way. No-fucking-body. You got that?"

Bobby just wasn't in the mood for Lenny's tough-guy bullshit. "Lemme fucking wise you up to something, Lenny—"

"Don't you fucking tell me nothing," Lenny interrupted. "Swear to God, Bobby, open that mouth again and I'll—"

"Oh fuck," Eddie said, pulling his plate closer. "Here we go again."

Bobby started to rise. "You'll what? Go ahead . . ." These things happen. Social clubs are Testosterone Central. These places are filled with very tough men who have been successful because pretty much they never took that first step backward. An argument between two guys like that is the definition of a real serious problem.

In this case they were saved by the ring. Vito answered the phone and shouted, "Hey, Bobby. It's for you."

Bobby sneered at Lenny and walked over to the phone. "Asshole," he muttered.

Lenny shot him the finger, adding, "Anytime, baby, anytime." He sat down and pointed at Eddie's bacon. "Gimme a couple of those strips."

As Bobby passed the radio, he turned up the volume. Franzone was on the phone. "Youse a very lucky man," he said. Cosentino had agreed to see him that afternoon. He was going to church, then afterward having a family dinner, this time with his legal family, at the Dew Drop Inn on Pacific Avenue. Bobby could have five minutes, no more. "Listen to me," the Hammer warned him. "This Cosentino, he's an important fellow and he makes time to see you. That's a nice thing. So you don't go there and do something to embarrass me, *capisce*?"

Bobby said he understood. What is, is. By the time he hung up the phone, he'd just about forgotten his argument with Fast Lenny. Lenny was shoving a strip of bacon down his throat. When Bobby saw him, he pretended to smack the heel of his hand against his forehead. "Fuck me," he said. "Ah fuck, Lenny," he continued, walking toward him. "I'm sorry. I got a lot of fucking pressure on me right now." And when he got about two feet away, he opened his arms— and then pretended to throw eight or nine quick jabs into Lenny's stomach. "Paisano," he finished, finally throwing his arms around the big man and kissing the top of his head.

"Yeah, that's good, that's nice," Eddie said, satisfied. "But don't you fucking kiss him back, Lenny. I can't stand that bullshit."

As Bobby put on his overcoat, Eddie sighed. Although no one had said a word about the phone call, in that mysterious way in which people know when something big is going down, everybody knew it. Eddie pulled the napkin off his shirt. "Hold on there a second, tough guy," he said. "I'll go with you."

Lenny asked between swallows, "You need me, Bobby?"

Bobby started to turn down their offers, then remembered that in this business one person was considered a victim, but two were a problem. "Yeah, c'mon, Eddie. You can drive."

Bobby waited until they were in Brooklyn before telling Eddie that he was going to meet with Cosentino. "I knew it was something," Eddie said, then asked without actually asking if this meeting had anything to do with the professor. It didn't, Bobby told him, it was about some other things. "Just be careful of that guy," Eddie warned. "He's a little, you know . . ." He pointed his index finger at his head and made some little circles. "Sometimes he ain't right."

They stopped for gas at an independent station in Flatbush. "A dollar fucking forty-two a gallon," Eddie said, marveling at the price. "Reagan just oughta go over there and take it from those A-rabs. They don't need it. Fucking camels don't use gas, right? They just make it."

Bobby reached across Eddie's stomach and handed the attendant a twenty. "I'll get it."

The Dew Drop Inn was a family restaurant masquerading as an old-fashioned tavern. It was as classy as its name implied. The walls were covered in cheap paneling, and above each table hung a stained-glass-colored plastic lamp. Even the ceiling was covered with faux tin paneling. It was not the kind of place in which citizens would normally expect to find a Mafia boss, but in fact, Two-Gun Tony had been eating there long before he got made, and it remained a Cosentino family favorite. On this afternoon there were three generations of Cosentinos gathered at a large round table in the corner. Four large men at a table in front of them—one of them the soldier Bobby knew named Jimmy or Johnny—formed an impenetrable barrier between the family and the rest of the place. Bobby spotted Two-Gun Tony immediately, sitting in a booth with his back against the wall, with several young kids, obviously grandchildren, seated on either side of him.

Eddie waited in the car.

Cosentino signaled to his bodyguards. Each one of them was bigger than Bobby. Two of them approached him and professionally patted him down. Jimmy or Johnny greeted him, "How's it going, Blue Eyes?"

"Going good," Bobby responded, raising his arms. Cosentino scooted the kids next to him out of the booth and slid free. He pointed to the kitchen and went through a swinging door. Bobby and Jimmy or Johnny followed. Cosentino was standing next to a cutting block, toying with a cleaver, when Bobby joined him in the kitchen. The cook and his assistant took off their aprons, wiped their hands on soiled towels, and left.

Cosentino slammed the cleaver down on the wooden board and greeted Bobby. Two-Gun Tony Cosentino was a small man, and thin, no more than five-seven, 135 pounds. His face was long and narrow, sort of flowing down into his long squared chin. His gray hair was wispy, but neatly cut and perfectly groomed. Overall he looked almost frail, helpless. And on occasion people made the mistake of equating his size with his strength. Cosentino, like Franzone, like just about all the men I knew from the old days, had enormous self-discipline and strength of character. He had come up with the legends: my father, Luciano, Gambino, that other little guy, Meyer Lansky. Most important, being from those days, he wasn't bound by the rules of acceptable behavior. As Eddie had reminded Bobby, there were a lot of people who thought Cosentino was crazy; and Tony knew that and used it. And probably even enjoyed that reputation. He understood that if people believed he was crazy, he could do crazy things and no one would be surprised. Usually, for example, when someone was caught stealing from the family, his punishment was immediate and final. One time, though, Cosentino caught a thief and used an electric jigsaw to cut each of his ten fingers—lengthwise, cutting through the middle of his fingernails to his knuckles. People who claimed they were there said he was laughing the whole time. Several times he supposedly disposed of people by wrapping them up with cinder blocks and throwing them alive into a cesspool. Laughing. Crazy. "So you got him, right? Where the fuck is that bastard?"

Bobby looked directly at the old man. "No, Mr. Cosentino, I don't have him. I got to tell you the truth: I don't know where the fuck he is. That's not why I wanted to talk to you."

Cosentino didn't react. Instead, he sniffled, cursed a cold, then wiped his nose with his wrist. "So what is it? What do you want?"

Bobby knew that Cosentino would never admit giving him up to the Russians, so he didn't bother asking that question. Instead, he leaned over and whispered, "I have great respect for you, Mr. Cosentino, I hope you understand that. So I'm gonna ask you this favor. I need you to give me the Russians that came to the funeral."

Cosentino leaned back against the counter, his hands grasping its top. His lips moved as he considered his response, but he didn't utter a sound. Finally he asked, "You think you know what you're doing here?"

"Yeah, I know."

"Bullshit. You got no fucking idea."

"I know I got no choice. That's what I know." Bobby knew exactly what he was doing. One word from Cosentino, a nod of his head, and Bobby was dead. Another piece of shit in a cesspool. He just didn't care. His voice was firm but constrained. And he left no room for doubting his intentions. "Those people . . . they took from me. What they did, it wasn't right. If you got a problem with me, fine, you deal with me. That's the way it's always been. I accept that." He leaned in close again. "I see your family out there, Mr. Cosentino. And you and I, we know that if anybody breathed on them wrong . . ." He swiped his hand across his throat. "That's what you'd do and don't tell me no. 'Cause I know. You have to, that's who you are. You'd follow them to hell." He stood up straight. "I'm not looking for any help from anybody. This is my thing. All I want is the names. And I got the right to ask this." Officially that wasn't true. Bobby wasn't made, he was an associate. He didn't have the same rights as a made man. But as a person who had earned respect his wishes had to be considered.

This presented a problem for Cosentino, a real serious problem. He wondered how much about all this Franzone knew. Franzone had spoken for this kid, which carried a lot of weight. He went back a long time with the Hammer. Cosentino wiped his nose again, sniffled, and replied, "Things happen, kid. I ain't telling you it's right, 'cause we know. But there's a lot going on here that you don't know dick about. All I'm gonna tell you now is that the thing that we're doing here is bigger than any fucking thing we've done. This is a new way for us, and if it happens the way it's s'posed to happen, it's gonna make a lot of people real happy. Now, you want a taste of that, you and the fat guy in the car outside, you earn it. You do the right thing by me and I'll find a place for you. We're talking here about more than you can earn in a lifetime. Two lifetimes. You got my word. But that's it. What's done is done. *Capisce?*"

There was nothing for Bobby to say. Cosentino had made his decision. Bobby was expected to honor it. That's the way of this world.

"*Capisce?*" Cosentino repeated firmly. Then he continued, "Let me tell you a story, kid. Long fucking time ago I set up a beautiful situation through some people down in Florida. Believe me, this was a fucking beautiful deal, a thousand, two thousand a week. Guaranteed. And it woulda gone on forever. But there was a guy down there who walked in after I did all the fucking work and took it over. It was all legal the way he did it, on the books. He had the right; there wasn't nothing I could do about it. So I waited, but I never fucking forgot. I waited sixteen years. Figure it out, sixteen years a thousand a week. And then, when the situation changed a little, you know what happened to that smug fucker?"

Bobby shook his head.

"Neither does anybody else. And unless somebody goes fishing in a shit pool, they ain't ever gonna find out." He took a step closer to Bobby. "*Capisce?*"

Bobby got the point. That whole thing he had been taught about tradition, about protecting each other, about family, it was all bull-shit. It was forever or until enough money came along. Cosentino thought he was for sale? Honor is like virginity: You can only give it up once. After that it was only about the price. *"Capisce,"* he agreed softly, telling his own lie.

Cosentino put his arm around Bobby's shoulders and led him out of the kitchen. "Now, what about that professor? I gotta have him."

"We're close."

"Close ain't good enough." They walked back into the main room, Cosentino smiling at his family. "Let me hear from you soon, okay." It was not a question.

"Yeah, sure."

Head bowed, Bobby left the restaurant. Cosentino watched him leave. Somebody was going to have to keep an eye on that fuck, he knew. He wasn't going to be permitted to screw up a billion-dollar deal. He was getting close to being out of control.

"Everything good?" Little Eddie asked when Bobby got back in the car.

Bobby shrugged. Nobody was going to stop him. "They been better," he said.

FOURTEEN

Connor O'Brien was pretty confident he understood the cognitive differences between men and women. Men thought logically, meaning neurons fired in a predictable sequence, straight as a road through the desert, roaring like the perfectly tuned engine of a Ferrari roadster. Women, however, thought chaotically, their neurons firing even less orderly than a box of bottle rockets on a burning fireworks barge. Women understood logical thought and therefore could pretty accurately figure out what men were thinking at any time. But a man could never guess what a woman was thinking because women just didn't think in any discernible pattern. So trying to figure out what a woman was thinking at any given time was about as easy as a blind man playing whack-a-mole.

This belief of his was the result of having been raised primarily by Mops, a woman who was just as likely to make him sit through a Bucky Fuller lecture at the 92nd Street Y as she was to surprise him with tickets in the Garden's blue seats for a Rangers play-off game.

Having this knowledge about women, O'Brien believed, gave men a distinct advantage. Men were smart enough to understand that they couldn't possibly figure out what was going on in a woman's mind, and therefore they never bothered to try. Women, however, were confident they knew what men were thinking at all times and often reacted to it before the man even knew what he was thinking.

Which is why Connor O'Brien went along with Laura Russo's

hunch that Peter Gradinsky was very much alive and hiding out with a former girlfriend. There was nothing to lose. Both the FBI and the Mafia, using all of the unique methods available to them, ranging from sophisticated technology to good old-fashioned leg-breaking threats, had been unable to find him. So why not try women's intuition?

Geri Simon had given Russo three names. But as they got ready to leave Simon's house to go to her office and get their addresses, Russo had stopped her and asked, "Geri, he's not here, is he? That really is your mother in the bedroom?" Truthfully Russo didn't believe Gradinsky was there, but she also assumed correctly that Simon would be flattered to be considered close enough and loyal enough— and attractive enough—to a man like Gradinsky that he would rely on her for help.

Simon had laughed so hard that she started coughing uncontrollably and had to put down her cigarette. "I wish," she had replied, looking daggers at the bedroom door.

After arranging for a car service to drive Simon home from her office O'Brien and Russo took her list of Gradinsky's former girlfriends downtown. While many agents working in the city relied on the subway system to move around, O'Brien clung faithfully to his car, remaining defiant even in the face of such familiar New York tribulations as being stuck in gridlock caused by Con Ed digging up a corner while watching the temperature gauge rising inexorably toward the dreaded red zone. In this particular instance he simply persevered, and rather than worrying about overheating, focused instead on their destination. "Come on, Russo, you really think he'd hide out from the Mafia at an old girlfriend's apartment?"

She looked at him with surprise. It was sometimes difficult to believe that men were so dense. "You still don't get it, do you?"

"Of course I do," he said firmly. He chuckled at that thought. "What are you, kidding me? Me get it?" And then he added casually, "Get what?"

She was enjoying this. "Why, Agent O'Brien, I'm surprised at you.

Peter Gradinsky isn't hiding from the Mafia." She waived away that thought. "The Mafia's easy. The problem he's got is a lot more complicated than anything the Mafia can do to him."

Somewhere, way in the back of his mind, he began to hear the tune, but he still couldn't identify the song. "Okay, you got me. Happy now? I give up. If he's not running from the wiseguys, then who's he afraid of?"

"Gradinsky got two phone calls that night, remember? One from Natalie calling from his office and the other one from Off Limits. From Cosentino, probably. We just assumed it was Cosentino's call that made him take off. Right?"

"Yeah? And?"

"Remember what we said, don't assume? Well, just suppose it wasn't that call."

He named that tune. "I like that," he said enthusiastically. "I don't know if you're right or not, but I like it."

"Think about it," she said emphatically. And then Russo sang the whole song for him. It turned out to be the old Hank Williams hit "Your Cheatin' Heart." "Gradinsky's at home with his wife when Natalie calls to tell him the good news." She self-corrected that thought: "Or maybe the bad news, depending on which end of the phone you're on. She's pregnant, and what's worse for the not-so-good professor, she's thrilled about it. The only thing he can think about is what's going to happen to his marriage and his career when Grace finds out about it. So he decides that the best thing for him to do is take off for a little while. Let things cool down a little."

"So where does Cosentino fit?"

"That's my point. That's where we were wrong. He doesn't. Interpreting for the Mafia was just like some kind of part-time job to Gradinsky. Who knows what he was thinking? Maybe he figures that if he doesn't show up, they'll just go ahead and get somebody else. It probably never even occurred to him that they would wonder what happened to him. That maybe the Russians grabbed him. I'll bet you he doesn't even know that the whole world's out there looking for him."

O'Brien finally squeezed past the Con Ed site. As a kid reading science fiction he'd loved the concept of two alternate universes occupying the same space at the same time but in different dimensions. What he never anticipated was that there really would be alternate universes, one inhabited by men, the other by women. In Guy World the facts as he knew them allowed only one conclusion: The mild-mannered university professor was fleeing for his life from the Mafia or Russian gangsters. In Girl World the killers were an afterthought; it was the wrath of women that had caused him to take off. It was astonishing to him that these worlds could be coexisting right in front of his eyes and he wouldn't even notice it. "Okay, let's say that's true. So why would he go to an old girlfriend's place?"

Laura looked at him as if he were visiting from another universe. The answer was so obvious she was amazed he couldn't see it. "What are you talking about? It's absolutely the perfect place to hide. You really think his wife or Natalie would ever call an old girlfriend to ask if she knew where he was? And have to admit that he'd walked out on them?" She dismissed the thought with light laughter. "Trust me, there's more chance of me becoming king of England. And I guarantee you that the old girlfriend is so flattered that he still needs her that she's happy to take him in for a while." She sneered at him disdainfully, "Ugh, men."

He laughed softly, shaking his head. She reminded him just a little of Mops, whom he had once described in a college essay as the only person he'd ever known who could figure out an orderly pattern in the Milky Way. If there was a loophole in Russo's reasoning, he couldn't find it. "You've got all this figured out, don't you?"

"It's logical, isn't it? I mean, think about it."

"We'll see," he said, refusing to commit. Woman's logic, he thought firmly.

Em Monroe was the first name on the list. She had worked for Gradinsky for six months, and then they had to let her go. "That was five years ago," Geri told Russo, then added, "I don't want to say they were an intense six months, but there's still claw marks in the walls from the day they dragged her out of the office."

"Well," O'Brien responded somewhat defensively when Russo told him the story, "the same kind of thing happened to me once. Except, instead of claw marks in the wall, she left half a carton of moo shu in the refrigerator." His whole face brightened as he added, "And that's still there too!"

Em Monroe, or "the zaftig Monroe," as she cheerily admitted to the two agents, was living in NYU housing with her three cats, Curly, Moe, and President Reagan, on Washington Square Park North. She was working as an associate professor in that school's highly rated Russian studies program. For some reason her cats were attracted to O'Brien, and Monroe had to warn Reagan several times, "Get off the agent." She explained that she hadn't seen or spoken to Gradinsky in several years. "Peter was a wonderful teacher," she told them, "and I learned a very important lesson from him."

Russo had the answer. "Don't fall in love with your teacher?"

"Exactly." Em Monroe actually laughed at the thought that she might be harboring him. "Trust me, that would be impossible," she said.

O'Brien wasn't really surprised to hear that. As he knew, intense relationships tended to end badly and permanently. "Why is that?" he asked.

"Peter was totally allergic to cats."

The second name on the list was Karen Abbot, who lived in an apartment in one of those high-rise window boxes on 30th Street and First Avenue and was working as an interpreter at the United Nations. It was early evening by the time they got there. Rather than allowing the doorman to announce them, they flashed their bureau credentials at him. "You got it," he told them, buzzing them into the building. The court probably wouldn't like it done that way, but this wasn't a criminal investigation. At times it was easy to forget that legally Gradinsky wasn't a wanted man, he was a needed man.

She lived on the fifth floor. There were two stickers on the door, a peace sign and a notice from a security system that the apartment was protected. Russo knocked on the door. A few seconds later it was answered by Professor Peter Gradinsky. Both O'Brien and Russo were surprised speechless. This was probably the only response for which they were not prepared. Gradinsky frowned and said, "You're not delivering the Chinese food, are you?"

"Peter Gradinsky?" Russo said.

He mumbled some phrase in a foreign language. O'Brien had absolutely no idea what he said, but it sounded profane. Connor introduced himself and "Agent Russo," but Gradinsky barely responded until he added, "FBI."

"FBI?" he repeated quizzically. "What's going on?"

A woman shouted from somewhere inside the apartment, "Is that the Chinese food, Peter?"

He shouted back to her, "No, Karen. It's the FBI."

"Really?" she shouted back, obviously not believing him. "Did they find our Chinese food?"

To O'Brien and Russo he said, "I'm sorry," and stood aside for them to enter. To the woman he yelled, "It really *is* the FBI."

"Oh," she said. The disappointment in her voice was obvious. But she recovered quickly. "Call me when the food comes, okay?"

Russo noted almost immediately that this was a one-bedroom apartment—and she was actually relieved to see several pillows and a neatly folded blanket on the floor next to a long couch. At least he was sleeping only with his wife and pregnant girlfriend, she thought—admittedly sarcastically.

O'Brien was somewhat surprised by Gradinsky, who seemed to be a much nicer guy than he had anticipated. The professor had an open, comfortable manner, projecting an aura of approachable competence. There seemed to be little artifice about him. As they sat down, O'Brien asked, "Do you know we've been looking for you?"

Gradinsky seemed genuinely surprised. "The FBI looking for me?

You got to be kidding." And impressed: "My wife must have some pretty important friends I didn't know about."

Russo responded, "This doesn't have anything to do with your wife, Professor."

"Actually we got your name from Tony Cosentino," O'Brien added.

"Oh crap," Gradinsky said. "How mad is he?"

O'Brien broke the news to him. "His people have been looking for you too."

Gradinsky's mouth fell open in astonishment. "You're telling me that the FBI and the Mafia are looking for me? Wow." He chuckled. "I mean, what happened to the Mounties?"

Russo briefly explained the investigation, artfully emphasizing some facts and completely avoiding others to make him believe they knew both more and less than they actually did. Among those things that she failed to mention, O'Brien noticed, was Natalie Speakman's condition. "So let's start at the beginning, Professor. Why'd you leave?"

He smiled wanly. "Can't we start at the end? The beginning is the difficult part for me to explain."

I'll just bet it is, Russo thought, I'll just bet. Sitting opposite him, listening to this man who had been the focus of her attention every waking moment for the past two weeks, she couldn't help feeling somewhat let down. For a man who had created such chaos he seemed perfectly ordinary. It was like meeting a gorgeous movie star at the supermarket checkout counter as she purchased a sixteen-roll pack of toilet paper. "Well, it would be better if you told us what happened."

He swallowed hard, then asked plaintively, "You've met my wife, right?" Russo confirmed that. Gradinsky hesitated, and as he did, some deep emotion swelled within him. As if he were a marionette and his puppet master had suddenly laid down his strings, his entire body seemed to droop. "This is very hard." He collected himself. "Grace and I, we have . . . Our marriage is . . ." He took another deep breath. "Wow, this is not easy." And with that, Peter Gradinsky began revealing the most intimate details of his life and his marriage.

Sometimes during investigations you learn a lot more than you need to know. Or you want to know. You sit there as impassively as possible listening to people reveal those secrets that have shaped and dominated their lives. The secrets that have caused them to live their lives so differently than they might otherwise have so desired. As an FBI agent your job is to take notes and plug the information into your investigation. You're not supposed to react, you're not supposed to show any emotion, be it sympathy or repulsion.

I've been in this position several times, listening to stories that made me want to cry or enraged me. The real difficulty, of course, is that as you listen to these people, you have to try to figure out how much of what they are telling you is absolute unadulterated bullshit.

O'Brien really did not want to hear Gradinsky's tale, but he recognized that it was the most direct route to the information he needed: what was going on between Cosentino and the Russians. And so he listened and took notes as Gradinsky slowly and painfully stripped away the façade of his marriage. According to the professor, one ordinary afternoon almost a decade earlier, without the slightest warning, his wife had casually told him that her feelings about him had changed. Actually it wasn't him, she explained, it was her. She had discovered, and here he quoted her quite specifically, "the other side" of her nature. Soon thereafter she began "what she always referred to as her journey of discovery."

Initially he had assumed she was just putting pressure on him to agree to have a child, even adopt one if necessary, but it soon became obvious that she was serious. In response he had begun "dating." That was the euphemism he used to describe his many affairs, "dating." Maybe she knew about them, maybe not; their unspoken agreement was that they would publicly maintain the fiction that they were happily married.

O'Brien kept his head bowed in his notebook. Russo focused on

trying to see how long she could look directly at the professor without showing any reaction.

He wouldn't have noticed her reaction anyway; his thoughts were
focused squarely on his broken marriage. "The ironic thing was that
after a few years we discovered that we really did love each other. Not
the fireworks kind," he said dismissively, "I don't know that we ever
had that. I guess I'm not that kind of person. More like the nice-fire-
on-a-winter's-evening kind. We just enjoyed being together. She
stopped all that other stuff." He smiled sadly and admitted, "And I
guess she thought I did too." He looked down at the faded wooden
floor and shook his head. "I didn't want to hurt her. But I couldn't
help myself." He closed his mouth and waited, as if deciding how far
to go. And then he blurted out, "Natalie Speakman? That girl you
met. She's pregnant." He nodded affirmation. "She wanted me to
leave Grace. I mean, how ridiculous is that?"

Russo did a fine job acting surprised. O'Brien professorily touched
the tip of his pen to his tongue, then suggested, "So? What? She was
going to tell your wife? That's why you took off?"

Before Gradinsky could respond, the buzzer sounded. "That's the
Chinese food," he explained. "The doorman knows the delivery boy.
He just lets him in." As he went to the front door, he shouted,
"Food's here, Karen."

While he was busy paying, there was a brief clamor from behind
the closed bedroom door. "Shoot," a woman said angrily. Then the
door opened and an attractive woman rolled into the living room in
a wheelchair. Straps around her waist and calves held her firmly in
the chair. Her purse was on her lap. "Let me get it this time, Peter,"
she said.

"Too late," he told her, holding high a large plastic bag.

Karen Abbot introduced herself to O'Brien and Russo, then asked
skeptically, "You guys aren't really FBI, are you?" After Russo replied
that they were indeed FBI agents, Karen looked at Gradinsky and
said, sounding slightly disappointed, "Oh, Peter, you haven't been

taking those secret documents home from the office again, have you?"

O'Brien glanced at Russo, who was absolutely startled.

"I'm kidding," Karen Abbot said forcefully when she realized they were taking her seriously. "It's a joke." Neither agent seemed convinced. "I swear, I swear on my chair."

O'Brien laughed politely. "I knew that. No, the fact is we're here because the FBI, the Mafia, and several Russian criminals have been looking all over the city for your friend here."

She laughed. "Yeah, right, nice try, copper. And I'm gonna put a rocket engine on this chair and win the Daytona 500."

"He's serious, Ms. Abbot," Russo said.

She looked at Laura Russo, her broad smile slowly disappearing. "Serious seriously?" Russo nodded. Karen collected her thoughts. "You mean Allen Funt really isn't waiting outside to surprise me?"

"This is for real," O'Brien said.

"Whoa, that's incredible," she said. "I swear to God, if I was able to stand up, I'd have to sit down." She spun her wheels around to face the professor. "So that's who you've been hiding out from? Oh, Peter," she scolded him, "why didn't you tell me?" She shook her head in amazement. "Only you could bring the FBI, the Mafia, and the communists together. That's so . . ." She searched for the proper word. "So . . . New York." She gracefully turned her chair to O'Brien. "The guy knocks on my door one night a couple of weeks ago looking all sad and tells me he needs a place to stay for a few days. We've been friends for a long time, so why not? Next thing I know he's got me doing wheelies on the promenade." She tsked, "Peter, Peter, Peter."

In response he reached into the bag and said brightly, "Egg rolls anyone? Let's eat before it gets cold." O'Brien started to object, but Gradinsky reminded him of the Rule of Dim Sum: Chinese food expands to meet all the people present.

Following his usual technique, O'Brien excused himself to wash his hands. This gave him the opportunity to get a quick look at the apartment. Observe it all, details later. The bedroom was handicap-equipped, with a railed hospital bed next to the window. A rudimentary pulley system hung from the ceiling, allowing Karen Abbot to support herself getting in and out of bed. The bathroom also had a range of devices to help her get around, but what especially drew his attention was a nicely framed unsigned pen-and-ink drawing hanging on the wall. It showed what was clearly a caricature of Karen in her wheelchair skiing down a hill. Behind her the chair had left two parallel tracks in the snow. At one point a tree had blocked her path—and the tracks had bulged outward and gone on either side of a large tree trunk. Below the sketch the artist had written, "Miracles happen."

The four of them sat in Karen's "dining alcove," a round table pushed into a corner. Gradinsky was particularly solicitous of Abbot, getting her an extra seat cushion to raise her to a comfortable height and even positioning her legs under the table, then serving her, from the hot-and-sour soup to the last pineapples.

It quickly became obvious that the professor did not want to discuss his complicated marital situation in front of Karen. But to the surprise of both agents, who were used to squeezing bits of details out of reluctant witnesses, he willingly poured out the whole story of his dealings with Cosentino. More than that, he clearly enjoyed talking about it, often looking directly at Karen as he did.

It was O'Brien who'd initially brought up the subject, asking casually while dishing out the fried rice how well Gradinsky knew Tony Cosentino. The professor didn't even hesitate to consider the consequences before answering. "I know him a little. It was a business relationship, that's all it ever was. What do you want to know about it?"

Russo's heart danced as she listened to him. It was as if she had discovered the Lost Dutchman mine. This was the mother lode. O'Brien wrote as fast as he could. Obviously Professor Gradinsky found it considerably easier to talk about the work he did for stone-cold killers than discuss the many ways he'd disappointed his wife.

As he explained, the "big megillah" had begun the night he and Grace were taken by friends of theirs to an Italian restaurant in Queens, a place named Gino's, to celebrate their anniversary. "We ordered a nice bottle of wine and I made an old toast in Russian to love and friendship. You know, the joy of the harvest, my mother's bosom . . ."

"The dignity of the ox," Karen added.

"Right. The, uh, courage of the Cossacks. You know those crazy Russian poets. So when I finished, this really big guy"—he shared what was clearly an inside joke with Karen—"big as a Catskill, comes along. Naturally his nickname was Skinny, Skinny Al D'Angelo." In a deep voice, apparently his imitation of D'Angelo, he said, "I heard youse talking commie. What is it you do?"

Karen Abbot laughed delightedly at his performance. Within the first few minutes O'Brien had realized that she was quite an unusual person. He considered himself an expert in reading body language, but this was his first experience reading wheelchair language. She used her chair as a prop, as other people might use their legs, rolling slightly backward in delighted response to a funny line, pushing closer when she wanted intimacy. Karen Abbot was, he finally decided, light on her wheels.

Meanwhile, Gradinsky continued, this Skinny Al had recruited him. He didn't really know what he was getting into until the first meeting. By the time he realized he was working for the Mafia, he explained, it was too late to do anything about it. He was working for the Mafia, "and," he joked, "I couldn't quit, because when the Mafia lays you off, they really lay you off."

Karen rolled backward as she laughed, and O'Brien and Russo smiled politely.

It was obvious to Russo that Gradinsky was not aware of Skinny Al's demise. She elected to wait until his story was done before telling him. But as she listened, it also became terribly clear that Professor Peter Gradinsky had absolutely no idea that he was trapped in a desperately dangerous situation. There would be no laughs at the end of this story. There was no escape for him. From this night on, his life was changed forever. He had information that both the mob and the Russians would kill to keep quiet. His eyewitness testimony would eventually put a lot of people in prison—that was an absolutely certainty. For the next few years at least, he would be forced to live in the shadows, showing up for law enforcement interviews, depositions, hearings, and trials. If he stayed with his wife, she would have to move with him to a secure and private location. They would not be able to communicate with friends or co-workers and would see members of their family only in carefully arranged meetings. His career at Columbia was finished. He wouldn't be able to work publicly as a translator anymore, although it was probable the bureau or the government would be able to utilize his skills. There was always a need for competent Russian translators. And Peter Gradinsky, sitting there eating his Chinese food, happy and smiling, seemed completely oblivious to all of that. Quite unexpectedly Laura found herself feeling sorry for him.

He'd met Tony Cosentino at that first meeting, which was held in a hidden room in the rear of a gas station. "You had to go through a really filthy, disgusting bathroom to get there. I think they keep it so disgusting so people won't use it. But once you got inside, the meeting room was really nice." His job was simply to sit in the back of the room, keep his mouth shut, and listen. Listen closely to anything the Russians said to each other in Russian, any little asides, any comments, any jokes, any expletives, any anything. And later, after the meeting, he would go through it all with Tony and Al and a couple of other men. This way the Italians got a lot of information that the Russians wanted to keep among themselves, and the Russians didn't know they knew it. The professor gave them an edge. For the meetings, Cosentino even gave him a name, and he was introduced as Peter Two Tongues. "That was their joke. If the Russians asked about it in English, I couldn't let them know I spoke Russian. I was supposed to tell them it had something to do with sex."

Karen rolled way back with that admission. Russo couldn't tell for sure, but she thought Karen was blushing.

O'Brien asked the million-dollar question. "So what were these meetings all about? What kind of business was Cosentino doing with the Russians?" Then he shut his mouth and waited for the million-dollar answer.

"Oh?" Gradinsky responded, somewhat puzzled. "I thought you guys knew all about that."

"We wish," Russo admitted. "Just that it's something to do with gasoline."

"Absolutely." Gradinsky chuckled to himself. "That's exactly what it's all about." He paused and looked at Karen. "You all right? Want a blanket?"

She was fine, she said.

"Good." Turning back to the agents, he continued, "Anyway, it seems like the Russians have been running this scam operation for a long time. It's based on the fact . . . See, a lot of people don't know this. I mean"—he tapped himself on the chest—"I certainly didn't, but apparently we use exactly the same fuel oil for home heating as we do for cars. Who knew gas was oil? But it's the same thing, same product, exactly. It comes out the same storage tanks, they just call it different things. The big difference is that the government doesn't tax the oil used to heat houses, but there's like forty or fifty cents tax on every gallon of gas."

Gradinsky was now in his teaching mode, O'Brien realized, lecturing to students he judged to be not particularly bright. He spoke with his hands, emphasizing each word of importance. And like a student anxious to please his professor, O'Brien scribbled away.

"It turned out that the Russians understood American business better than Americans. What they did was set up companies to buy heating oil. They didn't have to pay any taxes. They gave the company any kind of name, it didn't matter. That first company sold all the oil it bought to another company that they also started. The second company sold it to a third company. You got to understand, these companies existed only on paper. They were all owned by the same people. They didn't have any employees, they didn't have anything except a name and a mailing address. The fifth or the sixth company that bought it as home heating oil would turn around and resell it to the next company—as motor oil. Without collecting a penny in taxes . . ."

O'Brien stopped writing. This was like trying to take verbatim notes at a college lecture. He closed his notebook, leaned back, and listened with fascination. "It was called a . . . you know, a whatchamacallit," Gradinsky continued. It took him a few seconds to find the proper phrase. "A daisy chain. That company would sell it to another company and so on and so on, until eventually they would sell it to gas stations and just pocket the tax money. By the time the government figured out the whole thing, the company that bought it as home oil and sold it as motor oil was long gone. It was out of business, no forwarding address, no owners, no records."

"So what are we talking about here?" asked Russo. "Hundreds of thousands of dollars? Millions?"

Gradinsky laughed at that. "At least. And it looks to me like it's just about foolproof."

Karen went to the kitchenette and returned with cans of soda, which she passed around. "I understand all that," she said. "But I don't see what this has to do with the Mafia."

"They were the cops," he said, as if it were obvious. Then to the agents he admitted, "I guess I forgot to tell you about that part."

Rarely does an interview proceed so smoothly. It was as if a faucet at an oasis had been turned on; the information just poured out of him. As Russo listened, she began to understand that it wasn't only Gradinsky's life that would never be the same. This was a career-making case. This was going right to the top, and everybody who had a stake in it would go along for the ride. They were going to know her name, and O'Brien's too, of course, in Washington.

With so much money up for grabs, Gradinsky continued, several Russian crews began fighting for control. People were getting killed.

"Supposedly one group, not Kuznetzov's guys, another gang, threw somebody off the George Washington Bridge one night. They said they did it because he was some fly-by-night hustler." Then he added, "But it was only from the lower level." In an effort to stop this warfare the Russians hired Cosentino to act as a mediator. And when he had to enforce his decisions, he brought in members of his crew.

Gradinsky didn't have to tell O'Brien or Russo what happened next. Once Cosentino got a sniff of this kind of money, he wasn't going to settle for less than a full-course meal. He wanted all the way in. The question became how and when Cosentino planned to make his move, and O'Brien doubted the professor knew that answer.

The professor gave them everything, absolutely everything. Cosentino had been hired by a Russian named Vasily Kuznetzov. Vaseline, obviously. His partner was named Ivan Chernanko, "Something like that," the professor admitted. "These people aren't big on last names. I always referred to him as Barney Rubble. You know, from *The Flintstones?*" He paused. "He was a really bad guy. Not that the other ones were so nice, but him?" He shook his head. "Just a really nasty man."

When Gradinsky hesitated, O'Brien guessed that a particularly unpleasant memory had popped into his mind. Maybe something this Barney had done to leave that impression. Instead, though, the professor asked, "Are there any more sautéed string beans?"

Karen served him. As she dumped the last few string beans on his plate, she told him, "You're just full of surprises, Peter. Who would've ever guessed, you and the Mafia? It's amazing. It's like *The Godfather Meets Professor Higgins.*"

Russo prompted him to continue. "You were saying, Professor? Ivan, the second guy, the really bad one?"

He nodded to Karen. "Just like in the movies." And then to Connor, "He was a mean son of a bitch. Believe me, he's not someone I'd want after me. He used to . . . I'm not kidding about this, he'd sit there and sort of pick his nose with that little thing, that little piece of raised metal on the end of a gun, the thing you aim with. You know what I'm talking about?"

"Uh-huh," Russo responded, "the sight." She glanced at O'Brien—and caught him staring at her.

"I'll tell you one thing. He and Skinny Al didn't get along at all. No way. And Skinny Al was no day in the park either, believe you me. I think maybe they were too much alike. But it seemed like every time Skinny Al said something at one of these meetings Ivan would tell him to shut up. He'd scream at him that he was supposed to listen, he wasn't supposed to talk. He wasn't permitted to say anything." This time Gradinsky did a poor imitation of the Russian: "Don't you hear me no good? You say nothing. Nothing! Is not your place to speak, you fucking prick."

O'Brien opened his notebook and once again started writing.

The professor exhaled. "And then Skinny Al would yell at him, 'I don't got to listen to you.' You should've seen them, the two of them. Like bulls. There were a couple of times when they almost went after each other. People had to hold them back. One time . . . one time I remember Ivan said something in Russian to Vaseline. Basically he was saying, 'I'm going to kill that prick, I swear to God. He doesn't listen.' I forgot what I told Skinny Al that Ivan had said, but I definitely didn't tell him that. I didn't want to cause any more problems."

The professor talked long enough for Connor to get hit with the insatiable desire for a second round of Chinese food. Neither he nor Russo found it necessary to ask many questions. On occasion they would push the professor in a slightly different direction, but Gradinsky needed little prompting. He was a performer. He loved the attention. Loved it. And they gave it to him, as much as he desired. Maybe most important to him was the fact that Karen was so impressed by his tale—reinforced by the great interest in it shown by not just one FBI agent, but two.

Eventually he started running out of story. When Karen excused herself and went into the bathroom, essentially he was done. But there was one last piece of information O'Brien needed. "When they called you the same night Natalie Speakman called, what'd they tell you?"

"Oh, it was nothing. They were just telling me when the next meeting was. I was supposed to call them back the next day to confirm it. Obviously I didn't."

Thus putting in motion this entire investigation, O'Brien thought. "So when's the meeting?"

"What's today's date?" the professor wondered. Russo told him. "That's interesting," he said. "Tomorrow night."

While there was a mountain of detail still to be uncovered by investigators and, inevitably, prosecutors, O'Brien and Russo had the information they needed. Russo excused herself to use the telephone, leaving O'Brien alone with Gradinsky. "What happens now?" the professor asked.

"That's not really up to us," Connor replied, skillfully avoiding a real answer. "Maybe you'd better start getting your stuff together, though. I don't think you'll be staying here tonight."

"No, that's not what I meant. I meant, you know, about Grace?" He covered his face with his hands, a gesture O'Brien read as emotional exhaustion. "It's so damned complicated."

Connor tried to be helpful. "How about this? You could tell her you got caught between the mob and the Russians. That's why you took off." He shrugged. "At least it'll buy you a little time."

Gradinsky looked right at him. "And what do I do about Natalie?"

There was no way of avoiding that question. "That's a tough one, Professor," O'Brien said weakly. "What can I tell you? Sometimes things have a way of working out better than you think." He smiled sheepishly. "We sure do have a way of screwing things up, don't we?"

The professor responded with his own sad smile.

It was after one in the morning when Russo woke Slattery at his home. He answered on the second ring, not a hint of sleep in his voice. Matter-of-factly she reported, "Well, we got him." She covered the most important points in a few sentences.

Slattery was properly impressed. "Sounds like you people had an interesting evening."

"Mostly," she agreed, "but truthfully the Chinese food wasn't that good." Slattery told her to bring Gradinsky to the office. He would meet them there within the hour.

The professor packed his few belongings. Russo offered to stay with Karen Abbot until she could get someone there to assist her. In response Karen laughed. "Are you kidding? You know what this means?" she asked. Laura shook her head. "I finally get my bathroom back."

FBI agents meet literally thousands of people during their careers. They meet all kinds, good and bad, smart and stupid. And very, very few of them really stick in their memory. As Karen rolled with them to the front door, both O'Brien and Russo knew they'd met a force not easily forgotten. "Maybe we'll see you again," Russo said, meaning it.

"That'd be okay," she replied. She stayed by her open door as they waited for the elevator. When the elevator doors finally opened, she shouted after them, "Just remember, I'm the wheel thing!" And laughed and laughed.

On the drive downtown the professor was quiet for a long time and then asked, "Any idea what they're going to do with me now?"

O'Brien looked at Russo. He was elected. "Well, the first thing is to make sure nothing happens to you." He tried to find something promising to say but could think of absolutely nothing.

Finally the professor said something to himself in Russian. When Russo asked him what it was, he smiled weakly and said with resignation, "It's just an old prayer peasants used to say at the beginning of winter."

An hour later O'Brien and Russo were sitting with Slattery in his office. Another team of agents had escorted Peter Gradinsky to a safe house, one of several apartments the bureau keeps in the city for just such a purpose. Because Grace Gradinsky's telephone was tapped, he was not permitted to call her. Instead, agents were sent to her apartment to inform her that her husband had been found, that he was safe, and that he was in the bureau's custody. They were vague about when she would be permitted to see him. Soon, she was told, as soon as possible. She was also told that her telephone was being tapped by the familiar "person or persons unknown." She was warned not to tell anyone, including close friends and relatives, in person as well as on the phone, that Peter was safe.

The agents stayed with her, waiting for a decision from Washington whether she would be permitted to remain in her apartment with security or be moved into protective custody.

Slattery was quietly thrilled. He was not a man known for public displays of excitement, but by the time O'Brien and Russo walked into his office he was, he told them happily, "two Cokes to the wind." For him that qualified as a huge celebration. Slattery continued to amaze O'Brien. It was three o'clock in the morning, the man had gotten out of bed and raced to the office, yet from all appearances it could just as easily have been three o'clock in the afternoon.

O'Brien and Russo settled comfortably into the couch and began filling in the details. Russo did most of the talking. Slattery listened without comment, occasionally making a few notes. Laura took off her shoes, stretched out her long legs, and rested her feet on the coffee table, causing Connor to remember for the first time that entire evening that his partner was a very attractive woman. The sudden realization that he had finally accepted her as a very competent, reliable, nongender partner, rather than a pretty girl whom it was fun to work with, surprised him. The fact that an attractive woman was capable of making him forget that she was an attractive woman made her even more attractive to him. In this particular coupling familiarity bred respect.

When Russo finished, Slattery took a deep, satisfied breath. "Let me tell you, you guys did some great work. I mean great, great work." Then, compliments done, he got right back to business. "So what do you think? Where do we go from here?"

"Home?" O'Brien guessed.

"Nice try," Slattery responded. "But that's not why we're paying you people those big bucks." The evidence provided by the professor might put a lot of people in prison, he continued, but that alone would not be enough to prevent the Mafia and Russian gangs from forging a powerful alliance. "Cosentino, those two Russians, they're nothing. They're replaceable parts. Once the Italians make a deal with the Russians, it's not going to matter who signs the checks. Believe me, guys, if all we do is get rid of these people, there'll be dozens more lining up to take their place. We're talking millions of dollars here. What we've got to do is break up this romance."

It ended up being much more of an early morning than a late night. Several strategies were suggested, considered, and thoroughly debated. The most obvious—raid the meeting, arrest everybody you can grab, and throw the entire operation into disarray—was impossible. Raids took an enormous amount of planning, organization, legal support, equipment requisitions, manpower, rehearsals, and enough time for everyone involved to prepare a solid excuse in case things didn't work out. They had one day.

Normally Slattery would have written a long, detailed memo laying out the pros and cons of several possible scenarios and forwarded it to Washington, where it would be debated and analyzed, and several weeks or months later an action plan would be approved. Unfortunately they only had hours to make that decision. Agents assigned to the New York office liked to joke that by the time two bureaucrats at headquarters could agree on what time it was, it was already too late.

It was Russo who came up with the plan. "Whoa," said the very impressed Jim Slattery after she'd laid it out. "That's nice. It's great." Connor O'Brien was truly impressed by its symmetry: If Russo's plan worked, it would cause a schism between the Mafia and the Russians that would take a long time, if ever, to heal. It would force the bad guys to honor their own traditions or be exposed as frauds. It would permanently eliminate some very dangerous people with absolutely no danger to a single FBI agent. And it was remarkably simple to put into motion.

Of course, that's if it worked.

As usual, Slattery volunteered to take full responsibility for approving the plan. O'Brien knew what that meant: If it worked, Slattery would make sure O'Brien and Russo got the credit; but if something went wrong, he'd take the heat. Typical Slattery.

Rather than grabbing a few hours' uneasy sleep on office couches, O'Brien and Russo went home to dress for success. "Dark colors," he suggested as he dropped Laura off at her apartment. "You know, blood doesn't show up as well."

She ignored that remark. But with the car door half-opened and the dome light flickering, she asked, "No jokes, Connor, what'd you think of the professor?"

O'Brien considered that. "I think," he said evenly, "that he's about to get caught in a fucking shit storm and the poor bastard still thinks the sun's coming out. That's what I think." Laura mumbled a few words in agreement and got out of the car. As she did, he lowered the window and shouted after her, "On the other hand, that Karen Abbot's a real treat."

When he got home, there were eighteen recorded messages waiting for him on his answering machine. He was asleep halfway through number 8.

At one o'clock the next afternoon reasonably refreshed FBI Special Agents Connor O'Brien and Laura Russo were right back where they had started, on Elizabeth Street in Little Italy. They were standing in front of a faded brown steel door, the entrance to a nondescript one-story building. Large bay windows on either side of the door made it obvious that this had once been a shop of some kind, but white screens at the back of both of those windows made it impossible to see inside. It made no difference. O'Brien and Russo knew that this was the Freemont Avenue Social Club, the home of the Mafia crew headed by Henry "the Hammer" Franzone.

The two agents had been notified less than a half hour earlier by the surveillance team in the Country Club that Bobby Blue Eyes San Filippo had arrived and was inside. As they approached the brown door, O'Brien had whispered, "I hope you remembered to bring the cake."

"Just my luck," Russo had responded. "I need John Wayne and I end up with Soupy Sales."

"Hey, look at this," he said, pointing to the name slot above the buzzer, which read "J. E. Hoover." "I always wondered what happened to him."

Russo leaned on the buzzer. The two agents stood there waiting, assuming they were being observed by a security camera. Every few seconds Russo shifted nervously from foot to foot. The door was finally opened by a relatively thin, balding older man O'Brien recognized as George "Georgie One-Time" Nunzio. There was very little chance that Nunzio knew who they were, but he definitely knew they didn't belong there. "Yeah?" he asked, but not unpleasantly.

O'Brien replied, asking, "Can Bobby Blue Eyes come out and play?"

Russo shook her head in disbelief. Showing Nunzio her identification, she said professionally, "I'm Special Agent Russo, FBI. This is Agent O'Brien. We'd like to speak to Mr. San Filippo, please."

Nunzio's eyes traveled very slowly and obviously down and then up her entire body, stopping only to admire her chest. Then he grinned at her. "You got some nice body for a cop."

Russo didn't flinch. "Right. I'll bet you told my grandmother the same thing." She repeated her request, a bit more firmly. "Mr. San Filippo, please."

"Bitch," he said, closing the door.

As they waited, she turned to O'Brien, who was looking straight ahead, his lips puckered for a shallow whistle. "Don't look at me," he said, "I just work here."

About a minute later the door was opened about halfway. Bobby Blue Eyes San Filippo was standing there. His right hand remained on the inside doorknob. It was pretty obvious that he wasn't about to invite them in. He spoke directly to O'Brien. "What?"

This time O'Brien made the introductions. "There's a couple of questions we'd like to ask you, Bobby. We don't have a warrant, you don't have to talk to us. But I got a real strong feeling you'll be happy if you do."

While O'Brien was making their pitch, Russo took a good close look at San Filippo. It was obvious to her why women found him attractive. He was a dark, handsome man with chiseled good looks, about the same age as O'Brien, but in just about every way he was as smooth as Connor was ragged. His black hair was perfectly groomed, he was clean-shaved, and his piercing blue eyes contrasted with his bronzed Sicilian complexion. He was wearing what was obviously an expensive, highly starched white shirt and silk tie. And whatever cologne he was wearing, it was the right one. More than all that, though, he had about him an appealing aura of complete confidence.

San Filippo considered O'Brien's request. It wasn't that unusual. Agents and wiseguys speak with each other all the time. And O'Brien was hoping that his curiosity would be strong enough to overcome his apprehension.

"Come on," Russo urged him, "take a walk with us. Ten minutes, tops."

San Filippo smiled at her, his lips just barely parting. Unlike Nunzio's, his eyes never left her face. "This really's not such a great time," he said.

As Bobby Blue Eyes focused on Laura, O'Brien took a real hard look at him. He pegged him right at thirty-five, and looking exactly that. San Filippo was obviously one of the "new Mafia," the next generation of hustlers as concerned about their appearance as respecting the traditions of the family. His black hair was slicked down with some kind of goop that made it look about as natural as a statue's. He had shaved that morning, that was easy to see, but still he looked exhausted, and there was a real puffiness under his eyes—they looked like tea bags to O'Brien—that made him look unusually tired or sad. It was also pretty clear that to make his dull blue eyes stand out, his mob trademark, he was using one of those bronzing lotions that darkened his complexion a little too much Miami Beach. And whatever brand of cheap cologne he had slopped on, the pungent smell was enough to suffocate an elevator full of secretaries. He was wearing a starched white shirt with a high collar, and Connor guessed he was hiding a flabby neck. It all came together in a two-bit manner, giving him the unappealing aura of misplaced arrogance.

Russo lightly took hold of Bobby's left hand. "Please," she said softly, tilting her head innocently to the side.

San Filippo frowned. "All right," he said out of the side of his mouth. "Just gimme a minute."

As they waited for him, O'Brien found himself suffused with energy. He bounced up and down, finding it difficult to believe that Russo had actually reached out and grabbed the guy's hand. For an instant he wondered if he might be feeling a twinge of jealousy, but almost immediately rejected that thought. Long ago he had dispassionately examined the whole concept of jealousy and decided it offered no benefits. After that he had been able to keep it out of his system, so it couldn't possibly be the cause of the strange discomfort he was feeling.

San Filippo reappeared wearing a full-length camel hair coat and a black fedora. "Let's go," he said, closing the door firmly. The two agents flanked him as they walked toward Mulberry Street. "Either of you wired?" he asked, the kind of question defense lawyers cherished. O'Brien and Russo both said no. "Okay," Bobby said, "but everything's off the record, right? We got that straight?"

They agreed. The day was on the edge of winter, crisp and clear. O'Brien and San Filippo jammed their hands into their coat pockets; Russo wore white furry mittens. As they crossed the street, Connor began the conversation. "You ever hear of a Professor Peter Gradinsky?"

San Filippo made an exaggerated search of his memory. "Gradinsky, huh? Gradinsky? No, it doesn't sound familiar. What kind of professor is he?"

"He teaches Russian up at Columbia University," Russo said. "Okay, then, how about Anthony Cosentino? You know him maybe?"

San Filippo couldn't repress a weak smile. "You know how it is, maybe I met him once or twice to shake hands. Seems like a nice enough guy. We got some friends in common, that's all. What game we playing here?"

"Clue, it looks like to me," O'Brien said. "You know, Uncle Tony's in the basement with a hammer." Connor was enjoying this conversation. Even the subtexts had subtexts. But the only question that mattered was, would Bobby really understand the questions? They turned left on Hester. O'Brien waited for some reaction from San Filippo, but when Bobby failed to respond, he continued, "Okay, let me ask you this. Did you know an individual named Alphonse D'Angelo? Skinny Al?" He spread his hands apart. "A big fat guy used to hang around over on Bath Street."

Again San Filippo's whole body shrugged. "Sure, who didn't know him? Everybody knew that fat slob. Even the mayor, Koch, he knew him from when he was a councilman, I'll bet." For the first time he hinted at a touch of emotion. "It's a shame what happened to him." He glanced at O'Brien. "I hope you guys do something about that."

"We're trying," Laura interjected. "Believe me, we're trying." They were laying down a pretty obvious path, hoping he would follow it. She glanced down at the sidewalk, noticing the intricate web of cracks. The next question, she knew, was the rough one. She doubted very much that he saw it coming. They had spent considerable time that morning debating precisely how it should be asked. "Mr. San Filippo," she asked as dispassionately as she could manage, but even she heard the slight squeak in her voice, "what do you know about the murder of Pamela Fox?"

San Filippo took the question without breaking stride. He bowed his head but otherwise expressed no emotion. Even O'Brien admired his fortitude. Tough guy, he thought, real tough. They had learned her name the night before. The bureau had matched their information with NYPD reports to identify the victim. SA Bill Madden had confirmed her relationship with San Filippo by showing his mug shot to the landlord, who identified him as the legal tenant of the apartment and a frequent visitor.

When they reached the corner of Mulberry and Hester, San Filippo stopped and turned to face both of them. Then he angrily spit out the words. "Fuck you. Who the fuck do you think you are, talking to me like that?" He pointed a warning finger at them. "I don't care who the fuck you are. Come near me again, I swear to God you're gonna be real unhappy. Now, you got any more questions, you call my fucking lawyer." Then he angrily walked right between them, shoving them out of his way.

O'Brien shouted after him, "Hey, Blue Eyes, I got one more question for you. You ever hear of a Russian guy named Vasily Kuznetzov?" San Filippo kept walking. So O'Brien shouted a little louder. "Maybe you ran into him somewhere? A tall guy, scar on his face? The guy's a real lady killer, know what I mean?"

That's when San Filippo stopped. He turned his head toward them. "What'd you say?"

O'Brien and Russo walked toward him. It was O'Brien's turn to smile confidently. "Figure of speech, Bobby," he said, "figure of speech." He stopped a few feet away from the mobster. "I asked if you knew this Russian guy, Vasily Kuznetzov. Maybe I can refresh your memory. He runs this bootleg fuel business out of a gas station on Brighton Beach Boulevard—1405, I think it is." He asked Laura, while still looking directly at San Filippo, "That's it, right, partner— 1405 Brighton Beach Boulevard?"

"That's it," she confirmed. Then she asked Bobby, speaking in a normal tone, "You certain you've never been there? You'd remember. There's a room hidden in the back. You have to go through the men's room to get there? Doesn't ring any bells, huh?"

They stood about four feet apart. The expression on Bobby San

Filippo's face was one of bemusement. He heard them, no question about that, but they wondered if he got it.

Still looking only at him, O'Brien continued, "And doesn't he have this psycho partner works there too, Russo? Ivan something?"

She, too, spoke to Bobby while responding to O'Brien. "Chernanko. Wasn't he the guy always fighting with Skinny Al at the meetings between Tony Cosentino and the Russians? The one who swore he was going to kill him someday?"

O'Brien closed the gap between them by half, then lowered his voice and added, "I think that's what Professor Gradinsky said when we spoke to him last night. Remember? Was that before or after he told us that they were meeting there tonight?"

"Beats me, O'Brien," he said.

San Filippo inhaled deeply. With his right hand he took off his hat, and with his left he swept back his hair. And it appeared that he bowed his head slightly and closed his eyes. It was a gesture that might have been interpreted as a salute. Then he put his hat back on his head, adjusted it carefully, and wordlessly walked away.

O'Brien and Russo stood on the sidewalk and watched him go. And in a voice just slightly louder than a whisper, Russo said, "Bingo."

In his car driving back up to the office, O'Brien sang cheerfully, "My boyfriend's back and you're gonna be sorry . . ."

When he reached the chorus, she joined him.

FIFTEEN

What you gotta do, you gotta do.

Basically that pretty much sums up the wiseguy philosophy of life. The fact is that sometimes you just can't fugetaboutit. Not if you're a stand-up guy. And everybody knew that Bobby Blue Eyes was a stand-up guy.

As he drove with Little Eddie toward Brighton Beach, he didn't waste time considering the consequences of his actions. He didn't bother trying to balance his right to revenge with the precepts of tradition. Bobby knew well that even if he survived the next few hours, the actions he was about to take might get him whacked. He was going up against the interests of some powerful people. None of that mattered to him; if he didn't do it, he couldn't live with himself. What was at stake was his honor.

They didn't talk much in the car. Little Eddie hadn't hesitated when Bobby told him he needed his help. He'd asked a few questions, but "why" was not one of them. If Bobby asked, Bobby got. He had earned that respect from Eddie. And that didn't change even when Bobby told him, "Bring Myrtle." Myrtle being Eddie's favorite semiautomatic weapon. They used to joke that he took it out only on holidays—like St. Valentine's Day.

Bobby hadn't had time to work out any kind of plan. Pretty much, he was going in there naked. Whatever happened, happened. It had been only a few hours since the two FBI agents showed up at the front door of the social club. He'd been sitting at the card table, lost in his private sadness, when Georgie One-Time told him the feds were outside and wanted to talk to him. He described them as "a fucking clown" and "a bitch with some smart mouth." Normally Bobby would not have spoken to law enforcement without an attorney on his hip, but there was nothing normal about the last few days. Bobby had a lot of different things going on, and this visit could have been about any one of them. He was curious enough to walk to the door and find out what they wanted.

The guy agent was a real schlump. From his messy hair to his scuffed shoes there was not one thing about his appearance that looked like he'd put any thought into it; it was sort of like he was dressed out of focus. After introducing himself and his girl partner, this agent said, "There's a couple of questions we'd like to ask you, Bobby . . ."

While the guy made his pitch, Bobby took a look at the female agent. Maybe on other days he would have been more attentive to her—she was definitely attractive enough—but today wasn't that day. Today there was little room in his heart for that.

They asked him politely to take a walk with them. Initially he turned them down, telling them just as politely, "This really's not such a great time." But then the girl agent had taken hold of his hand and squeezed it gently. He couldn't tell if that was meant as sympathy or seduction, but either way it got his attention. If an FBI agent was desperate enough to flirt with him, it had to be really important.

Before they had taken three steps, he asked the proper legal questions. If he had gotten the wrong answers, he wouldn't have taken a fourth step. In response they told him they weren't wired and agreed that everything he said would be off the record, meaning they wouldn't use it against him. While that didn't provide any solid legal protection, if they were taping him, a jury would hear them lying, pretty much destroying their credibility.

O'Brien, the male agent, asked the first question. "You ever hear of a Professor Peter Gradinsky?"

The professor? Of course, Bobby thought, that's why the one

name sounded sort of familiar. These were the agents that that long-faced secretary, something Simon, had told him about. Yeah, right, the nice-looking girl and the grumpy-looking guy. A young Walter Matthau, that's how she'd described him. These people were also out there looking for Gradinsky. Had he ever heard of him? Cute, very cute. They already knew the answer to that question. But he made the decision that he wasn't going to help them. "Gradinsky, huh?" He repeated the name as if he'd never heard it before. "Gradinsky? No, it doesn't sound familiar. What kind of professor is he?"

They played the game, telling him what he already knew. Then they asked him if he knew Anthony Cosentino. Anthony? They sounded like a talking newspaper story. Mr. Anthony Cosentino. He couldn't help but smile. "You know how it is, maybe I met him once or twice to shake hands. Seems like a nice enough guy. We got some friends in common, that's all." This was total bullshit and he knew it and they knew it. So he asked them, "What game we playing here?"

O'Brien made a joke out of it, responding, "Clue, it looks like to me. You know, Uncle Tony's in the basement with a hammer."

A regular fucking comedian, Bobby thought. Don fucking Rickles. Then the agent asked if he knew Skinny Al. Alphonse D'Angelo. Bobby decided to throw him a bone. "Sure, who didn't know him?" he lied. "Everybody knew that fat slob. Even the mayor, Koch, he knew him from when he was a councilman, I'll bet." That'll get them running to the grand jury. Mayor Koch friendly with a wiseguy? Whoa, stop the presses. Bobby chuckled to himself. This whole thing was actually sort of amusing. On a day like today he needed it.

The girl agent was talking now. He looked her over again. Okay, he noticed, that Simon was right, she was nice-looking. She had some style too. She was wearing just the right amount of makeup; when you looked at her, you didn't notice right away that she was wearing makeup. Perfect.

And then her words ripped through him. "What do you know about the murder of Pamela Fox?"

Jesus fucking Christ. Keep walking, he ordered himself, just keep moving. Don't stop. Don't let them know nothing. Prick bastards. How the fuck did they find out about it so quickly? Keep walking, don't look at them. That Gradinsky bullshit, it wasn't about that at all.

And then, suddenly, he decided to confront them. They didn't have the right to come to him about this. This wasn't their fucking business. He stopped and whirled to face them. "Fuck you," he spit at them. "Who the fuck do you think you are, talking to me like that?" His anger was growing. He balled his hands into fists, digging his fingernails into his palms, his old way of making sure he didn't hit the wrong person. Maintaining control. A couple of people walking past stopped, then got out of there as fast as they could. Bobby pointed a warning finger at O'Brien, then practically screamed, "I don't care who the fuck you are. Come near me again, I swear to God you're gonna be real unhappy. Now, you got any more questions, you call my fucking lawyer."

Then he walked right between them, right between the two of them, like a defensive lineman going through the line after the quarterback, practically shoving both of them off to the side. Who the fuck did they think they were?

What the fuck was he doing talking to them in the first place? That was the mistake. That was what happens when you try to be a nice guy. They fuck you over. The fucking agent was yelling something at his back. A Russian name, Vasily someshit. At that moment Bobby didn't give a flying fuck about anything the FBI had to say to him. Only when he heard the agent call the guy "a real lady killer" did he get the message.

That was a lot more information than necessary to ask that question. Bobby stopped and spun halfway around. "What'd you say?" They couldn't intentionally be telling him what they were telling him. Not the Fucking Bunch of Idiots.

The guy was blabbing. "I asked if you knew this Russian guy, Vasily Kuznetzov. Maybe I can refresh your memory. He runs this bootleg fuel business out of a gas station on Brighton Beach Boulevard—1405, I think it is." They walked toward him. The guy had a real shit-eating grin on his face. He was talking to his partner but looking directly at Bobby. "That's it, right, partner—1405 Brighton Beach Boulevard?"

That was the right address, she said. Bobby just stood there, stunned into silence. They were actually giving up Pam's killer to him. He didn't have the slightest doubt about that. Holy fucking shit, this was an amazing thing. The FBI giving up a killer to the family. Somebody dig up Ripley, 'cause no one was gonna believe this one. 1405 Brighton Beach Boulevard. A gas station. Easy to remember. "There's a room hidden in the back. You have to go through the men's room to get there? Doesn't ring any bells, huh?"

They were giving him the road map. Telling him everything. Who would have figured? The FBI asking for help from him. Basically asking him to do the heavyweight work. He couldn't help smiling at that thought. The world gets pretty strange sometimes.

The guy continued talking, pretending he was talking to the girl but looking right at Bobby. "And doesn't he have this psycho partner works there too, Russo? Ivan something?"

The meaning of that was pretty obvious. They were warning him to watch out for the little fucker. The broad-shouldered guy. Even at the funeral the guy looked like a walking problem.

There was no question about what these feds were doing; the real question was, why were they doing it? The female agent, Russo, was still talking about the crazy guy, Chernanko. Shit, they were all crazy, those Russians; that one was just a little crazier than the rest of them. ". . . always fighting with Skinny Al at the meetings between Tony Cosentino and the Russians," she was saying. "The one who swore he was going to kill him someday?"

Kill him? Holy Mother. Bobby relaxed his fists. For just an instant his mind flashed back on the funeral. It was like he was standing right there again, a few feet away, watching the two Russians kissing Tony Cosentino. And the Hammer, the motherfucking Hammer, was laughing along with them. So they were the producers, he thought. They had made the funeral possible—by killing the featured guest. These thoughts were racing through his head at lightning-bolt speed. And then he settled on the one that mattered: Did Cosentino know?

Jesus.

He looked at the girl and saw the cold determination in her eyes. She knew exactly what she was doing. She was pushing him to kill the Russians. Both of them, her and her partner, they were putting the gun in his hand. Why? What was in it for them? If they had all this information, they probably had enough to make their bones in the bureau. This was stuff for the front page of the *Daily News.* The bureau loved this stuff as much as the reporters, they loved the publicity. And this situation? Pretty much your average Joe Citizen liked the Mafia, but there was nobody who liked the Russian mob. Not even the Russians. They were the enemy, the commies. So why didn't the bureau take them down themselves? Pam maybe? Getting even for Pam? Was it possible the FBI had a heart? That they wanted to do the right thing? That thought made him smile. Not in this lifetime. But nothing else made sense.

The guy came a few steps closer and said, "I think that's what Professor Gradinsky said when we spoke to him last night. Remember? Was that before or after he told us that they were meeting there tonight?"

The professor? They had the professor? If they expected that to have an impact on him, they were going to be real disappointed. At that moment the professor was maybe the last person in the world that he cared about. He was going to find Gradinsky for Cosentino? That story was very old news.

The fact that the big meeting was being held that night wasn't much of a surprise either. It was pretty obvious that was the reason Cosentino was pushing so hard to find him. He needed him before this meeting. It was almost funny. None of that mattered anymore, none of it. Finding the professor, the million-dollar deals, none of it. By the time he got done tonight, it would all be a sad memory.

He had all the information he needed. Whatever their reasons, the
FBI had given him the name of Pam's killer and told him where to
find him. Game over. Dealing with these agents was complicated. He
owed them big-time. Maybe he should be thankful: Without their
assistance he wouldn't be walking into a potential bloodbath. He
wouldn't be putting his own life up for grabs. Fine, he thought, I'll
buy them a table at the annual Mafia Dinner Dance.

It had been a long time since he'd slept. Seemed like a couple of
years, at least. He took off his hat and brushed back his hair. He
closed his eyes and for a split second he almost fell asleep on his feet.
His head dropped forward but he quickly jerked it back. Then he put
his hat back on, adjusted it to a jaunty angle, and walked away.

Fuck 'em, he thought.

A fender bender on the Belt Parkway had cost them a few minutes, but Bobby wasn't in a big hurry. There was no possible way the
meeting with Cosentino was going to start before ten o'clock and
probably it was going to be much later than that. Dinner first, always. He used the time on the road to explain the situation to Little
Eddie. When he started telling him about Pam, he couldn't help it,
his eyes teared up. As he had anticipated, Eddie didn't say too much
in response, mostly a few "bastards" and "motherfuckers."

Eddie ignored Bobby's tears. They never happened. Talking about
personal problems always made him uncomfortable. He much preferred situations that could be handled with a baseball bat, or in the
extreme, with Myrtle and her friends. He was curious, though, wondering what they had done to Bobby's girl. He figured Bobby probably wanted to know too, almost as much as he didn't want to know.

Bobby drove past the gas station three times to check it out. The
first time he went by the place Eddie said in surprise, "Gees, look at
that, willya?"

Bobby glanced at the gas station but saw nothing unusual. "What?
What?"

"High-test's only a dollar five. That's pretty fucking cheap."

Bobby ignored him. After the third drive-by he turned the corner and parked as far as possible from the streetlights. They were too far from the station to be noticed but close enough to watch the place. They sat there and they watched. It was impossible to see what was going on inside, but out in front a steady stream of customers took advantage of the low price. Bobby counted two attendants. A little after eight o'clock the outside lights were turned off. A couple of minutes later most of the lights in the office also went out. And a few minutes after that one of the attendants, an old-looking guy, came out of the office, got in a beat-up Chevy, and drove away. "He didn't lock it," Eddie noted.

"The other guy's still inside," Bobby pointed out. While they waited, Bobby checked out the entire area, watching for guards, cops, cameras, surveillance, or security of any kind. If it was there, he couldn't find it.

"How long?" Eddie asked. He affectionately patted his stomach. "You know, I gotta feed this thing every few hours."

Bobby couldn't help laughing. Little Eddie definitely had his priorities in order: friendship, food, then killing. In that order. Friendship first, always. Bobby didn't like to eat when he was in this kind of waiting situation. If he ate, he wanted something to drink. If he had something to drink, he was going to have to take a piss. If he had to take a piss, he either went into a soda bottle or had to get out of the car. If he took a piss in a bottle, he had to carry it away with him or leave it at the scene for the cops. Since he didn't like pissing in a bottle and he didn't want to get out of the car and give up his stakeout, he didn't eat.

Eddie was different. Eddie had cast-iron kidneys. He could drink a six-pack and pee next week. He was amazing. So Bobby was about to suggest that Eddie walk over to a deli they'd passed about a block away when the charcoal Firebird stopped at a traffic light almost directly in front of them. "Look at that," he said urgently, "look, look."

It was impossible to see who was in the car. The light changed and the Firebird went about thirty yards, then made a right turn into the gas station. It disappeared around the back. Bobby and Eddie watched and waited, but whoever was inside never reappeared. Bobby assumed whoever it was went through the bathroom into the secret hidden special room.

They waited in the car until Eddie's stomach growled. "Hey, don't blame me," he said, holding up his hands. "It speaks for itself."

"All right," Bobby said. He reached across the front seat and opened the glove compartment. Eddie had to push back in the passenger seat to give him stomach clearance. Bobby shoveled everything out of the box and onto the floor, then pulled open the false back. He took hold of the gun that was hidden there, then checked it to make certain it was loaded. "Ready?"

Little Eddie nodded toward the gun. "You got a silencer for that?"

Most people don't know it, but it's considerably more difficult to get a silencer for a gun than to get the gun. A lot of people improvise. If you know what you're doing, for example, it's possible to make a functional silencer from a plastic soda bottle. Or a cushion or a pillow. Bobby shook his head. "I didn't have enough time." He thought about it. "Maybe there's something in the trunk."

Once again he reached across the seat, this time pressing a button and popping open the trunk. As Eddie checked Myrtle, Bobby dug into the trunk. He was smiling when he got back in the car.

"What the fuck is that?" Eddie asked.

"What's it look like?" Bobby said. "It's the last one of those Cabbage Patch Kids I had, 'member?" He read the name on the "birth certificate." "This is Penny Nichols." He held up the doll. "Penny, say hello to your Uncle Eddie."

"Great," Eddie said, "fucking Looney Tunes. Now, what are you gonna do with that thing? Ask them to babysit?"

"Watch." Bobby carried a penknife on his key chain. He stuck the knife into the doll between its legs and cut it open. Then he reached in and pulled out some of the rag stuffing. Almost immediately the strong scent of turpentine filled the car.

"Open the fucking window," Eddie ordered. "That stuff stinks."

Bobby opened his window. "These is counterfeit, I guess." He tossed the rags out the window. Then he took his gun and twisted its barrel into the hole he'd dug. He waved the gun through the air and the Cabbage Patch Kid appeared to dance on it. "This'll work," he said, pleased.

Little Eddie started getting out of the car. "Yeah, the smell alone'll kill them."

Bobby took the ignition key off his key chain and put it on the floor, under the mat. If they had to get out of there quickly, he didn't want to waste time fumbling with his keys trying to find it. For the same reason, he didn't lock the car.

The gas station was in the middle of the block. The stores on either side of it were closed. Bobby and Eddie stayed on the far side of the street and walked down the entire block. Bobby's gun was in his coat pocket, the doll stuck headfirst into the other pocket, its legs sticking up in the air. Myrtle was concealed under Eddie's unzipped jacket. There was some traffic on that portion of Brighton Beach Boulevard, but few pedestrians. They passed a woman walking two dogs and a young couple holding hands and giggling. They looked across the street at the gas station. They didn't see anybody moving around at all.

At the far end of the block they crossed the street and turned right, walking back toward the gas station. The men's room was on its left, the side closest to them as they approached.

"Let's do it," Bobby said, and they walked purposefully, side by side, toward the station. They ducked behind the pumps, where they could not be seen from the office. Once they were safely in the shadows, Bobby took out his gun and Penny Nichols, then twisted the barrel of the gun between the doll's legs. Eddie took out Myrtle, checking to make sure the safety was off. And then the two men went to work.

Bobby led the way toward the office. At times like this you never know what to expect, so you expect everything. All of your senses are primed; you hear every sound, see the slightest movement; some people claim you can even smell your adrenaline pumping. The im-

portant thing is not to hesitate. To move with confidence. To keep
going forward.

The office was empty. The room was dimly lit by a low-wattage
bulb in a gooseneck lamp on the desk. They didn't bother trying the
door, assuming there was some kind of bell or buzzer system. They
moved past the garage doors. Somewhat surprisingly, all of the single-
pane rectangular windows were covered with sheets of white paper.
Somebody obviously did not want people to know what was going
on inside the garage. Scribbled in black marker on one of these white
sheets was the notice "Lifts Broken. No Repairs."

But as they moved past the last window, Bobby saw that the paper
covering it had flopped back. It was being held in place by a piece of
tape on the bottom corner, allowing him to see inside. The lights
were on. It was a typically drab auto mechanics work area. There
were two old-fashioned hydraulic lifts, the type with two parallel
long metal skids to support a car. The two ramps of the lift on the
left were lying flat on the cement floor, but the lift on the right was
holding a car about four feet in the air. Chest-high. It did not appear
to be broken, just shut down for the night with the car left raised in
position. Although Bobby's field of vision was limited, he scanned as
much of the garage as possible. And that's when it caught his attention.

There was a wooden workbench against the back wall. Scattered
on the bench top were well-used tools, grease-covered auto parts,
filthy rags, and a telephone. Stored on the lower shelf were more
tools, more parts, and more filthy rags. And one other thing. Bun-
dled into a ball, just another rag, and shoved into a corner was something bright powder blue. Whatever it was, its color stood out
against the drab work materials like carousel horses in the desert. The
color was unmistakable: It was the corporate blue used by Pan Am,
as recognizable as Coca-Cola's red or Camel's camel. In fact, it was
the precise color of a stewardess's uniform.

Bobby put a restraining hand on Eddie's stomach and whispered,
"I gotta check something." He backtracked to the office door. Very

slowly he pushed it open a few inches, waiting to hear an alarm. Nothing. He pushed it open a few more inches, then slipped inside. Holding the door still, he reached up and grasped the cluster of bells hanging on the back of the door. The alarm system. Holding them tightly in his hand, he opened the door and let Eddie inside. A large, noisy space heater warmed the office, indicating the attendant would be returning. Bobby pointed to the door, silently telling Eddie to stand guard. Eddie nodded. He stepped into the protection of the shadows and stood there, Myrtle warm against his chest.

A doorway separated the office from the garage. If there had ever been a door there, all evidence of it was gone. Bobby stepped through it and took one step down into the cold garage. He went directly to the uncovered window and refastened the paper, figuring no one outside would notice. Little actions like that can sometimes save a life. That done, he turned and took a good long look at the place. No matter where he looked, though, that ball of blue under the workbench wouldn't go away. In his mind it just grew larger and larger. He knew what it was, he just wasn't ready to confront it.

He ran out of time. Carefully avoiding the black signal hose that rang when stepped on, he walked to the back, to the bench. And he reached down and grasped it. He knew instantly. It was a Pan Am flight attendant's skirt, Pam's skirt. It had a couple of grease spots on it and was ripped in several places, but it was her skirt. He held it close to his chest. She had been here. Here, in this garage. They had probably grabbed her just as she was getting ready to take that flight to Paris. She was dressed for work. Fifteen minutes more, twenty maybe, she would have been out of there. Safe. Alive. He held on to her skirt, but he didn't want to think about her. What they did to her. What made her scream like that. He looked at the variety of pulling and hammering tools, he looked at the torch, at the hooks and the cutting tools. At all of them. And wondered. And then he neatly folded her skirt and placed it on the bench.

Seconds later he knew the answer. As he turned around, he was facing the front of a car four feet in the air, resting on the metal skids.

He took one deep cleansing breath, then headed back to the office. It was time to get even. He took four or five steps and stopped. Just stopped. It was the color, again, that got his attention. Caught in the hinged joint of one of the skids was a small ragged piece of Pan Am blue fabric. A piece that had been torn from her skirt. And he knew then what they had done to her. The cop had said it. "They crushed her," he'd said, "limb by limb. Her feet, her hands, arms, and legs." In his mind he heard that cop again and again. They crushed her. They crushed her.

Control, he thought. Control. A mammoth sorrow threatened to overwhelm him, smother him, but he wouldn't let that happen. This was a time to focus. He took two steps backward, but his shoes stuck briefly to the cement floor. Fucking grease, he figured. When he looked down, though, he knew how terribly wrong he was. He was standing in a coagulating puddle of a deep red substance.

If he was going to lose control, this would be the moment. Instead, he closed his eyes, feeling his despair being transformed into pure white rage. And rather than compelling him to strike out mindlessly, this rage empowered him. It took away his fears. It bestowed on him the invincibility of a man beyond caring.

Whatever happened, happened.

"Now," he said to Eddie. Taking hold of the bells once again, Bobby opened the door and they slipped outside. They moved in the shadows. At the corner of the building he paused, an infantryman on patrol. He looked around the side of the building. Clear. Both men stayed close to the wall as they approached the bathroom door.

They stood directly in front of the door. Bobby pushed the barrel of his gun deeper into the doll. He checked again to make sure his safety was off. Then he turned to Eddie, who whispered, "Fuck 'em."

Holding the gun in his right hand, he turned the doorknob with his left hand. As the door opened, he put his left hand on the doll's head to hold it in place. A large man was sitting on the toilet seat, fully clothed, an automatic weapon resting on his lap. When the man looked up in surprise, Bobby saw the gold crowns on his front teeth. The only thought Bobby had time for was how much this man reminded him of James Bond's Oddjob.

The attendant scrambled for his gun. Bobby coolly raised his right arm, aimed his Cabbage Patch Kid, and fired. One shot. *Pstew.* The doll ate most of the noise. Bits of cloth flew all over the bathroom. The bullet smashed through the attendant's gold teeth and exited the back of his head. He still appeared to be looking at Bobby, but he was already dead. His body slumped to the right, his fall stopped by the wall. He remained seated on the toilet, his dead eyes still open. The filthy tiled wall behind him was covered with blood spatter and tiny bits of brain matter.

Bobby watched the stain spreading with curiosity. Some people were superstitious about the blood patterns they created and examined them closely. Supposedly one wiseguy saw the Virgin Mary in a blood spatter pattern and never fired another shot. To Bobby this one looked mostly like a work from Picasso's abstract period.

Eddie pushed inside the bathroom behind Bobby and shut the door. Bobby took a quick look around. The place was pretty awful, so disgusting that even a dead body on the toilet didn't make it much worse. It looked like it hadn't been cleaned since the Flood. He glanced at the ceiling and the corners, searching for a security camera. If this bathroom was being watched, the camera was well hidden. His eyes professionally swept the room. Tiles were missing from the floor and the walls, there was a layer of caked dirt on the floor, both the toilet and sink were cracked. The sink was dry and stained brown. A filthy cotton towel hung limply from a broken dispenser. There was, however, a full roll of toilet paper sitting on the cracked toilet lid. Fortunately the familiar smell of gunpowder dampened the stench of urine.

"What're you, sightseeing?" Eddie whispered urgently. "Where's the fucking door?"

At first Bobby didn't see it. Then he looked at the drab, dirty raincoat hanging on the wall directly opposite the toilet. "There," he said. He pushed the raincoat aside, and beneath it, as he figured, was the doorknob. He took a few seconds to shove the remnants of Penny Nichols back down on the barrel of his gun, then put his left hand on the faded silver doorknob. "Ready?" he whispered.

"Just fucking go," Little Eddie told him impatiently, waving Myrtle toward the meeting room.

Bobby guessed it wasn't locked. There really wasn't any reason to lock it. The room was hidden and protected by a hulking armed guard; putting a lock on it wasn't going to make much difference.

He turned the doorknob without pushing open the door. It turned easily. "I'm going right and down," Bobby whispered.

Eddie was getting irritated. "Yeah yeah, just go, huh?"

Bobby pushed open the door to another world. Hidden in the rear of the dilapidated gas station was a high-tech conference room that more properly belonged in a Park Avenue law firm. High-back leather chairs were set around a highly polished oval mahogany conference table. A second row of chairs was arranged several feet behind this table. The walls were paneled in dark wood. There were no windows, but the room was brightly lit by mostly recessed lighting that gave it a warm reddish tint. For an instant Bobby was stunned by the contradiction in rooms, but recovered almost immediately and got out of the doorway, ducking down and to his right. Moving at full speed, Eddie followed him through the open door.

There were three men in the room. Two of them were sitting at the table, obviously waiting for the meeting to begin, their shoes resting comfortably on the mahogany. They reacted almost immediately. One of them screamed a single word in Russian. And then Bobby and Eddie began firing. Bobby's first shot hit the man closest to him, a fat, balding man sitting less than six feet away, in his left shoulder. The doll burst open, hurtling off the gun. The force of the bullet ripping through the Russian's body at close range caused his chair to begin spinning counterclockwise. Bobby fired again, through the back of the chair. The chair just about completed a full revolution and slowed to a stop. It was the Wheel of Misfortune. The Russian was dead before it stopped moving.

Simultaneously Eddie sprayed the room, laying a track of bullet holes the length of the table and straight up the far wall. The second man at the table, the stocky Russian with a blond flattop, dived off his chair and onto the floor. The third Russian, tall and thin, was standing on the far side of the table next to an open minirefrigerator. He reacted first. Whether he recognized Bobby or saw the guns, he was the one who shouted the one word of warning, then dived for the light switch on the wall. The recessed lighting went off, leaving lit only two floor lamps—one on either side of the room.

Seconds later the Russian on the floor began firing back. It was defensive fire, shots fired rapidly and wildly, firing to force the aggressor to take cover. As the Russian was firing up from beneath the table, most of the shots hit the top of the wall or the ceiling.

Eddie calmly moved out of the light. He figured it would be ridiculous for a man as big as he was to try to take cover, so he didn't bother. Instead, he laid down a rain of fire.

Wiseguys aren't Superman. Although just about every soldier is knowledgeable and comfortable with a wide variety of guns, they're not John Wayne. So most hits are pretty basic. Boom in the back of the head. That kind of thing. Nobody can practice for a gunfight.

Actual gunfights are extremely rare and almost never last longer than a few seconds—but for the shooters it will be the longest few seconds of their lives. Bobby had a big advantage: He was already ducking down to get out of Eddie's range of fire, so when the lights went off, he just kept going. He hit the ground, lay down flat, and kept firing. That meant his direct line of fire was below the table.

Nobody had time to aim. So what happened was pretty much luck. The stocky Russian was trying to scramble to his feet, still firing wildly, when Bobby's fourth or fifth shot hit him directly between his legs, taking off the head of his penis and one testicle. It was as if someone had burst a balloon full of blood; the blood just poured out of him. Frantically he tried to stop the bleeding by squeezing his penis. The excruciating pain forced him to try to rise up, but as he did, he smashed his head into the bottom of the table. He was unconscious when he hit the ground, falling face-first into a pool of his own blood. The coroner would not be able to determine if he died from the gunshot wound or choked to death in his own blood.

Little Eddie got the third one, the tall one, Vaseline. Once bullets start flying, it's impossible to predict their path with any accuracy. For example, bullets will bounce off the ground, one of the reasons that hiding behind a car when someone is shooting at you may not provide adequate protection. One of Eddie's shots bounced off the door of the minifridge, angled almost straight up, and smashed a bottle of vodka. The bottle exploded, and razorlike slivers of glass sprayed Vasily in the face. In that one instant he looked as if he'd just had the worst shave in history. His face was marked with dozens of small cuts. And when the vodka hit that raw skin, his face began burning terribly. He threw up his hand to try to wipe away the vodka and blood, and as he did, another bullet tore through his hand. It literally made a hole he could look right through.

"Quit! Quit!" he screamed. "Quit!" Seconds later he tossed his gun on the remnants of the table. Eddie had a hunch, yelling, "Throw the other one too." And after a brief pause a second gun landed with a clunk on the table. "Stand the fuck up," Eddie ordered. "Get in the light."

The entire shoot-out had taken no more than fifteen seconds. In about the time it takes to sneeze three times two men were dead, a third was wounded.

The Russian was obviously in tremendous pain. He stood up, holding his wounded right hand with his left hand, stuffing a handkerchief into his palm to stanch the bleeding. Curiously his hand did not bleed excessively. But rivulets of blood flowed down his face, the blood dripping onto the carpet like drops of water from melting icicles. A cloud of gun smoke hung over the room and everybody's ears were ringing. The floor was covered with shell casings. Neither Bobby nor Eddie bothered to pick them up. It didn't matter that they could be linked to specific weapons, since by the end of the night those weapons would no longer exist.

The Russian was muttering something to himself. Whatever he was saying, to Bobby it just sounded like gibberish. It didn't matter. In the same heavily accented English Bobby recognized from the phone call to the Freemont, Vasily asked for another handkerchief, for something to wipe his face.

Bobby picked up the remains of the Cabbage Patch Kid. The head was gone and what remained of the torso was practically ripped in half just above the midsection. It was still smoking. "Sure," he said, pulling out a turpentine-soaked rag and tossing it across the conference table. Vasily picked it up and used it to wipe his face.

Bobby waited patiently. Only after Vasily began screaming did he smile.

"You want me to do it?" Little Eddie yelled. Eddie was shouting because he could barely hear a word. It sounded like the Hunchback of Notre Dame was practicing the bells in his ears.

Vasily's screams dampened to a whimper. "Fuck you," he shouted at Bobby. Bobby did have to admire him. There he was, standing there with blood dripping from his face and hand, two guys dead on the carpet, another guy dead on the toilet, and he hadn't lost a whit of his arrogance. "That motherfucker Cosentino he cut off your fucking balls you kill me."

Bobby appeared to be considering that. "Maybe," he agreed.

"Fuck that, Bobby," Eddie shouted dismissively. "Don't listen to that asshole."

"Get your hands behind your back," he ordered the Russian.

Vasily looked at him smugly as he did exactly as ordered, believing that Bobby had taken his warning seriously.

Bobby yanked a telephone cord out of the wall, then pulled the other end out of the phone. He wrapped it around the Russian's wrists. "Move," he said, poking him forward with his gun. Vasily started talking, blabbing something about Cosentino, fuel oil, you and me, but Bobby wasn't listening. Instead, he picked up one of the doll's severed arms, grabbed a hank of the Russian's hair, and pulled back his head. When Vasily opened his mouth, Bobby shoved the doll's arm down his throat, shutting him up. As the Russian gagged, struggling to cough it out of his mouth, Bobby pushed him forward.

"What're you gonna do with this piece of shit?"

"Watch." They moved through the bathroom. The dead attendant had slumped off the toilet seat and appeared to be wedged between the bowl and the wall. The first flies had already appeared and were buzzing around the hole in his head. Bobby pushed Vasily out of the door. Vasily continued struggling to get the arm out of his mouth. Bobby held on to the Russian's hair with his left hand and prodded him forward with the gun in his right hand. He stayed in the dark as much as possible and pretty much pushed and prodded him around to the front of the gas station. He probably realized what was about to happen to him when Bobby pushed him into the office.

With his hands still bound behind him, he whirled around, lowered his shoulder, and charged into Bobby, trying to force him backward into Eddie. Trying to do anything to change the equation. Bobby fell back a couple of feet into Eddie, but Eddie was a wall. Bobby just stopped. The Russian charged again, but this time, just before he slammed into Bobby, Bobby smashed him in the head with the butt of his gun. He really didn't want to hurt him too badly; he wanted the Russian fully conscious.

The blow staggered the Russian. Bobby went right at him, kicking him hard in the balls, literally lifting him off the ground. He landed on his stomach; unable to cushion his fall with his hands, his face smashed into the concrete floor. His nose must have been splintered because blood immediately began gushing out of it. Bobby stepped over him and took hold of one of his feet, then dragged him into the garage, his face leaving a trail of blood on the floor.

At some point the doll's arm was jarred loose. The Russian started screaming in a mix of Russian, English and agony, the English consisting mostly of "motherfucker" this and "motherfucker" that. The actual threats—Bobby assumed they were threats from the tone— were screamed in Russian. Bobby paid no attention to him.

Eddie had no idea what Bobby intended to do, but nothing would have surprised him or, in fact, horrified him. In his career he'd seen some pretty brutal things done to people. Once even he had cut up a body with a hacksaw, then dropped the various pieces in different sewers. Bobby's reason for torturing this guy was a little light on the details, but that made no difference. He played on Bobby's team and Bobby knew the rules. Besides, it was just some Russians, and whatever they were doing, it probably wasn't right.

When Bobby dragged the guy into the garage, Eddie figured that whatever he had planned, it probably had something to do with the tools in there; he'd heard about some real crazy things people had done with tools. And why else drag the guy in there? It doesn't matter where you shoot somebody. The Russian in the bathroom was just as dead as the two Russians in the conference room.

Vasily was squirming and kicking like a hooked fish. He eventually managed to turn over onto his back. That was just fine with Bobby; he wanted this fuck to see every single thing that was happening to him.

Bobby dragged him across the floor until he was directly under one of the skids. He knew exactly where he wanted him to be—lying in that sticky deep red puddle. As soon as he let him go, though, the Russian began cursing at him—and used his legs to wriggle out from under the hydraulic lift. In response Bobby took a long orange extension cord off the bench. While Eddie stepped on the Russian's face to keep him still, Bobby methodically wrapped the cord around his legs tight as a mummy. When he finished, Eddie asked loudly—his ears were still ringing—"Where do you want him?"

Bobby looked at the hydraulic, and Eddie knew. Now, that's creative, he thought. He liked the whole idea. Following Bobby's instructions, he dragged the guy back, until he was right under the lift. "Here?" Eddie had a little problem moving around because his shoes were sticking to whatever that crap was on the floor. And when he stepped on the guy's face, the sole of his shoe left a purple splotch on his skin.

"No, no, no. Just his feet," Bobby directed, standing by the hydraulic control lever.

"Gees, Bobby," Eddie said with admiration, "you got some fucking sense of humor." Eddie turned the Russian about ninety degrees and pulled him back a few feet. He still wasn't certain he had him positioned exactly right. "Go ahead and try it," he suggested. "Let's see."

Bobby pressed down on the lever, and the lift began descending, bringing down with it a 3,577-pound Buick LeSabre. The Russian started shrieking in terror, struggling desperately to get loose. Once again Eddie put his foot firmly on the Russian's neck and pushed down hard. The Russian stopped squirming. His eyes opened wide in absolute terror as the skid came down lower and lower and lower. The skid was about a yard above his feet when Bobby shut it down. The Russian closed his eyes in relief. "Now what's the problem?" Eddie asked.

Bobby walked over to the bench and retrieved Pam's Pan Am blue skirt. He stuffed as much of it as he could manage into the Russian's mouth. "I can't stand that screeching," he said. Then he went back to the controls and once again pushed down on the lever. As it turned out, Eddie had positioned the Russian perfectly. The metal ramp carrying the Buick came down directly on both of his feet. He tried to splay them to the side with only limited success. The lift barely slowed as it crushed his feet. If the breaking bones made any sound, neither Bobby nor Eddie heard it. After squashing both feet the skid began pressing into his legs.

Bobby stopped the lift again. He wasn't feeling good or bad; at most he felt a small sense of satisfaction. He was doing what had to be done, putting the world right. The bad guy was being punished. This was simply an act of revenge.

He raised the lift up a few feet, then ordered Eddie, "Move him down a little more." The Russian was writhing in pain, his agonized cries muffled by the mouthful of cloth. Bobby tried hard not to think about Pam lying there, caught in this same torturous situation, but that proved impossible.

Eddie put a shoe on the Russian's shoulder and shoved him down two or three feet. The Russian was in too much pain to resist. The second time Bobby lowered the steel skid it came down directly on Kuznetzov's hips. Neither Bobby nor Eddie knew anything about physiology, so they didn't know exactly what kind of damage was being done. They didn't know if it would be fatal. They didn't even know if the skid was pushing his hips apart or crushing them straight down. It didn't make any difference. As Eddie watched, one thing he knew for sure was that this guy wasn't going to be dancing any time soon.

What they did know was that the hydraulic lift exerted a tremendous amount of downward force per square inch, and as a result the Russian killer was literally being squashed into the cement. It was like lowering a cinder block on a grape.

Bobby let the skid continue to press down on the Russian's hips until he stopped screaming. The lift had literally pressed the air out of his lungs.

And then he raised it again. By then the Russian was semiconscious. His lips were moving, but the only sound coming from him was a low guttural moan. Bobby had next intended to crush his chest, but that no longer seemed to have any real purpose. For a few seconds he even considered just leaving the Russian there to either live in excruciating pain or die slowly. But he pretty quickly dismissed that thought, knowing that if the Russian somehow lived, his only reason to keep breathing would be to kill Bobby. "All the way under," he shouted at Eddie.

Eddie grimaced. This was a pretty tough thing that Bobby was going to do. Not that it bothered him. He figured, what the hell difference does it make how you go so long as you go? And obviously this was how they made Skinny Al skinny. Once again he put a sticky shoe on the Russian's shoulder and jostled him a little bit farther under the hydraulic lift, until his head was directly beneath the left skid. And then Bobby pushed the lever down. All the way down.

Only the top half of the Russian's head was actually under the skid, and it provided no more resistance than an egg. Like everybody in the business, Eddie knew the legendary story of the big-mouth wiseguy whose head was crushed in a vise until his eyes popped out and rolled across the floor, and he had wondered if that was really possible. As it turned out, this didn't help him answer that question, because the Russian's eyes were covered by the skid. Bobby could actually hear his skull cracking when the lift pressed down on it. It sort of crackled like a piece of wood breaking. The only sound the Russian made as the skid smashed down on his skull was a high-pitched whine. But that stopped abruptly, sort of in midwhine, like somebody had pulled out his plug.

Eddie was absolutely fascinated by the whole thing. As he watched, a mass of reddish pulpy material oozed out from beneath the skid, blending into the substance already there. To Eddie it looked like the highway crap he usually referred to as roadkill soup. While nothing ever repulsed Eddie, admittedly this did make his stomach a little queasy.

Bobby had to force himself to keep his eyes locked on the Russian's face. It was like being in a horror movie. If he had felt even the slightest tinge of compassion for the Russian, he would not have been able to watch. As almost two tons of steel pressed down on the Russian's head, his entire body seemed to arch upward. The skin on the lower part of his face was stretched when the skid pressed down on the upper half, causing his upper teeth and gums to be exposed. Then Bobby looked at the Russian's tightly clenched hands. When they opened, exposing the bullet hole, he knew the Russian was dead. It was really important to him that he saw him die.

He turned off the lift. The bottom half of the face was still visible, his upper teeth bared like a skeleton's. "Ugh," Eddie chuckled defensively. "That's some fucking headache. Man, I'm not gonna be able to eat nothing for an hour."

Bobby spit at the dead Russian, who was lying on the cement in a spreading pool of blood and brain. "C'mon."

"You just wanna leave him there like that?" Eddie asked curiously. He wasn't used to leaving his work behind.

"You wanna scrape him up, go ahead. That fucking prick doesn't deserve it, though . . ." Bobby stood there staring at the remains of the Russian gangster. There was no reason to hide the body or clean up the garage. Bobby wasn't worried about the cops. Nobody was going to report this killing. The people who needed to know who did it would know. And if things got a little warm, if the law put some heat on him, there were these two FBI agents he knew who might just want to put in a good word for him.

The last thing Eddie wanted to do was scrape him up. "It's our funeral, I guess," he said, and laughed. He picked up Myrtle from the top of the bench, checked to make sure the safety was on, then shoved the barrel down into his waistband. His sports jacket covered the weapon. "Let's go."

Bobby was absolutely exhausted. This had been the longest few days of his life. Whatever was going to happen next, there wasn't anything he could do about it. The train was going full speed down the mountain. As they walked out of the office, Bobby said firmly, "Thanks for that. I owe you."

Eddie beamed. Tonight was one of those experiences that bonded men together forever. This wasn't an ordinary hit; this one people were going to be talking about for a long time. And they had done it together. Eddie was a realist, he knew his own limitations. He was a camel, a proud soldier who carried the load for other people and made a nice living from it. And that was fine with him. He didn't want or need the problems that came with being a boss. But Bobby . . . Bobby was smarter than most of the other guys. Bobby had a real shot at making it—and if he did, after tonight, Eddie was going with him. They made a great team. "It's nothing," he murmured.

They were still in the shadows, walking away from the pumps, when the first guy stepped out in front of them. "Stand still," he ordered. He was pretty much hidden in darkness, but Bobby assumed he was holding a gun. "Keep your hands where they are," said a second man, standing behind them.

Bobby instantly ran through the possibilities: No way they were cops, either NYPD or feds. They would have identified themselves immediately. That was the law; they had to admit who they were. So they weren't law. And they didn't speak with any accent, so they weren't Russians. That meant they were wiseguys. Almost for sure Cosentino's people.

"Oh fuck," Eddie sighed softly. He just hadn't expected forever to be so brief.

Bobby didn't back off. "Who the fuck are you guys?" he demanded. He had nothing to gain by being cute. Their only hope was to come right at him. Whatever they were going to do, they were going to do, and at this particular moment there wasn't jack shit he could do about it.

"Just wait," the guy ordered.

Bobby thought he recognized the voice. He decided to take a shot, "That you . . . Jimmy?"

"Shut the fuck up," Jimmy Smiles ordered.

Shutting the fuck up wasn't going to save his life. "I want to talk to Mr. Cosentino."

Tony Cosentino appeared almost magically, moving through the shadows. Bobby didn't even try to guess how long he'd been there and how much he knew. One thing was obvious: He was pissed off. He came right up to Bobby and jabbed his finger in his chest. "I fucking warned you, didn't I? Didn't I tell you to stay away?"

"Yeah," Bobby admitted, "you did."

"I told you that you didn't know what was going on, didn't I? Didn't I tell you that?"

Bobby nodded and took a deep apologetic breath.

"Now, you tell me, asshole, where the fuck is the Russian?"

Bobby hesitated. Within a few seconds Cosentino would know

that the Russian was dead. There was nothing he could do to prevent that. In a conversational tone he said, "Well, see, Mr. Cosentino, I don't think he's going to be talking to you. The truth is he's under a lot of pressure right now."

Eddie's mouth opened. He looked at Bobby with awe and admiration. Holy fucking shit, he thought, here this guy is looking death right in the eyes and he's got the balls to James Bond him.

"That supposed to be funny?" Cosentino said. It was not a rhetorical question.

Another guy came walking back from the office. "Tony," he said with a shudder in his voice, "you better come see this. They fucking squashed the guy's head under that thing . . . you know, whattya call that thing that lifts cars up in the air? They dropped it on his head." Then he made some kind of sound indicating his disgust.

"You fucker!" Cosentino snapped, getting right up in Bobby's face. His anger was so intense, so complete, that his only outlet was a kind of disbelieving laughter. Not only had Bobby disobeyed him, a capital crime, he had betrayed him. He had destroyed the biggest deal anybody could ever imagine. Even if he could whack him two times, three times, even then he wouldn't be close to even.

Bobby stood his ground, wondering for an instant if the Hammer might be a little jealous that he'd never tried this method. Actually he was pretty surprised to discover that he wasn't the slightest bit afraid of Cosentino. He figured that maybe because he was resigned to his fate he didn't have to worry about getting hurt. He already knew he was going to get hurt. That was a given. He was going to get hurt bad. And there wasn't too much he could do to stop it. So his heart was barely pounding. "Mr. Cosentino . . . ," he began.

"Shut the fuck up," Cosentino screamed at him.

Bobby knew he had nothing to lose. "The guy whacked Skinny Al."

"I fucking said . . . ," Cosentino warned, then stopped. Just stopped cold. Until that moment Bobby had never completely believed that you could see hatred. But that's what he was looking at, inches away. Pure white hatred. Cosentino finally took a step back, trying to figure out what to do. Jackie Fats was standing a few feet away. Jimmy Smiles was there. Three other guys were close enough to hear him. They all heard Bobby make that claim. And if he was telling the truth, he had every right to kill the Russian and anybody who tried to stop him. More than that, he had an obligation. It was a family matter.

Looking straight into Cosentino's eyes at that moment, Bobby learned one other thing: Cosentino knew that. He knew the whole deal and he took it. Cosentino had averted his eyes, looked down, looked away in shame. He knew that the Russian asshole had killed D'Angelo, and he had done absolutely nothing about it. If that could be proved, Cosentino was a dead man. A boss who allowed a member of his crew to be whacked and did nothing to avenge that killing betrayed the tradition. A boss who would sell the life of one of his people lost his honor, and without that he was nothing. A piece of shit.

Cosentino had to put up a defense. "How the fuck you know that?" he challenged him.

"I got people," Bobby told him. He couldn't exactly tell him that the FBI had provided that information. Nobody standing there was going to believe anything said by the FBI.

For his own safety Cosentino needed to end this conversation fast. He didn't know how much Bobby really knew, and with members of his crew standing right there he wasn't about to dig too deeply. He just might be digging his own grave. So once again he waved a warning finger at Bobby. "You better be fucking right about that. I'm warning you."

"I'm right," Bobby said confidently.

Cosentino looked around anxiously. There was no doubt in Bobby's mind that Cosentino desperately wanted to whack both him and Eddie right where they stood, but that would make people too curious for his future health. "I'm gonna find out," he promised, "and I swear to God, I swear, if you ain't right, I'm gonna break fucking parts you don't even know you got." He turned to Jackie Fats. "Let's get the fuck outta here."

Jackie Fats indicated the garage. "You wanna leave him there?"

"What the fuck do I care?" He pointed at Bobby and Eddie. "It's their problem."

Bobby and Eddie watched Cosentino and his crew walk away, walking backward, their guns still aimed at them. Only after they were out of sight did Eddie dare speak. And he laughed, he laughed incredulously. "He's under a lot of pressure? Are you out of your fucking mind? Are you nuts? I couldn't fucking believe it."

Bobby was feeling okay, which was about the most he could expect for a while. Pam was dead and nothing was going to change that. But so were the people who killed her, and the big one died hard. Eventually, he knew, Cosentino would be coming after him. No question. As long as Bobby was alive he remained a danger to him. And when that happened, he'd be ready for him. He'd deal with it. But Cosentino had to let some time pass first; he'd have to give people time to forget.

And Bobby was never going to forget. What you gotta do, you gotta do.

SIXTEEN

Connor O'Brien looked across the candlelit table at an absolutely stunning Laura Russo, who was smiling demurely at him. It was as perfect an evening as he could imagine. Diamonds of light sparkled in the wine goblets set in front of them. Around them handsomely dressed diners spoke only in hushed tones, to a background of soft classical music, punctuated on occasion by the distant clatter of silverware. He found it almost impossible to take his eyes off her. Jim Slattery, dressed formally, a white towel draped over his arm, poured champagne for each of them. Connor lifted his glass and said softly to her . . .

"I mean, you wouldn't have believed that fat slob. You should have seen him. Little Eddie was so hopped-up it was like he was shooting caffeine."

The deep gravelly voice punctured O'Brien's daydream and brought him back to reality. He and Russo—who was actually wearing a white turtleneck sweater—were sitting at a table in the back at ManPower, a gay bar in the West Village, with Jim Slattery and Special Agent Victor Valone. Valone was one of the bureau's most promising young undercovers, having successfully infiltrated Henry "the Hammer" Franzone's Freemont Avenue crew, where he was known as Vito Valentine or Vito V. To maintain operational security, his true identity was known to very few people other than Slattery, his supervisor, but he had agreed to a sit-down with O'Brien and Russo to help them close their case. Holding this meeting in the back of a

Greenwich Village gay bar substantially diminished chances that they would be spotted.

Valone was describing the scene inside the social club the afternoon following the killings at the gas station. The agents had seen the official transcripts, but Valone put flesh on the bones. "The guy was so happy to still be breathing that he couldn't stop telling the story. I mean, he even acted it out in like charades for the Duke. I swear to God, he lay down on the floor and made these like real ugly faces. And all of those guys around, they were making up jokes. Like Georgia One-Time goes, 'Hey, hey, I guess the Russian was pressed for time,' and then somebody else goes, I think it was Lenny, 'The Russian can't come, Tony, he's got a pressing engagement,' or 'You gotta say this about that guy, he definitely has a one-track mind.' "

Slattery laughed happily in all the proper places. Watching him, O'Brien decided that his laughter was as much real as it was supportive. There was no question about it, Valone's imitation of the Freemont Avenue crew really was funny, but Slattery was the kind of supervisor who would laugh at Little Lulu if he thought that's what his agents needed to hear. One thing Connor O'Brien knew for sure: After what Slattery had done, he was entitled to laugh long and hard. The man had put his career on the line in the most courageous way: He had nothing to gain personally and his reputation and career to lose. If everyone worked out perfectly, no one would ever see his fingerprints. Only if the whole operation went to shit would his involvement become known. Nobody at headquarters was going to risk their own career to defend him. If this plan had failed, he would have paid for it big-time. And if the whole story ever became public, he would still be as vulnerable as a turkey the day before Thanksgiving.

After O'Brien and Russo had set the showdown in motion by meeting with San Filippo, Slattery had picked up the telephone and pulled the twenty-four-hour surveillance off the gas station. He'd made up some bullshit excuse to get the agents away from there and didn't assign replacements. And with that action he had cleared the path for the bloodbath. It was an incredibly gutsy thing to do but absolutely necessary. For the plan to work, the agents working the stakeout had to be removed. If they had been there when the shooting started, they would have been forced to respond. It was a bizarre situation: FBI agents could have screwed up a deadly operation simply by doing their job, by trying to save lives. The setup was the gunfight at the Not So O.K. Corral.

If the media ever found out that Slattery had handed the Russians to the Mafia, that he had made murder possible, both he and the bureau would have been sliced, diced, and tattooed. Calling it a scandal would be like calling Vietnam a skirmish. And Special Agents O'Brien and Russo would have fallen into that infamous category best known as "What ever happened to?" If the real story was discovered, both of them had a real good shot at a secure job stamping license plates under federal supervision.

The only thing that could have saved Slattery was the growing suspicion in the bureau's personnel division that he never actually existed, as all traces of his paperwork had disappeared. It would have been extremely difficult for the bureau to fire someone who wasn't anywhere.

O'Brien and Russo had spent the night waiting anxiously with Slattery in his office, listening to reports on an NYPD radio. The best news they could hear was none; if the cops got a "shots fired" call, Slattery could start packing. Fearing it was going to be a long evening, O'Brien had brought in a couple of six-packs of Coke and big bags of potato chips and pretzels. The early part of the evening was quiet. In addition to the usual domestic disputes, missing children, car accidents, animal attacks, heart attacks, muggings, and excessive noise disturbances, a naked man in Brooklyn was seen walking down Kings Highway carrying a machete, an unidentified man in the Bronx was spotted going up to a rooftop with either "a small woman or a large child who was crying," two women in Queens were brawling surrounded by a group of men who apparently were betting on the outcome, and in Manhattan residents of a brownstone on East 77th Street were terrified because a resident's exotic snake had escaped its cage and crawled into the ventilation system.

O'Brien remained hopeful that they would sit there all night without knowing what happened at the gas station. If Vaseline was left standing, there was little chance he'd report the attack. There was no way the Russians wanted the cops anywhere near the gas station. Bobby Blue Eyes would just disappear: buried, burned, chopped, or dropped. He'd be given "the Hoffa." But if it was Bobby who survived, he'd have a much tougher time getting rid of the body or bodies and would probably be forced to leave them there. So unless the Russians provided special janitorial services, somebody would discover the carnage and make the call.

Three bites into a half-pepperoni with extra-cheese pizza O'Brien asked Slattery, "You got a horse in this race?"

Slattery shrugged. "Doesn't matter to me."

"Gees, you're tough," Russo responded with a touch of disbelief. "How about rooting for the old home team, you know?"

O'Brien frowned at that thought. "You mean like be true to your wiseguy?" He turned to Slattery and said in a slightly condescending tone, "She's just a sentimental fool. Besides, she thinks he's sort of cute."

"Fuck you, O'Brien," she said, and at that moment she meant it. Then she pleaded her case to Slattery. "It's pretty obvious, isn't it?" She looked at O'Brien and added, "Least it is to most people." Then, back to Slattery, passionately, "Just look at the facts, Jim. We got this guy by the balls. And whenever we need to, all we've got to do is squeeze." O'Brien winced and she ignored him. "He knows damn well that we can put him in a hole for thirty years to life. He'll have to talk to us. The Russian doesn't owe us a thing."

Jim? She called him Jim? Now, let's just hold it a second here, O'Brien thought. She's feeling pretty confident this evening, isn't she? And in fact, he knew, she was probably right. Ole Bobby boy could certainly help them out from time to time. But he also knew that it didn't matter to Slattery. As always, Slattery had his eyes fixed squarely on the bull's-eye. So long as somebody got killed in the gas station, and naturally the more bodies the better, it'd be a long time before the Italians and the Russians trusted each other again. If ever. Cosentino's dreams of an alliance controlling the billion-dollar bootleg oil business would be finished. This had all the makings of a beautiful feud. And that result was all Slattery cared about.

Admittedly O'Brien did hope it was Bobby who walked out of the gas station, and while Slattery would never admit it, Connor suspected he felt the same way. It wasn't simply the devil-you-know kind of thing, it was also the devil who knows all his fellow devils and speaks your language.

O'Brien was finishing his second slice when the police radio crackled with a report that an intruder with a knife was trapped in the vestibule of a brownstone on West 19th Street. Now, there's an easy one, he thought, no moral ambiguity there. Bad guy holding a weapon, caught in the act. Beautiful.

Every man and woman working in law enforcement loves that kind of case. It doesn't require any soul-searching. There's a bad guy waving a knife? You do whatever's necessary to bring him down. You become the bad medicine. Every cop knows the first order of business: Do harm to the bad guys before they do it to you. No shades of gray. It's those other types of cases that cause you to lie awake at night. This one, for example. This case had started so simply, a missing person case. Find the professor? That part was easy; everything that came with it was hard. It had taken more twists than a Philadelphia pretzel to get them from the Country Club to the meeting with San Filippo.

Maybe what was bothering O'Brien the most was that he had so willingly gone along with Slattery's plan. No questions, no reservations. In fact, he didn't just acquiesce, he had enthusiastically participated in it. Worse, he hadn't felt a pinprick of conscience. O'Brien adhered to a strict rule where pizza was concerned: two slices and done. And rarely more than once a week. Not this night, though. He finished his second slice and without any hesitation went for a third. Well, he decided, after you've broken every rule in the book—in *all* the books—by setting up a guy to kill or be killed, it's easier to have that third slice without feeling guilty.

He'd relived that walk and talk with San Filippo in his mind maybe a hundred times. Had they been straight with him? The honest answer to that, he had decided, was absolutely yes and no. Yes to the girl, no to Skinny Al. What'd they have on Skinny Al's murder really? A bullshit remark made in anger and repeated by Gradinsky. That was it. More than enough to make a DA laugh if you tried to make a case out of it. But that wasn't the way they'd presented it to Bobby Blue Eyes. For him it was the whole ball game, the whole shebang, a fait accompli. One commie killer delivered on a silver platter, *s'il vous plaît.* Oh, and by the way, here's where you find him. O'Brien wanted to believe that San Filippo was so determined to avenge the murder of the girlfriend that he would have gone ahead with or without the skinny on Skinny Al. But Skinny Al's murder gave him cover within the family. His killing was, literally, a lifesaver. San Filippo was a bright guy; he must've figured that out right away. What he didn't know was that the evidence proving that the Russian did it was as strong as air.

O'Brien wouldn't want to be on the receiving end of questions about that meeting in a courtroom. Um, tell me, Agent O'Brien, does the phrase "aiding and abetting" mean anything to you? He was pretty certain that the right answers were the wrong ones.

Sometimes he could just kill for a good old-fashioned perp with a knife.

The first call came over the radio long after the pizza crust was stone-cold. "Unusual activity reported at a gas station on Brighton Beach Boulevard." Two squad cars took the call. It was the address that caught Russo's attention. But there wasn't anything they could do about it, except wait. FBI agents couldn't respond to a seemingly ordinary NYPD radio call without attracting a lot of unnecessary attention.

It took almost forty minutes for the first patrol car to get to the scene. There was no sense that this was any kind of priority call—except to the three people sitting in Slattery's office. But within a few minutes the cops were moving at hyperspeed. "We got four men down," one of the cops reported in a nervously high-pitched voice. "Send the meat wagon. Shit, send everybody!" And then, just barely on the professional side of hysteria, he added, "You better get some gold badges down here right away. I never seen anything like this."

These police officers had absolutely no idea what they had stumbled into. To them it probably looked very much like a robbery gone real bad. The existence of a lavish conference room hidden in the rear would certainly raise their curiosity—it was pretty obvious this wasn't any ordinary gas station—but their initial assumption would most likely be that the Russians were running a gambling or drug operation. And that assumption would serve to support the robbery theory.

It was that last line, "I never seen anything like this," that sent cops scurrying to the scene. On the job cops see just about everything imaginable. It's the stuff they talk about quietly in the locker room and the bars. They see so much of it that eventually they become inured to human depravity. So when one of their own makes a claim like that, they respond. They all want to see something they've never seen before.

The remnants of Slattery's sense of self-preservation still proved stronger than his curiosity. An FBI supervisor showing up uninvited at an NYPD crime scene would certainly be noticed, so O'Brien and Russo went by themselves. By the time they got there, the gas station had been transformed into a crime scene. In addition to about two dozen officers and detectives, at least six different NYPD units were on the scene. Still, a steady stream of police cruisers and ambulances continued to arrive, some of them with their sirens wailing as if getting there quickly would make a difference. Spotlights had been set up on tripods, giving the gas station an otherworldly look of artificial light and elongated shadows. Yellow crime scene tape had been stretched between poles and trees to create a security perimeter, keeping the curious onlookers and the rapidly gathering—and loudly complaining—media storm at a distance.

The place was an organized mess. Radio reporters screamed questions at anybody looking even mildly official who passed within shout-shot of their microphones. The bodies had not yet been removed, and chalk outlines were being drawn around them. It would still be several hours before they were transported to the morgue. Forensic teams had been assigned to each body, officers were conducting an inch-by-inch search both inside and outside to collect all possible evidence, all types of measurements were being taken, photographers were recording the crime scene for potential use in a courtroom, in a corner of the garage an officer from media relations was helping a lieutenant prepare a statement, a department chaplain was wandering around to provide counseling for any officers disturbed by the brutality, and out on Brighton Beach Boulevard officers were trying to keep traffic moving past the scene.

In the hubbob O'Brien and Russo faded easily into the scene. Having worked in New York for several years, O'Brien knew a few of the cops, and they accepted his presence as normal procedure. Russo, however, was a new and pretty face, and several detectives made a point of introducing themselves. When either agent was asked what they knew about the Russians, they responded simply, "You know, they were around some people." Inevitably the cops nodded. Even if they didn't know, they knew.

O'Brien and Russo went around back first. They still didn't know the identity of the victims. The small men's room was lit up brighter than a movie set. The first victim was wedged between the toilet bowl and the wall. He'd been shot once, the bullet going right through his mouth, exiting the back of his head. That shot had obviously been fired at close range—there wasn't room for any other possibility. His mouth was open, a line of caked blood running from his mouth onto his lap, and a splash of dried blood was on the wall behind him. A small piece of gold, apparently the remnants of a gold tooth, rested on a crease in his shirt. An automatic weapon lay at his feet. O'Brien recognized the victim as the attendant who'd flirted with Laura. That he had obviously been sitting on the toilet with his gun on the floor made it clear to O'Brien that he had been totally surprised.

Normally, several hours after a killing the odor of death would already be permeating the air, but in this case the stench of urine was so strong it overwhelmed everything else.

O'Brien recognized the smell of the restroom from his previous visit. In his notebook he'd described it as "Eau de Yankee Stadium." "The guy must've had a wooden nose," he whispered in Russo's ear. "You see who it is?"

She grimaced. "Yeah." She had not seen enough dead bodies to have become comfortable with the sight.

O'Brien said judgmentally, "You ask me, he looked a lot better with the gold teeth." He took her arm and urged her forward, into the conference room. "C'mon." He was eager to see the hidden room. Big picture, little picture, he had been fooled completely, never suspecting there was a larger room hidden behind the bathroom. How the hell do you miss seeing a door? he asked himself. But he had no answer. Apparently they'd intentionally made the bathroom as disgusting as possible to discourage people from spending a second more than necessary there.

Both agents were stunned at the opulence of the hidden conference room. It was like walking through a bodega into Versailles. The large conference table as well as the paneling on the walls was a rich mahogany. Several avant-garde sconces affixed to the walls provided warm recessed lighting. There were two rows of chairs; eight tall leather chairs were around the table while a second row of smaller leather chairs—obviously seating for the assistants—was about four feet farther back. The room was crowded with the law. Several people were busy collecting evidence, while gawkers were hanging around to get a better look at the bodies.

The room had been shot up. O'Brien counted a line of seven bullet holes running right through the center of the table and several more holes going up the far wall. There were at least as many holes in the wall behind him and the ceiling, apparently made by the Russians returning fire. Most of the holes had already been circled and numbered in black marker for investigative purposes.

At first O'Brien saw only the body seated in the leather chair. The victim was partially visible, turned at an angle away from the door, his chin slumped onto his chest. Seen from this angle, he could have just as easily been sleeping as dead. He asked Russo, "Recognize him?"

She shrugged, then shook her head.

The plush carpeting on the floor absorbed much of the normal conversation, so even with more than a dozen cops working there the room was funereally quiet. " 'Scuse me," a detective said to O'Brien as he walked out carrying a clear plastic bag presumably filled with evidence. O'Brien politely stepped to the side to let the officer pass— and that's when he saw the second body sprawled beneath the table. He moved a couple of steps closer. The carpet around the body was saturated with blood. The victim was lying on his stomach, his face practically buried in a pool of his own blood, making it impossible to identify him from across the room. It didn't look like San Filippo, but O'Brien took a couple of steps closer to be certain. Russo was a step behind him.

Much of the torso was hidden by the tabletop, but the back of his head and his shoulders were visible. "It's not him," O'Brien said, with more relief in his voice than he intended.

Russo grabbed hold of his forearm. Her eyes were riveted on the body. "It's him," she said.

O'Brien was surprised at the intensity of her reaction. "No, it's not," he insisted. "It doesn't look anything like him."

She dug her nails into his arm. In her mind she was considering her fate. "No, no, not San Filippo." She closed her eyes and took a controlled breath. "Connor, that's the guy who tried to break into my apartment."

"Oh gees," he said involuntarily. "Are you sure? I mean, how can you . . . It can't be." She had never seen him so clearly flummoxed. "How . . . I mean, are you really sure about that?" His mind was racing, trying to find a rationale that made sense. What the hell was a Russian gangster doing trying to break into an FBI agent's apartment? That was supposed to be the Mafia's job. It made no sense at all.

"I'm positive. It's him." There was no doubt in her voice. "I saw the back of his head when he went down the stairs. Believe me, that's him." She couldn't take her eyes off the body, and deep in her mind all she could hear was a woman's long, awful scream.

A burly detective whom O'Brien had met at the beginning of his career during a bank robbery hostage situation squeezed between the two agents and the table. "How are you doing?" O'Brien said as the guy pushed by, identifying himself.

"Yeah," the officer said, "I remember. The Chase chase. How's it going?"

Good, O'Brien told him, then asked, indicating the body on the floor, "You ID that guy yet?"

The detective glanced at the corpse. "He's some Russian guy." He flipped open a spiral notbook. "Cher-nan-ko. Alexander Ivan Chernanko. He's got a hack license in his wallet but . . ." He shook his head. "He sure isn't dressed like a cabbie, is he?"

Laura finally looked away. "Any idea what happened here?"

The detective frowned. "Who the hell knows? These guys, they're into anything where they can make some money." He waved his hands to indicate the shot-up room. "I mean, c'mon, look at this. Looks like they really pissed somebody off."

O'Brien chuckled. "They sure did a job on them, didn't they?"

The detective raised his eyebrows. "On these guys? You kidding me? This is nothing, this is just the appetizer. You didn't see what they did to the other guy yet, right?" As he said that, he pointed toward the garage.

O'Brien and Russo shook their heads in unison, like the Captain and Tennille.

The detective let out a long, respectful breath. "Man, go get yourself a ticket. I promise you, this is one you ain't ever gonna forget."

While they had been in the back room, the police had used sawhorses to create a corral for the media. "Multiple homicides" is a magic phrase for reporters, always drawing a big crowd. As O'Brien and Russo walked around to the front, reporters shouted the headline questions at them—who, how, and how many—as they did to every cop who passed. The two agents ignored them, unobtrusively keeping their heads down.

Some smart cop had taped sheets of newspaper over the office windows to prevent photographers from using a telephoto lens to shoot inside, but it made the office feel even smaller and more confined. So many police officers were standing around it looked like a cop convention. A thin trail of blood led from the office into the garage, and a cop standing in the office repeatedly warned people about stepping in it. O'Brien and Russo carefully avoided it as they walked into the garage.

The first thing they saw once inside the garage was a late-model luxury car sitting on the ramps of the hydraulic lift, raised about three feet off the ground. They walked around to the rear of the car. O'Brien saw the body first. "Oh man," he said, sucking in a mouthful of air, "oh Christ."

"What?" Russo started to ask, then saw it. She covered her mouth with her fist.

The nearest ramp of the lift had been lowered onto the top half of the victim's skull, crushing it into pulp from slightly above the bridge of his nose. The victim's mouth was open, and a light blue rag was still stuffed into it, the color quite familiar. His facial skin was pulled way back, exposing his teeth and gums. He looked like a skeletal figure drawn by Hieronymus Bosch, the man of eternal agony. It was impossible to identify the victim facially—hopefully some dentist

would have his chart—but looking at his body, O'Brien was certain
he was taller and thinner than San Filippo.

Several cops were standing around the body, looking down at it
like curious visitors to an art museum. One of them was laughing
nervously. Somebody forced a joke about having stew for dinner.
Russo just couldn't take her eyes off the crushed skull, her fascination
easily overcoming her horror. There had been absolutely nothing in
her life to which this might be compared. It was more violent or
more disgusting than anything she had ever seen. It was unquestion-
ably unique.

Blood and pulp had flowed out of the crushed head into a murky
public, which was outlined by an irregular pattern of white tape affixed to the floor. Several other objects on the floor were also boxed
by the white tape, primarily to ensure that no one touched them or
stepped on them. One of them, Russo noticed, was the ripped and
blackened remnant of a Cabbage Patch Kid. Nudging O'Brien, she
pointed to the doll and asked, "What do you think that's all about?"

At just about any other moment of his life, that might have been
a great straight line. He could have reached into his grab bag of
snappy comebacks and pulled out the quasi-perfect quip. Not this
time, though, not this time. His heart just wasn't in it. "I don't know.
Nothing probably. Maybe it belonged to one of the mechanic's kids
or something."

She rolled it over with a steel pencil. "It's what's left of one of those
Cabbage Patch dolls. The ones they give the name to."

He got it immediately. "Well, well, well," he said, looking at it
knowingly. "Didn't we hear something about some guy trying to un-
load a truckload of those things?"

She looked around at the garageful of detectives poking and prod-
ding and measuring and photographing, searching for that one elusive clue that would put them on the trail of the killer. "Not that I
remember," she replied.

He chuckled, and this time he couldn't resist. "Right, I don't remember too."

The garage continued to fill with cops. Most of them would take a good long look at the corpse, shake their head, then go back to work. A couple of them had to race outside before they lost their cookies. This was rapidly turning into a major crime event. By now the media had learned that these killings had the required gruesome quotient to qualify for the front page, although they didn't yet have the details. There is nothing like a good old-fashioned gang war to sell newspapers! They were still merchandizing the St. Valentine's Day Massacre, and that had taken place more than half a century earlier. O'Brien knew the facts of life: Death is a marketable commodity. The more horrid the death, the more valuable it might be. The right quote or photograph or film clip could make a career. So the reporters stuck behind the barriers were desperately trying to make side deals for even a few seconds of access or, failing that, for detailed information. The early bidding was centered around Yankees and Knicks tickets and dinners at trendy restaurants, items that cost the newspapers and broadcast stations exactly nothing. When the reporters got a whiff of what was inside, the bidding would go a lot higher.

As always, O'Brien tried to take in the whole picture, details at six. It was a lot tougher than usual—ignoring a body with a crushed head was about as easy as ignoring the ball at a basketball game. But as he looked around the garage, nothing else of consequence stood out. It was a garage, dirty and drab. As in any repair shop there were quite a few grease-covered tools and rags scattered about. The blue rag again caught his attention. He recognized the color, the Pan Am blue, and figured it was from one of those in-flight blankets that are always a few inches too small, no matter how short you are. There was no obvious reason it would be in the garage, but it made sense: Pan Am flew to Russia from New York.

Among the tools in plain sight were a mallet, several pairs of pliers, a set of screwdrivers, a power drill and a selection of bits, a file, a hacksaw, and a jigsaw. O'Brien clasped his hands behind his back, an old crime scene habit that prevented him from distractedly touching a piece of evidence, leaned over, and examined the working end of each tool. This was one time that he really was apprehensive that he might find what he was looking for.

"Anything?" Russo asked.

"I don't think so." He stood up, and with a sweep of his hand asked, "So what do you think of your boyfriend now? He's got some temper, huh?"

She forced a feeble smile and said sadly, "Men." She sighed deeply. "Just when you begin to think you understand them, they drop a car on your head." She swept back her hair with the palm of her left hand. "Seen enough?"

"I guess," he said. That one little involuntary gesture, that little feminine thing she did, the way she brushed back her hair and then shook it free, that unexpectedly got to Connor O'Brien. It awakened his protective instincts—the whole caveman thing—and made him acutely aware of how close the Russians had come to grabbing her. The questions that followed in his mind were pretty obvious: How close had she come to ending up on that cement floor? How did they identify her? What were they looking for? Did they think she knew where Gradinsky was hiding? And at the end of every unanswered question was the one that mattered: What would they have done to her? He shuddered, literally. It was his job to protect his partner and he had failed. Maybe she would have protected herself. Maybe. "Sure, let's get out of here."

He put his hand lightly on her back and gently guided her toward the door in a most gentlemanly way, being very careful to make sure neither of them stepped in the drying blood.

Only on television and in the movies are all the loose ends tied up at the end of a case. In reality, even after the best possible outcome there are always questions that will never be answered. Most of the time it doesn't matter, although it can lead to some uneasy moments during a trial. What makes it difficult is the fact that criminal behavior isn't predictable. Criminals follow no discernible patterns. Motives tend to be more ragged than smooth; they have a lot of sharp edges in unexpected places and very often don't seem to make sense. Sometimes even criminals are perplexed by their own actions. So chances were pretty strong that Connor O'Brien and Laura Russo would never know why the Russians had attempted to break into her apartment.

As they strolled in thoughtful silence toward their car, the herd of reporters shouted questions at them: What's going on in there? How many bodies? Is it true you found a bucket of severed hands? One reporter for a local TV station seemed especially furious, screaming at them in a vaguely threatening tone that his viewers had "a constitutional right" to see film of the dead bodies.

O'Brien fell asleep easily that night, although as he later admitted to Russo, "I dreamt about dragons all night." Russo decided to sleep on her living room couch for reasons she could easily explain. But she was awakened several times by clanking sounds coming from the aged heating pipes and noises either real or imagined from the hallway.

The next few days raced by in a bureaucratic blur. O'Brien and Russo spent long hours in the office preparing voluminous reports in which they told the story of the operation in complete detail. They attended numerous meetings with FBI and NYPD officials alarmed by the possibility of an Italian-Russian criminal alliance, as well as Federal Department of Transportation executives investigating the billion-dollar bootleg fuel oil business. But in all the reports they filed, and during all the meetings they attended, they never mentioned having met with Bobby Blue Eyes San Filippo.

The "Brighton Beach Massacre" did make a front-page splash. The New York newspapers and local news stations reported that the killings were the result of "a turf war threatening the increasingly homogenous community" (*New York Times*) between Russian gangsters, "many of whom spent years being tortured in Russia's infamous gulags" (*New York Daily News*), for control of "the lucrative drug business" (*New York Post*) in the "ethnically isolated Brighton Beach section of Brooklyn" (*Village Voice*). They got most of the gory details of the killings right but failed to get any photographs inside the garage. An NYPD spokesman announced that detectives had developed "significant leads" and had "several suspects under surveillance." They anticipated making arrests within the next few weeks. But he added that Brighton Beach remained "a safe neighborhood in which local residents play an active role in protecting people and property."

Slattery guided them through the bureaucratic maze. Having traveled this road before, he knew all the dangerous curves. A task force consisting of FBI, NYPD, and DOT investigators, in addition to federal prosecutors, had been set up to squeeze every last bit of juice out of this case. Slattery had somehow managed to mollify a score or more of ambitious FBI officials anxious to get their names associated with this investigation; he set up those meetings that couldn't be avoided and made sure O'Brien and Russo got all the support they needed to ensure that their reports were as complete and accurate as possible. But as he knew, "possible" covered a lot of territory.

He also made certain that his agents remained in the center ring as the investigation got rolled up. At lunch on the third day, for example, he brought them up-to-date on the complicated life of Professor Peter Gradinsky. The professor had taken a few days to settle into his new life. It appeared that he was considerably more frightened of his wife than of the entire Mafia. He asked the bureau to arrange his first meeting with Grace in prison so there might be a thick piece of Plexiglas between them when he told her about Natalie's pregnancy. When he was informed that prison was much too dangerous for him, he reluctantly agreed to meet her at the safe house—on the condition that an armed agent remain with them.

As it turned out, the professor had little to fear from his wife. Having experienced what life would be like without her husband, Grace Gradinsky was in a deeply forgiving mood. With the agent sitting between them trying hard not to be noticed, Peter Gradinsky told his story as he wanted it to be. "Remember all those papers I was bringing home? The ones marked Top Secret?" he said as honestly as he could lie. "I've been working undercover for the FBI for the last four-teen months. I infiltrated the Mafia and the Russian gangs." As the clincher he added, "I love you very much. Really I do."

It wasn't clear that she believed him, but she did accept his story without asking a single question. "I really missed you," was what she told him.

He explained to her that he was in what was called protective cus-tody, which he described as a sort of friendly arrest. The bureau was going to move him from New York to San Diego, where he would spend at least the next few months being debriefed by the FBI, giv-ing them all the details of his undercover work. While he was in pro-tective custody, he wouldn't have to go to work and the government would pay all his expenses. Basically he was going to lie in the sun by the pool and answer some questions. He'd emphasized that he had specifically asked for a place with a pool. And then the professor looked at her lovingly, took her hand—the agent sitting between them figured he was about to tell her about his affair with Speak-man—and asked Grace to come with him. "I want us to start a whole new life together," he said, adding romantically, "in the sun."

And as the agent explained later, he never saw the rest of the story coming. The professor continued, "I want us to be a real family. You know what? I've got this crazy idea." He paused, as if this thought had just popped into his head. "It'll be absolutely perfect. Perfect."

She was enthralled. "What? Tell me."

With all the enthusiasm he could muster he blurted out, "Let's adopt a baby!"

The agent didn't know who was more surprised, Grace or her. At first Grace was flustered, telling him that she was too old to raise a child, but by the time their meeting ended and she'd gone home to pack, she was convinced this was the most wonderful thing that had ever happened to her. Finally she was going to be a mother. She did wonder if they would be eligible to adopt a baby. "Let's be honest," she said. "I'm already in my . . . my early forties."

"Oh, don't worry about that," he reassured her. "You know, with all the work I've done for the government, I think they owe me a pretty big favor."

Professor Gradinsky remained in custody at an undisclosed location, pending his relocation. Russo was duly impressed by the man. "I can't believe he's actually going to pull this off."

O'Brien said he was betting against him. "You don't really think Natalie's just going to hand over her baby, do you?"

As impossible as that seemed, Laura Russo believed that where the professor was involved, pretty much anything was possible.

In fact, the professor's situation was probably not as dire as it had originally appeared. After a few days it became apparent that he probably wouldn't have to testify against the Mafia. Few—if any— prosecutions would result from this operation. The Russians' bootleg fuel operation was as dead as they were, so none of them would go on trial.

Several charges could be brought against Tony Cosentino, but the only one that really had a chance to stick was conspiracy to defraud the government. And that would be tough to prove—it's almost impossible to prosecute someone for what they might do in the future. The most Gradinsky could do was put Cosentino at meetings in which criminal activity was discussed, but thus far there was no corroborating evidence. It was kind of a murky area and it looked like Cosentino was going to skate.

The professor also had nothing to fear from the Russians, obviously, and not a whole lot more from the mob. The Freemont Avenue crew had no interest in him, and Cosentino couldn't afford to make a move until he got a good look at the hand he was playing. And when he realized it was good enough to keep him in the game, it was pretty doubtful he'd risk drawing the joker.

In Washington there was considerable debate about just how much information to provide to the NYPD and the Brooklyn DA's office. It was apparent that a pretty solid murder case could be made against Bobby Blue Eyes San Filippo, but any investigation and trial would inevitably involve the conduct of James Slattery, as well as

Special Agents Connor O'Brien and Laura Russo. There were rumors bouncing around headquarters that Slattery had provided confidential intelligence to Mafia soldiers. If that was true, Slattery would be indicted. If convicted, he might end up serving more time than any member of the family. And while there was a reasonable chance that San Filippo would be convicted, there was little doubt that the bureau's already fragile reputation would be devastated. This was a story the media would love: the FBI feeding information to a known killer, resulting in three deaths. That would sell newspapers for months.

The trade-off, destroying a respected supervisor's reputation and perhaps resulting in a criminal prosecution, as well as greatly damaging the bureau's reputation, in return for putting a wiseguy in jail for killing three gangsters, didn't seem to balance out. While the final decision about just how much cooperation the bureau would offer local authorities would be made by headquarters, there was no great clamor for Slattery's head. Even if they could prove he existed on paper.

So until one of the local authorities came up with irrefutable evidence that the rumors were true, headquarters would watch with interest and shallow enthusiasm—and without volunteering any additional information.

There was a pretty strong chance the NYPD would never be able to make a case against San Filippo. Generally mob hits don't get solved. Nobody ever got arrested for the St. Valentine's Day Massacre, for example. This one quickly faded back several pages in the newspapers. Without a single lurid photograph to print—not even the blood-soaked carpet being carried out by a grim-faced detective—this story just didn't have that old pizzazz. Four Russian bad guys got whacked. Nobody much cared. It wasn't going to cause a problem for the mayor or chief of police if these killings went unsolved.

San Filippo would walk. Nobody in the bureau was taking any bets on how long, though. The Russians would have to go after him.

They had to retaliate. Even Vaseline's enemies. If the Mafia was permitted to destroy a multimillion-dollar Russian operation and kill four men without paying a price, the life of every other Russian gangster would be in jeopardy. That was a fact of family life.

Admittedly O'Brien and Russo continued to wonder about Bobby Blue Eyes. It was impossible to suddenly forget all about him. That would be like listening to the *1812 Overture* and leaving before the cannons and bells. It just felt incomplete. The daily reports from the Country Club were filled with interesting tidbits—it was like a mob gossip column—but not nearly enough to satisfy their curiosity.

Which was why Slattery had arranged this very meeting at a gay bar with Special Agent Valone. But O'Brien and Russo were stunned when Slattery introduced them to him. Neither agent ever suspected that the somewhat dense ass-kissing Vito V was an FBI undercover agent rather than a legit young wannabe. And they were duly impressed. Looking at him, O'Brien figured him at twenty-six or twenty-seven, mostly because he knew it would have taken him several years to complete his training, get this assignment, and gain admittance to the social club, although he looked more like a teenager struggling to look old enough to buy a six-pack. The age didn't matter at all, O'Brien decided. Special Agent Valone had more balls than a bowling alley. And his were bigger too.

"Eddie just couldn't shut up about it," Valone reported. "It was like he was living on borrowed breath. He needed to get it all out. It was like an eruption of nervous energy. But Bobby . . . you know, truthfully Bobby's not a bad guy . . ."

Except, Connor thought, for the occasional mass murder.

". . . but this wasn't him. It was like he was there but he wasn't really there, if you know what I mean. They didn't just blab out all the details, they didn't tell me anything, just that something big went down. We didn't know the whole story until it was in the papers."

O'Brien asked, "What about Two-Gun? You hear anything about him?"

Valone in person was quite different from Valone on tape. Russo was surprised that she had been completely fooled by him. The warm-up act turned out to be the star of the show. "And Franzone, how'd he react to the whole thing?" she asked.

Valone sipped his watered-down rum and Coke. "Bobby and Franzone spent a lot of time holed up together. I can't tell you what they were talking about, but whatever went down between them, Franzone was pretty pleased. There was definitely a lot of hugging going on." He paused and smiled at his next thought. "Now, Two-Gun Tony, that was a whole different thing. He was totally boxed in. Figure it out, when you're playing for the visitors and the home team gets whacked, people are gonna figure that your team had something to do with it. I think it's fair to say that Cosentino was sweating caviar. Eddie was telling me that Cosentino called Franzone four or five times minimum, and then one of his guys, Joey Black, showed up at the club with an envelope."

"Cosentino was making a payoff?" O'Brien asked. "That's interesting. For what?"

"Nah, it wasn't a payoff." Valone pressed his thumb against his index and middle fingers and shook them like he was talking to the dice. "It was a tribute. That was the beautiful thing about this all. No matter how pissed off Cosentino was, and you know he had to be steaming, he couldn't touch Bobby or Eddie." He waved his hands in the air. "I mean, what they did was completely the right thing. These guys had whacked Skinny Al, so we . . . you know, I mean them, the wiseguys, they had the right to get even. But there was a lot more than that involved. Now, this is according to Franzone. He called us all together for a meeting." He looked at Slattery. "I'm sure you guys got this one on tape, right?"

Slattery nodded, then told O'Brien and Russo, "We got the transcripts in this morning. If you want to see them, I got them back in the office."

Valone continued, "Cosentino figured the Russians might be coming after his crew, so he wanted to have as many friends as he could get. He needed Franzone. That meant he couldn't touch

Bobby or Eddie. In fact, Franzone told us that Cosentino was making noises about going into the fuel oil business together. It was
pretty amazing."

"So what about San Filippo?" O'Brien asked.

"That was the piece of resistance. Franzone knew how much he
owed Bobby." He paused and shook his head at the wonder of fate.
"So they opened up the books for him. Bobby's gonna get made."

O'Brien and Russo stayed at the bar a lot longer than they had
planned, even after Slattery and his star undercover had left, even
after the place had filled up and Russo was getting a lot of curious
glances. While O'Brien was busy pontificating about the symmetry
of it all, Russo took a good long look at him. She noted that he used
the same word, "fairness," in three consecutive sentences, something
he would ordinarily not do. There was a lot to like about the guy, she
finally decided, although he could probably do some work on his
sense of humor. He was unusually quiet—for him—in the car. He
was definitely glad for San Filippo. Bobby Blue Eyes was a stand-up
guy. Being made, being inducted into the Mafia, came with certain
privileges—and it just might save his life one day.

For O'Brien, San Filippo might prove to be an extremely valuable
connection. Bobby was moving up the ladder toward real power in
the family. And there was no way he could ever tell anyone about his
connection to the bureau—a situation that might prove extremely
beneficial to the bureau in the fugure. It was decided, as Slattery explained, "to leave him there and let him grow."

More than all that, though, Connor O'Brien was contemplating
the irony of the situation. Growing up, he'd played all the fighting
games: cowboys and Indians, Superman and Lothar, Star Fleet
against the Romulans, Yankees and the Red Sox, the FBI against the
mob. And in all those games it had been easy to separate the good
guys from the bad guys. Almost always, he played the good guy. As
a special agent of the Federal Bureau of Investigation he was no
longer playing a game. He had become a good guy.

He was sorting all this out in his head as he drove uptown. It turned out that sometimes, to be a good guy, you had to do bad things. In this case, for example, to achieve an important and legitimate objective, he'd sort of pushed a guy into a shoot-out. People had died. And they had died brutally. Connor knew that he'd broken all the good guy rules and gotten away with it. And the only reason he was able to do it was that the bad guy was true to some strange family code. All that stuff about honor and loyalty that they believe in.

Sometimes good guys do bad things, and maybe sometimes the bad guys do the good things. A couple of drinks after a long drought can make a situation like this seem pretty complicated.

O'Brien was so deeply immersed in his thoughts that he drove right past Laura's block. He was almost to his own apartment when he realized his error. "Oh man," he told her, "I'm sorry. I don't know where I was." The smile on her face was so welcoming that he completely forgot she was his partner in the anticrime business. He sighed and corkscrewed up his courage. "Want me to take you home?"

She looked at him like he was crazy. "Forget about it," she said.

ACKNOWLEDGEMENTS

The authors would like to acknowledge the encouragement and support of our agents, Frank Weimann of the Literary Group and Mickey Freiberg of Acme Talent and Literary Agency. We also very much appreciate the enthusiasm of our editor, Rick Wolff, who was able to recognize this unusual project and gently lay upon us a steel glove to help us along, as well as the many people at Warner Books who were always there with a welcoming smile.

David Fisher would especially like to acknowledge the never-ending support and encouragment of his wife, Laura Stevens. He would also like to thank Jerry Stern of Columbus, Ohio, and Tom Jones of Pittsburgh, Pennsylvania, for the kind use of their cyberspace storage depot, which proved far superior to his own refrigerator, and Karen Greenfeld for making cyberspace appear. He is also very grateful to George and Kathy Hicker for putting up with him—or, actually, putting him up. And of course Belle Stevens, who was right there behind him—right behind him—the whole way.

Bill Bonanno would like to acknowledge the culture and tradition from which he comes, that gave him the strength and guidance to enter into and complete such an unusual collaboration. No man can rid himself of his heredity and his environment, as well as the accident of birth that preordained his destiny. It has been an extraordinary voyage of calm and stormy seas, but the sun has always shined on him. For that, he would truly like to acknowledge all those people who traveled this road before, carrying with them their ideals, and created a well-worn path.

Joe Pistone would like to acknowledge the long and deep friendship and support of all those individuals with whom he has long and valued relationships. They know who they are. And finally,

Hiya Gailie!